THE
SNAKEHEADS

Mary Moylum

A Castle Street Mystery

THE DUNDURN GROUP
TORONTO · OXFORD

Editor: Doris Cowan
Copy-Editor: Julian Walker
Design: Jennifer Scott
Printer: Transcontinental

Canadian Cataloguing in Publication Data

Moylum, Mary
    The snakeheads

"A Castle Street Mystery."
ISBN 0-88882-225-1

I. Title.

PS8576.0994S53 2001   C813.'6   C2001-901943-2   PR9199.4.M69S53 2001

1   2   3   4   5   05   04   03   02   01

Canadä

THE CANADA COUNCIL | LE CONSEIL DES ARTS
FOR THE ARTS | DU CANADA
SINCE 1957 | DEPUIS 1957

ONTARIO ARTS COUNCIL
CONSEIL DES ARTS DE L'ONTARIO

We acknowledge the support of the **Canada Council for the Arts** and the **Ontario Arts Council** for our publishing program. We also acknowledge the financial support of the **Government of Canada** through the **Book Publishing Industry Development Program** and **The Association for the Export of Canadian Books,** and the **Government of Ontario** through the **Ontario Book Publishers Tax Credit** program.

Dundurn Press
8 Market Street
Suite 200
Toronto, Ontario, Canada
M5E 1M6

Dundurn Press
73 Lime Walk
Headington, Oxford,
England
OX3 7AD

Dundurn Press
2250 Military Road
Tonawanda NY
U.S.A. 14150

prologue

Darkness. BJ loved darkness. That was when the city came alive. In the daytime, people were too busy drudging for a living. But at night, everything was exposed. The night stripped them of their phoniness, their veneer. The night revealed them for what they were. He had read somewhere about crucial events in history occurring at night. He wasn't surprised. He already knew it: stabbings, muggings, rapes, and murders all happened under the cover of darkness.

BJ and Harry were sitting in a rusty white van in front of a tony townhouse, just watching. The street was quiet. BJ held a pair of binoculars to his eyes as Harry panned the neighbourhood with a long telephoto lens. In the house next door, a woman was exercising on her Stairmaster. In another house across the street, several kids were eating a pizza in front of a television set. BJ fiddled with the radio, he was getting antsy. Two hours and counting and still no sign of their target. They needed to know whether the judge lived here alone or with a woman. If he lived with a woman, they needed to know her itinerary before they planned their next move. So far, so good. They had tracked down the judge's address from newspaper clippings and city hall records. They knew the month and year he had bought the townhouse, how much he paid for it and the remaining mortgage on his property. Harry's interest in his enemy extended to the smallest detail. He even knew about the judge's relationship with his ex-wife and his children and all about his work on the Immigration and Refugee Commission. In the age of information technology all of that could be downloaded from the net. In prison, with plenty of time on their hands, they learned to cruise the internet; they had discovered a wealth of information about people, which they downloaded and saved for further use.

BJ took a last drag on his cigarette and flicked the ashes on the floor. He had to admire his good friend Harry. All those years in the Pen, Harry never lost sight of his goal. Instead Harry's rage had fed on itself until it had reached Old Testament proportions. The righteous wrath of an executioner. BJ smiled. He had no problem with that. Hell, he could recount all the crimes he himself had committed without a flicker of emotion. He had been in and out of jail for most of his forty-five years and had the tough-guy look to go with it: shaven head, scarred arms, bulging muscles, and tattoos of girls and guns everywhere on his body.

BJ turned toward his friend, whose eyes were fixed on the house, as if by will alone he could conjure up the judge who had done him wrong years ago.

For another half hour they waited for something to happen. Finally it came in the presence of a well-dressed man walking toward them, with a woman on his arm.

Harry smacked the back of his hand against BJ's shoulder and said, "It's him!"

BJ took a good long look at the guy. He felt a vibration in his chest, a catch of breath. He wished they could do the job now, tonight. But what if the bitch spent the night with the judge? Shit! It meant they'd have to keep up the surveillance, find a night when the she wasn't sleeping over.

BJ grinned at his friend. He was wired now. He always felt like that before a job. In this case it was justified. Didn't the Bible say an eye for an eye? No one had paid the price for the man's crimes, yet. But soon, soon, someone would.

chapter one

Months of surveillance on an agent smuggler called Shaupan Chau had finally panned out. But, in the end, the sting operation had gone wrong.

Nicholas Slovak stared dully out the car window. It was not quite four in the morning. Good thing he didn't have to drive. He knew he should be used to the routine by now, should expect the unexpected. But this was worse, much worse, than usual.

He was aware of Dick Asler glancing over at him repeatedly. Was he looking for signs of emotion? Maybe the silence was making Asler uncomfortable, because apropos of nothing he suddenly started to talk:

"Last thing we need is a repeat of the *Moon Star* disaster. What did that end up costing the American taxpayers? — over five mil, to house a hundred illegal migrants. The mayor of Seattle was ticked to no end. That wasn't the kind of tourism he wanted."

Nick kept his eyes on the bleak highway landscapes

they were passing. The sky was getting light. He could tell he was making Asler nervous. The guy normally didn't bother to make chit-chat.

"This week alone," he continued, "I netted a truck-load of fucking Africans hiding under crates of lettuce and tomatoes. There were so many of them that we ran out of cells in Detention, had to let a few of them post bond and turn them loose. Won't ever see them again. They'll disappear underground. You can bet good money on that."

Asler was a U.S. detention and deportation officer stationed in Buffalo. In his thirties, he was a few years younger than Nick. He'd been sent to meet Nick at Niagara Falls, New York, and take him to the crime scene on the U.S. side of the St. Lawrence River, seventy kilometres from Montreal. They were in the same line of work, but on different sides of the border. For both of them, the priority was to stem the flow of illegal aliens into North America. Nick was the Canadian counterpart of Asler's boss, so he apparently thought he should try to take Nick's mind off what had happened. It wasn't working.

"We moved fast on this one," Asler rabbited on. "We separated the ill and the infirm from the healthy. The snakehead is in a separate cell. In fact INS has already begun processing the illegals for deportation. The bosses want them out of the country pronto. Before the human rights lawyers and cultural groups twig to the whole thing. We even got the snakeheads. How often have we gotten lucky like that? One's dead and the other in lockup." He tapped the steering wheel to the beat of country and western music playing on the car radio.

Nick didn't respond. He hoped his body language was sending a clear message that he didn't want to talk about Walter Martin's death right now. Didn't want to talk, period.

Just by listening to Asler's tone of voice, Nick knew the guy had been at his job a couple of years too long. In another place, another time, Asler would be pumping gas or driving a bus. He was a decent man, not particularly bright, the son of a mason. Policing the border was like enlisting in the army for guys like him. They sacrificed their lives for the good of their country, and not only in wartime. To Asler, illegal migrants were the enemy, and he always met his quotas to deport. Last year his personal stats showed that he had caught over seven thousand people who had been either trying to enter the U.S. illegally or had overstayed their visas.

The numbers just kept going up. Illegal border traffic went both ways, but seventy percent of the traffic was from north to south. The U.S. Attorney General was not too happy that illegal aliens often used Canada as a conduit for entering the U.S. These rising statistics were fast becoming a bone of contention between the U.S. and Canada. As they said in the vernacular, the shit rolled down. On the political side, the Prime Minister passed the flak down to the Immigration Minister, who in turn passed it directly down to Nick, warning him that his team, the investigative and enforcement unit of Immigration and Citizenship Canada, had to deal with the problem. It was in his court now. But how the hell did you police thirty million visitors who entered the country? How did you ensure that they all left when they were supposed to? Worse, there was no efficient way to track the untold thousands who stayed illegally and were swallowed up by the vastness of the North American continent.

"We tried to get the guy, Nick. The one we did get went nuts, wouldn't stop shooting. Ignored the direct orders of the U.S. government. One of our sharpshooters took him out with the first bullet. Head shot.

What do these people expect? We'd roll out the red carpet for them?"

Nick saw little point in explaining his belief that the law must be served with detachment. "You were in the papers this week over some other shooting."

"We've had quite a few of them lately."

Nick let out a breath but held his silence. The U.S.-Canada Immigration Operation was a joint cooperative effort. To maintain working collegiality, Nick refrained from making comments about the use of excessive force.

Fifteen minutes later, they pulled up in front of a two-storey concrete building. Nick knew the border control checkpoint well. It was fenced at the back with heavy wire around the detention centre where those apprehended on immigration arrest warrants, or caught using false documents, were held. Ideally, detainees were housed there until their country of deportation had been identified. The next step was to contact their country of origin to obtain entry visas so they could be deported back home. In many instances, those with the worst criminal offences were refused entry visas by their country of nationality for their return home. Who could blame them? Nick knew that many of those countries did not have the resources to feed their hungry, let alone attempt to rehabilitate criminals and psychopaths. Depending on their criminal records, they were either locked up or were released, turned loose on society again. Those who were granted freedom were warned to check in with Immigration on a regular basis. But plenty of them were never seen again. They disappeared "underground."

Inside the station, Nick recognized Jim, a supervisor of border operations who was a couple of years away from retirement.

"Where are the detainees?"

"I'm doing paperwork on some of them right now. Want to help me with these body bags?" asked Jim, running one hand through his thinning grey hair.

"Not really. But tell me the numbers."

"Thirty-six males, two of them minors. Five females, all young. Hard to tell their ages. They're all Asians."

Nick's eyes wandered to the sliding glass doors and the black body bags being loaded into another van.

"What about them?"

"Four illegals dead. They either didn't know how to swim or they were old and terrified of water."

"Any of the illegals in lockup speak English?"

"Nobody's admitted to knowing the language."

"What good is interrogating them if we can't communicate?" asked Nick, flipping through the manifest. "Book a couple of interpreters for this afternoon."

"Nick, I got news for you. There's no more money in the budget for interpreters for illegals. We can't afford it. Congress downsized our budget this year."

Nick was saved from venting his opinion by Asler's timely return. Instead he asked, "What about the snakehead who was killed? Was he our guy under wiretap surveillance?"

"Yeah, it looks like him." A team of immigration officers on both sides of the border had been tailing the suspect for several months.

"How about the others? Are they in lockup?"

"One gunshot wound was flown out on a Med-Evac. Surgery at Canadian taxpayers expense. Engle, the big cheese, made that decision."

Another way to stiff the poor Canadian taxpayer. Nick changed the subject, "You're telling me one of the snakeheads got away? How did that happen?"

Jim replied, "I wasn't part of the sting operation. Better talk to Asler or Engle about that."

Back on the road, Nick took in the passing scenery. Growing up in Rochester, New York, he knew this area like the back of his hand. Finally, turning his gaze on Asler, he said, "Okay, tell me how it happened."

"The craft had already docked. According to one of my officers, Martin gave the order for them to come ashore single file. That was when somebody started firing."

"So, five people are dead counting one snakehead?"

"You should see how many illegals they'd crammed into that boat. They panicked and when they started throwing themselves into the water, it got crazy. People piled on top of each other because they couldn't swim. Four of them drowned in less than five feet of water. It's amazing to me that more didn't drown."

Nick said, "I'm telling you right now that I'm going to order an inquiry into how one of my officers got killed. I'm going to order the works. I want ballistics testing from all the guns."

Asler kept his eyes on the road. "I'm the first to admit that we made mistakes."

Nick, facing the younger man, asked, "What the hell went wrong? I've lost a top-notch officer. How the hell did that happen?"

"We're talking two in the morning when the whole damn thing went down. Seems like a long time ago even though it has only been six hours. We made the damn mistake of thinking there were only two agent smugglers. After the shootout we started rounding up the illegals into vans. Your partner, Walter, announced that he was going to take two officers aboard. They were assembling a team to comb the craft when a shot was fired. Walter was at the head of the line. He was killed instantly."

"Why the hell didn't you guys know there was another smuggler aboard?"

"Ah, shit, Nick!"

Nick waited.

After a moment of silence, Asler continued, "We exchanged fire with the third snakehead and we know he took a hit because there's blood on the side of the boat. But he got away."

"Got away? I don't understand how he could've gotten away. One injured snakehead against an army of officers armed with night vision goggles and guns?"

"We've been scouring the water ever since. Given that our smugglers are gooks, I wouldn't put it past them to swim half the St. Lawrence Seaway underwater."

It hit Nick again that Walter was dead. A good friend and colleague was dead. He turned away from Asler to hide the emotions pooling at the back of his eyes.

They turned onto Highway 37 and drove in silence for a while. The Mohawk signs along New York State Highway 37 gave warning to the Federal Bureau of Investigation, U.S. INS, and Immigration Canada against travelling any further. Mohawk guerrillas had been known to shoot at vehicles passing through aboriginal land. Nick was happy to deal with the Crees, Blackfoot or Micmacs any time, but in his opinion the Mohawks were a trigger-happy bunch. Still, he'd done his best to establish a working relationship with the Grand Chief and the reserve police chief. If their own police could control the smuggling of illegal migrants through Mohawk land, so much the better. Unfortunately, the traffic was too lucrative a business to be anything but a source of temptation to certain members of the community.

Large wooden "No Trespassing" signs marked the entrance to the Akwesasne Indian reserve, warning FBI and New York state police to stay off Indian land — a smuggler's paradise of twenty hectares of islands and hidden inlets spanning across Ontario, Quebec and the U.S. borders. Like the U.S. Border Patrol, they ignored the trespassing warning.

Asler swung the SUV onto St. Regis Road and they headed due north to the St. Regis Mohawk Tribal Reservation. Knowing what they knew, neither man spoke to the other. Periodically Nick would finger his bullet-proof vest, reminding himself that most of his vital organs were safe. Unless, this very minute, someone was lining up the crosshairs of a telescopic sight on the back of his head. He sat tensely, observing the houses and farms they passed, keeping an eye out for armed Mohawk warriors.

As they pulled up beside another four-by-four in the dirt parking lot by the boat landing, Jimmy Longbull, Grand Chief of the Mohawks, turned to see who else was appearing uninvited on Mohawk land. A stocky man with long black hair in a braid that fell down his back, he was leaning against the side of his pick-up truck and watching the cops and officials down by the water. He raised a hand in greeting — to Nick only. Longbull didn't care for Asler, who had never acknowledged his authority as Grand Chief by sharing information with him.

"Longbull, how goes it?"

The two men slapped each other on the back in a gesture of genuine warmth.

As if on cue, Asler walked away to join his INS colleagues.

When he and Longbull were left alone, Nick apologized for the presence of the police. The Grand Chief nodded his acceptance of Nick's apology, still keeping a wary eye on the activity on the riverbank.

"Did your people see or hear anything of the shootout early this morning?" Nick asked.

"Sure, my people heard the weapons fire. But that ain't nothing new." Longbull shrugged. "Every day we hear automatic fire. People know better than to go out on the St. Lawrence at night. If it ain't the automatic guns that will cut you down then it's the smugglers' speedboats that will cut you in half."

"So you don't know what happened out there?" asked Nick, pointing towards the St. Lawrence River.

"I'm telling you, Nick. Sure, there's been cigarette and people smuggling here before, but this time there's no Mohawks involved. I spoke to some of my people right after those INS officials told me about it. They say they don't know anything about this smuggling job."

As usual, nobody knows anything, thought Nick. It wouldn't surprise him in the least to learn that the Mohawks had sold docking rights to agent smugglers bringing in their human cargo. Outwardly, Nick accepted the Grand Chief's explanation, and followed the crook of Longbull's finger as he pointed towards a group of old men and women standing underneath a weeping willow.

"They don't like to see this. People aren't proud that this stuff is going on. They feel shame about this, eh? But you know the economy the way it is, some folks get desperate and make money whichever way they can, just to put food on the table, eh?"

"Longbull, I understand. No need for you to defend the actions of others. You're only the chief and not your brother's keeper," Nick said in a conciliatory tone. He knew putting people on the defensive was no way to get answers on the identities of those who killed Walter Martin.

Longbull smiled at him, then motioned another man to join them. "Nick, you remember Ronald Thunder?"

Nick cocked his head to the man in the mirrored aviator-style sunglasses walking towards them.

"The police chief. I remember."

His relationship with the police chief was more complicated. Thunder had always been formal and uneasy with him, as he was now. "Nick," said Thunder in greeting. "I got nine patrol officers, which is not enough to cover twenty hectares. First we deal with cigarette smugglers. Then the booze. Now they're moving people. What am I supposed to do, eh?"

Pushing his luck, Nick asked, "How many illegals has your reserve taken in?"

"Nick, you know where we are? An illegal could come ashore in somebody's backyard right here on Canadian soil. By the time he reaches the road in front of one of those houses," Thunder pointed, "he's already on American soil."

Sounding defensive already, said Nick to himself. Instead, he replied, "Thunder, I understand. You can't police everybody in your community twenty-four hours a day."

Thunder appeared to be satisfied. "People in the community have to earn a living. As police chief I ask myself, which is better? Cigarette or booze smuggling, or people smuggling? The thing is, eh, the smuggling of people ain't a headache for us, 'cause they're just passing through. It's funny how they come from faraway places but it seems like they always know somebody in our community. One guy last month came from Nigeria. He sends a fax asking for Eagle Willie to pick him up at the church in Buffalo. You know that one? Casa Marie something, I think. Now, if you ask me, how come people from places like Timbuktu know the names of some of our people here, eh? Mohawks don't have that kind of resources to handle this level of traffic from organized crime."

Nick stared hard at Thunder. Was the police chief trying to tell him something about Eagle Willie or organized crime? "What makes you think organized crime is involved in running illegal border traffic?" he asked.

"I hear rumours."

"What kind of rumours?"

Thunder shrugged his shoulders and lit a cigarette. "I've arrested a few of our people and they say they got into moving people from their big city connections with mob types in New York. You make what you want of that, eh."

Nick wanted to tell Thunder that he was full of shit. Instead he focused on his surroundings. He had been here hundreds of times before on immigration and smuggling operations. He could walk the narrow path hugging the water's edge with his eyes closed. This was cottage country. A fine place for a picnic or fishing trip. But not today. He took a couple of steps back, moving away from Thunder. Talking to the man always produced more questions than answers. It was an exercise in frustration. Nick turned away, saying, "Good talking to you. Let's follow up later."

With each step, he moved closer to the spot where Walter had died. If it wasn't for the yellow tape, he would never have known that the place was a crime scene. Nothing said violence and death had happened here mere hours before. There was just the sunshine, the fresh morning breeze and the sound of water lapping gently against the river shoreline. Closer to the spot where Walter Martin fell, Nick could see flecks of blood on the blades of grass, and patches of soil stained red. That was all but it was enough. He wiped his face with the back of his hand. He remembered when Walter first joined the unit. The summer of '92, when they'd worked a surveillance mission together, some of the deportations they'd carried out, the big immigration visa scam that had taken them to Holland. After that, there was Algeria, gathering information on those suspected of committing various atrocities. He remembered how Walter had always been ready with a joke under the most trying of conditions, his persistence in tracking down those with a multitude of IDs. Then two years ago Nick had promoted Walter to head of border control operations.

Shit, Walter. Why weren't you careful like always?

Several of the officers looked at him with a sad, unwavering gaze, and one man put a hand on his shoulder. Nick knew they would have liked to offer words of comfort but didn't know how.

Suddenly a car pulled up about a hundred feet from where he was standing. Two women emerged, one in combat fatigues. He immediately recognized Kelly Marcovich by her cropped brown hair and lean muscular frame; the other woman was her assistant, an evidence technician. Kelly was one of his key U.S. counterparts in the fight to control people smuggling on both sides of the border. She called out to him and waited for him to catch up.

"I'm sorry, Nick." She wrapped both arms around him.

"I'm all right, Kelly."

Together they stooped under the yellow tape and entered the crime scene.

Allan Engle, the district director of the United States Immigration and Naturalization Service, turned to greet Nick as they approached. "I'm sorry about Walter, Nick. Good man, he was."

Nick nodded. No one was in the mood for small talk. When he found his voice, he put the question directly to Engle. "What've we got?"

"Several cartridge shells around the area where the shooting happened. And another on the boat."

"How many shots were fired on each side?"

"About fifteen cartridge cases on their side. Automatics and semis down below. A high-powered rifle hidden in the galley. The usual stuff you'd expect to find. Everything's being tagged and bagged to be shipped to our forensics centre. We'll e-mail you the list."

Nick would have preferred to send the evidence to the forensics lab in Canada, but he only said, "Put a rush on the results."

"The best part of it is, we found a box full of phony Canadian visas to enter the U.S. There was also a box of Ontario driver's licences complete with photos of the migrants."

"A lot of work went into producing that," said Nick. "Photo ID with their names. Authentic or phony?"

"If it's phony, it's pretty good copy. We won't know for sure until we do testing," replied Engle.

"Did you manage to get anything out of that snake-head?" asked Nick.

"Nope. And we're not interested. He's all yours," replied Engle with a shrug of his shoulders.

"Why the Christmas present?"

"'Unofficially, Uncle Sam isn't interested in paying his medical bills. Officially, it's jurisdictional. The snake-head has landed status in Canada."

"You're kidding me?"

"The guys back at the station are trying to confirm it as we speak. And if that's the case, I don't need the hassle of dealing with your justice department."

Nick met his gaze.

"Marcovich here will process the paperwork so we can ship him to you."

"We'll take care of it," said Kelly. "Top priority. I don't need more headaches for my officers. The month's just beginning and already we've intercepted over a dozen smuggling jobs. Five were booze and cigarette related. Lots of drug trafficking and other illegal substances."

"You know what they say — with smugglers, the commodity is incidental," answered Nick. "Have you interviewed any of the undocumented aliens yet?"

"Yeah, but they ain't talking. Not even to a woman. Too scared. We'll have one last go at them before we deport them back to their country of origin. If anything of interest comes up, I'll keep you posted."

"Thanks, Kelly." He joined the evidence tech who was combing the area one last time.

Later that evening, driving back into Canada alone, he felt suspended in the darkness of the night, strangely detached even from the fatigue and grief he was experiencing, while another part of his mind was actively engaged with the realities he came face to face with every working day. In the world of human cargo trafficking, borders and security checkpoints had become mere inconveniences to be circumvented with forged passports, lies and guns. The going rate to be smuggled out of a country like China was fifty grand. The illegal-alien smuggling racket was hugely profitable, generating roughly $580 million a year for its bosses. It was a syndicated multinational operation stretching from China, Hong Kong, Vietnam, Thailand and Sri Lanka right into Central America and Eastern Europe.

In the past fifteen months alone, four converted cargo ships had beached in the United States, Canada, New Zealand and Australia. And it was Nick's job to stop the relentless wave of illegals from rolling into Canada. He had set up a surveillance operation and put Walter Martin in charge. Walter's team had set up wiretap surveillance on the dead snakehead, Shaupan Chau. Now both men were dead.

He'd have to start all over again. From the beginning. Except this time he was going after the ringleaders.

chapter two

When counsel was inept, when the witnesses were lying or had destroyed crucial evidence, when the asylum seeker had extreme criminality attached to his name and file, Grace Wang-Weinstein still did her best to keep the displeasure from her voice, and allowed no impatience or anger to show in her face. She did her damnedest to treat everyone who appeared in her hearing room with fairness and dignity. But the deck was pretty much stacked against petitioners who tried to cheat their way past her. It had not always been easy, but over the years Grace had learned how to assume the mask of judicial calm, and to cloak her feelings in the language of due process, procedural rules, and penal proportionality.

This morning's case, unpoetically titled B45690, promised to be a severe test of her acting ability. The police had barricaded the street below on either side. Only officially sanctioned vehicles could park in the metered spots. A squad of RCMP officers maintained

crowd control in front of the building, while inside a
retired Russian civil servant, his face twitching in the
bright light of the hearing room, sat nervously in a witness chair, waiting to testify.

After taking the oath to tell the truth, he tried to
explain how when he arrived in Canada he had a savings account stuffed with twenty-one million dollars.
Grace listened patiently to his attempts to be ingratiating as he described his wonderful good luck in his
financial ventures in wonderful, welcoming Canada.
Maybe if she was younger she'd be gullible enough to
believe that being a Russian bureaucrat was a lucrative
proposition. Here was a refugee claimant with no vis-
ible means of support, and yet within a year his $21
million had grown to $90 million. His counsel made
his arguments in a bullying tone, perhaps hoping to
impress this female judge, who was probably a financial ignoramus, with his assertion that the money came
from market gains on technology stocks. But the wiretap evidence was irrefutable. Months of eavesdropping
by RCMP agents had established that in Russia he had
had ties to the KGB, and that he now had even closer
ties to a biker gang, with whom he had been setting up
a merchant bank on a Native reserve for the purpose
of laundering drug money.

Scattered on the table before her were fat accordion
folders bulging with loose-leaf documents — immigration
officers' observations and notes, pleadings, news clippings, and FBI wiretap evidence. You would think, Grace
silently complained, keeping her irritation to herself, that
it was a black-and-white case for deportation. Add four
lawyers and you had anything but. Money could buy you
a lot of things, including in this case two pre-hearing
conferences and two six-month delays while the claimant
consolidated his financial gains in the country of his

choice. His legal advisers were past masters at the art of stalling. By the time the case was wrapped up, it could be five years. Grace knew damn well that if she rendered a negative decision this morning, the high-priced lawyers would immediately file for leave to appeal her judgment at the federal court. With a current backlog of two years and counting, Vladimir Vladimirovich would be back in business without a care in the world.

Sometimes Grace's friends would ask her what it felt like to sit in judgement of others seven hours a day, five days a week, to hold other people's future in her hands. When she was first appointed a judge on the Immigration and Refugee Commission, she had been excited to think that she could be the one who gave desperate people the chance to make a new life, granting them asylum and citizenship in one of the most prosperous countries in the world. She would be the one who deported false refugee claimants back to the place they came from. The stars in her eyes were long gone, but she still honestly tried to give every asylum seeker a good kick at the can.

And when she was asked what it felt like, holding the lives of others in the palm of her hand, the answer depended on who was asking. To the public and press, her response was, "My determination is based upon my findings of fact and the relevant legal issues." To friends and family, she was more likely to confess that it scared the hell out of her. Every day, she was in the hot seat. She never knew which case would land her on the front page of the morning paper. And the worst of it was that a wrong decision could send a failed asylum seeker home to face uncertainty, poverty, or even death.

Right now, an hour into the proceedings, the hands of the clock seemed to have stopped. Counsel for the claimant and counsel for the government were engaged in a point-counterpoint match over the admissibility of documents to be entered as exhibit items.

The clerk's monotonous voice read into the microphone: "The arresting immigration officer was Nick Slovak. However, the minister's representative is not present. In his place representing the Immigration Department is Rocco Corvinelli."

Nick's name went through her like an electric shock, but her impassive expression did not change. She had not disclosed that she knew Nick. In her opinion, that private fact had no bearing on the case, and the last thing she wanted was more excuses for delay in the Vladimirovich case. She endured another hour or so of posturing by the lawyers, which was really only done for the benefit of the claimant — who was paying for the show — to demonstrate that his counsels' billable hours were the real thing. The unspoken fact was that it made little difference if duplicate or similarly situated evidence was entered as exhibits. All parties had read the documents, and the damage was done.

The fifth package of documents was from Nick's office. His signature was on practically every piece of paper in the stack. That meant that the claimant's removal from the country was something that was being taken very seriously by his department, the Enforcement and Investigation Unit of Immigration and Citizenship. The message was that she should give those exhibit items of evidence a full measure of consideration. Nick really didn't have to emphasize the point so heavily, Grace thought. Cases involving gangsters who thought Canada was a nice, safe place to launder dirty money were not something she took lightly. But that was Nick.

"I've got a dozen affidavits, all attesting to my client's sterling business reputation and his high moral character, that I'd like to enter as evidence," announced one of the opposing counsel.

She flashed a look of impatience at the young lawyer. "More duplication of evidence we don't need, counsel. I suggest we enter only those affidavits that will allow for cross-examination of the witnesses."

A few strands of hair fell across her face. Removing an elastic from a package of documents, she used it to tie her hair back in a ponytail. She rarely thought about her looks these days. It took too much energy and time to look good. As it was, she didn't have enough time to do all the things she wanted to do in a day. Nor did she have the inclination to spend hours at the makeup counter or beauty salon.

"But, your honour," the older of the lawyers intervened, smoothly, "these affidavits are from businessmen who live all across the country. They can't afford to take time to fly in and support my client's asylum claim, but their statements are very significant to this case."

As Grace looked down on him from the bench she could feel her lip cynically curling up at one corner. Over the years she had grown to dislike lawyers who earned their living by representing the criminal elements of society.

"Mr. Dalton, the Immigration and Refugee Commission is mindful of the time schedules of witnesses. That's why we have video conferencing. The video conference calls will be set for next Wednesday." Turning to the refugee claims officer, she asked, "Any objections, Caldwell?"

"None," said the RCO, who was obviously pleased at the discomfiture of the claimant's lawyer, and was trying unsuccessfully to suppress a smirk tugging at the corners of his mouth.

And so for the rest of the morning she continued to allow four grown men to bicker in a kind of intellectual ritual. Corvinelli was there as the immigration department's police officer and witness. The RCO meant to be impartial but it was important that he uphold his place and retain the respect of his legal peer on the other side. Dalton and the other opposing counsel were vested with defending a man's right to remain in the country. When a case went south, the claimant would be deported and denied the right to return to Canada. In many cases that meant breaking up a family. His wife and children would have the choice of remaining in Canada or going with him into exile in whatever country would accept them.

Every day, Grace sat on the bench and listened to the terrible stories of the persecuted, and the elaborate lies of the ambitious. Secretly, she rooted for the genuine asylum seekers, hoping their lawyers would not be too incompetent, and delighted whenever their right to stay in the country could be proved. Every day, she was torn between emotions and intellect. On bad days she separated fathers from their children. Other days, she was merely interpreting and enforcing the law. So much depended on the merits of each case; when claimants were charged with crimes in Canada and abroad, she knew, though she tried to be fair, that their fate depended on how hard-hearted she was feeling on that particular day. Sometimes the press lambasted her for cruel, inhuman decisions. At other times she received death threats for her left-leaning sympathies and being too soft on crime.

Grace had long given up trying to please everyone.

chapter three

Walter Martin had been given a funeral befitting a well-respected peace officer. Hundreds of law enforcement officers attended, many on motorcycles. Traffic was snarled up for a good two hours in uptown Toronto. When it was over, Nick headed back to the office. The mood there was grim. He spent the rest of the morning on the phone, talking to his immigration and law enforcement counterparts around the world, seeking information.

When Officer Philip Wong appeared at his door, Nick, still on the phone, held up two fingers. Wong impatiently paced the hall until Nick hung up.

"What is it?" snapped Nick.

"I've got an informant who'll talk about the snake-heads from the Martin operation. He owns a travel agency in Chinatown."

"Which Chinatown?"

"Little Chinatown, Gerrard and Broadview. I

made kind of an informal deal. He's been charged with trying to bribe an immigration officer for the purposes of buying entry and exit visas. I told him if he talks we drop the charge."

Shortly after one in the afternoon, Nick and Philip Wong were heading east through the city. Wong navigated the van through heavy traffic and crazy jaywalkers before turning down a side street and stopping in front of a travel agency with a sign reading Adventures to Go. They parked in front of a produce and fish shop; the odour that greeted them bluntly announced that fact.

Gerrard Street East attracted Vietnamese, Laotians, Cambodians, Chinese, Bangladeshis, Pakistanis, and Caribbean immigrants. Nick didn't belong to any ethnic minority group in this neighbourhood. "Philip, I'm counting on you to do most of the talking if English is a problem."

The travel agency was empty except for a middle-aged man who sat behind a pile of brochures. He rose from his chair and bowed when they entered.

"Hum Byng," said Officer Wong, speaking Mandarin, "I want you to give my boss a full explanation, everything you told me. Remember, this is your chance to save yourself three years in the slammer."

Hum Byng bowed again and nodded nervously. "We work on commission. As brokers or salesmen. In Mandarin, we're called *shetou*, agent of snakehead ..."

Wong translated for Nick. "He's a genuine travel agent, but he makes a little money on the side moonlighting as a broker to a snakehead. He's sure that his contact works for a huge smuggling syndicate. Nick, the way he describes it, it's like an Amway pyramid scheme. He has no idea who the big players are. He only knows the name of his contact and what he looks like. Contact goes by the name of Tu."

"Chinese?" asked Nick.

"No, Tu's Vietnamese," translated Philip.

"How did Hum find this Tu?"

Wong spoke to Hum Byng, then told Nick, "Tu found him. But he hasn't seen Tu in almost a month. Tu's the one who always initiates contact. No one knows where he lives. Tu is a big-time people smuggler. But this Tu is not the kingpin in the people smuggling pyramid."

The travel agent spoke in rapid Mandarin to Philip, who translated to Nick. "He said this is Tu's territory. When he's in town, the smuggler hangs out at several of the noodle houses on this strip."

Nick, watching the man nod and smile, said, "Tell him we won't charge him with breaking any laws if he continues to cooperate. Tell him we want him to come down to our offices and look at the photos of snakeheads and smugglers we've accumulated. Maybe Tu's in there."

Wong translated, then turned to Nick. "He said he'll come after work tomorrow. I gave him our address."

Back in the van, Wong asked, "What do you think?"

Nick looked out the window as he spoke. "He really hasn't told us anything new. Except now we know for sure that we're dealing with a multimillion or even billion-dollar illegal empire that looks like a huge pyramid scheme. With a Vietnamese connection recruiting legitimate business people to work as brokers. It says a lot for human ingenuity. What we don't know is whether we're looking for one ringleader or several. It may be one huge operation, or a network of independent agents or cells. There's still a lot of questions we don't have answers to."

Nick paused. Philip did nothing to fill the pause until they were midtown at Bloor and Bay. "I'm not holding out much optimism that we've got a mugshot of this Tu character."

"You never know," answered Nick, "sometimes you just get lucky."

"I've got to head out to Regional War Crimes in Etobicoke. Is it okay if I let you off here?" asked Philip.

"No problemo. I'm on home turf here. I'll stroll through the university and grab a bite to eat."

Lunch was a street-vendor hotdog dripping with mustard and relish. As he passed a storefront window, Nick checked his reflection. No obvious mustard and relish stains on his shirt or face. But there was the unmistakable shadow of stubble on his face. It had been over twenty-four hours since he shaved. That would be his excuse for his pathetic appearance these days. His faded black chinos and dark shirt with the bleach stain on the left cuff reminded him that he was also on the slippery slope of the dress code.

When he first joined Immigration and Citizenship he wore a suit and tie every day — until he learned, first-hand, that a tie could become a lethal weapon in the hands of an uncooperative deportee. Now he wore casual clothes to work. What was the use of throwing good money away on a suit only to have it damaged in a scuffle? His mother always said she'd never heard of a high-flying department head who dressed the way he did, but fortunately, his aging parents still lived in Rochester, New York, where Nick had grown up, so he didn't have to pass his mother's inspection often. Sure, he should probably dress in a manner befitting his position, but since the budget cutbacks in his department, which had been downsized to half its investigators, he had become a quick-change artist. He had one set of clothes for meetings and paperwork, and another set for confronting death in the field. It was standard department policy for all field investigators to wear body armour, but sometimes even a bullet-proof vest didn't help. Like the time he went to deport a Somali warlord and found himself being clubbed with assorted kitchen utensils and household furniture by the warlord's four wives and many children. Then they tried to push him out a twenty-first-storey window. Working in pairs was no guarantee of safety either. Only last month, he and another enforcement officer had gone to the home of an ex-cabinet minister from Haiti to hand the man arrest and deportation papers. His partner wrestled with the man's dogs while Nick fought off a two-hundred-pound bodyguard who came at him with a dirty hypodermic and a mean set of teeth.

When he had joined the department a decade ago, inoculation against hepatitis had been standard procedure. Now standard procedure included — in addition to the body armour — face masks, flak jacket, side arms and a mobile phone to call for police backup. But you could take all the precautions you could think of, and sometimes that still wouldn't be enough. Look at what had happened to Walter Martin.

Nick left the subway at the University Avenue station and dashed across four lanes of traffic. He was running late for his meeting with his friend RCMP Captain André Dubois. Their association had been long and fruitful, extending all the way back to Nick's days as a prosecutor. Dubois had always been his first choice as an expert witness in cases involving organized crime, having spent his entire career investigating it. In the seventies Dubois had worked on major undercover operations to bring members of the Mafia and their crime bosses to justice. He had spent time in the eighties tracking down Italian and Latin American drug traffickers. In the wake of the collapse of the Soviet Union in the nineties, he had been assigned to monitor the emergence of the new Russian criminal class. When the U.S. Congress had passed the Immigration Bill, Canada had joined with the Americans to form a joint task force to combat organized crime by non-citizens. As the president had said on television, it was a threat to our borders and national security. The day after Clinton's speech, Dubois had been made the director of the RCMP Organized Crime Task Force.

Dubois was already sitting in the Mocha Java coffee house with a pot of caffeine and his favourite rag, the *Toronto Star*.

"Couldn't you have picked a better place to meet?" asked Nick looking around him.

"You know how I need an afternoon shot of caffeine in my veins. Look at ya." Dubois wagged a finger at his friend. "You could use a quick 100 cc of caffeine in your bloodstream, too."

The coffee house, Nick pointed out, was packed full of hired guns coaching their clients one last time before they made their way into the courthouse around the corner.

"Are you kidding, Nick? I can't think of a better place than this. When we're in a place like this, we're with the people."

Nick rolled his eyes and grinned. It was the first time he'd smiled in days he realized. "Give me the homeless any day."

"True. The defeated are much easier to handle than the self-righteous and the arrogant," said Dubois.

"So, got anything interesting out of that botched illegal alien operation?" Nick ordered a pot of cream to go with his coffee.

"Sorry, I couldn't talk to you at the wake."

"Hey, I was in no shape to talk to anybody," replied Nick.

"Yeah, I noticed."

Nick kept his feelings under wraps as he stirred his coffee with a stir stick.

"You know the dead smuggler your officers were tailing?"

"Shaupan Chau. I remember."

"Well, I ran his fingerprints through CPIC. He also went by another name. Sam Tan. Under Tan, he had a criminal record as long as your arm."

"Why doesn't that surprise me?"

"Well, this is gonna surprise you, Nick. VICAP had him listed as a tough and violent son of a bitch and a Flying Dragons gang member. But he made his money as a hired gun to the highest bidder whenever a gang needed to do something particularly vicious to a victim. His name's been linked to at least a dozen homicides. He was out on parole when he was doing the smuggling job."

"How come we didn't pick up the Tan alias before we requisitioned the wiretap?" asked Nick.

"Because we're short-staffed and overworked? Because the fucking feds axed our budgets and allocated our crime-fighting money to tax collection instead?"

"You said it. We're embittered misfits. Let's not go there right now," said Nick.

"I hear ya." Dubois bit into a muffin and spoke with his mouth full. "We raided Shaupan Chau's house. Found a cache of AK-47s tucked into a hidden compartment in his bedroom."

"He was out on parole and collecting AK-47s?" said Nick, more to himself than Captain Dubois. They both knew that the Russian firearm was the weapon of choice of Vietnamese gangs for a number of reasons. Many gang members had been trained on the AK by their Soviet masters. It rarely jammed and was easy to clean. "The smugglers are Vietnamese?" he asked Dubois.

"Yeah. It's funny. I didn't think the Chinks ever worked with the Vietnamese."

"Hey, it's one big global village now. They can't speak each other's language, but they all accept U.S. currency."

"Ain't that the truth," replied Dubois, slurping his coffee. "The RCMP collected that snakehead from the Americans like you asked. Engle's staff shipped him to us late last night. We ran his fingerprints. He goes by the name Gee Van Tung. Couldn't find any other aliases. His crime sheet isn't in the same league as Shaupan but he's a Dragon triad member all right. Born in Vietnam."

"Hmm," said Nick rubbing his chin. "I just came from Gerrard East. Spoke to a travel agent who works as a commissioned salesman for a human smuggler called Tu. I wonder if Tung would know anything about that?"

"Don't know, but we can ask," said Dubois, scooping up donut crumbs with two fingers. "The other thing is, Tung has a reputation as something of a bungler."

"A bungler? What kind of bungler?"

Dubois chortled into his coffee. "You're gonna love this story. Coupla years ago he shot off the end of his dick with a .45 he had kept stuffed down the front of his pants. Walked into emerg with some story about being in a shootout. But gunpowder marks on the inside of his pants told a different story."

"Jesus, no kidding!"

The two men laughed so hard that they spilled coffee on the table and themselves. Nick wiped his eyes with the back of his hand, and asked, "What about a search of Gee Tung's house?"

"The OPP did the search. Turned up diddly-squat. Someone sanitized it before the cops got there. Another thing, we analyzed the blood from the side of the boat. Type O. Doesn't match any of the smugglers or aliens, but we'd already assumed that. Also, no new hospital admissions of patients with bullet wounds on either side of the 49th parallel with type O blood."

"André," said Nick. "I refuse to believe that Walter's killer can just get away. He's somewhere. Possibly hiding in Toronto, Montreal, or Vancouver. Or even New York or San Francisco. Any city with a large Asian population would allow him to blend in. We're going to have to call in the FBI and maybe Interpol on this one."

Dubois picked up on the hard edge in Nick's voice. "Because of Walter, you're going for the jugular on this one?"

"Damn right I am," replied Nick. "Let's see if Interpol or the FBI has a file on this Gee Van Tung."

"Well, I got something that could be of interest to you. We found a telephone number in Gee Van Tung's pocket. We ran a trace. It's a Toronto number. Belongs to the Mandarin Club. Could be something, could be nothing. Wanna run it from your end?"

"Sure. What is it? Gang hangout?" asked Nick as he flipped open his notebook and jotted down a few entries.

"Some of my officers think it's a den of illegals working under the table."

"I'll check it out myself."

"I'm flying back to Ottawa on the four o'clock. Gonna interrogate Gee Tung. The RCMP's already moved him to the West Detention Centre. Wanna sit in?"

"Wouldn't miss it for the world."

"My flight from the island airport leaves in less than two hours."

"That gives me just enough time to check something on our database," replied Nick.

"How about we hook up at the airport? I've got a few things to wrap up, too."

Back in his office, Nick logged into the Citizenship and Immigration Database, which held the records of hundreds of thousands of resident aliens. The system supplied, at a glance, information on how, when, where and under what class a person had entered the country, and his or her current immigration status. This morning the network was slow. It meant that there were too many officers across the country logged into the system running background checks.

Patience had never been one of his virtues but in this case Nick endured the lengthy transmission delays. If Gee Tung could lead him to the identity of Walter Martin's killer, then justice would be served, and from a department standpoint, a blow would be struck against the global trade in human trafficking. He thought about how much things had changed since his first year in enforcement. His predecessor had been reamed, by the minister of immigration himself, when Canada was caught off guard and 158 South Asians waded ashore in Newfoundland to claim refugee status. A hundred and fifty-eight was nothing these days. Last year, over five thousand people claimed refugee status at Canadian airports.

A couple more clicks of the mouse and he was finally in the system.

Gee Van Tung had entered Canada when he was ten years old under the Family Reunification Program in 1979 at Mirabel Airport. A few more keystrokes and he learned that the entire family had landed immigrant status, but there was no record of citizenship. That meant Gee Tung could be deported. Next, he opened a deportation file to execute the removal of Gee Tung from the country. But in this case, Nick was prepared to trade information for asylum — if Gee Tung came across with the information he wanted. Granting asylum wasn't within his jurisdiction, but he'd cross that bridge when he got to it.

Detention centres had never ranked high on Nick's list of favourite places. They were worlds unto themselves. Sterile buildings that housed deportees prior to their removal from the country. Drug dealers, serial killers, kidnappers, war criminals. Once you had been inside a detention centre, the rose-coloured glasses were off forever. The Ottawa West Detention Centre was situated on what had once been prime farmland. Swell, thought Nick. Displace crops for crooks. He wondered if the politicians had ever offered that choice to the voters.

The armed security guards, electric fences, high tech security codes, and magnetic identity cards were for others. Nick was waved through without the usual checks.

Corridors were heavily monitored by overhead television cameras. A female guard escorted them past several sets of airlock doors and into Gee Tung's cell.

"Look at that. The perp's got private accommodation at our expense," said Dubois, breaking the silence for the first time since they walked into the detention centre.

The prisoner lay on a bunk bed, hooked up to an IV bag. One leg was bandaged up to his thigh and elevated at an angle. At the sight of Nick and Dubois, the passive look on his face changed to one of alarm.

Dubois had never been a fan of prisoners' rights.

"I'm with the RCMP and he's with Immigration," said Dubois, and waited, lighting up a cigarette. In the lengthy silence that followed, Dubois took a few drags and then pulled up a chair across from the prisoner. The staring match had begun. Nick preferred to stand. He leaned his back against the wall with an air of detachment as he sized up the prisoner. Gee Tung was about thirty years old, thin, and had a scar that ran the length of his face from his left eyebrow down past his ear.

Dubois observed the prisoner through a cloud of cigarette smoke. He was a master of the art of silence as a weapon of intimidation, knowing that imagined threats could be worse than reality.

Halfway through the cigarette, Dubois finally opened his mouth. "Let's understand each other, Gee Tung, so no mistakes are made. And don't give me any crap about you not speaking English. Okay? You pull that cheap trick on me and I'm going to knock your front teeth out. We know you've been in Canada since you were a kid. We know a lot about you but we need to know more about your friends. My associate here is gonna vouch that I've been known to use a little touchy-feely to get the job done."

The prisoner lay on the bed, mute and passive. He gave no indication that he understood.

Dubois continued, "We have two options in dealing with you. We can charge you with conspiracy to kill an immigration officer. You'll probably get life for that. Or you can cooperate with us and we'll give you a deal."

"I didn't kill anybody." His voice was faint.

"We know that. We know killing and attempting to kill are two different things. Now that night on the boat, there were three of you. You, Shaupan and the snakehead who got away. The one who got away, what's his name?" demanded Dubois. He grabbed the prisoner and pinched his cheeks painfully together. "I want the name of the third snakehead. Ballistics tells us the slug that killed the immigration officer wasn't from your gun or from Shaupan's. That means the third guy was the killer. What's his name?"

"I want to see my lawyer. After I see my lawyer, we talk."

Dubois's eyes were pinpricks of anger now. He turned to Nick and said, "What did I tell you about

these bad-ass foreigners? They got their rights and privileges down pat. Don't care diddly-squat about their
responsibilities to the country that welcomed them with
open arms." He turned and casually delivered a sharp
hand to the prisoner's mouth.

"Excuse me, you little fucker. This ain't no legal
aid clinic here, so don't you pull that line on me again.
Understand that? No calls to any scumbag lawyer until
I get some answers." Then he was in Gee Tung's face
again. "We found that telephone number in your
pocket and traced it to a place called the Mandarin
Club. We know from police records that you're a
member of the Flying Dragons, and that you've moved
up a coupla notches from being a foot soldier. So
gimme the dope. What's the Flying Dragons'
connection to the Mandarin Club?"

"I want to see my lawyer."

Hand raised ready to strike, Dubois said through
clenched teeth, "What did I just tell ya, you sorry piece
of shit?"

"They'll kill me if I talk."

Dubois pushed Gee Tung's head into the concrete
wall.

"And if you don't talk they'll kill you anyway, just
to be on the safe side. If I don't kill you first. Either way,
you're a dead man if you don't cooperate with us. Look
at it this way. Cooperate and we'll save you from life
imprisonment and possibly extradition. We'll cut a deal
for you and give you protection." Dubois paused.
"Otherwise, first you go to prison, then we kick you out
of the country." He smacked the prisoner hard across
the side of his head with the back of his hand.

Nick didn't move or speak. He could see that the
prisoner was frightened. Ordinarily he would have
intervened at this point, before any real damage was

done. He wondered how far he was prepared to let Dubois go. Would he let him beat the prisoner half to death to get the information they wanted? He thought he might, if it would help them find Walter's killer.

"Okay. Okay, I'll talk. The Mandarin Club is under Dragon roof."

"Speak English. What's this Dragon roof stuff?"

"The Flying Dragons give protection to the Mandarin Club from other gangs."

"Now, why the fuck would the Dragons want to do a thing like that?"

"That's the deal they have."

"Who inked that kinda deal?"

Nick winced at the sight of Dubois raising his hand to strike the prisoner again. Unable to shift his position lying on the bed, Gee Tung raised his hand feebly to block the blow.

"I don't know. I don't know. All I know is the Dragons give protection to the club, and they use one of the karaoke rooms for meetings."

"You're telling me that the Mandarin Club is the official hangout for the Flying Dragons?"

"We go to the club. We go to sing karaoke and to play mah-jong."

"No, stupid!" snapped Dubois, whacking the prisoner across the side of his head. "Did ya use the club for gang business? Like did ya plan the illegal alien smuggling operation there?"

"Gang members never do business in their homes. They want to protect their families from reprisals later on."

"Then how often did you and the other Flying Dragons members meet at the club?"

"Sometimes once a week or twice a month to sing karaoke."

"I don't want to hear about stupid karaoke singing! I want to know if protection money also exchanged hands at the club? Christ almighty!" Dubois swore at the prisoner and then turned to Nick. "I can't believe someone this stupid could plan a smuggling operation worth half a million."

"I don't know about protection money being paid."

"Bullshit! Who's your contact at the club?"

"The general manager. We call him when we want to book the karaoke room."

"Is that how you guys do business? You book a karaoke room?"

The prisoner nodded.

"What about your pal who pulled the trigger on an immigration officer and got away?"

A terrified look came over the prisoner's face.

Dubois spoke softly now, but his voice was full of menace. "You're gonna be a dead man. We're your only hope. Cooperate and we'll give you immunity from extradition to the States."

Nick touched his friend lightly on the shoulder to subtly remind Dubois that extradition was not in the cards. Even if the U.S. wanted to extradite a permanent resident of Canada, the police did not have control or influence over the parole board or jurisdictional issues like extradition.

"I'm afraid. They'll kill me."

Nick spoke for the first time. "I'll kill you myself. What's the name of your friend who killed the immigration officer? Give us that and a good description of him and I'll make sure you get a good plea bargain arrangement. You may even get to stay in Canada."

"Li Mann. His name is Li Mann Vu."

"Good," announced Dubois. "I'm glad we've reached an understanding 'cause you see, I ain't into this police brutality stuff. I only use it when I have to. Get my drift?"

"One more thing," said Nick, "ever hear of a smuggler called Tu?"

"No. Never."

For the next two hours, the three men worked with a police artist via a video conference call to make a composite drawing of Li Mann. After the video equipment was disconnected, Dubois answered the call on his pager.

Driving back into the city in Dubois's RCMP cruiser, they rehashed the interrogation.

"That guy's no mastermind," said Nick. "For sure he's not the ringleader. I wonder if there's any connection between Tu and the snakeheads in this operation?"

"The question is, who is the mastermind? It's either this Li Mann guy or someone else behind the scenes."

"From other cases that we've cracked, it's usually someone who doesn't like to get his hands soiled," said Nick.

"And he's got the money and the contacts to make a good living out of it. I'd profile the guy as someone living on a net income of several million bucks a year, in five-star hotels, while he puts up his clientele eleven or twenty to a room," returned Dubois. His foot was heavy on the gas and the speedometer needle was touching a hundred and fifty. "I'll cross-reference our police networks and see what I can come up with. When I get back to the office, I'll run Li Mann Vu and this Tu through CPIC and every enforcement database and see what happens."

"Those could be aliases. I'm not banking on that turning up much."

Dubois turned sideways to look at his friend. "It's gonna take some digging. It's one thing I learned as a Catholic. These guys all get their comeuppance in the end. You trust me on that, Nick."

Nick said nothing. Memories of Walter Martin weighed heavily on his mind. He was a man in mourning, who only wished he could mourn openly. For Walter, and all the others who had died in the line of duty. It weighed on him now like unwanted baggage.

"Where to, my friend?"

"Drop me off at the Chateau Laurier. I'll catch a cab to the airport from there."

For the next hour he wandered through the capital like a man lost in a trance. He moved where his feet took him, revisiting familiar places. What he really wanted was to pick up the phone and call Grace. But so much water had flowed under the bridge since they broke up. It was painful to realize that he was travelling through the world all alone. He felt as if he had ten men's loneliness trapped inside him.

Back in his hotel room, he changed into his running gear. He ran for the high of it. To feel the pounding of his heart against his chest. On a deeper level, he ran to forget the bullshit and craziness of the workday. And to try to blow her out of his system. Usually it worked, but not today. He was in her town.

He stared at the phone one last time before heading out to the airport. No, he wouldn't call her. What the hell was he going to say? That he was in town, and how about a drink?

Instead he closed the door behind him and hit the button for the elevator. Get it through your head, pal. It's over. Long past the point of blaming her. He could only blame himself for not being wiser. For not knowing, until it was too late, that her ambition on the bench far outweighed any love she had ever had for him.

chapter four

It was a hazy morning, promising a bright, hot day. Grace took a cab to work. Her fourteen-year-old Volvo had broken down yet again, which meant two days in the shop and another six-hundred-dollar bill. What she needed was a new car. A Toyota Camry or the latest BMW would be nice, except for one small problem. In her family, the Wang-Weinsteins, Japanese and German-made cars were still referred to as "enemy" cars. Her parents had been mere infants when the atrocities in their former homelands occurred, but the history of it all still lingered in their minds. In any case, with her luck she'd drop forty thousand dollars on a BMW and within a week it would be on a container ship to the Middle East, Hong Kong, or Russia. That's why a rusting Volvo, supplemented by taxi cabs whenever it was in the shop, was still much cheaper and less complicated.

"This block will do. Drop me off here."

Three years had programmed her for the walk, which took her across O'Connor and up Bank Street. From there, she turned down Slater towards an uninspiring thirty-seven-storey concrete building. A silver and black sign proclaimed "Immigration and Refugee Commission".

The IRC sat four blocks south of Parliament Hill, a mere ten-minute walk away from the political machinations it had been set up to bypass. Back in 1989, the commission had been created with noble intentions, as an arm's-length agency, to determine who was or was not a refugee under the 1951 Geneva Convention. The year she had been appointed was the same year the commission had earned the distinction of being just about the most vilified government agency in the country. Knowing that, she had still accepted a political appointment to the bench. Why? Ambition — and naïveté. She had wanted to grant asylum to every deserving, downtrodden soul from every wretched country in the world. And besides, what else could you do with a law degree and a doctorate in anthropology?

It was easy to tell when an immigration or human-smuggling story had hit the front page. The lobby became a circus of newshounds. She did her best to look unimportant and anonymous as she threaded her way through them towards the bank of elevators. At the security desk, she discreetly flashed her ID badge to the men guarding the agency from subversives, and from the public it was supposed to serve.

On the nineteenth floor, she slipped past cubicles of overworked civil servants who laboured in silence, bent over desks covered in paper and case files. There were days when she still thought that the taxpayers were getting their money's worth from all these young prosecutors, stern moralists bent on carving out careers, weeding out bogus asylum seekers from the genuine article.

"Grace!"

She turned around and came face to face with Mark Crosby, one of her least favourite colleagues. Crosby was a womanizer and plotter; when not on the bench, he spent his time scrounging around for cheap feels and political gossip.

"What?" she barked.

"I hear you're assigned the Vladimir case?" he asked, leaning against the door outside her office.

"What's it to you?"

"Need a second-chair? I could be of help to you. Given that last year, I was in Russia for three months with Immigration." He glanced at the banker's boxes of documents stacked outside her office waiting to be returned to records.

"Well, thanks, but no thanks."

Not put off by the lack of friendliness, he continued, "I'm heading out to Vancouver this afternoon to try a boatload of Filipino sailors. My second-chair is down with the flu. Wanna run away with me?" he winked. "I checked. You got nothing on the docket."

"No. I'm busy," she snapped, giving him the once-over. Black horn rimmed glasses, double chin, and an ever-growing paunch. Why on earth should she be interested in him? She found his sexual interest in her almost insulting.

She pushed past him as she walked into her office, a nine-by-nine foot place of chaos, crammed with bulging files and more banker's boxes of documents. It wasn't luxurious by any stretch of the public's imagination. However, this was the cubby-hole where she had produced her best work, the legal decisions that had held up at the Federal Court.

"Grace, you really could use my help on the Vladimir case and I can use yours on the Filipino sailors' case. I don't see why you're not keen to work together."

"The fact is, I'm not into office romance. I've said it once. I'll say it again."

"Come on, Grace. What's a gorgeous girl like you doing all by yourself? You know how it could be between us."

She glared at him. "I don't want to hear how you feel about me. Let's not go there. We've got a nice working relationship, so let's keep it at that."

"What about the hotel room I've already booked for you?"

"What? What?" She was royally pissed. "Cancel it! Cancel it right away! I don't need that kind of cheap gossip hanging around me." She wagged her finger menacingly at him. "Do something like that again and it's grounds for a harassment charge. Send me an e-mail when you've cancelled the hotel room. Jesus!"

Without another word she buried her head in the file sitting in the middle of the desk, hoping he would go away. Mark Crosby had a sharp mind for spinning clever legal arguments, but she found him irritating. Unfortunately for her, he was somewhat infatuated with her. At the same time she could see the loneliness in his face. She wondered if he could see the loneliness in her as well. They were both workaholics, partly because they both had little going on in their private lives. He probably interpreted that as common ground. The fact of the matter was, he just didn't appeal to her.

As she reached for the second package of exhibit items, the phone rang.

"Ms. Wang-Weinstein? This is Cindy Black from the law offices of Richard and Richard. We're seeking a postponement of Thursday's case."

"May I ask why?"

"We need time to line up the witnesses. Immigration refuses to accept the authenticity of the passport and birth certificate. The lawyers want to explore identity through witness testimony."

I don't know how witness statements can vindicate your client when it's clear from the documents that he's a liar, Grace wanted to say. Instead she answered, "I suggest you call scheduling and ask for a hearing date next month. I'm not willing to postpone it further than that. And I want to see those witness statements at least a week prior to the hearing."

"You'll get them. I appreciate this, Ms. Wang-Weinstein."

"You're welcome."

She knew that refugee claimants were often quite prepared to violate the Immigration Act by producing forged or stolen identity and immigration documents. It was predictable, yet dispiriting. Four years on the bench had made her weary of photocopies presented as "original documents," or identity papers that were torn or had incomplete stamps and seals or faded lettering. That was the problem with the job. After a while, compassion fatigue set in, closely followed by cynicism. Nothing surprised her. She had seen it all before. Prosecutors and judges who spent too many years in the business became masters of the same worn-out, exasperated expression.

After she hung up, she reached into her briefcase for the morning's *Globe and Mail*. Immigration and refugee stories were now a sign of the times. Populations were on the move, displaced by war, natural disasters, famine — who could have guessed that her Ph.D. dissertation on mass movements and resettlement of displaced peoples would position her in a growth industry? Wanting to make a difference in the world, she had accepted a contract with the United Nations High Commission for Refugees to study mass migration in Europe. That was the year when Europe had to deal with an influx of millions of people leaving the former Soviet Union. In the course of her two years with UNHCR, which spanned seventy thousand interviews with asylum seekers, she had learned two facts. One, people migrated. For whatever reason, they wanted a chance to live in another country that offered them better economic opportunities. Two, when too many people migrated, prosperous countries responded by shutting their gates through tougher immigration laws. But people were desperate, and willing to do anything. They would use fraudulent documents, pose as other people, become indentured slaves as nannies or sweatshop workers or prostitutes, run drugs, run guns — anything to earn hard currency to pay for passports and air tickets.

In Geneva, one of her tasks had been to deal with the press, who tended to be unsympathetic to the plight of refugees. Often, she would link them up with various field officers: people who worked on certain cases or remembered a story that stayed with them. Grace thought about the case that still resonated through her life after all those years, like the incoming tide that washed driftwood onto a beach. She would never be able to forget the face of that young woman. The case had played itself out at customs in Sweden. A young Iranian woman and her baby had been smuggled out of Iran by agent smugglers. They had stuffed her and her baby into a cargo trunk. When customs officials pried open the top, they found the woman buried underneath a bundle of rags. During the trip, the baby had suffocated. Mouth to mouth resuscitation could not save her infant. The young mother had seized her one chance to escape from Khomeini's henchmen, who had executed every member of her family, only to find herself being charged with criminally negligent homicide by the Swedish authorities, and sent to jail.

Grace despised agent smugglers. To her they were no more than criminals living off the desperation of others. But she knew that those desperate people in Third World countries often saw them as saviours. And sometimes, she grudgingly had to admit, they were.

She grabbed a second cup of coffee from the lunchroom and scanned the papers. This was the third immigration story splashed all over the front page this month. More often than not, she read the feature stories not for the news, but to see if the reporters got the details right. The lead story this week was about a people-smuggling ring that was jointly smashed by U.S. and Canadian immigration officers. A migrant vessel had been intercepted around Akwasasne. Nick Slovak's colleague, Walter Martin, had been killed in the shootout between INS agents and the snakeheads. Even the papers were calling them snakeheads now. She preferred the term alien smugglers. The dead smuggler, Shaupan Chau, had been granted refugee status by the IRC in Montreal, back in the mid-1990s. Thank goodness she hadn't been the judge who heard his case. Blank passports and Canadian visas were found on the boat. It must have been an inside job in some embassy somewhere. How else would they have gotten their hands on blank passports and visas?

There was an adjoining article about Nick. It described how he had spent the last couple of years running undercover operations against agent smugglers. There was a picture of him at the bottom of the page. She soaked up his image; looking for subtle changes since they had last seen each other. The photo didn't do him justice. In the flesh, he exuded energy and intelligence. She remembered the first time she had laid eyes on him. He was her idea of handsome: deep-set, piercing grey-green eyes, a serious, sensitive face, mop of brown hair falling over a high forehead, the way his clothes hung on his five-foot-eleven frame. He moved with an easy grace; she knew that he either played or had once played a lot of sports. He turned her on. Taking him to bed was easy, but a real extramarital romance wasn't something she had planned. A brief encounter had morphed into something deeper. In the beginning, on impulse, she had lied to Nick about not being married, and then she had to go on lying. What a fool she had been. At first it was easy to do, living in two different cities. He always called her on her pager. But then one day he had called her office and her secretary had inadvertently provided him with her home number. David, her husband, had answered the phone. Nick had ended their romance. He told her he wasn't interested in a three-way relationship. Not long after that, David, too, left her and filed for divorce.

After the break-up with Nick, she rationalized that there was no way their relationship could ever have worked. In the world of immigration, there were two opposing sides. Those like Nick who stopped the barbarians at the gate. And adjudicators like her who granted them asylum and let them in. In their nine months of sleeping together they had both been crossing into enemy territory.

A few months later she had presided on a case in which Nick had represented the minister's office. He had spent months building a deportation case against a female member of the Iranian mujahedin. However, in Grace's opinion the middle-aged woman didn't fit the profile of a terrorist. In her legal decision, she had written that living in a mujahedin neighbourhood wasn't the same thing as actually being a bomb-throwing member of an underground army. Forced to choose between love and the exercise of her own judgement, she really had no choice at all. She could not convict a woman she believed was innocent because she was in love with the prosecutor. Nick was outraged, and his office treated her as *persona non grata*. He hadn't returned any of her calls. To make matters worse, the left-wing ideologues had been triumphant, using her legal decision as a moral victory in their propaganda war with the right-wing ideologues over the issue of refugees.

Staring at the photo of Nick, she was filled with regret and desire. It was too late now to pick up the phone. Too much time had passed and events had driven them too far apart. The connection between them was broken.

chapter five

Nick was on a first-name basis with agents of the FBI, CIA, Interpol, MI5, MI6, Mossad and half a dozen other police forces around the world, but one of his most frequent working partners was his old friend, Detective Steve Kappolis of the OPP. Kappolis commanded the fugitive squad, which investigated and tracked down criminals from other countries who had chosen Canada as a hiding place. The last case they'd worked together had involved a phony document ring that was doing brisk business in the reproduction of passports, *propiskas*, health insurance cards and other documents for illegals who were living under false identities. Nick knew he could count on Kappolis. The detective was not one to play the information-sharing, power-playing jurisdictional games that provincial and federal enforcement agencies often indulged in.

Nick figured if the killer of Walter Martin had not been a criminal before he entered the country, he was a criminal now. And within twenty-four hours Kappolis had gotten a police search warrant for the Mandarin Club.

The world of clubs held no allure for Nick. The only one he had ever belonged to was Hart House, the alumni association at his university, and he guessed the Mandarin Club wouldn't be much like Hart House. According to the current month's issue of *Entertainment* and the scribes of the city's gossip columns, the Mandarin was an expensive and glamorous new place where Asian hip-hop and celebrity types hung out. The membership fees alone spoke of a closed world of privilege, where those with money and leisure could afford to pass the time exchanging gossip over mai tais and margaritas.

Detective Steve Kappolis parked his unmarked cruiser at the end of the block right under a tow-away sign.

Apart from its prime location, there was no mistaking the aura of exclusivity which extended right down to the sidewalk: the building was sixty thousand square feet of marble opulence, with a raised roof and nine-metre cathedral windows. A flashing sign underneath one of the windows promised karaoke five nights a week.

"Tacky," said Kappolis. "Big red canopy. Flashing neon. Looks like a bordello, if you ask me."

"This is how the yuppies fool themselves that they're not going into the red light district." Nick patted his hip pocket to make sure he had his wallet.

"Let's not mention the warrant right away. I want to get a feel for the place before everyone makes a run for it or destroys evidence."

"I'm with you," Nick answered.

"We're the run-of-the-mill customers who want to check out the girls and the booze before buying memberships. The only problem is, it's four hundred bucks just to get in," said Kappolis.

"Four hundred bucks! No club is worth that."

"Nick, this ain't the time to be cheap, my friend. And don't count on me, because this is an immigration matter. The requisition originated from your office. Remember?"

"I'm sure glad I made that trip to the bank machine," grumbled Nick.

They extended their wrists and receipts to the doorman who wordlessly unhooked the rope. Nick tried to make out the Chinese characters stamped on the back of his hand as they climbed the wide circular staircase to the first floor.

"Let's keep tax evasion in mind if nothing else pans out," remarked Kappolis as he eyed a couple of Hollywood actors with their dates, tall, slender birds of paradise in five-inch stilettos, impossibly uncomfortable clothing, and blue eyeshadow.

"White collar crime isn't at the top of my agenda here," replied Nick dryly. "I'm here for a certain matter of justice."

Kappolis cast a brief look at Nick's set face and wondered if "revenge" might not be more a more accurate term.

Clouds of opium smoke and other illegal substances assaulted their nostrils. Not even in the old days, before he became respectable, had Nick ever frequented places like this, but in fact, the club was giving him a feeling of déjà vu. It took him back to his posting in Thailand in the eighties, when he was a young intellectual-property lawyer working for a Boston firm. One of his clients had been a big-name New York fashion house that wanted to put a stop to the Asian knock-offs that were costing them millions in lost revenues. His investigation had led him to the bars and whorehouses in the red light district of Bangkok where he saw the knock-offs being worn as a uniform by every bar girl. Those years of working and travelling through Asia came wafting back to him, bringing a sharp nostalgia for that Eastern culture, with its mix of tranquillity and cruelty, devoutness and grasping ambition, beauty and squalor.

Kappolis gave him a reality check by poking him sharply in the ribs. "You wondering where the money came from for all this? I just found out from that guy over there that this place has three separate nightclubs. I could get used to a place like this."

"Well, don't even think about it. It's not in your budget."

"Speaking of budget, bet they uncork a lot of pricey champagne here. And none of this cheap Baby Duck stuff."

"Come on."

A frosted-glass door led into a cavernous disco lit by flashing coloured lights and a gigantic overhead glitter ball. The walls were tastefully plastered in nineteenth-century Chinese art. A slim, tuxedoed young woman croupier presiding over the blackjack and roulette tables tried to entice them over to play. They ignored her to admire the singer in the daring sequined number who was belting out a Chinese torch song.

"My Cantonese isn't as good as yours. It's hard to get worked up about a song if you don't understand the words," said Kappolis.

"Never mind my Cantonese. Don't look now, but over there ... notice anything funny?"

"Yeah. I thought the courts had banned lap dancing. Obviously those with moolah think they're above the law." Kappolis pointed at the stage. "Look at the mirrored floors. Now look at the videocameras. Holy shit! Girls with no knickers! Real kinky."

"Asian nightclubs tend to be like this. I remember when I lived in Japan. In the Shinjuku district of Tokyo,

Roran Shabu Shabu was an exclusive all men's dining club. None of the waitresses wore underwear. You paid $36,000 a year for the privilege of titillating yourself."

"Nick, you telling me that this is real tame by comparison? I want to go upstairs. Maybe it gets kinkier up there."

They ignored the singer in the skin-tight micro mini who was pouring her heart into a microphone for the second floor club, done in Italian wrought iron.

"Crowd's different. A lot of Armani suits," Nick observed.

"For some, there's never a recession," replied Kappolis.

"Probably not their money. They're on expense accounts."

The waitresses were dressed as schoolgirls in white shirts and micro kilts with baggy white socks.

"This is paedophile heaven. I should send Vice over now," commented Kappolis.

"Before we do that, let's check out the top floor."

The third floor, billed as "Ecstasy Club," was a cokehead's paradise. They walked through a set of red doors to find people in an array of positions and states of undress shooting stuff into their veins and inhaling substances up their noses. In another opium-filled room were several couples making out on floor mats.

Kappolis pointed to a man lying prostrate on the floor with his shirt opened. "I know that guy," he whispered to Nick. "He's a city councillor. He was on television just days ago talking about family values. Can you believe it?"

They stood by the door, taking it all in. A voluptuous bottle blonde in a latex body suit and a leather whip was dragging a middle-aged man around the room by his dog collar.

Nick whispered, "I read somewhere that dominatrixes make good coin whipping and brutalizing their clients."

Off in one corner was a bearded man stretched out on the floor smoking an opium pipe. In an alcove, a young woman in little more than stilettos and a pair of surgically assisted breasts was entertaining a half-dressed drunk.

"That's it for me. I've seen enough," said Kappolis.

"I agree. Casino gambling on the first floor. Half-naked politicians. Women with no underwear. If we don't shut this place down right now, our asses could be hauled before a public inquiry questioning our behaviour in coming here."

"Right. Our pensions are at stake here." Taking out his cellphone, Kappolis made the call for uniformed officers, and plenty of them.

Nick led the way back down to the first floor. It took less than three minutes for two squad cars to pull up at the curb. At the sight of uniformed cops, Nick pulled out his ID and asked the nearest bartender, "Who's in charge of this place?"

"That would be the general manager, Andy Loong."

Nick remembered what the snakehead Gee Tung had said about the general manager being the conduit.

"We want to see him. Now!"

Andy Loong turned out to be a hip young Asian dressed in pink and lime green, sporting coloured hair and a pair of earrings.

He stared at the search warrant and protested at being shut down. "We have a bona fide licence to operate the club. Our clientele is very respectable."

"Yeah? Is that so?" Kappolis's tone was cocky.

"Our guests are all very legitimate people. District attorneys, supreme court judges, business owners and movie moguls. This a very legitimate establishment. See those photos on the wall?" he pointed to a row of black-and-white photographs of prominent people.

"We don't care about your who's-who list," said Nick. "What I want to know is, what kind of joint you're running?"

"This is a private club for people of high class."

"Class thing, is it?"

Kappolis's sarcasm was lost on Andy Loong. He continued in an earnest tone. "Entry is for members only. Our initiation fees are five thousand with annual membership at three thousand. Right now we have a waiting list for membership."

"I'm sure you do," answered Nick. "Who owns the place?"

"Mr. Sun Sui."

"Where is he? Where did he get his money?"

"Mr. Sui is at home this evening."

"Pick up the phone and call him. Tell him to get his butt over here right now," demanded Nick.

"He doesn't like to be disturbed at home."

"Tough shit," said Kappolis in a menacing tone.

Loong quietly complied, punching in a set of numbers on Kappolis's cellphone. Nick took the phone out of Loong's hand, and listened for a few seconds. "His bloody voicemail. The guy's not home. I don't feel like leaving a message when the element of surprise works a hell of a lot better," he said to Kappolis.

"Getting back to this membership business," said Kappolis to Loong, "how about letting us have a look at that membership list of yours?"

"I can't do that. That's private information. I would have to ask the members first."

"We got a search warrant, Mr. Loong. I hope your immigration status is regularized. Or you better start praying."

The general manager sighed. "I'll give you a computer printout. You want it right now?"

"Yeah, after we're done with the questions. I see you're peddling sex and drugs on the third floor."

"Those are massage rooms. We have permits for that. And I can't say exactly what goes on behind closed doors."

"Yeah, yeah. Heard that excuse before."

"The girls are dancers and entertainers. If they want to sell sexual services, it's up to them. It's got nothing to do with the club management or policy."

"Is that so? Well, this is an immigration investigation. And I want to see their working papers. Or else I'm gonna shut the place down for the evening. And maybe permanently."

"That's a big loss of profits. I assure you they're all here legally. All have working papers. Why close down the club if I can prove this? What you're doing isn't good for business. Everyone has paid good money ..."

"Mr. Loong, we've heard enough," snapped Kappolis, impatiently.

"Mr. Sui is with the immigrant investor program. You can't do this to him. He's a very important man. Immigration Canada promised him lots of help if he invested in this country. That is what he is doing. The club needs to stay open." Loong was still protesting as the uniformed cop escorted him out of the room.

Nick and Kappolis carved up the interviews with the eight police officers from backup, but kept Loong for themselves. Saved him for last. It was a tactic they learned early in their careers.

The first entertainer was a pretty and petite woman going by the name Niin Tran.

"What documents do you have to confirm your immigration status in this country?" Nick asked, scanning her documents which gave her age as twenty-four. However, the girl in front of him looked no more than seventeen. Nick made a notation in the side margins to look into the matter. Sexual exploitation of female minors was a very serious offence in his book.

The second entertainer looked nothing like her photo. In the photograph she was wearing spectacles and a white blouse. Whereas the woman before them had dark, kohl-rimmed eyes, no glasses, and spiked hair the colour of a flaming sunset. Her lipstick was a dark shade, almost black, a colour they had not seen on lips before, and her skimpy sequined outfit barely covered her body. Kappolis and Slovak could not stop staring until they noticed that her stage companion was dressed in an even skimpier costume that left nothing to the imagination. It was not every day that they came across big-breasted Orientals.

"Implants," whispered Kappolis to Nick.

Nick stared harder. He had never seen a woman with breast implants. Could this be the real reason why men paid such stiff initiation and membership fees? After the two girls, they interviewed two young males who could easily have passed for the opposite sex.

"Nick, it took me a while to figure out they were guys."

"Yeah. Let's not linger longer than necessary with these people. There're too many of them and I don't wanna pull an all-nighter."

Nick retrieved his laptop from Kappolis's car, and started banging out notes with mathematical precision. Full names, nationality, dates they entered the country, the dates their foreign authorizations were due to expire, visa numbers, the whole shebang. When he lifted his eyes from the keyboard, he noticed that the woman sitting in front of him had legs that were far too thick for a dancer. He didn't believe that she had ever danced a day in her life before coming to Canada. He was trying to keep an open mind, but the only thing believable about these girls was that they all came from backward economies.

"How did you learn about getting a job here if you're from Thailand?"

"Advertisement in newspaper in Thailand."

"Who's your employer? Who pays you?"

"The general manager, Mr. Loong, looks after us. He pay us once a month. Put money in our bank accounts."

By the time they finished interviewing all the girls, Kappolis and Slovak were immune to half-naked bodies.

"Even the bouncer's an import. It doesn't take a lot of brains to be a bouncer. We got unemployment at ten percent and we're bringing in Third World thugs to be doormen?" asked Kappolis.

"I'm going to have one of my officers look into these work authorizations."

When Andy Loong sat down, he asked for permission to smoke, and lit up a cigarette with trembling hands. Nick registered the man's nervousness without looking up from the pile of witness statements. "Are you a landed immigrant, sir," he asked, "or here on a work permit? Please produce your documents for verification."

"I am a landed immigrant."

"May we see your landing card?"

Andy Loong pulled a dog-eared piece of paper from his billfold.

"Tell us about the club's relationship with the Flying Dragons triad," asked Kappolis.

Loong's face became noticeably paler. "Some who come aren't respectable people, but there's no way to deny them entry when they're paid up in full. As long as they abide by the rules, we have no problems. I know nothing about triads."

"Don't fuck with us," said Nick. "We weren't born yesterday."

Nick studied Loong as he closed his eyes, trying to pull himself together.

"Okay. This is Dragon roof, but we don't pay protection money."

"We hear the club's giving free services to the Dragons."

"Where did you hear that?" he asked defensively.

Nick shrugged.

Loong's hands were trembling. "Please, you don't understand. I'm not involved in these things. This is a job for me. I don't want my employer to think I'm not doing a good job. I could be in trouble because good jobs are scarce."

"Knowledge and involvement are two different things." Nick tried his best to sound sympathetic and intimidating at the same time. "Tell us what you know. Your cooperation will be rewarded. *So far*, you've committed no offences." Nick allowed the emphasis to sink in.

"We're under a Dragon roof. The Flying Dragons started getting in for free when Lo Chien triad tried to roof in on the club. Mr. Sui wasn't interested in paying protection money to Lo Chien. Lo Chien attempted to kidnap Mr. Sui one night, and some Dragon gang members who were drinking at the club helped foil the kidnapping attempt."

"Did you report the kidnapping to the police?"

"I didn't. I don't know if my boss did or didn't."

"Why did the Dragon gang members help Mr. Sui? Tell us about his relationship with them?"

"I don't know. It's not my place to ask questions. I only know that he allows the Dragons the use of the club. They come for drinking and karaoke."

"Does anyone else get free membership to the club?"

"Not that I can remember."

Nick produced mug shots of Gee Tung and Shaupan Chau. He also showed Loong a sketch of Li Mann. "Recognize any of these guys?"

Loong looked at the pictures blankly. Nick repeated the question.

"No, I don't think so."

"The drugs on the third floor, who supplies them?"

"What drugs?"

Kappolis glared at the general manager. "Don't fuck with us. We ain't stupid. You're already down on charges of prostitution, association with criminal elements. You don't need drug trafficking and soliciting. The way I see it, you've already racked up about seven years' worth of charges."

"We don't supply drugs. The clientele bring their own and we look the other way."

"This is a copy of your membership list? Everybody's name is on here?"

"Yes."

"It better be." Nick stuck the list in his notebook computer case. He stood, and nodded briefly to Kappolis, who pulled out a pair of handcuffs from behind his back.

"Okay, Loong," said the detective. "Let's go down to the station. I gotta book ya."

A few minutes later Nick and the detective were outside the building, leaning against the railing as they compared notes.

"In my opinion, tits and ass is nothing more than a cover to run a human smuggling operation. When you get beyond the girls without underwear, you're dealing with the same bullshit of moving bodies here from the Third World," said Nick.

Flipping the pages of his notebook, Nick wasn't thinking about the street scene, but he registered a brief flash of white in his peripheral vision as the Chrysler sedan with the tinted windows came towards them. Out of sheer reflex they hit the ground at the sound of gunfire. Thank God for Kevlar vests, Nick thought, as he struggled to get his gun.

Then, as quickly as it began, it was over. Nick picked himself up, put his hand to his head, and felt the stickiness. Blood. His left temple above his eye was bleeding — he'd been hit by flying debris. It took another moment to realize it was nothing serious. Kappolis, too, was in one piece. But Loong was dead. He was lying flat on his back, eyes open, blood pouring from holes in his head and stomach. Another bystander was also dead, and half a dozen were shot and bleeding. The officer beside him had been shot, but was alive. Nick, being the closest, did what he could to staunch the flow of blood from the man's wounded leg.

They spent the next hour loading bodies into ambulances and seeking out eyewitnesses.

chapter six

"... the death toll from last night's drive-by shooting in Toronto has gone up. A third person has died in hospital. The incident is the fifth drive-by shooting in that city in the past three months. Crime in this city seems to be way up. And a good proportion of it is committed by foreign elements who've managed to elude your department for almost a decade. Would you care to comment on the situation?"

A television camera crew had caught Nick trying to flee through the back doors of the Immigration Building.

"What situation are you referring to? If it's the drive-by shooting, the police and the RCMP Organized Crime Task Force have apprehended several gang members from a competing triad. Warrants have been issued to do search and seizure of their premises. Everything's under control."

"What are you going to do about criminals from other countries coming here illegally?"

"I'm glad you asked me that," said Nick. He looked anything but glad.

Grace hadn't seen or spoken to him in seven months, but from the televised image she could see that his face was bruised and bandaged up as if he'd been in a bar brawl. She felt her eyes tearing up. She couldn't help it. The sight of him filled her with tenderness and yearning. Just about every case he worked on had left its mark on him, like a soldier in a nasty war.

"Unfortunately it takes an incident like this to get the public's attention. I don't want to alarm anybody, but sometimes people wilfully destroy their passports and claim asylum. When that happens we really don't know who the hell they are. And once they leave the airport, there's virtually no way we can police them. Unless of course they commit a crime and get caught. I'm sorry I can't talk further. I've got to run to a meeting."

There was a two-second shot of Nick diving into an unmarked police cruiser.

Grace turned off the television. Nick Slovak and his department were in deep trouble, and not just from a public relations angle. Suddenly, a case about a botched human smuggling operation had taken a 360-degree turn. One dead immigration officer and a drive-by shooting that had claimed the lives of innocent people. She wished she could help him out. But she couldn't just call him up out of the blue.

She sighed. Once upon a time she had had two men in her life. Now she was dancing solo. She was a woman alone, without the benefit of husband or children. She had a nice house, but it was devoid of photographs of a handsome husband and laughing bambinos. All she had was her career, her ambition, and her mortgage. There were days when life looked pretty hollow.

The phone rang, startling her out of her thoughts. The call display on her kitchen phone showed her workplace number. Couldn't they leave her alone even for one day? She wasn't scheduled for any cases.

"This is scheduling. The deputy minister would like you to sit as second chair on a case, the one that's in the news about that snakehead."

"Which one would that be? There seem to be so many."

"Gee Tung, the one implicated in the murder of an immigration officer. Maybe last night's drive-by shooting, too. The deputy minister wants to expedite the case. Speedy deportation. Mark Crosby's presiding and they want a second chair. Your name came up."

"Can I think about it? I'll call you tomorrow."

"Just talk it over with Crosby. We called him at the Vancouver office. He should be back on the eight o'clock flight tomorrow. All you've got to do is secure his consent."

She mulled it over as she cleaned her kitchen. Cases like this didn't come along every day. It had all the ingredients of a good movie plot: immoral alien smugglers, Asian triads fighting over gang turf, drive-by shootings, nightclubs where dancers doubled as prostitutes, raids on seedy rooming houses packed with young illegals. Not to mention a handsome immigration officer in charge of the investigation.

She narrowed her eyes in thought as she opened a tin of cat food. Face it, Grace. You want the case. It's a reputation maker. Whoever hears the case will be queen of the heap.

And not only that, it was the perfect bridge to meeting Nick again.

She called Crosby at home and left a voice-mail message. After cleaning up the kitchen, she decided that it was to too nice a day to waste in front of a monitor and keyboard banging out legal reasons. She would bike down to Chinatown and pick up a few grocery items for dinner; she was out of sesame oil, soba noodles, and green tea.

A stroll through Chinatown was like a stroll down memory lane. The hanging barbecued ducks in the window and boxes of fish and dried goods displayed on racks on the sidewalk reminded her of her many childhood trips to Vancouver's Chinatown with her mother. Stopping in front of a shop window full of spices and dried herbs, she stared momentarily at her reflection in the glass. While she had inherited her father's thick wavy brown hair, her facial features were a composite of her parents, a blend of West and East.

She made a mental note to call her parents on the weekend, when they were back in the country. Now that they were retired they spent their summers travelling, and for the past month they had been visiting her mother's ancestral village of aging aunts, uncles and cousins. It was no holiday of pleasure. It was more a pilgrimage of guilt and obligation to those left behind the Bamboo Curtain.

Last year they had spent a month in Israel. It had been William Wine's second trip to the Red Sea in his sixty-nine years. His father, Grace's paternal grandfather, had been born Aaron Weinstein, but changed the family name when they emigrated to Canada. Aaron Weinstein had opposed Hitler at a public rally, and was jailed as a political enemy of the Nazis. In 1941, he, his wife and their children escaped from Germany with the Gestapo on their heels. Only after they had arrived safely in England did they learn that Hitler was deporting Jews to the death camps. Their entire families were gassed at Auschwitz. After the war they sailed for

Vancouver. But it was not a happy tale of survival and immigration. They were never able to cope with the fact that they had left parents, brothers, sisters, and cousins behind in Germany to perish.

In very British Vancouver, with their German accents, they tried to pass themselves off as the English Mr. and Mrs. Wine. But their son William, Grace's father, knew the act was wearing thin. When he married Kim Wang, he abandoned his adopted English name, assumed her family name and converted to Buddhism. He tried hard to erase his past, because he was ashamed to be Jewish; it humiliated him that he came from a race of people that were despised and hunted down. Completing school forms for Grace and her sister distressed him; he could not bear even to write the word "Jew". When Grace turned sixteen, he had confessed to his daughters that they were half Jewish. He explained that he had renounced his Jewishness to protect them. The story of how he and his two brothers, sister and parents had left Germany tumbled from his lips. For the first time, he talked about the remorse and shame he still felt because he had been unable to save the lives of his cousins, his grandparents, and his aunts and uncles.

It was ironic, really, Grace reflected, as she surveyed the traditional medicines displayed on the shelves of a Chinese drugstore. Her father was a physician, who had practised medicine as a family doctor for over thirty years. He had helped others, but was unable to help himself. He never got over his nightmares or his distrust of people.

When she was seventeen, without asking her father's permission, Grace took the original name of her paternal grandfather as her own, hyphenating it with her Chinese name. She was who she was; she was proud of her Jewish ancestry. Her father told her he admired her courage, but he himself would never acknowledge his background. Fifty-eight years after fleeing Germany, he had never gone back.

But he and Kim had been to China several times. Kim Wang's family was less dysfunctional, but they too had a history of political persecution. Grace's grandfather, Rei, had served the last emperor in the Forbidden City, and in 1925 the warlords who were controlling Beijing had put him under house arrest. Then during the Japanese invasion Rei's past with his emperor employer brought him under the scrutiny of the Japanese, and he was imprisoned. His daughter, Kim, spent her childhood in various labour camps until she escaped in a bold act of defiance. She was sixteen, and had been sent to a farm commune between Canton and Hong Kong. One day when the Revolutionary Guards were absent from their post, she decided to make a break for freedom.

The way Kim remembered it, she had walked until she found herself in a village with a train station. When the train pulled in, she sneaked aboard and rode it to the end of the line. From there she walked in the dark to avoid the checkpoints and the border control guards and their dogs. It was a starless night when she finally reached the ocean with the bright lights of Hong Kong beckoning to her. There was no one with a boat to take her across, and so, being young, strong and fearless, she decided to swim. She was in the water for many exhausting, despairing hours before reaching the city, but in the end she made it to shore.

She found work in the sweatshops and managed to learn English on the side. It was in the textile factory that she met and married her first husband, a Shanghanese. After their marriage, they emigrated to Canada where he was sent to manage a China-sponsored retail operation in Vancouver. The marriage was difficult, and Kim enrolled in a nursing program to learn a trade, in order to support herself. After her graduation she and her first husband separated amicably, and a year later she met William Wine at the Vancouver General. They married, and two years later Grace was born.

Kim Wang had travelled a long way from her days in the gulag, and she had reinvented herself more than once. At the age of fifty-five she had assumed the role of matriarch of the Vancouver Benevolent Society. Grace had always admired her mother, who was in every sense her own person. Long ago, Kim had freed herself from the restrictions that prevented her from living the kind of life she wanted. She had escaped from a prison camp and travelled to a new country. She had chosen the man she wanted. And all in the days before women's lib.

Grace could not say the same about her own life. Shame on you, she chastised herself. As a beneficiary of the women's movement, she had had it easy, compared to her mother. And what did she have to show for it? House, mortgage, career, cat ... but no husband. No Nick.

She sighed. She'd better get over to the office, do some serious work this afternoon. Work late. Get her mind off romance.

Crossing the park, Grace remembered that Mark Crosby lived a short walk from the office. Now that she'd decided she wanted to work on the case — wanted to see Nick again, truth be told — it occurred to her that she should drop in on him tomorrow. His plane got in at eight, and by nine he'd be home. Then she could tell him she was taking him up on his offer to work on a case together as long as he didn't think she was taking him up on his other offer. She was eager, now, to speak to Crosby and make sure he didn't give the second chair to anybody else.

The drive-by shooting made headlines in all the papers. The public was outraged and the immigration department's toll-free number was ringing off the hook. Television, print, and radio reporters were calling the investigative and enforcement unit for interviews and updates. One of the support staffers wheeled the television from the conference room straight into Nick's office. Nick flicked it on with the remote.

The mayor was quick off the mark, holding a press conference about last night's shooting. "Our system of deporting undesirables is obviously not working. There are too many people abusing the system. Criminals from all over the globe know Canada has an open door policy...."

Nick knew exactly where the mayor was going. His remarks about cleaning up crime in the metropolis were very familiar. City elections were two years away, but he was already working on his re-election strategy. Now the mayor was joined by another elected official and the police commissioner himself. They took turns offering sound bites to the press.

Nick called Rocco Corvinelli into his office.

Rocco looked sharp in his suit and tie. Nick had hired him fresh out of grad school with a psychology degree, of all things. But then he had always hired people with diverse backgrounds as immigration officers. Creative thinking scored high in his book, and he also looked for tenacity. Given that immigration and customs officers were among the few enforcement officials with the right to search anyone or anything without a warrant, he expected his staff to hold up as witnesses under gruelling cross-examination by a defendant's lawyer. Rocco was smart, and he was also something of a bulldog — another positive trait, in Nick's book. In his first few months on the front lines at Terminal 2, Rocco had scored a cold hit that resulted in one of the largest airport drug busts ever.

"How many calls have we logged?"

"Over five hundred so far on our toll-free line. Frothing at the mouth, most of them. Want to deport every coloured face out of the country. Scary, actually," said Rocco, leaning against the door.

Nick nodded. "Racism flares up when stuff like this happens. This is what we're gonna do. The press will want to bypass Public Information for the inside scoop. That will be you."

For the next half hour, Nick briefed Rocco on what to give to the press on the investigation Immigration was conducting into the drive-by shooting.

"We pick two reporters. Print and television. The *Globe* and CTV. I want you to leak to them that we're running our own checks on the Flying Dragons triad members. We think the shooting wasn't really about alien smuggling, it was about gang warfare and fighting for turf. That way we toss the ball back into the police commissioner's lap."

"Why are we leaking it to those two reporters?"

"First of all, we need to buy time. And secondly, we want to put a reporter or two in our debt. That will make the other reporters jealous, and they'll chase the story that much harder."

"I don't quite follow."

"We want the reporters to push the investigation. Any information they find will help us. One of them will be sharp enough to track down the owner of the Mandarin Club. And hopefully we get who we want in the spotlight."

Rocco's eyes opened in amazement. So that was how spin worked. Manipulate the press to get them investigating a few leaks Nick fed them. Massage the message, give them a bagful of half truths, and stand back. With luck, they'd get a lot of new information.

"We're buying time until we finish our investigation. Remember, we never lie. We just withhold some information until the time is right. We need time to organize our investigation."

"Okay. I follow."

"Good. Handle the media scrum this afternoon. Don't let the reporters trip you. Watch yourself with that reporter from the *Times*. Jamie Singh. He likes to ask the same question ten, twelve different ways. Then when you give a wrong response he'll correct you. And you trip yourself by talking too much. Giving out more information than you meant to."

Rocco nodded.

"Jamie's one of the sharpest reporters around. English is his first language — don't let that Sikh turban of his fool you. Remember, be very careful with him."

After Rocco left, Nick tried to close a few files. But he couldn't work. He needed to clear his head and think. He needed oxygen. Everything was racing too fast for his brain. Instead of hiding in his office, he dodged out the back of the building and took a walk. Why had Andy Loong been gunned down last night? Who knew about the raid at the Mandarin Club? Just himself, Kappolis and the squad cars waiting in the side street. He didn't think it was an inside leak. Was he being followed? He looked behind him as he walked along King Street towards Spadina Avenue. Or had someone inside the club made a quick exit when the raid began? That seemed more likely. The police had tried to seal off all the exits, but they didn't know the precise layout of the building. Supposing this someone knew what was going down, quickly got out, and alerted the head honcho, who ordered the drive-by hit on Loong. Why? To silence him. Whatever Loong knew had died with him. What the hell did he know that was worth his life?

He power-walked up Spadina. As he crossed the first set of lights, he played back what he knew because too many theories were spinning around his head. The Mandarin Club's membership list had not turned up Li Mann's name or anything close to it. Unfortunately, he had no idea if Li Mann was a real name or a nickname. Some cultures, like the Somalis, used nicknames in the place of real names. To Nick, they were all aliases designed to confuse law enforcement officials, nothing else.

Chinatown was a sea of life, sounds, smells and people. Nick grabbed a bite to eat at a street vendor's stall. He could remember when Spadina had been the heart of the Jewish community, defined by delis and garment factories. After the Jews had moved up and out, the Chinese had moved in. The Yiddish theatre had been replaced by a movie theatre featuring kung fu movies. The old Jewish synagogue had been converted into the Chinese Community Centre. But in the last few years, immigration had altered the four-kilometre stretch again. Now the Chinese were following the Jews and the Italians in their migration to the suburbs, and the Vietnamese were taking over the area, giving it yet another identity as Little Saigon.

He detoured around large trucks unloading and delivering boxes of fresh produce and cases of frozen fish to the crowded shops and street markets. Before the crosswalk, he elbowed his way through a throng of shoppers who were busy checking out T-shirts, fake Rolexes, and other knock-off merchandise. Waiting patiently for the streetlights to change, he curiously eyed a pair of young Asian girls on the other side, hair bleached reddish-blonde. One of them sported a nose ring, while her companion had a ring through her belly button.

Crossing the street and walking past the synagogue, Nick noticed that it had been transformed again; this time into a pool hall. He didn't know why it bothered him but it did. A lot of things were beginning to bother him. Particularly about the case. Officer Philip Wong had left a voice-mail message that he had some evidence that the shooting might have been done by a rival gang, the Vietnamese Lo Chien.

Maybe. But Nick was far from convinced that Loong's murder was really about gangs rubbing out the ethnic competition. If so, what about the timing of the hit? Coincidence, or what? Maybe the Lo Chien gang had been hired to take Loong out to keep him from talking to the police. That seemed plausible. But then, who bought the contract hit? He went over and over the facts, trying put them together in a way that made sense.

All he could do was keep pushing. Stay in touch with Dubois. Maybe Kappolis would have some ideas about where to go next.

In the back of his mind one persistent, maddening thought never went away: that Walter Martin's killer was still out there somewhere. So far, the son of a bitch had gotten away with it.

chapter seven

"Where're you now?"

"I'm calling from the Toronto airport," replied the General.

"We're in trouble," said a voice on the other end. "Big trouble. Have you read the papers?"

The words seemed to clear the General's mind, reminding him of the events of last Friday. They revealed to him the risks he had to take and the limited options that were open to him. Standing at a payphone without his gun, the surprise and fear hit him with a freshness he had almost forgotten.

"Call me when you get to New York tonight," the distant voice continued curtly. "If you don't call, then I'll know that you didn't make it. Remember the place in New York's Chinatown we talked about? Go and stay there for awhile until things cool down. Or until I tell you otherwise."

And then the line went dead.

As he passed through the metal detectors at passport control he was glad he had discarded his weapons before boarding the airporter bus for Pearson International. He stifled his mind not to think anymore. After all, he knew the procedures and route well.

"The length of your visit?"

"One week."

"Business?"

The official handed him back his boarding pass.

"Family. I'm going to visit my niece and her children," Li Mann Vu lied.

"Hope you have a good flight."

Li Mann Vu nodded his head and smiled as he picked up his brand new, carry-on luggage. In fact, he smiled for the first time in a week. Exactly a week ago he was shot and hunted like an animal. Running through the woods on all fours, swimming underwater like a fish, eating seaweed, sleeping under the stars. He had become an animal. That's how he had survived, and he was right under their noses.

So far, so good. He had managed to evade the authorities. They didn't call him "the General" for nothing. He sat on the deck of the frequent flyer lounge, staring up at the night sky. He felt at home watching the planes flying in and out. The lights from the radar control tower and the aircraft reminded him of flares and tracer bullets arcing across a night sky. It reminded him of another place and time.

In April 1966, the war machine was in full force and the Communist leaders had drafted him into the army to fight his South Vietnamese brothers. His entire high school class had been drafted and posted to the same reconnaissance unit. They were young and didn't believe they could die. Until they saw the American death machines swooping down from the sky. He was seventeen then. They promoted him to unit commander and sent him on a mission to destroy the American Black Horse Division. The ambush came when they were crossing the Le Thuy River. Without any kind of warning the American Huey gunships descended. There had not been enough time to run for the cover of the forests. By some accident of fate he alone had survived. He was wounded, but his entire unit lay around him, dead or dying, including Phan, his sister's husband, who was also his best friend. Young men he had known since childhood. He had had a responsibility to every one of them. They were his comrades, and he had failed them all. He had dug graves for them with his bare hands, but he knew he should have died with them.

He had bound up the wound in his leg with his best friend's shirt, and forced himself to trek through the malaria-infested jungles. Days later, when he had reached his village, he found that it had been napalmed by the Americans. Nothing was left but charred ruins. He became a man defined by what he had lost, a man with nothing more to lose. He re-enlisted, volunteering only for the most dangerous missions. Life and death became one.

He had first made himself known to the Americans in 1969, in an attack on Phnom Khai, an Air America stronghold south of Phnom Penh. When the ten-hour barrage of rocket and artillery fire was over, nineteen Air America commandos were dead. For that, he had been promoted to the rank of general, and sent into Laos to find and destroy a U.S. Air Force radar installation. It took several months of tracking, but he managed to locate it at a mountain site at Phu Phai Thi. He would never forget the explosion of grenades and bombs going off all at once. It had reminded him of celebration fireworks. By the time the Americans had pulled out of Vietnam, he had shot down more than his fair share of the eight-thousand U.S. fighter jets. He was proud of that. The memory brought a smile to his lips.

The war had ended over twenty years ago, but for Li Mann Vu peace would never come. He hadn't taken a life in a long time. The ability to kill without hesitation or remorse had merely lain dormant until the night he had shot that immigration officer. He had been shot, too, but the bullet penetrated only flesh and muscle. In spite of the pain, he had managed to swim a couple of miles downstream to the home of one of his mules, Sally Grandfeather. She had sheltered him in her house while law enforcement officials on two continents issued warrants for his arrest. She had paid for the doctor from Detroit, who had made the trip across the border to remove the bullet from his shoulder. On the fifth day when he was better, she had bought him a one-way Greyhound bus ticket to Toronto.

He gently touched his shoulder. It was still painful to the touch. It was too bad the smuggling operation had failed when they were caught at the border. Sally Grandfeather needed the money she had been expecting to receive for housing the migrants while they were in transit to New York City. He would speak to the boss about paying her anyway. After all, she had kids to feed. It wasn't her fault the operation had gone wrong.

The General thought it was hate that kept him alive. The United States government had destroyed his country. A quarter century later, hate still ran deep in his veins. He hated the Americans for the suffering and pain his people had endured during and after the war. And he pitied his South Vietnamese brothers who had believed the lies and empty promises of the Americans. The marines had quickly fed his southern brothers to the dogs when he and his comrades surrounded the walls of Phnom Penh. Thousands tried to flee by boat, but had lived only to be lost at sea or interned in refugee camps around the world. Those who managed to get to the promised land often found themselves forcibly repatriated by Western governments.

Since he had started in the people smuggling business, he had assisted in over two thousand entries into the United States. It was a kind of revenge. Because the Americans had destroyed his country, he would move people into theirs. He brought them into the U.S. by ship, plane, cars, and trucks. He arranged transportation for them all — the dispossessed of his own and other countries. He was paid huge sums of money, but he didn't do it for that.

His flight landed on time at JFK Airport. Li Mann took his place in the queue at customs and immigration. He handed the customs officer a Malaysian passport which he had reproduced himself, carried with his own photograph. He was nodded through without a problem.

Nick, Kappolis, and Dubois were seated at a corner table in a greasy spoon at Bloor and Bathurst. Kappolis was describing the raid his fugitive squad had staged the night before. "We got this informant, good at his work. Not everybody can do it, but this guy's really cut out to be a snitch. He's smart and he's angry. You need nerves of steel to penetrate your own community, betray your people. This guy, Cam, has the nerves. Twenty-four years old, born in Laos, and already served three years for knifing a man to death."

"Three years for murder, that's all he served?" Nick found that hard to believe. "Obviously he had friends in high places."

"Nah, nothing like that." Kappolis paused a moment before going on. "Cam was used by the higher-ups to kill a member of a competing triad. After a year in prison awaiting trial, Cam decided he'd been stupid to maintain his silence, protecting his masters who had hung him out to dry."

"So he plea bargained to serve only two years?" Nick whistled to himself as he pushed his chair back from the dining table.

"Sort of. He signed a contract to become our snitch. Released last year and already did a couple of assignments for us. Wears a wire. Looks like your average Asian guy in the street. So right after the drive-by we sent him to check out a grocery store in Chinatown II."

"Oh, yeah. I saw a blurb on some surveillance job in that area that came across my desk," said Dubois, raising the beer mug to his lips.

"No one told me or my department about this snitch or the surveillance job." Nick assumed an indignant look.

"At that time Nick, it wasn't an immigration matter." Kappolis drained back the rest of his malt before continuing with his story.

"Nick, law enforcement isn't required to tell Immigration everything," said Dubois.

"That's real comforting to know," answered Nick, looking anything but.

Kappolis pushed a handful of French fries into his mouth. "So we had him under twenty-four-hour surveillance for a full day, the works — an inside inspection by Cam, checks on all movement in and out of the store, and a photographic record. We were across the street in a carpet cleaning van, with a telescopic lens. Every visitor was logged. Anybody who spoke to anybody was monitored were listed."

"What did you get?" Nick asked impatiently.

"There were shopkeepers making their weekly protection drop offs. The old men, I'm guessing. Some Lo Chien gang members. No sign of the bosses. We waited till all the ducks were lined up. The raid was timed for midnight. We were gonna get them in their own backyard."

Kappolis wolfed down the rest of his hamburger. "We got photographs taken earlier in the day by the surveillance team. The store was a front for the Lo Chien gang, which was a big player in the extortion and prostitution racket. Cam, the snitch, told me that Lo Chien is trying to muscle in on the people-smuggling racket. The Flying Dragons control it now. All we wanted was information and pictures, and maybe make a strategic arrest or two. The SWAT team was just for intimidation. Nobody was supposed to get killed."

Nick passed his plate of half-eaten burger to the waitress. He was not hungry.

"But then this red Corvette cruises down the street and two mean-looking Asian guys get out and check out the carpet cleaning van. I got a bad feeling about that, I can tell ya. Then when two more guys climb out of the car with ammunition belts and semi-automatics over their shoulders, I figure guess what, guys, we've lost the element of surprise. And less than a minute later, we hear bullets ripping out the windows of parked cars in the back alley where our other guys were.

"So I give the signal, and the SWAT team blows through the front door, returning fire. Then it was all over. A damn miracle, in my book. None of the shopkeepers got killed but all four Lo Chien gang members who returned fire are dead."

Nick sighed. In his opinion the raid had been a big mistake, and Dubois, who was hearing about it for the first time, looked as if he agreed.

Kappolis was doing his best to placate Nick. "No worries, Nick. The precinct's got a reward out for snitching on the community. Stuff will come in on the Flying Dragons. Give it time."

"Problem with that sketch of Li Mann is that he looks like every and any Asian man," said Dubois.

The conversation paused when the waitress appeared with a pot of fresh coffee. They watched her refill their cups. As soon as she left, Nick said, "All we've got is Gee Tung. At this point I'm prepared to plea-bargain with him. Offer him a deal if he betrays his friends."

"Nick, I wouldn't trust the quality of his information." Dubois scowled. "Maybe he led us astray with that sketch of Li Mann. I mean, how else to explain a country-wide arrest warrant on both sides of the border, and we got diddly squat. I wouldn't trust him. What makes you think scum like that are gonna help us indict their own people?"

Nick threw up his hands. "Then what the fuck have we got? At this point I'm prepared to try anything."

"When's the Mandarin Club owner coming in to see you?" asked Dubois.

"Tomorrow morning at nine sharp, with his hired gun."

"That should be something," said Kappolis, lighting a cigarette.

"I never count my chickens until they're hatched."

"Okay, Nick, I'll talk to Gee Tung when I get back to Ottawa. But don't hold your breath. I'm willing to bet good money that composite he gave us was pure bullshit."

"Even if he's prepared to deal," said Kappolis, "how the hell do we know that he isn't stringing us along just to avoid deportation back to Vietnam? We've all seen that script before."

"True. But why don't we get the information and then assess the quality of it?" Nick was annoyed and his voice was starting to rise.

"Nick, we ain't deaf. No need to be shouting the place down," Dubois said testily.

"I want a conviction in Walter Martin's death. I want Gee Tung to testify as a key witness in a prosecution case against Li Mann and his cohorts for Martin's death, smuggling illegals into the country, abusing immigration permits, the drive-by shooting and other triad activities. I'm prepared to cut a deal."

"That'd be a real deal with the devil, Nick. You want to turn loose one of the snakeheads who killed?"

"I'm not turning anybody loose! It's a two-pronged strategy here, Dubois. You put the squeeze on Gee Tung. I'll put the squeeze on the Mandarin Club owner. Let's see what we come up with. That's all I'm saying," said Nick, holding up his hands in a gesture of surrender.

Just then the national news came on the TV over the bar. The police raid was the lead story. The restaurant owner turned the sound up slightly and the two men turned to watch. Store windows blown-out. Police cruisers pockmarked with bullet holes. Body bags wheeled into ambulances. Nick couldn't take any more of it. He got up and changed the channel on the television, pissing off a handful of pub patrons.

"So much for trying to squeeze the competition for information on Li Mann and Sun Sui. Couldn't your boys have taken one of those Lo Chien thugs alive?" asked Nick.

"When the bullets are coming at you, you don't think about saving one thug for later. All you want to do is get out of there alive, go home and see your kids."

"In other words we're doing our best and still coming up zero," Nick said. "I'm back at square one."

The offices were empty. The civil servants had long gone home. The building was quiet, almost spooky, except for the hum of the ventilation system.

Grace swivelled her chair and hiked her feet on the window ledge. She opened the file and reviewed her notes for a pre-hearing conference. The Federal Court had overturned the deportation order of a Tamil Tiger and he was claiming refugee status. According to her notes, he had been involved in two bombings in Sri Lanka eight years ago, and feared political retribution if he returned. He had lived in Canada since then, under a deportation order and without refugee or landed immigrant status. On the other side of the coin, through eight years of a lengthy appeals process, he had married and fathered two children. In many respects, he was a model citizen, volunteering his time as a church janitor and doing community service, while working days as a dishwasher and cleaner in a restaurant. The restaurant, church and his community supported his application to stay. The petition ran to over five thousand names. Nick's office had rejected his request to remain in the country on humanitarian and compassionate grounds.

She sent an e-mail to scheduling for a hearing date followed by a second e-mail to Nick's office, asking if they wished to revisit their department's decision in light of the fact that the claimant had not committed crimes in this country, taking into consideration the interests of his wife and children. What Grace really wanted to do was call Nick. But this case was the wrong pretext. She knew exactly what he would say. *We have repeatedly denied him permission to remain in the country as a refugee or land-*

*ed immigrant. He was issued temporary minister's per-
mits, and now the permits have expired. We don't offer
asylum to people who are facing prosecution back home.
The asylum process isn't meant for criminals on the run.
Getting married and having Canadian-born children is a
ruse. Seen that before. Sorry, Grace. Time's up. The
claimant must go home and face the music. End of story.*

She imagined Nick saying those words. Then she
remembered him saying other words, looking at her
with love in his eyes.

The phone rang, ripping the silence like a torpedo
and pulling her back from her private grotto. She
jumped, upset the file on her lap, and scattered paper all
around her.

"Ms. Wang-Weinstein?"

"Yes?"

"This is Rocco Corvinelli. I just read your e-mail
and no one in scheduling is picking up. I want you to
know that your hearing date isn't convenient with us.
Could you move it forward by another two weeks or so?
Our plate is very full at the moment. After Labour Day
would go better for us."

Grace flipped through her docket. "Fine, I'll send
another e-mail to scheduling."

Swell. Another complication in mending their relationship. After the phone call she couldn't concentrate.
Time ticked by as she sat at her desk, frustrated and
undecided. Her professional and personal lives were col-
liding, and not in the way she desired. Collapsing the
files and dumping them back into the filing cabinet, she
closed her office and headed for the bank of elevators.

Outside the building, the sky had deepened to the
colour of prairie rose. The humidity had dissipated.
Checking that Crosby's address was in the pocket of her
suit jacket, she set out to walk over and drop in on him.

She was an hour early, but there was a marvellous book-
store along the way. She could stop and vanish into a
book for an hour any time. And right now, she needed
to be in another headspace.

BJ and Harry were sitting in the van on the arrivals deck
at the Ottawa airport. Harry lit another cigarette. He
had smoked ten in the last hour and a half.

"I thought you quit," BJ said.

"I did. I quit when I got out of the pen. But I started up again two months ago." Harry looked pale, sick-
ly white, under the parking lot lights. He was sweating
profusely, nerved up for his revenge.

"Relax, man," said BJ, in an easy tone. "I never
seen you like this before."

Harry threw his half-smoked cigarette out onto the
pavement. "I hate summer. Too hot and humid. I used
to like it, when I had the kids." And in the same bitter
tone he repeated Crosby's name several times.

BJ had heard the whole story from Harry while they
were bunking in prison together, heard it so many times
he knew it all by heart. Knew all the details and could
play it back in his head like it was a movie he'd seen.
How Harry's family, his wife, four-year-old daughter,
and a seven-month-old baby son had all been taken
away from him. Killed by a drunk driver. Harry was
depressed, living in no-man's land. All his life, he'd told
BJ, he just wanted to be a good citizen. His expectations
weren't so high: a house, a wife, and kids running
around the back yard.

BJ had heard all about the accident. It had happened on Highway 40 outside Troy. Harry couldn't
remember the impact, but he did recall being thrown
clear out of the car, then blacking out. The next thing he

knew he was lying in a hospital bed with several broken ribs, broken shoulders and arms and a punctured lung. And his wife and little children were dead. After his release from the hospital, he tried to commit suicide in his empty farmhouse, but he was saved by the neighbour down the road.

The driver who had destroyed Harry's family and his life had escaped criminal charges on a technicality because the police investigating the accident had screwed up on the evidence-gathering process. Harry tracked him down, broke into his house and shot him to death with a .44. If a victims' support group hadn't taken up his legal defence, he would have been convicted of murder and jailed for life. Instead, he served time for manslaughter, and while he was in prison, with plenty of time on his hands, he had enlisted BJ's help and done some research. That's when they had learned that the renegade driver who had killed Harry's entire family had been slated for deportation from the country. But it had all been overturned in immigration court by Mark Crosby. In other words, Mark Crosby had signed the death warrant on his wife and kids.

BJ had been given early release for good behaviour. A few months later, Harry got out too and came looking for his prison bunkmate. He'd asked BJ to help track down Mark Crosby, because he wanted to kill the guy. BJ had no problem with that.

They watched a tour bus disgorge over a hundred seniors through the revolving doors.

"That's his plane," said BJ, directing Harry's attention to the Air Canada flight circling for a landing.

Harry said in a hoarse, strained voice, "Stay here. Give Judge Crosby time to collect his bags."

Harry and BJ tried their best to look unobtrusive in the crowd. That wasn't easy since Harry was a big guy, tall and wide-shouldered.

"Did you put enough money in the parking meter?" Harry asked. "The last thing we need is a parking ticket from some stupid cop. Or to have our van towed."

"Yeah, yeah," snapped BJ. "Quit worrying."

"That's him. There, he's moving through the queue," said Harry, a few minutes later. They watched as Crosby collected a suitcase. Now he was ordering a limousine. Only the best for a jerk like him, thought BJ bitterly.

"You're sure it's him. The guy we saw last time had glasses. I don't want to be following the wrong guy."

"It's our guy," replied Harry. "Go get the van. If it's not him, then we go straight to Crosby's address and wait."

As the limousine pulled away from the curb, BJ edged the rusty white van with the tinted mirrors out of the parking lot. Harry jumped in, and they followed the limousine, not too close, but not more than five car lengths behind either.

"We don't want to lose him." Harry was still chainsmoking.

"Relax. I know this city like the back of my hand," said BJ. They hadn't spent good money on long distance calls to Crosby's office to learn his travel itinerary, and driven all the way to Ottawa, to lose sight of their prey.

"He's changed a bit. Gotten fatter," said Harry.

"The good life, man. Eating, drinking, and chicks." BJ grinned, rubbing his hands together.

"Keep your eyes on the road, and your hands on the steering wheel," ordered Harry. "I don't want to lose him."

For the remainder of the drive Harry clammed up, keeping his eyes on the limousine ahead of them. That was okay with BJ. There was no need to go over the details of the job.

Trailing at a safe distance, they observed the limo pulling up in front of the townhouse. They watched the judge getting out and paying the driver. When the limo pulled away from the curb the van moved forward to take its place, parking right in front of the victim's door.

As Crosby was pushing open his front door, BJ and Harry walked quickly and quietly up behind him.

"Are you Mark Crosby?" Harry asked in his hoarse voice.

"Why do you ask?" asked Mark Crosby, turning around. His mouth fell open as he stood staring at the gun pointed at his chest.

"Get into the house," ordered BJ.

Crosby didn't get the chance to ask how they knew his name or his address. Meekly, he obeyed their instructions.

BJ closed the door behind them.

chapter eight

The following morning, Kappolis showed up bright and early in Nick's office with two large cups of Costa Rican coffee. The Mandarin Club owner had a nine o'clock interview with Nick in his office.

If first impressions are what counts, Sun Sui blew it right off the top by arriving late for his interview with Nick and insulting him.

"You're over an hour late." Nick made a show of looking at his watch.

"So? You're a public servant. Aren't you here to serve the public?"

Nick inwardly cursed Sun. Arrogant son of a bitch! Looking him over, Nick came to the opinion that Sui didn't come across as someone victimized for protection money by Asian triads. He looked like what he was: a successful investor immigrant, the kind Australia, Canada and the United States were all trying to woo. He was dressed in an expensive grey silk suit, designer suspenders and European brogues.

At the sight of Sui's lawyer trailing behind, Nick knew for sure the interview was headed downhill. Of all the immigration and refugee lawyers Nick knew, Don Verster was the one he admired the least. The two men took each other in with hostile looks.

"Good morning, Mr. Slovak. I see we meet again. How long has it been since the Ibrahim deportation case?"

"Not long enough," replied Nick.

Kappolis glanced curiously from one man to the other, but he kept his thoughts to himself. As if reading his mind, Verster threw him a suspicious glance.

Nick explained the detective's presence. "Detective Kappolis and I frequently work together on immigration cases. It's usual practice for him to sit in on my interviews and assessments. You could say he keeps me in check. Makes sure that I'm not violating anybody's constitutional rights."

Verster gave Kappolis the once-over. Kappolis gave him a friendly smile and handshake. From Verster's expression it was hard to tell if he had bought Nick's bullshit or not.

The real reason Kappolis was present was because Nick needed a witness, or nothing Sui said could be used as evidence. The interview wasn't being recorded; it couldn't be without Verster's consent, and he wasn't likely to give it. Nick couldn't testify, no way he could appear as a state prosecutor and a witness on the same case. But Kappolis could be called if necessary.

Nick had decided to take a polite approach at this point, and not make any direct accusations about gang activity or illegals. As Sun pulled out one of the client chairs across from the desk and seated himself, with an air of composure, Nick got the definite impression that the man before him was an old hand at official interviews. Most non-citizens were downright uneasy in the presence of immigration officials. Not Sun. One more reason to dislike him.

"This interview is part of our follow-up to our investor immigrant program. I've reviewed your application and I've got a couple of questions regarding the Investor Immigrant Application you filed in Hong Kong several years ago. You stated in your application that you intended to open a restaurant and nightclub."

"Yes, that's correct."

Nick studied the papers in front of him. He said in a careful tone, "From my personal tour of the Mandarin Club ..."

"Your personal tour?" Verster interrupted in a belligerent tone. "A thousand or so applications and you, head of the investigations and enforcement branch, are giving my client personal treatment? Well, Mr. Slovak, from where I sit, that smells like you've got my client under the microscope. Why's that?"

Obviously the courteous, go-slow approach was not going to work. "Because it looks more like a strip club for lap dancing and solicitation than a sit-down, knife-and-fork, eat-in establishment."

"It's an entertainment palace, Mr. Slovak."

Sun Sui sat, full of ease, watching his lawyer answer the questions.

"It caters to those who want to eat, sing karaoke, dance or watch others dancing. My client's market study told him Toronto was like New York and L.A. And there was an excellent opportunity for this kind of business. Any business-school grad would be able to see the common sense of taking advantage of market conditions."

Nick raised an eyebrow. "Oh, is that what this is? Trafficking in people and prostitution takes advantage of market conditions?"

"Are you making a finding of fact, Mr. Slovak? Or are you merely smearing my client's good name?"

"The evidence we have is this. Two hundred and sixty-three foreign work authorizations have been issued since the club opened two years ago. Mr. Sui may or may not be aware of what's going on at his club, but that number seems excessive. I don't think there's any shortage of women in this country willing to work as exotic dancers. And my staff has been looking into how many of these so-called entertainers have claimed asylum when their visas expired. From our checks so far, quite a few."

Sun Sui spoke at last. His English was only slightly accented, his voice well-modulated but defiant. "Yes, some of my girls have made that decision. And yes, my girls do more than waitressing. It's something along the lines of a supper club, and I agree their outfits are very thin. Go to another club like mine and you'll find that's customary. However, I don't see myself as a trafficker in people. Or girls for that matter."

"Then what are you?"

"I'm a businessman. An employer of beautiful girls from small villages all over Asia. I offer these girls the opportunity to leave their backward lives and see more of the world. If they wish to use their beauty to find husbands here I see nothing immoral in that."

Sui was a guy who could think on his feet.

"Girls without underwear, giving extra services like blow jobs. You see nothing immoral in that? Turning village girls into prostitutes isn't immoral in your book, huh?"

"I don't pressure them. Those girls who want to make extra money, offer extra services. They are show-girls. Perhaps they look like prostitutes to you. That doesn't mean they are prostitutes."

"You know what they say in this country? If it walks like a duck and quacks like a duck, it is a duck."

"Sun, don't say another word! Mr. Slovak doesn't have the best of intentions here."

"Oh, come on, Verster!" Nick slapped the file folder against the corner of his desk.

"This meeting is over," said Verster, standing up. "My client hasn't broken any laws or immigration regulations. He filed 263 applications to bring in a bunch of good-looking women on temporary work permits. If you think that's abuse of procedures, it would be more productive of you to question your own immigration officers on why they signed them off."

Nick stood up too. "Your client peddles drugs on the third floor of his supper club."

"My client does not peddle drugs and has never observed anyone selling illicit substances in his club. And he'll testify to that under oath, Mr. Slovak. So what if his business venture isn't politically correct and his club isn't a highbrow affair? Mr. Sui isn't a politician courting votes from the morally conscious middle class like yourself."

Nick brushed this aside. "Whether the drugs were free or for sale is a moot point. The fact of the matter is, drugs were being used there. In my book, prostitution and the possession of drugs are offences under the Immigration Act as well as the Criminal Code. There is also the fact that casinos are known to be big money-laundering operations."

"You know what you sound like, my friend? Like you're out to redeem yourself after the tongue lashing you received on television from the mayor. If you think you have any evidence against my client, I suggest you file criminal charges. We'll deal with that. But I'm not wasting Mr. Sui's time by listening to innuendo and veiled threats."

Nick took a deep breath. "Please, sit down, Mr. Verster. There are still a few matters we have to discuss." The last thing he wanted was to be accused of intimidation or brutality. He knew he'd have to exercise discipline in nailing the owner of the Mandarin Club because the rich and powerful rarely served their time. They hired other people to do it for them.

Verster, after a look at his client, sat down again. Nick allowed a moment to pass as he shuffled loose papers inside a file folder. "You've brought your tax returns for the two years you've been in the country as I requested?"

Sui said nothing. Verster seemed to be doing all the talking now. "What exactly are you investigating? If you're looking into income tax irregularities, I assure you there aren't any. My client's accountant will meet with you if that's your concern."

"I'd like to look at them now, counsellor. To see what exactly the club's writing off in terms of expenses."

"Isn't that more a function of the tax department than an immigration matter?"

"Reviewing tax returns of non-citizens falls within the ambit of Immigration. I suggest you review your copy of the Immigration Act, counsellor."

"Christ almighty, Mr. Slovak. Can't get my client on one thing, try another, is that it?"

Nick ignored Verster, turning his attention back to Sui. He really didn't care if Sui was cheating on his taxes. But he wanted the man who had shot and killed Walter, and if he and Kappolis had to charge Sui with running a prostitution racket and tax evasion, so be it, he thought. The damn problem with Gee Tung's information was that apparently Dubois hadn't read him his rights. That meant his evidence was largely inadmissible in court. But even if Li Mann had pulled the trigger, Sui probably bought the bullet. All they had to do was find evidence connecting the two together; it would probably lead directly to Li Mann's doorstep. It sounded simple, but Sui was a man with a thousand tricks up his sleeve.

"That drive-by shooting outside your nightclub. Was it a result of gang war over turf between the Flying Dragons and Lo Chien? Do you know anything about that?"

"I only know what I've read in the papers like everybody else," Sun said mildly, making eye contact with Nick and Kappolis.

"In other words you have no knowledge of or participation in the Flying Dragons, or of any gang rivalry with Lo Chien?"

"None."

Nick knew from Sun's body language that he was lying.

"Where the hell are these questions coming from? Are you accusing my client of being a triad member? This is just too fucking much!" barked Verster, jumping up from his seat.

"No, Don. Let me explain." Sun held up his hand. "Yes, Mr. Slovak, you're right. We do have a problem with the gangs in Hong Kong. The Lo Chien wanted me to pay protection money in Hong Kong and Taiwan. I refused. Now they're pushing me in Canada. In Taipei, I tried to get into the movie business. They firebombed my studio there."

"Did you report this to the police?"

"No."

"Why not?"

"What would they have done about it? The Taipei police could do nothing. And if we had called the police here, Lo Chien would be angry enough to torch my club. And then what would I tell the club investors? Sorry, your rate of return is zero? I couldn't do that.

That would push me into bankruptcy. Besides, I'm Chinese. We don't wash our dirty laundry in public."

The look of annoyance etched on Verster's face seemed to be permanent. "I fail to see how petty gang rivalry impacts on my client's immigration application."

Too bad those Lo Chien gang members were killed in that shootout the night before last, Nick thought. Their testimony on the Lo Chien triad might have been interesting. Nick paused, then, in a controlled voice, he continued, "Gee Tung, one of the agent smugglers we captured at Akwesasne said he belonged to the Flying Dragons. And that the Flying Dragons had an arrangement with the Mandarin Club. The police reports indicate that the drive-by shooting outside your club was turf warfare. I'd like Mr. Sui to tell us what he knows about these incidents."

"Now you're also accusing him of colluding with snakeheads? On top of the prostitution, immigration fraud, and tax evasion?" Verster fumed.

"I'm accusing him of nothing. This is an investigation only."

"Bullshit! In the space of over an hour, you've managed to accuse him of being a pimp, triad member, drug pusher, agent smuggler and money launderer!" Verster's tone was belligerent. "You keep this up and I'll have you and your department up on charges of defamation of character and harassment."

The two men had a brief staring contest. Pretending he'd won, Verster sat down again, snarling.

Kappolis, Nick noticed out of the corner of his eye, seemed to be finding this amusing. The detective had always had big problems with lawyers. Leaning on the desk, Nick asked, "So what we were told isn't true? Your club isn't under a Dragon roof?"

Verster was livid. "What the hell are you implying now, Mr. Slovak?"

"Don, please, let me fully explain. Yes, I pay protection," said Sui pulling out a sheaf of press clippings from his suit jacket and handing it to Nick. "Here my friend Ray, who was in the karaoke business in Seattle, narrowly missed death. He refused to pay protection money to the Sun Yee On triad. I know another club owner in Vancouver Chinatown who wasn't so lucky. He refused to pay protection money and was gunned down as he was getting out of his car."

Why the hell was he backtracking now? Nick wondered. A moment ago, he'd denied all knowledge of these matters. "Mr. Sui, when I asked you earlier if you knew anything about the drive-by shootings outside your club, you said you didn't. Now you're telling me otherwise."

"I didn't think it was relevant. I thought I was coming to sort out an immigration and tax matter."

"I see," said Nick, but the tone of his voice said, "You're lying."

"You understand, the Dragons saved my life when Lo Chien gang members burst into my club last year and tried to kidnap me. Naturally I am grateful. But how could I explain this complicated relationship to the police? Would they understand my cultural obligation to repay that debt? Since the Dragon members liked coming to the club, I gave them free use of one of the rooms. The bookings are done through the booking attendant. I'm not involved in day-to-day operations. I'm sorry that I misled you earlier. I had hoped to keep everything simple and uncomplicated."

"Isn't it convenient that your general manager Andy Loong can't corroborate this evidence?"

Nick's sarcasm appeared to be lost on Sun, or he chose to ignore it.

"Yes, it's unfortunate. I was very distressed about his death. I told my staff to cooperate fully with the police. But since I wasn't there," Sun shrugged, "I can't help the police in that matter. And as for Lo Chien, I really don't know whether they were targeting us for protection money. It may be true. But I didn't know. Andy took care of such things."

Maintaining the same disbelieving tone, Nick went on, "I'll lay my cards on the table if you will, Mr. Sui. Could you please explain to me why one of the snakeheads from an alien-smuggling operation we busted last week happened to have the telephone number of your establishment in his pocket?"

Verster thumped his fist on Nick's desk. "Mr. Slovak, I fail to see what possible connection this could have to my client. The smuggler probably meant to make reservations for dinner or karaoke." Verster's voice was dripping with sarcasm. "Is there anything else you want?"

"Actually, there is. We'd like Mr. Sui to take a blood test. Blood was found on the smugglers' boat, which doesn't match that of any of the migrants or smugglers. Mr. Sui, I hope you'll agree to that."

"He most certainly will not," Verster said in a menacingly tight voice. "I'm not letting you go any further with this fishing expedition, trampling over my client's constitutional rights."

Sun interjected. "Please let me explain something. I understand that you're saying that the telephone number of my club was found in the possession of these men. You must understand that my club's booking number is unlisted. Members have to carry the number around with them."

"Then you're saying this snakehead is a member of your club?"

"He might be. The membership list has over a thousand people. Unlike your department, the club does not check to see if applicants have a criminal record."

"I'd like you to tell me where you were on the night of August twelfth, last Friday."

"As I told you, I'm trying to expand my movie business. So far, we've produced three films in Taiwan. One of them won an honourable mention at Cannes. *In My Mother's House*. You should rent it." Sun flicked lint off his trouser leg. "On August twelfth, I was at home working with one of my lead actresses. We were revising a script for a movie in which I've invested five million dollars. It will be shot next year somewhere inside China. I haven't quite figured out the precise location."

"And what's the name and number of this actress?"

"Suzie Wong."

Nick laughed out loud in disbelief.

"That's her screen name. And if you want her phone number, sorry, I don't have it with me."

Nick leaned back against his chair and scrutinized Sun. Reading him was like looking for invisible ink. Trying to trap him one more time, he reached inside the file folder and passed Sun a photo of Gee Tung.

"Have you seen this man at your club, or anywhere else?" Nick passed him a black-and-white mug shot of Gee Tung.

Sun Sui held the photo between his hands and studied the face in the photo. Showing no sign of recognition, he replied, "No, I don't think I know him."

Keeping his eyes on Sun's face, Nick said, "This man is a member of the Flying Dragons triad. Your club number was found in his pocket. He's also one of the agent smugglers who was caught in the weekend operation I mentioned. One of our senior immigration officers was killed. You probably read about it in the papers."

"No, I don't read the papers every day. I must've missed that story," Sun replied in an even voice.

This time the lie was obvious. Sun was good, but not that good.

"My last question to you pertains to the investor application you filed in Hong Kong. It appears that you never filed a tax return while you were a resident of that city. I'd like to hear the details of how you made your money to start two nightclubs."

"Mr. Slovak," Verster burst in, "I fail to see the relevance of these questions. What does it matter if Mr. Sui filed tax returns in Hong Kong or the kind of jobs he held."

"The relevance of the question is to ascertain sources and approximation of income. As we both know, profiting from the proceeds of criminal activity is against the law. In fact, assets from the proceeds of crime can be confiscated under IPOC ..."

"Don't threaten my client with IPOC, Slovak. You know what I think of IPOC."

The two men glared at each other like boxers in a ring. The Integrated Proceeds of Crime program had been set up by the RCMP to seize the assets of drug traffickers and organized crime rings. Since the 1980s it had been expanded to include drug smuggling and illegal immigration rackets. Nick had clashed with Verster when the lawyer was acting for a Somali warlord, Ibrahim, who had come to Canada and reinvented himself as an agent smuggler. He had brought tens of thousands of Somalis into Canada illegally, and they had paid him back by committing welfare fraud on a massive scale.

Nick and Dubois had used IPOC to confiscate Ibrahim's savings accounts, totalling over three million dollars. Verster had argued the case all the way up to the Supreme Court, accusing the government of using IPOC as a tax collection agency. In court, Verster had called Nick a "tax collector with a gun." The Bar and the multicultural groups picketing outside the court room had labelled Nick a Nazi, and had stuck swastikas on the sidewalk in front of the Immigration Building.

Verster's eyes were now angry slits. "You know Mr. Slovak, you're trying to pin every crime in the book on my client but you don't have a shred of proof to make a case. And you won't find any evidence, because there isn't any." Verster leaned over Nick's desk. "If you don't cease and desist this nonsense, I'm going to sue the pants off you and your department for defamation of character of a prominent member of the multicultural community."

With Herculean effort, Nick refused to rise to the bait. In a voice of deadly calm, he said, "I wouldn't advise you to play the race card like that, counsellor. You never know who'll get hurt."

"I don't need to play any card. All I have to do is file the appropriate papers and we'll see you and your department in court. Then we'll see who gets hurt."

"Oh? Is that a threat, counsellor?"

"It's a statement of fact." Verster glared at him, his mouth twisted in an angry snarl.

After Sun Sui and his lawyer had left, Verster slamming the door behind them, Kappolis said, "Verster was scared. See how quickly he jumped at you like that?"

"Yeah. The big question is, how did a country bumpkin from Communist China bankroll two nightclubs in Hong Kong? We're talking pre-takeover days here. What's his rags-to-riches story? If we find that out, we'll learn a lot."

"What're the chances of that?"

"Slim. We'll put in calls to our embassies in Asia. But filing an annual tax return isn't a big thing in those countries. I'm not holding my breath."

"What next, Nick?"

"If I get enough evidence linking Sun to Walter's death, then we're going with prosecution. If not," Nick shrugged his shoulders, "then we move for deportation."

Long after Kappolis left, Nick sat in his office contemplating Sun Sui's immigration file. It reminded him of another file. A Russian businessman who turned out to be the head of some Moscow mafiya. In Sun's case, he didn't have enough evidence to make an arrest. At least, not yet. Still, he had reason to believe that Sun Sui was a member of an organized crime gang, that he was involved in trying to smuggle those illegal migrants across the U.S. border, and that he had bought the bullet that had killed Walter. All he had to do was prove it.

He leafed through Sun's immigration file. It was frustrating how little information and few pages it contained. He had seen thicker files on family sponsorships. He skimmed through it again. Apart from the excessive foreign work authorizations, there wasn't even enough evidence to get Sun on illegal immigration. Or drug dealing for that matter.

The Flying Dragons gang was involved in people smuggling. The question was, how to link Sun Sui to the Dragons, and to prove that he was an agent smuggler himself? Gee Tung gave oral evidence on that. But Dubois and Gee Tung's lawyer were locked in a stalemate over Gee Tung repeating these statements in court. It was that damn witness protection program they were fighting over. Dubois's promises of court testimony in exchange of federal witness protection were coming back to haunt them. Getting into the witness program was a matter for a law enforcement committee, and it was very doubtful that Gee Tung would fit their criteria for protection. You could maybe persuade one or two people to your way of thinking, but not an entire room. He was partly relieved to hear that Gee Tung hadn't made the cut into the witness protection program. After all, the snakehead was caught committing federal offences and participated in Walter's death. Why should he get away with all that simply by giving testimony? And what if his testimony failed to indict and deport?

Hold that thought. A ripple of anger washed through his body. He closed his eyes and breathed deeply. Then he forced his thoughts into order. Build a case on circumstantial evidence. Did he have enough? No, it wasn't a question of enough. It was a case of consistent circumstantial evidence. And consistent was the operative word.

He pondered all of these questions and issues down the steps to the subway station. As he got into a half-empty car, a plan was beginning to take shape in his mind. The more he thought about the sex-slavery angle, the more he liked his idea. Bottom line, he wanted Walter Martin's killer, alive or dead. From past experience, he knew better than most that there was more than one way to skin a cat.

Grace sucked in her breath. She needed a moment to regain her composure. Mark Crosby was dead. What the hell had she gotten herself into? In hindsight, Grace knew she should not have agreed to second-chair the agent smuggler case. Her other mistake was to walk into Crosby's house. Yes, that was her biggest mistake.

André Dubois and his team of RCMP officers, a forensics team, detectives from homicide and selected members of the press were traipsing through Crosby's house, while Grace sat outside in a police cruiser answering the same questions over and over again.

A crowd of curious bystanders stared from beyond the yellow police tapes discussing who the killer could be as they watched the medical examiner pull up with an ambulance to take the black body bag to the morgue. After a while the homicide detectives took her back inside the house, where they grilled her some more.

Grace sat at Mark's kitchen table watching the forensics team down on their hands and knees looking for DNA evidence of the perpetrators and other clues.

They wanted to know about her relationship with Mark Crosby. The reason for her visit. Was it her first time in his house? Did she notice anything out of the ordinary? Then she was forced to reconstruct everything, moment by moment, from her arrival at his house to the moment when the police got there.

Dubois pulled up a chair across from her. "Let's go over it one more time."

Grace groaned.

"You saw no one when you came in."

"That's right."

"How did you get into the house?"

"The door was partially open but I rang the bell anyway. When there was no answer, I simply walked in."

"And what did you see?"

"His suitcase was in the hallway. I called Mark's name but there was no answer so I walked through the first floor. When I got to the sunroom ..." Grace stopped.

Dubois had seen Crosby's body sprawled on the white rug in the sunroom. "What did you do?"

"I dialled 911 on my cellphone. I was careful not to touch anything."

Dubois put his notebook back in the outside pocket of his uniform. "Tell me why you were at his place again?"

Grace realized that Dubois was watching her reactions closely. She wondered what was the right response. She shook her head. "It was a work related matter. I was supposed to sit second-chair on one of his cases."

Dubois looked sceptical. "Couldn't you have waited till tomorrow to discuss work at the office?"

"In hindsight I should've."

Dubois was about to say something when a detective who had been questioning the neighbours walked in, and motioned for his attention. "Neighbours say he was an okay guy. But a lot of them didn't like him as a judge," he said, reading from his notepad.

"Whaddya mean?" Ignoring Grace, Dubois turned his attention to the cop.

"Too left-wing. Too soft. He let a lot of refugees into the country. Several of his cases had criminal records. Some of them were up on murder charges. Like the guy who held up a convenience store this year. According to the fella living in the white house across the street, a lot of right-wing groups hated him. Used to protest every now and then in front of his house. Police would have to be called in and disperse the commotion."

"In other words, a lot of folks were up to date on his legal decisions," said Dubois.

"Yeah. He wasn't well liked. Finding the perp is gonna be like looking for a needle in a haystack," said the younger detective.

"My thinking is, he got whacked by someone who was negatively affected by one of his left-wing decisions," said the older detective.

"What about that, Ms. Wang-Weinstein? You and your friend get a lot of death threats?"

"Yes, we do. We get so many it's hard to take them seriously." Everything about the situation seemed unreal to Grace, except the hollow feeling in the pit of her stomach.

"Takes a lot of nerve to kill somebody on a fairly busy street. How the hell did the perps know that he had just gotten off the plane?" Dubois answered his own question as he flipped through the papers on the clip-board. "Could only know that if they were following him. Do we have profiles of wacko amateur groups? Let's check his answering machine at work and visit his office. See if he had any death threats there."

"I'll look into it. I'll call the telephone company and get a record of all incoming and outgoing calls for the past week."

"Other than that, all we can do is speculate. Until some group claims responsibility," commented the younger detective.

"Ms. Wang-Weinstein, your help is greatly appreciated," said Dubois. "All I have to ask you to do now is come down to the station with me and give us a written statement."

"No problem," said Grace.

Ushering Grace out, Dubois closed the door behind him and ducked underneath the yellow tape. "Crosby may have been an asshole on some of his court decisions. But he didn't deserve the death penalty."

Discovering the body had been bad, very bad, but being forced to relive it under police interrogation was almost worse. By the time she left the police station, it was almost ten at night. She was shaking, emotionally and physically wrung out.

Thank God she did not have a case to deal with tomorrow. She decided to call Ellen Winkler. She didn't feel inclined to go home to an empty house. She

needed a friend who would understand and not berate
her. Her friendship with Ellen had started a little more
than four years ago. They had met in the sauna at her
health club. In that hot, surreal atmosphere, sitting
naked wrapped in white towels, faces covered in a
clay aromatherapy masque, the two women had discovered they had a great deal in common besides the
legal profession. Ellen was a federal court clerk, and
like Grace she was single. Within minutes of meeting,
they were swapping biographies and gossip about all
the weird and wonderful men they had known.

She had a hunch that Ellen would still be at work,
reviewing court applications and drafting legal decisions. Most days, her friend called it quits at ten, ten
thirty. She dialled Ellen's number, and began to pour out
what had happened to her from the beginning. As soon
as Ellen understood what Grace was telling her, she took
control. "Where are you? You're less than ten minutes
away. Meet me here," she ordered.

Grace hailed a cab to the Federal Court, where Ellen
clerked for Justice Angus. After paying the cabbie, she
dragged herself up the wide stone steps. She was in no
mood to admire the imposing edifice of stone and marble. Nor the Latin inscriptions pertaining to justice sten-
cilled in ornate script on the granite stone face above the
building. Grace waited in the handsome lobby with its
neo-classical columns. In less than five minutes, a short
woman with dark, tight curly hair appeared from
behind a large pair of oak doors.

"How terrible for you," Ellen said, holding out
her arms.

They embraced like sisters. "Where to?" asked Ellen.

"I haven't had dinner. And I need a stiff drink. Let's
go to one of those cafés along the canal?"

"Grace, you're exhausted. Come on," said Ellen,

motioning with her chin for Grace to follow, "never mind a café, we'll go back to my place and put our feet up."

"Sounds good to me," said Grace, linking her arm around Ellen's.

chapter nine

The glittering art-deco ballroom, decorated to evoke the opulent style of Shanghai in the 1930s, was crowded with fashionably dressed members of the country's Asian business elite. The black-tie fundraiser for the Yung Kee Foundation was one of the few high-profile events that drew the society types together with the corporate and the political heavies. This year the charity ball was being held in the penthouse of the Asia-Pacific Bank.

At the last minute, Grace had decided to come. Taking a little time off to see old friends and have some fun might help her stop brooding over Crosby's murder. In the last few days she had thought of little else. Crosby had been the most left-wing adjudicator on the bench. Was there any significance in that? Why did she have the awful thought that she would be next? She could not shake the sense of foreboding.

In no mood to shop, she wore the same strapless red organza gown as in the previous two years, hoping no one would notice. As she stood in line for drinks, she ran into an old acquaintance from her days on the Asia Business Council.

"Sandra. Good to see you."

The two women air-kissed each other, then Grace stepped back to examine the other woman's dress. "Daring Sandra. Burnt velvet with large see-through patches." Grace gave a wolf whistle. "I wish I had the bod."

"Darling, you do!" exclaimed Sandra Lim. "Your problem is you've no courage."

"No, Sandra, it's the fact that I'm not a hundred and five pounds. Who's that woman over there? The one dripping in jewels?"

"That's Angela Kwok. She used to be the mistress of that Taiwan tycoon who had the license to manufacture computers for Compaq, Dell, or whatever. It's all the same to me."

Grace eyed the voluptuous woman. She was with an aging Caucasian, who kept a possessive arm around her waist. "Who's the man?"

"Big real estate developer. He likes that type," Sandra whispered conspiratorially. "Attends every year with a different bird on his arm."

"Sandra, you know everybody."

"That's because I'm one of the ladies who lunch, my dear." She laughed.

They moved around the room, sampling the hors d'oeuvres that elegant young waiters offered on silver trays. Grace noticed heads turning to look at them. Sandra was looking spectacular.

"Who's the old white guy that has people lining up ten deep to shake his hand?" asked Sandra, biting into a crab cake.

"That's Senator Goldman. In fact, I see that the political and business communities are well represented here. Oh shit! There's my boss."

"Who?"

"The immigration minister himself," answered Grace, grabbing Sandra by the elbow, swinging her around in another direction, "and I don't want to say hello. We'll just ending up talking shop. In fact, all I really want is to get as far away from work as possible."

"I can't blame you. It must be dreadful to be tied down to a nine-to-five job."

"Try seven to seven," Grace corrected her.

Sandra gasped. "Really?"

Grace grabbed a second glass of wine from a waiter in a penguin costume of black coattails and white linen, and swivelling her head discreetly, did a quick head count of government officials, political lobbyists and foreign diplomats. "Do you know these people, Sandra? I can see hustlers of every stripe, all networking away like crazy while pretending to celebrate a worthy fundraising cause. How many of them are friends of yours?"

"Put like that, none of them," said Sandra, laughing. "But, Grace, I see quite a few politicians here. Maybe you should be networking, too."

"Why? They're canvassing for votes in the next election. And panhandling for campaign contributions to finance their next election campaign."

"Grace, you're such a cynic. We want them here. Business people need a chance to lobby for deals, concessions and lower taxes."

"Spoken like a true spouse of a business entrepreneur," said Grace dryly, and reaching for a dim sum treat from the wagon going around the room, let her gaze pass over the throng. A man in a well-cut suit was staring back at her, but her cool glance didn't connect with his. Turning around, she could feel his eyes burning into her back. She couldn't tell whether his interest in her was sexual, romantic or political, and she didn't care, but she didn't like the way he had been watching her for the past half hour.

"Let's check out the next room where they're auctioning off goods," she suggested.

The adjoining room was crammed with high-priced furniture, jewellery and other items, all with big price tags. Grace admired an Oriental room divider of carved rosewood, but the listed bid price made her gasp aloud.

They walked around the room, admiring the *objets d'art*. "See all those guys over there?" Sandra whispered, discreetly indicating a group of prosperous-looking men, "you can bet that their wives wait patiently at home every night with the burnt moo shoo pork while they paint the town red with their mistresses."

"I guess it's a good thing we're not married to any of them. Who's the Chink talking to our trade minister?"

"That's Rick Huang. He runs a import-export conglomerate. He's his own PR machine. He thinks he's the conduit for most goods moving between Asia and the rest of the world. Sells everything to everybody. From computer notepads made in Taiwan to air missiles to Iran, so they say."

"So, not someone you'd want to be seen with in public. Wouldn't surprise me if the intelligence community has his phone lines tapped."

"In other words, you want me to say no if he asks me for an introduction to you?" joked Sandra, patting Grace on the arm. "I see my husband waving his arm off. He probably wants to introduce me to some business associate. Catch you later. Look, your friend Wa Sing is here."

Catching his eye across the room, Grace smiled and waved to the old man, who lifted a hand in greeting and moved toward her. Every few steps, he had to stop to speak to someone. Her mother's friend looked like an

Oriental gnome with a white goatee, in an expensively tailored suit that was a size too big for him.

"Planning on gaining weight?" asked Grace, as she wrapped her arms around him. Wa Sing came up to her shoulders in height.

"I'm helping a tailor friend get established. He's doing his best." Wa Sing kissed her on the cheek. She watched his gently expressive face as he told her about his tailor friend's difficulties. When her mother, Kim, had met Wa Sing in Hong Kong in the 1950s, a bond had quickly developed between them. But it was neither romantic nor sexual in nature. Rather, Kim Wang and Wa Sing discovered, to their delight, that their families had known each other as far back as the early 1900s. At that time, Kim's uncle and Wa Sing's father had been early members of the Communist Party. In the 1920s the two men were sent by the Chinese Politburo to study Marxist-Leninist thought in Moscow; both embraced Russian communism and wanted to adopt certain elements of it in their own country. Their political allegiance had disastrous consequences for them later, when they were accused of spying for Russia and sentenced to re-education camps in the Chinese gulag. Kim never saw her uncle again.

In Hong Kong, Wa Sing and Kim lived in the same ghetto, and belonged to the same group of refugees who had sought the safety of the Colony during the war with the Communists in southern China. The prejudice they faced under the British helped shape their ideology. Like many, they believed that it was their own people, not the English, who had transformed the colonial backwater of Hong Kong into an Asian powerhouse.

After Kim married, she lost touch with Wa Sing until, years later in Vancouver, she was in Chinatown buying vegetables one day, and ran into him on the street. To a traditional Chinese person, a coincidence is never just a coincidence. They interpreted their meeting again as a sign that the continuation of their relationship would bring good fortune.

The story of Wa Sing's coming to North America was the classic story of the ragged émigré who rises to riches. At first he struggled to support his family by working in Chinatown as a rice and tea peddler. In 1966, with his life savings of nine thousand dollars and another ten borrowed from the community, he bought himself a car dealership. By the seventies, with the arrival of the Vietnamese boat people, his business had increased tenfold, and in the mid-eighties he reinvented himself again as the head of an Asian conglomerate with offices in Vancouver, San Francisco, Beijing, Shanghai, Hong Kong, and Taipei. His empire spanned car dealerships, savings and loan institutions, aviation companies and health care. Last year *Forbes* had nominated him as the forty-ninth richest man in the world, and he was part of an elite Cantonese group that wielded significant financial and political power. Not bad for a man who had arrived in Canada with nothing but the shirt on his back and a grade three education.

Kim had always said Wa Sing was a strong individualist who played by his own rules, but his generosity to those less fortunate had been part of his character as long as she had known him. When his only son died in an automobile accident, he had reached out to the community for solace and they had rallied to his side. In gratitude, he established a foundation to assist Asian-Americans. His benevolence was legendary. Grace owed her political appointment to the bench to his intervention on her behalf. Quite a few politicians were said to have benefited by his influence and aid, although that, unlike the scholarships and relief funds, was not publicized, and no politician, to Grace's knowledge, had ever admitted it in public. Over the years she had been curious about who, besides herself, he had helped. But there was no polite way to ask.

"Haven't seen you in a while. Where've you been?" Grace asked. "Closing some mega deal somewhere in Asia?"

"No, I was in San Francisco. I was going to Guangzhou but had to reschedule. I can't leave the country right now. Too much is happening."

Grace nodded without asking him for details. She had heard the rumours in the Chinese community that he had a mistress tucked away in some remote place like Wuhan or Nanking.

The music cut their conversation short. After the band stopped playing, Wa Sing said, "I want to introduce you to someone."

"Who?"

"A charming man." Wa Sing took her hand and led her through the crowd. "You know how happy your mother would be if you were to settle down soon. Too much independence is not good for a woman. This is Sun Sui. Sun, Grace Wang-Weinstein."

As Grace shook hands politely with the pervert who had been staring at her all evening, a young man in a tuxedo materialized at Wa Sing's shoulder and said a few words to him in a low voice.

"Excuse me, Grace. Back in a minute." Wa Sing moved away into the crowd and Grace was left alone with Sun Sui. He was a handsome Oriental, dressed expensively in a beige silk shirt and Armani suit. Not her type. Up close, his charm looked fake.

"Good to meet you," she said coolly. "Are you from here or visiting?"

"I'm from Hong Kong. But I have businesses here in Canada, so I must be here. You can't run businesses from a distance." He exuded self-satisfaction. Obviously humility was foreign to him.

She gave him an artificial smile. "Others have said that."

"You're a judge on the immigration bench, I hear. Fascinating work. A lot of people must offer you money to swing your decisions in their favour."

Did he really expect her to answer that? The man was a menace. What she really wanted was to get away from him, but rudeness to Sun Sui would show disrespect for Wa Sing, who had made a point of introducing them and would (she hoped) be back in a moment or two. So she simply changed the subject and told him about herself. How she had grown up in West Vancouver, and had downhill skied every March break at Whistler. How she had attended undergraduate studies at UBC before moving east to Toronto to pursue a doctorate. He sucked it all in, with that ingratiating smile of his, as if by paying close attention he was doing her a huge favour.

She was immensely relieved when Wa Sing returned and butted into their vacuous conversation about commerce in Asia. "How is your mother's health?"

"Despite her arthritis, she's doing pretty well."

Wa Sing turned to Sun and said, "I knew Kim Wang, her mother, back in the old country, when we were fleeing the Communists. Now everyone wants to do business with them," he cackled. "Western companies are salivating over those billions of consumers, because China is the biggest and last market left to crack. Yes, Grace's mother was something in those days. Kim proved to everyone how courageous and strong she was when she escaped from behind the Bamboo Curtain. She swam all the way into Hong Kong harbour!"

Grace noticed how Wa Sing's eyes became animated

as he spoke about Kim. The old man was really fond of his long-time friend.

Turning to Grace, Sun asked, "Does your mother live with you?"

"No." She refused to volunteer any more information to a stranger, but to her chagrin Wa Sing said, "No, her parents live in Vancouver. A beautiful house overlooking the ocean that they bought for a song when Grace was a baby." Wa Sing gave her a playful pinch on the cheek.

She blatantly looked at her watch. "Wa Sing, I'll see you later, at dinner. If you gentlemen will excuse me, the auction is about to start and I don't want to miss it. I'm going to bid on the Chinese screen."

Sun Sui pressed his business card into the palm of her hand. "If you're not successful in getting the screen, I can get you an exact copy. I would be pleased to have lunch with you."

Fat chance, she thought, as she made her escape.

Nick got back to his office to find Rocco Corvinelli standing outside his door.

"First thing I want to say is, you did great handling the press."

"Thanks," said Rocco, beaming from ear to ear. "That Singh fellow isn't so bad. We broke the ice by swapping ethnic jokes. He thought it was a hoot that the name Corvinelli is as ethnic as Singh. He said I looked like a swarthy Sicilian."

"Glad you two got on. A connection to the press is useful. Particularly him."

"Yeah, a few Mafia jokes, and we were best buddies."

"Better you than me," Nick replied, giving him the once-over. Yep, Rocco could easily pass for a Mafia enforcer. He was a muscular bull of a man, the kind of guy you would not want to meet in a dark alley. In the business of enforcement, that was a plus.

Rocco dropped onto the beat-up sofa that Nick had managed to confiscate when they were redoing the first-floor lobby, and waited as Nick picked up his voice-mail messages.

There was an angry message from Dubois, his RCMP counterpart. "You were right about the little shit. Gee Tung was released on $200,000 bail today and he and his lawyer have already talked to reporters about us using police brutality on him. And get this. He's suing us on the grounds that we violated his constitutional rights, and not only that, he's also pulling the multicultural angle, the race card shit! I'm holding a press conference of my own to give the facts to those left-wing reporters. In the mean-time, process those deportation papers, and let's put the creep on the next plane back to Nam. We don't need shit like that in this country. Call you again later."

So much for key witness evidence from Gee Tung. A week had passed since Walter Martin's death and the trail was getting colder. Hanging up the phone, Nick fixed his gaze on Rocco. "What about the rest of those foreign work authorizations I asked you to check out?"

"I went through the last batch. Twenty-seven of the entertainers applied for asylum when their permits weren't renewed. All twenty-seven were turned down. Five of them appealed at the federal court and lost their appeal. We sent them removal notices."

"Did we deport all of them?"

"Not one of them showed up to get on the plane. We ordered warrants for their arrest, but ..."

"Rocco, what're you telling me? That we never exe-cuted those arrest warrants because we couldn't keep track of their whereabouts?"

"Yeah. Worse, I was talking to one of the police detectives in New York's Fifth Precinct. He tells me that several of the girls are plying their trade on Forsyth Street in New York's Chinatown."

Nick rubbed his temples as he stared out the window. "If we add up the numbers, we have over five thousand failed asylum seekers facing deportation that we can't find?"

Rocco nodded his head with a grim look.

"At least half of them have already sneaked across the border to New York," wailed Nick. "Let's keep this under wraps. The last thing I need is a diplomatic kafuffle with Washington over illegals using Canada as a back door to get into the States. In the meantime, have the clerk run a complete search on the numbers, do the paperwork with Metro Precinct to have the Mandarin Club girls picked up. We're going to shut down the Mandarin Club temporarily."

"Boss, are you serious?"

"We've only got a few options open to us to prevent them from going underground. That would be a public relations disaster for us and the government. Having them in lockup buys us time to find evidence that Sun's abusing foreign work permits as a people-smuggling tactic to get them into North America. We need that evidence to build a case against Sun Sui as a smuggling kingpin. Then from that evidence, we take what we need to charge him with Walter Martin's death. Unfortunately, we'll have to deport the girls back to their country of origin."

"On what charges do we pick them up?"

"Whatever sticks. Expired working papers. Underage prostitution. Lap dancing. Possession of drugs."

"Shit, Nick. We're squeezing a bunch of girls so we can go after one guy? We're going to have every damn feminist in this country down our throat."

"I'm not happy with the decision either but we're just doing our jobs, Rocco."

After Rocco left, Nick stayed in his office working until it was past eight, making good progress on some of the files sitting on his desk. After he'd done enough paperwork for one day he dialled the number for the embassy in Hong Kong.

"Jon Keiler around?" he asked.

"He's on summer holidays," replied the secretary for the immigration unit at the embassy.

"How can I reach him?"

"Mr. Slovak, my boss doesn't file his holiday plans with staff."

"When's he back?"

"In a week."

"Tell him to call me ASAP."

His anxiety over the Mandarin Club file was giving him a headache right between the eyes. This case and Walter's death gave him the feeling that he was a warrior going into a losing battle, and more than anything, Nick hated to lose. If he hadn't gone to law school he would have been a cop, maybe a wrestler, anything that allowed him to fight the good fight. That's why he had always loved the job. He went through his notes again, his jaw tightening as he read. After closing the file, he made up his mind. He was going to send a message to smugglers and illegal migrants and all those who abuse the immigration system that there were serious consequences for doing so. He was going to make an example out of Sun Sui.

His phone rang. He glanced at the call display. Dubois. He picked up the receiver.

"Nick, I'm buried in paperwork. If I could take early retirement tomorrow, I would." His friend's voice was raspy with fatigue.

"Dubois, I'm buried in a file myself. Get to the point."

"My counterpart at the American embassy in Hong Kong told me that Sun Sui used to date the daughter of the Flying Dragons crime boss there. The Dragons are into drug trafficking, people smuggling, prostitution. Nothing good. Our boy's got no crime sheet, but he's sure got connections."

"That would explain the wads of cash in his bank accounts," said Nick, getting up to stretch his legs. He stared at the rush-hour traffic snaking up University Avenue. There were benefits to working late after all.

"I'm going to follow up on this conversation when Keiler returns from his holidays."

"One more thing. Kappolis told me he got orders from you to lay 209 criminal charges against the owner of the Mandarin Club and his so-called entertainers. The club's membership list is full of movers and shakers. Tread carefully there, boy."

"Just doing my job, Dubois."

The RCMP officer chortled at the other end. "A lot of good civil servants have been downsized for doing their jobs, Nick. Because their job didn't jibe with some politician's game plan."

The thought had occurred to Nick. He knew politicians bent the rules when it suited them. In his own modest way he tried to make the immigration system fair and transparent. The problem was the applicants with money and political connections who got to bypass the system.

"Hey, I ran into your ex-girlfriend."

"Grace?"

"I don't want to get into your personal life, but ... were you serious about her?"

"Why do you ask?" He shrugged to his reflection as he stared out the window. "I thought I was. But she

was just slumming. Looking for fun on the side."
When Dubois didn't speak, Nick said again, "Why do
you ask?"

"She went to a colleague's house, found him dead,
made the 911 call. Autopsy report indicates here that
he'd been killed minutes before she showed up. Body
was pretty warm. If she'd been at the victim's house any
sooner, she might not have got out alive herself."

"Is she okay?" His heart seemed to stop beating,
then started up again in a rush. He could feel his legs
giving way under him. He pulled his chair over to the
window and sat down.

"As okay as anybody can be after walking into a
dead body."

"Suicide?"

"That would be simple. Nah, he was murdered.
Victim's name was Crosby. Shot once through the heart.
Lab running ballistic tests as we speak."

"Any suspects?"

The RCMP officer snorted. "Nothing. It's shaping up
to be another cold case. No fingerprints, hairs, hair folli-
cles, pubic lice, nothing to take for DNA testing. Nada!"

"What the hell was Grace doing at the victim's
house?"

Dubois was silent for a long moment.

"Surely she's not a suspect!"

"Well, the officers found her a little evasive. Like
she was hiding something," Dubois replied.

Abruptly, Nick sat forward. "I see."

"This is gonna hurt, Nick, but the detective that
interviewed her, and myself included, thought she was
having an office affair with this Crosby."

He had to work to hold down his emotions. The
thought of Grace sleeping with another man was
painful. So much for the passage of time.

"Sleeping around like that in those circles impairs judicial impartiality or something like that."

"Could be just a random act of dropping in to see a colleague," said Nick, coming to Grace's defence.

"The detective nosed around her workplace. People who knew them both said she and Crosby weren't exactly pals. This is what I can't figure out. Maybe that was just an act they put on in the workplace to hide their affair. You know, everything in this world is timing. I'd like to know what was so important about meeting Crosby that she had to get to his place right after his plane touched down. She even had his exact flight number."

"Hmmm. Interesting."

"Let's just hope whoever pulled the trigger didn't see her. Because the last thing we want is to have him, or them, come back and finish the job."

Nick hung up the phone in a state of disbelief. First Walter was killed, and now Grace chanced upon a dead body. He dialled her home number, but there was no answer. And he didn't feel like confronting her in a voice-mail message. After all, who the hell was he? Nobody in particular — just a civil servant confronting a judge.

In a state of emotional vertigo, he walked out of his office. A colleague called out to him, but he didn't stop. No banter, no flirting with the clerks in the bullpen. He took the elevator down.

Theirs had been a complicated relationship, and she was a complex creature. At times too complex for him to figure out. They had met during national training week at Immigration. It was the one week in the year when the Commission judges and immigration officers could mingle without repercussions from the Bar Association, which frowned on its members fraternizing with immigration officers, whose outlook could taint the thinking of the Commission members. The five days of grudgingly permitted social contact was allowed under the guise of professional development.

Nick had been one of the speakers at the interrogation techniques workshop. He could hardly have helped noticing her because she barraged him with questions — good questions. He had always found a woman with a razor-sharp mind sexy. He couldn't guess her age. He thought she must be in her mid-thirties — she had lost the bloom of youth, but she was extremely attractive.

Over coffee, they discovered how much they had in common. They were both children of refugees. His parents had fled Czechoslovakia, ending up in Rochester, New York. Her father's family had escaped out of Hitler's Germany, and her mother's people had fled the Communists too late. They had both missed out on communicating with their grandparents, because the older generation didn't speak English, and as children, they had refused to speak their mother tongue, and now regretted their childish stubbornness. They compared notes and found that a similar mix of idealism and circumstance had drawn each of them to their respective vocations.

On their first date at a Japanese restaurant they had laughed themselves silly trying to play ethnic one-upmanship at the sushi bar; each trying to gross out the other. She had won when she bravely popped the raw octopus tentacles into her mouth. He drew the line at eating squishy fish eyeballs.

It was true that he hadn't had a relationship in close to four years before their fateful meeting. He'd applied a simple test to any woman he found at all interesting: would she date a man without a car? He couldn't believe how many of them failed. Living within walking distance of work in the heart of downtown, he didn't see the point of dropping thirty thousand to own a car when he could rent the latest model whenever he wanted, and without the hassle of car repairs. And he figured any woman who cared more about him pulling up in front of her house in a set of wheels than she did about him, himself, wasn't worth the trouble.

Grace didn't mind taking the subway or a taxi. She said it made her feel young and footloose again. Besides, she made him blissfully happy in so many other ways. The truth was, he hadn't felt such happiness in a long time. Kappolis had said that his happiness was directly proportional to the emotional deprivation he'd been feeling when they met, but Kappolis was the original hardboiled anti-romantic. Anyway, maybe they'd both been emotionally deprived. She had stayed on an extra week in Toronto. And when that wasn't enough, they had impulsively walked into a travel office and bought air tickets for Malta. While it lasted, it had been pure happiness. And then it all came crashing down to earth.

He could still feel the pain of it. She had lied to him from the very beginning. Less than four months after their Malta trip, he called her at home because he wanted to hear the sound of her voice before getting on a plane to Turkey to investigate a phony passport ring. It had been a hell of a shock to find himself talking to her husband.

She had lied to him once. What would stop her from lying to him a second time? Nothing, he answered himself. He didn't know what the hell she was involved in but Dubois was right — not only had she lied, she had also taken privileged information on a case he had told her about in bed and used it against him and his department. There had been hell to pay on that one. The director general had given him one hell of a tongue-lashing.

No, he had to confront her when her defences were down. The truth was, he still cared about her. But being her second-string man was definitely out of the question.

After a walk around several blocks, he went back to work. Yes, he wanted to see her again. But it had to be on his terms.

BJ hated surveillance work and Harry was driving him crazy, wanting him to do more of it.

Harry wailed, "Why did the broad have to show up at Crosby's place, right then?"

"She looked right at us," said BJ.

"That doesn't mean she can ID us in a line-up."

"If we're not sure, we whack the broad," said BJ. "She coulda seen the van. Maybe it's just damn fate for her to die too."

"We can't go about whacking people left and right."

"You want to go back to the Pen?" asked BJ, cleaning his fingernails with an X-acto knife.

"BJ, we don't want to go back to prison. On the other hand, we just can't go about killing people. First, we got to figure out who she is. That way, we can watch her. Then we got to run into her again, see if she remembers us."

"How do we find out who she is?"

"Easy. We knew where he worked. We watch the workplace again. See if she works there."

"She coulda been the girlfriend."

"Nah, she was in a suit. Girlfriends don't go on dates in business suits, BJ."

"Whatever you say, Harry. When we catch up to her again, I say we whack her. Take care of the problem then and there."

"Only if she can ID us."

BJ continued cleaning his fingernails. He didn't want to argue with Harry but he thought his friend was chickening out on him. Any moron knew not to leave witnesses alive at the crime scene. The killing of a judge was a big-time offence. "You whacked one. What the hell is two?" said BJ, inspecting his nails. He had no problem with icing the broad. One thing for sure, no damn way he was going to spend another day in the Kingston Pen. The leg irons and handcuffs were still fresh in his mind.

Yeah, no damn way he was going back there.

chapter ten

"Boss, I think you better stay indoors today." It was Rocco was on the phone.

"What?" mumbled Nick. His brain was in another dimension.

"How bad can it be?" He pried his eyes open. Outside the bedroom window, the sky was sullen, gunmetal grey. His clock read 5:59 a.m.

"Turn to CHKU 99 to get the full flavour. The shit is worse than we expected. The feminists and multicultural groups and civil rights activists are all yelling. They say we had no right to put those girls in lockup last night. Plus, one of the girls is on the loose. She escaped our officers during the raid. Afraid she got away. We got an immigration warrant out for her arrest as we speak. Cops are doing their best to find her."

Nick told Rocco he'd be in touch soon, and hung up. He turned the dial on his bedside radio one twist to the left. He was fully awake now. A female voice blared,

"... the girls are themselves victims. It's not fair to charge them with prostitution and move to deport the victims when the owner of this club, who's nothing more than a pimp, is running around scot-free." The announcer came on, identifying the angry speaker as the spokesperson of a women's shelter.

More and more callers commented on the issue. At least half the country was against him. Several minutes later, his phone rang again. It was the concierge downstairs warning him that a mob of people and reporters were lying in wait for him on the street, outside his condominium building. The thought of being a prisoner in his apartment held no appeal. He would die of cabin fever.

He called the concierge back. "How about letting me use the service elevator and exit?"

"I'm not supposed to. Well, okay, just this once."

Several minutes later he reached the subway, lungs aching. He caught his breath as he waited for the west-bound train and assessed his situation. How the hell was he supposed to know that putting fifty girls in lockup was an unspeakable offence against political correctness? He was just doing his job.

Every move he made toward catching Walter Martin's killer seemed to be taking him farther away from his goal, not closer to it. Every witness he'd tried to secure had been killed or ran away, and now this eruption. He'd have to spend valuable time and energy putting out more brushfires on the secondary issues.

After two stops, he got off and briskly walked towards his refuge at Odansky's diner, his favourite breakfast joint. Who would think of looking for him in a mom-and-pop greasy spoon?

Albert Odansky waved to him from the kitchen, peering out through the window that allowed him to survey his customers.

Nick waved back, making a beeline for his customary cubicle.

"Morning, Olga. I'll have the usual."

The usual meant two eggs sunny side up, two fat sausages and whole wheat toast. Olga poured him a cup of coffee in a chipped stoneware mug.

The whole city had become one big temple for those with money. The Caffé Galleria down the street was done in funky colours and expensive stone floors, and the coffee came in Italian glass and cost four dollars. He'd only been to there once, when it had first opened. No, he preferred the greasy spoon. There was something comforting about a place that hadn't changed since it opened its doors in 1964. The Formica-topped tables, plastic booths, swivel stools at the counter and the green linoleum floor were as he had remembered them from his student days at St. Mike's. In those days, $1.05 for breakfast was all he could afford. Now the best high-cholesterol meal in town was still cheap at $2.50.

Like his parents, the Odanskys had fled the Communists for Canada. They had escaped the Ukraine in the middle of the night and had found asylum in Saskatchewan. When they had first arrived in the country, they had found work as farmhands. After moving to Toronto, and more years of saving and scrimping, they had finally bought the modest diner on College Street. He smiled as he lifted his empty coffee cup to Olga who came over to pour him a refill. The Odanskys were living proof that the country had been built on decent, hard working immigrants. People wanting to immigrate here weren't all like Sun Sui. He shouldn't forget that.

After paying the bill, he headed east towards University Avenue and the Metro Precinct.

Kappolis, with his feet up on an open drawer, was on the phone working another case. Nick eavesdropped

long enough to hear about a fugitive who had re-entered
the country illegally six times after he was booted out.
He was wanted by his home country for embezzlement.
Nick didn't want to know any more. He could only
devote a hundred percent of his concentration to one
case at a time. He walked down to the water cooler and
got himself a drink of water.

Kappolis hung up and called out, "Nick, where did
you go?"

"I'm here. Thought I'd give you some privacy."

"I don't need any privacy," he replied, flipping
through a stack of computer printouts. "I heard about
your troubles. I've been trying to reach you for the past
hour. Where were you hiding?"

"I wasn't hiding. I was having breakfast."

The detective gave him a look. "Oookay. Good to
hear that you're taking things in your stride."

"How else?" said Nick.

"You know you're in deep shit, don't ya?"

"Steve, I acknowledge only one thing: that you can't
win these days. First, I get in trouble with the mayor for
not doing my job. Now I'm in trouble for doing my job,"
said Nick, shrugging his shoulders. He then grabbed a
chair that was leaning against the wall and pulled it up
to Kappolis's desk. "Give me a status report. How's our
search going?"

Kappolis threw up his hands. "In the beginning we
got no sightings. Now we have two boxes of reported
sightings of our guy Li Mann. Personally, I think people
are trying to bullshit us for the reward money."

"Surely there has to be at least one promising tip
buried in those two boxes," said Nick.

"Nick, we've got leads. They're just too vague to
follow up. What the hell do you do with a lead where
the caller says he saw a guy matching that description

boarding a bus. A bus going where? The caller doesn't know. Or when? Maybe yesterday he says. Or maybe a week ago." The detective hunched up his shoulders and turned the palms of his hands out. "We wasted time on one lead that seemed like a hot tip. Wrong guy."

"Being ethnic doesn't help. To most Anglos, all ethnics look alike. That's probably why there're so many sightings of him," said Nick.

"Nothing comes up on motor vehicles registration or social security or the credit bureau. Officially he doesn't exist, doesn't have a driver's licence, a health card or a credit card. But we know that isn't true."

"Anything interesting on Gee Tung's surveillance?"

"Nada. I suspect he knows he's being watched and is on good behaviour," said Kappolis, loosening his tie. "So, you going back to work?"

Nick got up and adjusted his chinos which were sticking to his body.

"Where else? I've got too much damn work on my desk. I'll take my chances with the special interest groups. So watch for me on the news tonight." He gave a humourless laugh as he walked out the door. As he left the station, he was relieved to see that there was nobody waiting to pounce on him.

He sneaked into his office through a side entrance. At his desk, he saw that he had two calls from the Immigration and Naturalization Service in New York regarding a Sri Lankan gunrunner they'd arrested at JFK. Not now, he thought. After cleaning out his messages, he went down to the cafeteria and grabbed a pop. Back in his office, he concentrated on the case at hand. The evidence he did have against Sun didn't look good. More holes were beginning to appear in his case against the man. The problem was, for every bit of information gathered, a whole lot of new questions opened up. Sun was obviously abusing the work authorizations, but where the hell were the visa officers at the Canadian and American embassies? Were they asleep at the switch? Didn't they see that the Mandarin Club was running a scam to bring people to North America?

Everything came right back to Immigration. He knew he should take the case upstairs and discuss it with the director general. But if he did that, he would be ordered to downplay or even drop the case against Sun. The director general's answer to incompetence and stupidity was secrecy. The DG didn't want to know about the dumb mistakes immigration officers made in the field because he didn't want the public to know. And Nick wasn't going to drop the case. Sun was all he had to lead him to Walter Martin's killer.

Li Mann flew out of La Guardia and into Pearson International. Seventy-five minutes flying time from New York to Toronto. He had no problems leaving the country six days ago. Why would he have problems re-entering the country? Nor was he frightened by the thought that the city would be crawling with cops hunting for him. He had been hunted before, by American soldiers and CIA operatives in the jungles of Nam, and by DEA agents in the Golden Triangle in Thailand. So what else was new?

He took a taxi downtown to the ferry docks. The meeting place was on Toronto Island. Half an hour later, he was strolling on the Ward's Island boardwalk. The wind rolled in from across the lake.

The General was dressed for the rainy weather; rubberized slicker and runner shoes. His companion, the Red Prince, had difficulty keeping the fedora on his head. Li Mann could pass himself off as a day labourer walking with his master.

"We have no choice. We must act." Li Mann's voice was firm.

The Red Prince looked at the General in consternation. "I'm in no hurry. I need to consult — "

"Consult what, the stars?" the General asked curtly. "Let's not be foolish, and let's not be dabbling in religion at this point. We can't afford to have our best-laid plans derailed by a few immigration officers."

"I don't want the shedding of more blood! It's bad enough that you killed that senior immigration officer."

"That was unintentional. I had no choice," replied the General, as he examined his scarred hands and chipped fingernails. He didn't like the direction of the conversation. It was difficult working with civilians. They knew nothing of military tactics and strategy. Li Mann Vu prided himself in these things. He appraised his walking companion at a glance. The Red Prince, for all his education and connections, was essentially a weak man. The General looked upon him as a peacock. All he cared about was the cut of his suit and the art of a business deal; little else. The General shook his head in private disgust, but the reality was he'd have to work with what he had.

"We need at least another fifty million to complete the joint venture real estate deal in Macau, but if we move now we could lose everything. It's all over the news. Immigration officers are on alert in both countries. We can't afford to lose another cargo ship," said the Red Prince. "But then again, we can't afford to lose three hundred migrants at fifty thousand a head."

"The sweatshops on East Broadway are clamouring for more bodies. I already told some of the businesses down there that we were going to wait it out."

"That decision was not yours to make." The Red Prince curtly reminded his companion.

They walked several yards in silence. Every few steps, the Red Prince tossed pieces of stale bread to the flock of geese that followed them.

"We have a more pressing problem and I want you to take care of it."

"I could smuggle him into New York. I think we should send him down to Fuzhou Number One street for retraining," argued the General.

"It's not our job to provide retraining. He's a loose cannon. He could destroy everything. Is that what you want?" It was a rhetorical question. The Red Prince didn't expect an answer. Nor did he get one.

Neither man spoke as they retraced their footsteps back to the ferry.

"I'll contact you in a few days," said the Red Prince. "I don't need to remind you that you don't have supreme authority here."

Li Mann flinched as if he had been struck. For a long time he stood on the dock and watched the ferry pull away, until it became a dot on the horizon. Theirs was not a relationship of equals. But if the Red Prince thought that a former military officer would accept being subservient to a civilian for long, he had a surprise coming. For now, though, the General preferred not to rock the boat.

He plotted and argued with himself as he waited for the next ferry. The boat, when it came, was almost empty. In the dark, he could see the rain coming down in sheets. When he boarded the streetcar for Kensington, the General knew what he had to do when he got off.

chapter eleven

O ne of the hardest things Nick had to do was show respect for judges for whom he felt nothing but contempt. He had been hoping to buy time and build his case against Sun when he filed the deportation notice. But when he heard that Kenneth Egan would be presiding on Sun Sui's case, he knew the deck was stacked against him. The left-leaning Egan had made his name by leading the good fight for conjugal rights for prisoners and generous welfare payments to single mothers.

Nick had decided to go ahead with the deportation hearing, hoping to save taxpayers at least a million dollars by prosecuting Sun now, even though he didn't really have enough evidence. Andy Loong was dead. Gee Tung had changed his mind about trading information for a lighter sentence, and he wasn't talking. Neither were any of the entertainers from the Mandarin Club. One of them, Niin Tran, still had not been found. And Li Mann, whoever he was, was still at large.

As Nick took a seat in the old Courthouse, a man in wire frames and moustache approached carrying an expandable briefcase. He introduced himself as Jeremy Klein, and added, in a gently apologetic tone, "Department of International Trade. I thought you should hear it from me first, but I'm supporting Mr. Sui's claim to remain in the country."

Nick's jaw dropped. Holy shit! What the hell was going on? How could Immigration deport a man that the Trade Department wanted to protect?

He looked down at Klein's card, then stared as he moved away and seated himself next to Sun Sui's lawyer. Sun Sui himself was nowhere to be seen. Probably didn't want to show up in court like a common criminal.

Judge Egan opened the morning's proceedings, intoning from the bench, "Mr. Slovak, I've read your pleadings and exhibits. Frankly, I'm somewhat confused on exactly why you want to remand the appellant into custody prior to deportation. Because I don't see a case for deportation here."

Nick watched Judge Egan peer at him over the top of his bifocals.

"Given the pleadings, I want to remind the Immigration Department that we're not living in a police state. What I see in these documents is the use of unnecessary force and fascist tactics."

"Thank you, Your Honour." Verster threw Nick a gloating look.

Without missing a beat, Nick argued, "Your Honour, it is the argument of the state that the appellant is a member of an inadmissible class. There are reasonable grounds to believe that he has committed offences both outside and inside Canada, and these offences could be punishable under any Act of Parliament by a maximum term of imprisonment of ten years or more."

Verster immediately jumped to his feet. "Your Honour, I submit that it is a question of fact whether my client Mr. Sun Sui participated in any of the alleged activities as stated on the deportation order and the Immigration Department's package of exhibit documents. I further submit that it is a question of law whether these alleged activities constitute sufficient evidence by way of complicity or membership in a criminal organization to warrant the application of the exclusion clause."

Judge Egan glared down at Nick from his pulpit. "Counsel is right, Mr. Slovak. What says the Immigration Department on this matter?"

Verster threw Nick another gloating smile.

Nick prayed he would be struck down by a bolt of lightning. Keeping his voice even, he said, "With all due respect, Your Honour, I'd like to refer to the documents here ..." He went over the little evidence he had, trying to make it sound like more than it was.

When Nick finished speaking, Verster launched into his arguments without looking at his notes; he had done his homework. "I've read the documents Immigration has submitted regarding my client's alleged activities as a people smuggler and his alleged use of his nightclub to bring in asylum seekers under the guise of entertainers and sex workers. However, there is no documented evidence that my client directly participated in any illegal smuggling operation bringing in any illegal aliens on any cargo ship or any transportation vessel at any time. Your Honour, it was the Immigration Department that approved all of those foreign work authorizations for the Mandarin Club. Nor is there any evidence that my client is a member of any crime group such as the Flying Dragons. However, the very same Immigration Department is levying such charges against my client without proof. My client finds this deportation order against him to be vexatious. In this regard, I'd like to call as my witness one of the government's own lawyers."

Jeremy Klein stood, casting a nervous look in Nick's general direction. With a flourish, Verster introduced him. "This witness is a government lawyer from the Department of International Trade. He has prepared an affidavit from the minister's office which indicates that my client is held in high regard by the prime minister's office. My client, Mr. Sui, has advised the Trade Department on several occasions regarding trade in Asia. I would like these documents entered as exhibit items because they reveal my client's value to the economy of this country. At the same time, I think we can also infer my client's good character because under no circumstances would the government of this country have dealings with a crook or criminal."

Nick was stunned, and inwardly raging. It was all too typical of government for the left hand not to know what the right hand was doing. But in this case the right hand was stabbing him in the back.

Outwardly, he tried to look unmoved, but the rug had been pulled out from under him. Still, he charged in, aggressively dismissing Verster's arguments. "Come on, counsel! I really fail to see the relevance of this. Trade and people smuggling are two different issues. The Immigration Department's case against Mr. Sui isn't affected by these touching testimonials."

"Your Honour, Mr. Slovak is on personal mission to find the killer of an immigration officer, and has allowed his desire to find a culprit to cloud his judgement. The Immigration Department has tried to shut down my client's business by locking up his employees in detention. Furthermore, the police and the Immigration Department Enforcement Unit have harassed and perse-

cuted my client. I feel that there is a reasonable appre-
hension of bias and abuse of power on Mr. Slovak's
part. It is my considered opinion that Mr. Slovak is
motivated by animus against my client in determining
whether Mr. Sui should be judged as a member of an
inadmissible class."

Nick was apoplectic, but he tried to maintain his
cool. As he listened to Jeremy Klein describing Sun Sui
as a man of good character, honest and trustworthy,
and a valued advisor to the Trade Minister on the next
Team Canada trade mission to China, Nick knew the
fix was in. He had lost. The case was over in under
two hours.

Judge Egan peered down from the bench. He ruled
that there wasn't enough evidence to arrest and deport
Sun Sui. Worse, he also ruled that there wasn't conclu-
sive evidence to prosecute Sun Sui on criminal charges
of prostitution, money laundering, people smuggling, or
any of several lesser charges of criminal activity.

Nick took deep, steady breaths, trying to stay calm.

"It is my opinion that a jury properly instructed
would not convict the accused," Judge Egan concluded,
and with that remark discharged the case against Sun Sui.

The only concession Egan made to Nick was to order
that Sun Sui hand over his passport for a short time, to
prevent him from leaving the country while Nick continued his investigation and any possible involvement by Sui
in triads, immigration fraud, and drug trafficking.

Nonetheless, Judge Egan's decision, in favour of the
appellant, was a kick in the teeth.

Nick went for a long walk to detoxify his mood. The
sky was overcast, the clouds seemed to hang low, no higher than the treetops. He walked past City Hall, past the
glass and steel towers of the big banks. When he dragged
his feet back to his office, it was just before 1:30 p.m.

Erma, his secretary, asked, "Are you okay, Nick? You look lousy."

"I'm fine, Erma."

But he wasn't fine. The entire investigation was unravelling from every direction. Not to mention all the other cases that were hanging over his head, a dozen of them that he'd set aside to concentrate on the one that mattered to him. In the middle of everything was tomorrow's squash game with the M-16 officer at the British High Commission, which he should really cancel, but wouldn't because he needed the physical release of smashing a rubber ball against a wall.

In all of this, the man who killed Walter was still at large. Was it possible that his grief and anger over Walter's death really was clouding his judgement as the horrible Verster had said? He put a hand over his eyes and massaged an aching spot on his forehead. Maybe he really was burned out; it had been a possibility for long time, but he'd been unwilling even to think about it.

Rocco popped his head around the door frame. "You got a call from the INS in New York. Seems they've been trying to reach you for over a week. Here's the number." He dropped a pink slip of paper on Nick's already cluttered desk.

"Thanks," Nick muttered. He turned on his computer before dialling the New York number. Playing phone tag, he left a message before hanging up.

"Erma, please make a fresh pot of coffee and zap this stale muffin for me." He handed her an oversized blueberry muffin that had been sitting on his desk for almost two days.

He adjusted his Obus and tipped his chair back, resting his feet on the window vents as he stared out at the world outside. How could this Li Mann character be so elusive in this new age of computer technology where privacy had

gone the way of the dinosaurs? Anyone could be tracked
down. It was just a matter of time. Maybe he wasn't looking in the right country, he ruminated. He hated to call his
counterparts in Washington and concede defeat. It could
cause trouble, even a diplomatic tiff between the two countries. But what if Li Mann had fled into the United States or
had a base somewhere in the States? Assuming that he was
the top dog of the Flying Dragons, how stupid or audacious
would he have to be to travel under his own name?

Not wanting to call it quits yet, he did a quick cruise
through VICLAS, the new violent crime linkage analysis
system. He typed in Li Mann's name in half a dozen
variations and waited for the search. He liked VICLAS.
It was a database of signatures of criminals' *modi
operandi*. It had given law enforcement agencies great
success in identifying suspects. It had recently identified
the killer in a 1983 murder of a teenage girl. But for
Walter Martin's killer, it turned up nothing.

Munching on his blueberry muffin, he logged into
ORION, a geographic profiling system that Dubois had
raved about even though it was still in the testing stage.
Last year, the RCMP had used it to pinpoint the residence
of several members of Persian Pride, an Iranian organized-
crime gang operating out of Vancouver. Several cups of
coffee later, there was still nothing.

The phone rang. He tapped out of ORION before
picking up.

"I heard the news on the radio. I don't know what
to tell you, Nick." It was Kappolis.

Nick hit a few keys to exit the program as he
briefly gave his friend the details of what had occurred
in the courtroom. "I still can't believe it. Egan didn't
even reserve judgement. Such a public case, you think
he'd at least make a pretence of reserving judgement for
a couple of days."

"Why would Egan let Sun Sui off so quick and easy? You think he's in somebody's pocket? Hey, Nick, maybe the Trade Minister's in somebody's back pocket."

Nick was silent for a moment, contemplating the possibility as he remembered Klein's testimonial. "I don't know," he said, wiping muffin crumbs off his desk, "but here's what I'd like us to do. Put Sun under twenty-four-hour surveillance. You think you could have several teams on him around the clock?"

"No problem. I'll add Li Mann's name to it. That way the surveillance requisition will come through pronto when we find him."

"That still won't help us if Sun has leverage with the Trade Minister. His getting off could have something to do with this Team Canada trade mission to China later this year. I think I'll put a call in to the Trade Minister myself."

"I don't understand it, Nick. I'm just a cop, maybe you got to live in the nation's capital to get it, but if one half of the government is spending millions to stop these migrant cargo vessels from entering the country, and here you are, trying to deport these agent smugglers, why does the other half of the government come up behind you and nip you in the ass? As a taxpayer, I can tell you, we need smaller, smarter government. Not some bloated bureaucracy spinning out of control and crammed with mediocrity."

Kappolis had a point, but Nick wasn't up for a political discussion right now. He made the excuse that he had to return his messages. But Kappolis's words wouldn't go away. The more he thought about the government, the clearer the feeling became. He needed to be in Ottawa where these half-assed political decisions were made.

Rummaging through his recycling box, he finally found what he was looking for. An invitation to the

Immigration Minister's summer tea party! It was time to confront a few people.

chapter twelve

She scooped up the mail and carried Buzby into the house, closing the door behind her. Bills, more bills and a letter from David, her ex. Just what she needed! Here she was in a house with a fat mortgage, that she couldn't sell for love or money without losing a quarter of her equity, trying to cope with the pressures of living in an unforgiving economy. And no second income as backup. If she had known all this would happen, she might even have stayed married.

No, no, she wouldn't, she quickly corrected herself. That was over.

They had outgrown each other; it was a stage-of-life thing. That was her problem, she outgrew things — jobs, friends, husband. She had met David when she was seconded to the UN office in El Salvador. He was first secretary to the American ambassador. They had met at someone's Valentine's party, and had hit it off. After a three-month romance they had tied the knot. In hind-

sight, it was a co-dependent relationship that had survived only because friends and family were far away.

Coming home after a decade abroad had been culture
shock for them both. After years of negotiating with rebel
fighters and military dictators, David had found the chattering classes and language fanatics of the Canadian capital excruciatingly parochial. He also whined about the loss
of his favourite perks. Gone were the Mercedes, the uniformed chauffeur, the ten-thousand-square-foot mansion,
the retinue of servants. Worse, he had blamed her for the
loss. He frequently reminded her that he had turned down
the Washington posting for this provincial place.

What could she say in her own defence? She had
wanted to return to Canada. Her many years abroad
had nurtured a rosy image of home as a wonderful place
where everything worked: telephones connected you on
the first try, road crews fixed potholes, supermarket
shelves were always stocked full of food, and there were
no power outages. But the home she came back to was
a country fractured by separatist politics, a city rife with
crime, and a property tax bill that reflected the bur-
geoning welfare rolls.

Further cracks soon appeared in her relationship
with David as they found themselves arguing over who
was going to cut the grass and shovel the driveway.

She tore open David's letter. She was glad he was
doing okay. It meant an end to any last twinges of guilt
she might have felt about her affair and their divorce.
She knew from previous letters that he was posted in
Budapest, playing the part of the grand Pooh Bah again.
But she *really* didn't want to hear the details of his
romances — he had even sent her photographs of his
conquests! This latest one was obviously the *Lolita* type
— she was half his age. Grace tore the photo in half and
tossed it in the wastepaper bin.

After a late dinner, she sat down, intending to work on her case files. But she was too tired to even open the accordion folders. Tomorrow. As she piled the dirty dishes in the sink, she heard a strange sound outside her kitchen window. It sounded like the scraping of branches against the garage. Her imagination? She moved slowly across the room, going from window to window, and listened. No, she told herself. It must have been a little animal — a raccoon or squirrel. She wouldn't let her mind play tricks on her. Still she remained standing in front of the window, looking out into the darkness.

She inhaled sharply as she glimpsed a sudden movement in the lilac bushes. Was someone spying on her? Before Crosby was killed, she hadn't really paid much attention to the death threats the IRC received every time a stay of deportation was granted. Now, just about any little thing was enough to spook her. She stood like a statue staring out the window, hoping and praying that a cat or raccoon scrounging for food would let itself be seen and calm her nerves.

BJ wanted to smash through her glass windows and kill her with his bare hands. All because his new running shoes were ruined tramping through her backyard. There was the stink of manure to them. At least, the surveillance on Crosby's workplace had paid off. They now had her name, address and telephone number. That was important if you wanted to whack someone.

He stood behind the shrubbery and wondered what kind of folks did not put up curtains on their windows. The high and mighty, pretentious folks. Well, they got what was coming to them. No privacy and much more.

He watched her standing in front of the window.

Tell me Lady Judge, are you scared? Scared of me or the sound of broken branches?

BJ saw the cat sitting on the kitchen counter, and wondered what kind of folks allowed animals to prowl on eating surfaces. Middle class folks, he answered back. When he watched middle class folks, BJ was glad that he was raised working class. But he didn't always feel that way. When he was a kid, the middle class kids at school used to make fun of him and the way he dressed. And the peanut butter sandwiches he brought to school every day.

Now he was getting his own back. From the house and the street, BJ knew the bitch was middle class. That was reason enough to hurt her.

Kappolis called him at 4:20 a.m. He ran out of the house and hailed a cab. The cabbie, a recent émigré from Islamabad, barely spoke English, and Nick had the damnedest time giving street-by-street instructions to the Metro Precinct. He gave him a big tip anyway.

The interior of the precinct, with its bare walls, fluorescent lights and vinyl tile flooring worn by countless footsteps looked much the same in the middle of the night as it did at noon.

Kappolis was standing behind the public counter. Seeing Nick, he gave a weary wave.

Nick crossed the lobby. "What happened? The guy's been out on bail less than a week, and now he's dead? And in Toronto? I thought he lived in Montreal."

"He got on a bus to Toronto, according to a bus ticket stub they found in his jean jacket."

Nick shook his head. "Obviously somebody besides us was watching his movements. They sure didn't want him to talk. Just like Andy Loong."

Detective Kappolis finished marking the report he was working on and jerked a thumb over his shoulder. "I got the cruiser out back. Let's go. I'll fill you in as I drive."

"The call came to this precinct?" asked Nick, holding the door open for his friend.

"Yeah, you just missed the reporting officer who interviewed Gee Tung's girlfriend. His shift ended half an hour ago. I chatted with him and got a copy of his notes. According to Tung's girlfriend, she met up with him at the bus station and they took the subway back to her place. Inside, she started cooking dinner. As they were sitting down at the table, two thieves in ski masks broke through the door. According to her, they asked where was the jewellery. When Gee Tung and his date said they didn't have any, the two assailants shot him several times and fled without taking anything." Kappolis walked half a step ahead of Nick.

They walked across the impound yard full of cars last driven by thieves, drunkards, killers, or more moderate citizens who had run afoul of the law.

"They shot him more than once and didn't take anything? They can't even spend the effort to make it look like a real robbery. The Flying Dragons are tying up loose ends. I wonder who's calling the shots? This Li Mann character or our friend, Sun Sui?" asked Nick, as he climbed into Kappolis's unmarked cruiser. The downtown streets were still hopping, but as they left the central core the action thinned to empty.

"The detective down at Metro Division 14 who took the call wrote it off as your average home invasion. Which means they aren't going to blow resources on finding the perps."

"What was Sun Sui doing when it went down?" asked Nick.

"I'll check with my officers. But don't get your hopes up high 'cause I got a fleet of cars watching him. Two men apiece. For the past two days, Sun has spent it mostly in his condominium. However, a bevy of gorgeous gals have paraded through his pad. With their résumés."

"Résumés?" asked Nick.

"Yeah. You should see the slinky dresses on these gals. Whoa!"

"More entertainers? Actresses?" asked Nick.

"Who knows?"

"Any male visitors?"

"Nope," replied Kappolis, keeping his eyes on the road. "The only times he left his pad he walked to Chinatown for lunch. The undercover guys watching him said he bought a paper and ate alone at a noodle bar or dim sum house. Then he circulated through some of the shops on Dundas, talking to a handful of shopkeepers."

"Maybe he's trying to extort protection money from them."

"Two of my undercover guys are going to check in on these shopkeepers later in the week. The next team tracked him as he went shopping. Tried on suits, shirts and stuff. Spoke to no one other than the sales help. Then came home. If he put the hit out on Gee Tung, it certainly wasn't in person or on the phone. The only calls he made were to girls and his banker."

They stopped at a red light. A streetcar rumbled to a stop behind them.

"Except for one afternoon when the surveillance team lost him for about an hour and a half."

"Lost him? How?"

"Sui went to the fair. The cops watched him buy a ticket for the roller coaster ride. They watched him get in line. Both officers declined to do the ride. Twenty minutes later, our boy evaporates into thin air." Kappolis tapped impatiently on the steering wheel as he waited for the lights to change. "The team stationed outside his condo said an hour and a half later our boy turns up at his condo carrying a bag of candy floss from the fair."

Nick pushed the hair back from his forehead. "Did he give the boys in blue the slip or was it incompetence on the part of the surveillance team?"

Kappolis shrugged his shoulders as he put his foot on the gas. "Who knows? All I know is, we've got no suspects in Gee Tung's death."

"What about the ME?" yawned Nick. He could've used another hour of sleep.

"Yeah, the medical examiner is expecting us about now. I was told not to get there too early 'cause Dr. Dillon's got to drive all the way into the city from the 'burbs."

"I don't see why I need to be here," said Nick.

"Orders from the precinct commander. He's covering his ass on this one."

They pulled up in front of the morgue and parked in a tow-away zone. Kappolis didn't care for traffic cops, nor did they strike fear into his heart.

The medical examiner, Dr. Dillon, was already dressed in green surgical scrubs, his plastic goggles dangling under his chin. He was a tired-looking, middle-aged man who had clearly been rudely interrupted from his sleep when the call of duty came. Nick twice caught him yawning into his latex gloves.

"Follow me, gentlemen. We'll take the elevator down to the autopsy room."

They grabbed two lab coats hanging on hooks and rode the elevator down to the bowels of the building. The minute Nick went through the gleaming steel doors, the smell hit him hard in the nostrils. Years in the business, and he could never get used to the smell of death and formaldehyde.

The medical examiner asked the two orderlies to remove the body from the bag and lift it onto the gurney. Nick stood at a respectful distance and stared at what was left of the victim's head. The ME followed his gaze.

"At first glance, it appears that he was shot at least three times at point-blank range. One at the back of the head and two in the chest. One of the bullets punctured his left lung. At such close range, one bullet was enough to make death instantaneous."

"Thank you, Dr. Dillon. I hadn't realized that the victim took three hits."

"Oh, yes, he did. But I'll be able to tell you more after a more complete examination. We'll be getting started on that in a few minutes."

"Fine by us."

Nick's eyes wandered over to the hanging scale, the rows of gleaming steel instruments and the jars of chemicals lined neatly in the glass cabinets. In a few hours, the late Flying Dragons member would have been dissected, weighed, photographed and fingerprinted. What was left of his head would be examined for wound patterns. The bullets would be extracted and marked for ballistics. Although he had attended many an autopsy, he would never be comfortable seeing a chainsaw applied to a human body.

"Do you want to watch?"

"No, the autopsy report will do just fine. I'll pass on sitting in on this one," said Nick. He knew that the autopsy report, photographs and all information would be given to the detective in charge.

"I'll courier it to your precinct, detective," said the ME without looking up from the forms he was filling out.

They jaywalked across two lanes of traffic towards a corner doughnut shop that catered to the graveyard shifts of hospital workers and other night owls.

"Fine way to start the day," sighed Kappolis.

Nick grabbed a table by the window while the detective went to get coffee at the counter. It was five thirty and the city was already stirring to life, with early morning traffic and garbage trucks beginning their rounds. The street was like an empty stage set waiting for the play to begin. Soon office workers would be scurrying toward their day jobs. Then in the evening they would go home to their pets and a stack of bills in their mailboxes. What was the point? He felt heaviness descend on him. He couldn't shake the feeling. It was invisible, but there, like poison gas that hung in the air, slowly permeating the pores and lungs of the unsuspecting. Life was short. You were born, you struggled and you died.

Was his life any better? In some respects his life was worse. He has been pilloried in the press every day for the past week. The hate mail from special-interest groups had hijacked his e-mail address. He would give anything for a vacation right now. He had the same dreams as every man: once upon a time he had had a wife and a home. Now he was willing to settle for a little bit of love and waking up to a warm body.

Kappolis returned with a tray of freshly brewed coffee, jelly doughnuts, and an early edition of the *Star*. Neither man was in the mood for small talk. Nick flipped through the paper while Kappolis checked out the fellow with the floppy hair and ripped jeans who was munching on a croissant at the next table.

They ordered refills. After the second hit of caffeine it began to feel like night was turning to morning.

"What exactly is this case about?" asked Kappolis. "Illegal migrants? Or the snakehead that brought them here? Or is it about triads? Then there's Walter's murder and the Mandarin Club tie-in."

"I wish I knew," sighed Nick. "Who knows if Sun Sui is a human smuggler or just an honest guy with a fucking arrogant streak? Does he belong to the Flying Dragons? Maybe," shrugged Nick. "We don't know. Then there's Li Mann. What do we know about him? Well, he's got great survival skills. Took two bullets and swam the length of the St. Lawrence, evading German shepherd sniff dogs and infrared tracking systems. Where did he go from there? We don't have a fucking clue!"

Kappolis looked glum. "I'd like to know how he cleaned himself up because there're no hospital records of an Asian man with bullet wounds being admitted for treatment in either country. The guy must have a pretty good network to house him. We got an international warrant on him and no sign of the perp." The detective shook his head. "That's the mark of a professional criminal for you."

Nick chewed on a stir stick as he observed the other patrons. "Look at the Italian fellow over there holding hands with that pretty nurse on her coffee break from the hospital. She looks what, Thai? Filipino? The ethnic mix in this city makes it a perfect place to hide out. Jamaicans rubbing shoulders with Colombians and Syrians. And they're probably working side by side with Pakistanis in some biker-owned restaurant." Nick pointed to two men getting into their car across the street. "Look at those guys. They look like Eastern-European mafia thugs. Maybe they are, maybe they aren't. The point I'm trying to make is, Toronto is as cosmopolitan as New York, Los Angeles or San Francisco. Looking for Li Mann is like looking for a needle in a haystack."

"That's a really depressing thought, Nick." Kappolis looked glum as he lifted the coffee mug to his lips.

Nick dusted off the icing sugar before he bit into his second doughnut. "You know," he said, "I still can't wrap my head around it. I go to court with evidence linking the appellant to criminal activities like prostitution, selling illicit substances and membership in a triad. And I find that the case has morphed into a trade issue. And Sun walks away. Big fucking deal we're holding his passport."

"For the government to show up and give Sun a character reference, that speaks of political interference, man. They don't do that for just anybody," said Kappolis. "I feel we got to tread carefully here, Nick."

"I feel the case is going south. That Walter's murderer is going to get away with the crime," Nick sighed. "And that hurts me."

"We've already got a wiretap on Sun's home phone and the club's main number. I'll run a check to see how many other numbers he's got. Put a tap on that too," said the detective.

"Good idea. For that, I'll treat you," said Nick as he reached for the bill.

"Where to now?"

"Gonna head for the office and get a head start. I've been getting messages from the INS at Kennedy Airport for the past week and some."

"A week? And you haven't called them back yet?"

"I got a lot on my plate. Can't return every call promptly. Besides, I'm afraid these people are trying to create more work for me. Every call I get is turning out that way."

He chewed a toothpick as he walked past a group of people hanging around the corner. Then a bus pulled up and they climbed aboard. He continued walking, jay-walking across the street in the direction of Bathurst.

Dressed in a chequered shirt and dark slacks, he blend-
ed in. Nobody gave him so much as a glance. He could
always count on that in downtown Toronto, Montreal,
New York, and Los Angeles. But then he was good at
disappearing in a crowd.

After the war, Li Mann had nothing and no one. He
wondered why he had survived. As the years passed, his
life became an instrument of his vengeance. With the
American trade embargo against his country, his people
were isolated from the world, dying of disease, poverty,
and despair. No medicines for the sick, no hope for the
young. All they needed was money.

How could he help to feed his people? The answer
came to him one day as he was trekking up the valley
towards Chang Mai. Starting that day, he worked to turn
his village around. By the late seventies every farmer in his
village was growing opium poppies. With wealth came
new schools, a hospital, and two temples for prayer.

The American government didn't understand drug
trafficking — that it was a supply and demand equation.
As long as the demand was there, the American government could never destroy the supply. People would
import it because other people would buy it, at whatever
price. Stupidly, the police believed that the illegal trade
could be crippled by going after the big drug lords. But
the demise of the few drug cartels in Asia had been a
bonanza for the hundreds of small traffickers like himself.
Dead or jailed traffickers were immediately replaced by
their competitors.

Li Mann shook his head, talking to himself as he
walked. No, the Americans didn't understand that it
was easier to infiltrate two or four cartels. How could
DEA agents infiltrate hundreds of drug trafficking
groups? Logistically, it was impossible. Then there was
the matter of race. A bunch of white guys could not run

covert missions in Third World countries without being noticed. That's why the war on drugs had failed. And why the North American war on illegal people smuggling was doomed to fail.

He strolled down College Street, pleased to see that the Latinos were slowing taking over the place. He heard sounds of Spanish being spoken. He stared into the faces of the new émigrés. The Mexicans, Cubans, Guatemalans, Nicaraguans, and Colombians had arrived from the Third World. The thought brought a smile to his lips. Already, they had forged their identities on their newly adopted city. On this stretch alone, there were two coffee bars, a cooperative handicraft shop and a tortilla factory.

At the next corner he saw a parked police cruiser. Li Mann touched the pistol tucked inside his pants as he quickly lowered his face, eyes to the ground. Shuffling in the opposite direction, he quickly ducked into a Colombian restaurant. The room was dark and smoky. He squeezed in at the bar, at a discreet distance from the entrance, and ordered a beer and bowl of bean soup.

He listened to the jokes and tried to follow the conversation around him. But his Spanish was rusty. He liked the Colombians. His history with that country had coincided with his alliance with the Flying Dragons. It had all started with the American-ordered hit on Pablo Escobar. With Pablo gone, the Flying Dragons in Hong Kong had gotten a toehold into Latin America by linking up with the Cali cartel. The big break came with America's war on drugs. That meant the mass destruction of cocoa plants. The Colombian drug traffickers then cut a deal with the Flying Dragons to import opium poppies. Li Mann had been put in charge of negotiating with the paramilitaries. Within five years, he was delivering poppies to rich landowners and major drug traffickers. In Colombia, they were one and the same.

Within another five years, the Flying Dragons had penetrated the Colombian government. Entry and exit visas became a mere formality. Less than eight months later, a deal was struck to move illegal aliens from Asia to Colombia. From Colombia, they travelled by bus, plane, and boat into the United States and Canada via Mexico. The next step was a piece of cake. The poor migrants paid off their passage by working as mules, bringing drugs into North America.

After slurping hungrily on his soup, he cleansed his mouth by chewing on a coffee bean. He watched the patrons come and go as he studied the bill. Li Mann wanted more than anything to return home to his beloved country. But orders were orders, his work was not finished here yet. He pulled out the newspaper clipping from his shirt pocket and critically studied the "wanted" picture of himself. The sketch artist had made his nose too large and his mouth too thin. He wondered if the mistake had been deliberate on Gee Tung's part. Now he would never know. He re-read the article and wondered about the immigration officer that was hunting him. Maybe he should find him and watch him for a while.

After he slapped a couple of bills down on the counter, Li Mann walked down the street towards the pay phone. First he would do a little research. Picking up the phone, he asked directory assistance for the telephone number of the Immigration Department.

Just before two in the afternoon, the phone rang on Nick's desk. He was moody and glum, and wanted to be left alone with his paperwork. For a minute, he wasn't going to answer the call until he saw the call display.

"Good thing we wanted to give that speed boat a second look," said Dubois on the phone.

It was hard to understand the RCMP officer with his mouth full.

"What the hell are you eating?" asked Nick.

"A BLT sandwich. I'm sitting in a diner on Vanier talking to you on my cell."

"Well, don't talk with your mouth full of food," lectured Nick. "How on earth could our American friends have missed the evidence?"

"For the sake of diplomacy, let's not ask. Anyway, we found a coupla strands of hair on a bar of soap that was wrapped in a zip-lock bag under the bathroom sink. Obviously the owner of the soap had no intentions of sharing it with his comrades and clients. I've already sent it over to the lab for analysis. See what turns up. We'll match it against the DNA taken from Gee Tung and the dead snakehead, and the illegal migrants."

"Let me know if anything interesting turns up."

chapter thirteen

"Hello, Nick."

He saw her face, heard her voice. He had dreamt of this moment. "Hello, Grace."

The sight of her in the midnight-blue velvet dress he remembered so well evoked powerful feelings. Her hair was long and loose, the way he had always liked it. She was the most elegant woman in the room. He wanted to touch her again, but he couldn't, not here, not even a handshake.

He moved toward her. Up close, she was as he had remembered. All teeth, hair and tan.

"It's been a long time, Grace."

"How have you been, Nick?" She planted a kiss on his cheek.

Her physical contact left him breathless. "Good. You?"

He caught a whiff of her perfume. It was the same scent she wore that last time they had made love.

Standing next to her, he felt suspended in time, as if he had never left her.

"I've been watching you on the news, Nick. You've been keeping busy."

"Yeah. You too?"

He could barely manage to speak, beyond monosyllables. He had detained double-homicides, deported drug traffickers, and prosecuted tough cases. But here he was, acting like a social misfit on his first date.

"Well, our inventory is up past seventy thousand cases," he said.

She took his hand and pulled him aside. "We're in the path of traffic."

The coolness of her skin, the kiss on the cheek, the touch of her fingers, and already he was emotionally wrung out. God help him for the next hour or two.

"It's a lot." He bobbed his head up and down like a dumb dog.

"I was beginning to think that you'd stopped coming to Ottawa. I miss our sushi lunches. You know I still haven't found a replacement sushi companion."

She favoured him with one of her slow, seductive smiles showing perfect teeth between fabulous lips.

"Would you like to do sushi? I'm here for two days."

"I hoped we could do more than sushi," she said boldly.

This was what he had been dreaming of, but he was afraid to respond. Instead he said, "I heard through the grapevine that the IRC has a huge backlog of cases, too."

"Shhh. According to our Commissioner, backlog is a dirty word. We're trying to keep the lid on the exact number."

"Where are they all coming from?"

"The civil war in Yugoslavia. We've got asylum

claims from both sides. It's hard to separate the victims from the perpetrators," said Grace. "Too many lies, and no one has clean hands."

"I'll keep my job, thank you," said Nick.

"Hey, I heard through the grapevine that you were dating your secretary."

"The things people gossip about on e-mail. She's a single mother with boys. I took them to a hockey game. I don't consider that a date. I was just playing uncle."

"I apologize for believing that bit of erroneous gossip." Grace smiled at him again. It made him feel faint.

"What about you? I heard you were seeing someone. Dating one of the department's senior legal counsel."

"Three evenings at the symphony. Jealous?"

"Can't help it. You know, you ruined it for me with other women." He said it in jest but it was the truth.

There was a moment of uncomfortable silence between them. Grace looked away, apparently disconcerted by the honesty of his remark.

"I could use a drink, Nick. How about you?"

"Good idea," he grunted.

They stood in the drink queue at the bar and made small talk.

"Tell me, what kind of cases are you working on, Nick?"

"The usual. You don't really want to know."

"I only know about the one that's been in the papers."

"Yeah, an illegal alien investigation. It's eating up a lot of my time and energy."

"I can tell by the dark circles under your eyes."

"It was bad," he said, "when Walter was killed."

The touch of her fingers on his face was like a jolt of electricity. It made him jump.

When it was their turn at the bar, she said, "I'll have

a Dubonnet on the rocks."

He mumbled something about a Jack Daniel's while he psyched himself up to resist her. He had worked out his strategy on the flight up. He would go for limited honesty: letting her know details of the Crosby murder while he tried to find out, discreetly, what she had been doing at Crosby's townhouse. He needed to know the level of her involvement in whatever it was that had gotten Crosby killed. Too bad he was so nervous and tongue-tied. It was hard to sound cool and professional when her physical presence was affecting him so powerfully. The worst of it was she knew it.

"It's crowded in here. Too many people networking each other to death. I don't think we're here to network our way to the top. Let's go outside. I'm told that our minister has one of the best gardeners in the city. Let's check out the quadrangle."

Before he could refuse she slipped her arm through his and led him through a pair of French doors and down the steps towards a maze of a garden.

"I'm not keen on getting lost in this rain forest." He aimed for humour. "Do you know where you're going?"

"I'm leading you down the garden path," she laughed.

"I believe that."

She tossed him a sideways glance and smiled at him. Taking his hand, she guided him towards a fountain with a stone cherub spouting water from his mouth.

"I heard the news. You lost the case against the Mandarin Club owner, Sun Sui. Humiliation wasn't bad enough, you had to go for public humiliation. Ten times worse."

"You got it," said Nick, screwing up his face.

"Hey, my people wrote the book on shame and humiliation." She laughed but her eyes were serious. She wanted to mention that she had met the appellant Sun Sui, that people were trying to set her up with him — but she didn't know how to insert that bit of information into the conversation. It wouldn't be welcome news. So she let the moment pass. "What happened?"

"The judge threw out the case. All the allegations are true but I couldn't prove it. Didn't have enough evidence. But I know in my gut the appellant is bad news. Ever get that feeling, Grace?"

"Yeah, our sixth sense doesn't let us down too often."

They had slipped easily back into their old familiarity. Without thinking, she put her hand in his, and they strolled through the jungle of cultivated flora and fauna.

"I love gardens. I wish I could afford a full-time gardener."

"You don't have one?" He mocked her. "Who's that Portuguese guy, Manuel, then? Your butler?"

"Manuel's not a gardener. He's a weed puller. Comes once a month for half a year to fertilize the soil, repot and replant, and rip out the weeds. That kind of thing."

"Grace, that would be most people's definition of a gardener."

"No, Nick. There's more to being a gardener."

"I'll take your word for it since I've never had a gardener myself." He has always ribbed her on the class divide and her bourgeois habits.

She continued, "Amazing how they got hibiscus to grow in this climate." She pointed to a row of small pink flowers. "See those over there, Nick? When I lived in Africa, they grew everywhere. They're so common they're considered weeds. We used to call them outhouse flowers because they grew like crazy around outhouses. The name escapes me at this particular moment. And this one here, this is scented. I had a part-time gardener when I lived in

Kenya and I asked him to plant me some of these at the front of the house. It's from the jasmine family. Come close and smell this."

She leaned close to him, giving him a good glimpse of cleavage. "Smell that. Isn't it great?" she asked, pushing a flower up his nose. "I had some planted outside my front door. I use to sit and watch the sun go down inhaling this wonderful intoxicating scent."

She was away, lecturing him on gardening, hybrids and soil texture.

"Those marigolds are twice the size of the ones in my garden. I bet it's a different hybrid. They're just like the ones I had in Africa. Marigolds help ward off insects like mosquitoes. People plant them around their houses. Much better than inhaling insecticide, don't you think?"

"You're a veritable weedpatch of gardening information."

Her fingers played with the sleeve of his jacket. "There're lots of things you still don't know about me. If only you would give yourself the opportunity to find out."

He changed track and tried to cut the sexual tension between them by taking the conversation a hundred and eighty degrees.

"I heard you were the one who made the 911 call over Crosby's body."

"News travels fast."

He looked at her. "What were you doing at his house?"

She turned her eyes away. "You don't want to go there."

But he refused to be put off. "I do, Grace. You could've gotten yourself killed. I care."

"I appreciate your caring, Nick. It's kind of you."

"Kindness isn't my primary motivation."

Their eyes met. They really were reading each other's

minds. "It was stupid of me to go to his house," she said. "I could have waited till the next day at the office. Ever ask yourself how come intelligent people sometimes do really stupid things?"

"Well, we all have our stupid moments."

Without looking at him she said, "I went to his house thinking I could use him. I went to sell him on the idea of making me second chair on that Asian case you're working on. I thought it would give my career a boost for reappointment on the bench. And I knew you were representing the state. I thought it would be a good way to run into you again."

"Oh." He was flummoxed, at a loss for words. He had asked for honesty and now he didn't know how to respond to it.

"I did it for my career, and you, in that order. What I wasn't counting on was finding him dead."

He put his arms around her and they walked to the end of the stone path where they came across a pair of Adirondack chairs.

"I need to sit down. My feet are killing me. Do you know what it's like to squeeze five toes into a space designed for four?"

He bit his lip to keep from laughing and shook his head.

"You should try it sometime," she deadpanned.

Nick examined her shoes. "These heels aren't so high, only three inches. My secretary hobbles to work every day on four-inch stilettos. Don't women own any sensible shoes?"

"I wanted to look nice for you."

Her vulnerability touched him. He replied, "You look more than nice. You always look fabulous."

She turned towards him and in a voice full of insecurity she asked, "You think so? Middle age is going to be awful. I'm far from fifty and already the security guard calls me 'ma'am' I mean, what kind of word is that?"

He reached for her. "You'll be a great-looking fifty-year-old."

"You think so?" She kissed him.

The next thing he knew, his tongue was in her mouth, tasting the liquor on her breath. The feel and scent of her body induced both anxiety and delight in his brain.

"Ummm. I missed you, Nick."

"I missed you, too."

"Where're you staying?"

"The Lord Elgin," he replied between kisses.

"Hmm. I haven't been there in a while."

"Is that a proposition, Grace?"

She gave him a knowing smile. "Only if you want it to be."

"I do. I haven't had anybody since we broke up."

"That's your own damn fault!" She kissed him again.

"I don't know why, but women find me dull. They think I'm a real nerd."

"Not me." Between kisses, she pulled him out of the low-slung chair. "Let's get out of here."

"What's in the cards for us, Grace?"

She took him by the hand. "First, just to get out of here."

He almost had an accident trying to drive with one hand. He had little recollection of what route he took or where he parked the car. By the time they got out of the elevator, his tie and shirt were completely undone.

"Can't you wait?" he asked, struggling to open the door with the hotel key.

"Patience was never my strong suit," she laughed as she struggled with the buckle of his belt while he worked the room key.

Feverishly, they undressed each other, mouths and fingers exploring.

"God, I've missed this," he moaned.

They left a trail of discarded clothes in their wake as they sank into the bed. Their bodies fused into one. They had both needed this for so long. Now the dam of lust and passion was broken, there was no holding back. Entering her body was like an electric shock of pleasure. There was no need for words to pass between them. They existed in their own world, forgetting everything but the moment.

"I'd almost forgotten what great sex feels like," he panted in her ear.

He came quickly the first time while she grabbed at his hair and screamed her way to orgasm.

Afterwards, neither of them spoke. They snuggled in each other's arms. He knew what she was thinking and said, "No, we didn't handle it well our last time together. I'm sorry about my boorish behaviour of not returning calls. And when I wanted to talk to you again, you weren't returning my calls."

"You were angry with me for deceiving you about my marital status. I understand. I probably would've reacted the same way if I were in your shoes. Let's not rehash this, please, Nick."

"Apology accepted." His lips sought hers again.

The rest of the night melted into a kaleidoscope of pleasure and passion. But as keenly as his body felt the ecstasy of release, part of him held back. He had always loved her. But he still suspected that he had to be wary of her.

Nick sat opposite Jeremy Klein at a corner table in the restaurant the international trade lawyer had picked for their meeting.

They regarded each other in silence. Nick was still bitter about being screwed by his own government. Finally he spoke. "I bet you do real well in trade negotiations. Talking out of both sides of your mouth. Promising the moon and delivering nothing."

"If I were you I wouldn't take this personally," said Klein. "We're both lackeys for our political masters. We do their bidding. New government comes in, and we undo what we've been doing for the past few years. Guys like us don't make the rules. We just play by them."

"I'm not sure I know what rules we're playing by."

"Listen, Nick, I can see you're pretty riled about losing your deportation case. But don't take this out on me. Thank your lucky stars I'm sitting here talking to you. If I had requested clearance to talk to you, we both know I'd be turned down."

Nick's mind was working on the fact that in part of the government, Sun Sui was a bad guy. And in another department of the same government, he was being flattered and courted as a saviour.

"Elections are coming up," said Klein. "We both know what's on the table. The government wants to get re-elected, so they want to look good. Lower taxes boost the economy. So they're looking for mass-market countries like India and China. We need middle men to open doors for us, to say the right things in the right people's ears."

Jeremy Klein emptied the bottle of beer into his mug, then he looked around the restaurant to make sure that he had not been recognized before he continued speaking. "I appreciate the work you're doing. At the same time I'm doing my best to lay what cards I can on the table for you, Nick. You have to appreciate that the prime minister goes on another trade junket in the fall or spring."

"Team Canada going back to China?" asked Nick.

"Yeah. That's where your appellant Sun Sui comes in. Unfortunately for you he's well connected inside China."

"How so?" asked Nick, raising his mug to his lips.

"That I can't say."

"Can't, or won't?"

"Both."

"Gimme a hint. Communist Party connections or criminal connections?" asked Nick.

"Come on, Nick. You know in some countries there's no difference between the two."

Nick squinted his eyes at Klein and wondered if the other man was trying to convey a message to him. "You mean, like Russia?"

Klein nodded. Both men laughed, breaking the ice a little further.

Nick wondered if Klein would help him nail Sun Sui after he'd outlived his usefulness to the trade-deal makers. He also wondered what information he could get out of Klein right now. "Okay," he said, "let's say I buy what you're saying. I still have a couple of questions I need answers to. How did a newcomer to this country who was once a country bumpkin from a Communist backwater get to know the movers and shakers in government? I know people born here, families going back generations, and they can't even get their city hall councillors and senators to return their phone calls."

"We met him through the Asia Business Council. We try to buy as many memberships in these business and community associations as possible, and China's going to be the flavour of the month for the next ten years."

Nick made notes as Klein talked. But the Asia Business Council must have thousands of members. How do you connect to the right people?" he asked.

"Our connection there is one of the old guard in the Chinese community. A past president of the council. His name is Wa Sing."

"How do I reach him?"

Klein held up his hands in a gesture of surrender. "That I can't help you with." He drained the rest of his beer. "That's all I'm going to tell you. If you repeat any of it, I'll deny that we ever met. Bear that in mind."

They left the restaurant separately. Nick drove like an automaton, following the signs and directions Grace had given him. With time to kill as he waited for her to finish work, he took her bike out for an hour. The river scenery on the Parkway was lost on him as he pedalled.

Klein's words had too much staying power. Nick's mind kept coming back to the question of what people would do for money and power — the kind of power that kept you in political office.

The trouble with this case was that it wasn't any longer about a boatload of illegal migrants being spirited out of a Third World country to North America. He wished it still was. Instead it had become something that was rotten to the core. He smelled political interference all the way up the food chain. In the name of justice to an old friend, he knew he would not turn back. But he would have to tread carefully.

After dinner, he wanted to tell Grace about his day. He wanted to unburden himself, and tell her everything. But he couldn't. He'd have to edit out all those bits of information that were state secrets of the international trade department. He sighed. This was one of the things that had doomed their relationship the first time around.

"Okay, Nick, what's eating you?"

"Work."

"I get it. You can't talk about it. You don't trust me. You think I'd use the information against you in some hearing," Grace said defensively. "Or maybe, blab to some newspaper."

"No, that's not it," he said, trying to reassure her. "I'm trying to work out the puzzle pieces in finding Martin's killer."

"Getting any closer?"

"Not one bit," he laughed bitterly.

"Well, to take your mind off work, you can putter in the garden with me."

Meekly, he followed, lugging bags of manure and compost in the direction of the Siberian irises.

"Use the wheelbarrow, Nick."

He kissed her on the neck. "You don't want a lover, you want a slave."

She pressed her lips to his. "That's not true. But sweetie, could you also get the other bags of black soil from the garage?"

An hour later, sipping iced tea on the deck, she said, "It's your last night in town. Where do you want to go? What sights do you want to see?"

"I'm not here to play tourist," he said, putting a hand on her thigh. Her skin was hot beneath his fingers.

"Ohhh. So, what do you want to do?" she asked innocently.

"How about a tour of your bedroom?"

The smell of her came back to him, overpowering him. He watched her undress. Her body still shocked him, as it had that very first time together in his condo — the smooth tone of her skin, the sleek muscles of her stomach and legs, and the triangle between her thighs could arouse him even if he were in a comatose state.

His mouth on hers, his hands on her breasts. Soon their gropings dissolved on the living room floor, with him on top. They gasped and crushed each other as they came together.

They made love again. Afterwards, they lay hugging, contented. The release, the two beers he had had with Jeremy Klein, the wine they'd had with dinner, along with his frustration over work had taken their toll. He closed his eyes and slept. In his sleep, he dreamt of many things, sometimes twitching like an animal in the throes of memory. He dreamt of his childhood, his mother's stories of fleeing the old Czechoslovakia, of climbing up steep rock faces, of running surveillance missions in anonymous cities.

But most of all, he dreamt of his friend and colleague, Walter Martin.

chapter fourteen

Nick flashed his way through John F. Kennedy Airport and hailed a cab for Elizabeth, New Jersey. Kelly Marcovich and Tom Bergen, the area port director for the Immigration and Naturalization Service, were on hand to meet him at the three-hundred-bed detention facility. He followed them down a long concrete corridor full of overhead television monitors. The sound of their footsteps echoed on the stone floors. He could remember when the place first opened in 1994 to handle the growing population of detained inadmissibles prior to their removal from the United States.

"We're getting your overflow. You seen the stats, Nick?" asked Kelly, picking up a stack of computer printouts. "Refugee smuggling is steadily climbing. The guys at JFK tell me that the numbers will soon surpass drug running as the *numero uno* illicit international business. In the past month alone, we netted a couple of thousand undocumented travellers."

"What about the alien smugglers? The snakeheads. Catch any of them?"

Kelly shook her head briefly, and Bergen, who was preparing a visitor's badge for Nick, released a dry laugh. "Boy, I'd like to get my hands on those creeps." He lifted his hands and made a twisting motion. "But there is something you should check out. In the past couple of months alone, we've caught a lot of undocumented travellers carrying Canadian addresses. Some of them were even carrying the same address. A couple of them were definitely terrorists, wanted in their home country."

"The very same address?"

"Go figure." Bergen nodded and rolled his shoulders in one fluid motion. "We figure the Sri Lankan we got in detention might be useful to you. After you talk to him, we're extraditing him back home for blowing up some minister with a home-made bomb."

"What tipped you off? One of your dogs sniff dope on his crotch?"

"Nah, the officer at the inspection booth ran his passport through the scanner. The machine-readable portion was tampered with. It wouldn't read."

"And he had a Canadian address on him?"

"Two addresses and a complete set of fraudulent Canadian documents. Driver's licence, health insurance card. Plus phony greenbacks."

"The other reason we called you," said Kelly, "is the marks on the documents. Like I told you, they're similar to the ones we found on the illegals we stopped at Akwesasne, where Martin got killed."

"Sounds interesting," said Nick, trying not to get his hopes up high.

"Even if he is, you people can't have him," said Bergen. "The Sri Lankan government's expecting him back day after tomorrow."

He handed Nick a visitor's badge.

"Tom will take you to the interview room," said Kelly, putting a sympathetic hand on Nick's shoulder. "I hope you get something useful."

Bergen set off with quick precise strides down the hallway and into another wing. On the way there, he briefed Nick on the details of the interrogation that the customs officers had conducted at the airport.

"His real name is Humair Subrathnam. He tried to pass himself off as Greek. Didn't speak a word of it though."

Humair Subrathnam sat waiting in the visitors' room. A confused look settled on his face at the sight of Nick and Bergen. He rose to meet them.

"Sit down," barked the guard standing behind Humair.

The illegal alien sat down again.

The guard said nothing more as he walked out of the room and took up his post outside the opened door.

"I need a cigarette," said the Sri Lankan illegal.

"You'll get a cigarette after you repeat the story you told us to this gentleman here," said Bergen.

"I don't remember what I told you."

"Sure you do."

"I need a cigarette first to help me remember."

"No, you don't. You're doing just fine. But we'll do one better. We'll give you an entire pack of cigarettes if you repeat your story."

"What part of the story you want to hear?"

"Tell us about the bombings."

"Which bombings? Blowing up of the minister's Mercedes with him inside? Or the bombing of the police station?"

"Why did you do it?" asked Nick speaking for the first time.

"Why? Because we want a separate homeland."

"Terrorism isn't the way to go. You know, the Tamil Tigers have done a lot of damage over the years. Last year, there was a series of car bomb attacks. This year, you guys bombed a military minibus." Nick shook his head.

Silence.

"Tell Nick about the stuff we found in your luggage at the airport? The bomb-making manual? The garrotte and the maps? What were those for?" asked the INS director.

Silence.

Nick picked up the police dossier Bergen had placed on the table. "Interpol described you as a university-educated man who is suspected of killing at least twenty-nine people over more than a decade of car-bombings and machine-gun attacks. This Toronto address you had in your wallet, I'm guessing now, that this is the address of the Tamil Tigers operation in Canada?" asked Nick, leaning forward.

"Yes. I'm supposed to hook up with them in Toronto. They're expecting me."

Nick didn't say anything for a minute as Subrathnam's words registered in his brain. When he spoke, his voice was softer, his manner friendly as his fingers riffled through the pages of the dossier.

"How the hell did the Tigers get you out of the country so fast? The airport cordoned off. Every road had checkpoints."

Subrathnam, still looking pleased about the cleverness of the plan, said, "The travel agency that looks after the Tamil Tigers got me out on somebody else's passport. In transit, I was given the Greek passport that was taken away from me here in New York. I'd like to have that cigarette now."

"Just a few minutes more," replied Nick. "What about the money in your suitcase? Who's that for?"

"They told me in Colombo to deliver the money to the Tamil Tigers' office in Toronto. I think the money is to buy weapons. My job was just to carry the money."

"What about the bomb-making manual? The garrotte and the maps?" asked Nick.

"For a training camp in Canada. Since there's no bomb-making manual, I was told to bring one. The same with the garrotte. The map of Sri Lanka pinpoints all the possible target locations back home."

"Fucking terrorist. Last thing we need is another World Trade Center bombing. After you're finished with him, he's on the first damn plane out of here." Bergen handed Nick a slip of paper. "This address was found with the phony money. Your people can check it out."

"Were you intent on committing any terrorist acts in the United States or Canada?"

"My job is to carry out orders. If those orders came, I wouldn't question them."

Nick knew about the suicide bombers inside the Tamil Tigers. The illegal alien's answer did not surprise him. Instead, he concentrated on the telephone number in his hands.

"This is a Montreal address. Who were you meeting there?" Nick looked at the illegal alien curiously.

"A man who was supposed to meet me at the airport here in New York. I was told that if I missed him, to call that number."

"Who is he?"

"Someone who would give me a new identity, and transport me to my new home."

"What about his name?" asked Nick, as he burnt

the Montreal address into his brain.

"I was not told his name. The address and number belongs only to him. All I know is, he's Vietnamese."

Could it be the elusive Li Mann? Nick levelled his gaze at the illegal, eyeball to eyeball. "You say that you don't know his name. Do you know what he looks like?"

He shook his head wearily. "I've never met him in person. I've only seen a photograph of him once. At the travel agency."

Nick turned to Bergen. "You got a cigarette on ya? Dangle it in front of him."

Bergen pulled out a pack of cigarettes that was rolled up his left sleeve.

Nick took the police artist's sketch of Li Mann out of his briefcase and showed it to the prisoner. Subrathnam held the sketch in his hands for a long moment before he spoke.

"It could be him. It could not be him."

"What the hell kind of answer is that?" demanded Bergen.

Nick lowered his voice. "Take another good look at the sketch. Jog your memory."

The illegal alien's mouth fell open. "I don't know. I'm not sure. It looks like him. A sketch isn't the same thing as a photograph."

That was the frustrating thing about black-and-white sketches. No wonder they couldn't locate this Li Mann. Still, it was a lead. "Light the cigarette and give it to him," said Nick.

Outside the concrete block of corridors, Bergen turned to Nick, "He pretty much sticks to the same story."

"Thanks. I owe you one."

Nick made his way down to the boarding gate for the commuter flight back to Canada. There was bounce in his step all the way home.

Grace passed through a lobby filled with surveillance technology before coming to a bank of elevators. Before stepping into an elevator, she quietly flashed her orange and black name tag to desk security. Without waiting for clearance, she hit the elevator button for the penthouse. On the top floor she was released into a posh lobby of richly stained wood and French period pieces. A large, dour receptionist in beige pointed her towards an Italian leather sofa.

"I'll let the commissioner know you're here."

Jean Cadeux was the head of the Immigration and Refugee Commission. She had only met him twice. What she knew about him could fit onto a rolodex card. He had been an obscure professor at a small university before landing the crowning patronage plum at one of the highest-profile agencies in the country. However, his claim to fame was largely based on his networking skills and francophone lineage. If race was the issue that defined the United States, then the separatism in Quebec was the one that defined Canada. And Cadeux had benefited handsomely from the debate over the issue of Quebec sovereignty. Grace found it ironic that someone who couldn't even find Algiers on a map was anointed as head of an institution that determined the fate of Third World peoples. But such was the world of political patronage.

"The Commissioner is ready to see you," announced the receptionist, a slavish woman who oozed loyalty and deference for her master from her every pore.

Grace followed her through a richly stained glass door and into another palatial space lined with extraordinary works of art.

"Have a seat and the admin assistant will come out and collect you."

Collect her. Yes, indeed, the man was a collector. She absorbed her surroundings and noted the eighteenth-century French furniture and the Fragonard by the door. The last time she had been invited here was last year. If only she had a video camera. The accoutrements of wealth and pretension were everywhere. The taxpayers hadn't skimped on any piece of furnishing. Every wall was covered in abstract paintings by artists more famous in Europe than in their native Canada. The Queen Anne cherry end table was laden with expensive coffee-table books, which had probably never been opened. But what did it matter, as long as Cadeux's handpicked furnishings conveyed to the visitor that his tastes were several cuts above those of the average man on the street? That was his insecurity. Her superior had strived all his life to be several cuts above the average Joe. And so he was, though only because the average Joe would never conceive of dropping two hundred thousand dollars to furnish a single office.

She had been summoned here on two previous occasions. First, to be formally greeted when she was appointed to the Commission. Second, when Cadeux requested that she preside on a case involving the ex-wife of a former Bulgarian diplomat. Her husband had left her for another woman, and she was claiming asylum on the basis of persecution at the hands of the new President of Bulgaria. The claim had been without basis; she simply wanted to stay in Canada. Since the woman came from a powerful family, and from a country that was one of Canada's largest trading partners, the politicians on the Hill had suggested to Cadeux that the claim go forward on gender grounds. Behind the scenes, the feminists who controlled the gender standing committee in the House had done a quid pro quo with the boys on the standing committee on gun control. It was a win-win situation for the players on the Hill, the public had only been factored in by the spin doctors at the last minute in their press communiqué. If the public only knew half the shenanigans that went on up there!

And now she was here for a third audience with the commissioner. She flipped through the current issue of the *Economist* and cynically wondered what case he was dumping on her this time.

The door to the inner sanctum opened.

"Grace, please come in."

The commissioner, waving away his assistant, was greeting her personally.

"Hello, Jean," she said in a neutral tone that conveyed nothing. For occasions such as these, she donned her Oriental mask of "inscrutability".

He led her towards the slab of handsome black marble that functioned as his desk. To reach it, she had to traverse several wool and silk rugs with unique Islamic designs. Facing the window she observed that he had one of the best views in the nation's capital; a spectacular panorama of the Rideau River, the Parliament Buildings and the Gatineau Hills.

He cleared his throat.

She waited for him to speak. Why should she make conversation? He was the one who had summoned her here.

"Coffee? Or would you prefer tea?"

"Coffee's fine, thank you."

"Coffee it is. Bring a pot," Jean ordered the still-hovering secretary as he sat down opposite her in a leather wing chair that matched the one she sat in.

"As you know," he began, steepling his long fingers, "the issue of criminal non-citizens weighs heavily on the minds of the public. Given the recent headlines about human-smuggling operations, we're in a bit of a hot spot."

That was an understatement, Grace thought.

His secretary returned with a tray: silver coffee pot, sugar bowl, cream jug, and Limoges demitasses.

"We've had quite a few upheavals in the past few weeks," Cadeux continued. "I know you were to second-chair the deportation appeal case of that snakehead apprehended in that smuggling operation. Now we've learned from Immigration that there's no case, because the snakehead's dead."

"How?"

"A home invasion, according to the police report."

Grace released a sigh. She was beginning to think all of these killings were the work of one crazy madman. But a home invasion of an Asian? Well, it was possible. The crime was becoming fairly commonplace.

"However, it seemed that an appellant who recently won a stay of deportation has decided to file an asylum claim. He feels that Immigration is conducting a vendetta against him, and he has a business to run. I might add that he's a prominent and successful businessman. Not to mention, at least a hundred employees count on him for their livelihood. It would be a shame for him to be removed from the country, and to begin the process all over again."

Grace could guess where the conversation was going, but she had to ask anyway.

"Who's the appellant?"

"His name is Sun Sui. The owner of the Mandarin Club. He's become something of an entertainment mogul. Apparently, he's also in the process of moving much of his movie-making operation to Canada from Hong Kong. I believe the Chinese are like the Indians, they have an enormous appetite for home-grown action films. I was contacted by one of the trade advisers over at International Trade and told that Mr. Sui adds a lot of value to our economy. If we don't help him, he'll simply move his entertainment empire down to L.A. And we don't want that, do we? "

"What good is economic value if he's a criminal?"

"On the contrary, Grace. Our embassy in Hong Kong ran extensive searches on all applicants wanting to emigrate. Mr. Sui came out squeaky clean. I've got the records on that."

"But he's under the Immigration spotlight in a very big way."

"Our boys in Immigration are very zealous. Besides, when a case hits the fan, they must look as if they're exerting themselves to bring justice. Else the public will lose all confidence in our institutions."

"If so, why doesn't the claimant file in Toronto? Why another city?"

"He intends to live in this city. And I assume his lawyer has advised him to put some distance between himself and a particular Immigration manager, though that's speculation on my part. In any case, International Trade has pressed me to provide assurances that the case will be competently handled."

She knew what was coming: he was going to dump Sun Sui's refugee claim in her lap. Now that she was back with Nick, she really shouldn't take the case. Truth be told, just by resuming her relationship with Nick she was already committing judicial impropriety. To go further and actually preside on a case where he represented the state in an adversarial role would not just be improper but was a clear breach of judicial impartiality. Not to mention the fact that she'd met the claimant socially at the Yung Kee dinner, which, if not strictly her fault, still looked bad. But how could she refuse the case without disclosing her relationship with Nick? The repercussions might be severe if she was found out. Still, why should she ever be found out? No one knew about her earlier affair with Nick. At least, she hoped they didn't.

She mulled the question over seriously as Cadeux ranted on in his self-important way. The consequences of disclosing her connection with Nick could be a public reprimand and dismissal by the ethics counsellor. However, if she kept the truth to herself, she would have a chance to be on the inside of a historic case. And maybe render a landmark decision. Who wouldn't want that?

Could she — as Nick's lover and as a member of the same cultural community as the claimant — actually maintain professional impartiality and objectivity? She was sure she could. But there was still the matter of appearances. The optics weren't so good. She might appear to be biased, but weirdly, toward both parties. It was a conflict-of-interest situation, on a very public case. Could she get away with it? What if the newspapers found out?

Someone might leak to the papers that she'd been seen with Sun Sui socially. But she had been no more than polite to him, and had not returned his phone calls. Maybe she should mention that to Cadeux, right now, and insist there was no conflict of interest. But that would open her up to further scrutiny. Or worse, public scrutiny. The problem with honesty was it sometimes made you look guiltier than you really were. But if she didn't disclose the facts, and the press got hold of it they would make it out to be far, far worse than it really was. A real can of worms.

She looked at Cadeux over the rim of her cup. This was the moment to be honest. But — tell the truth to Cadeux? If she liked him, maybe, or even trusted him. As it stood, she was one of his least favourite adjudicators because she wasn't into the sucking-up he expected from his subordinates.

As if reading her mind, Jean Cadeux said, "A word of warning. I saw you at the minister's tea party standing at the bar with that departmental manager from Immigration. I don't want to see you chattering with immigration officers like this Mr. Slovak. His beliefs are too far to the right for him to be a trusted friend of this government."

"I try to overlook ideology when I'm socializing."

"In our job we can't afford to be social with everybody."

"Thanks for the advice."

He looked at her, trying to look through her. She let the moment pass. She tried to think of excuses to weasel out of the case.

"As we both know, Asia is not my geographic region of expertise."

He made a dismissive gesture with his hands. "I realize that. But you've a secondary interest in that region, don't you?"

"Not really."

"Surely you're familiar with the political history?"

"Just because I'm half Chinese doesn't make me half an expert on China. I wouldn't want to expose how limited my knowledge is in a public case such as this. I'd hate to screw up and embarrass the Commission." She racked her brain to come up with a more convincing excuse.

"This public case demands a competent adjudicator. Not to mention a hearing that's expeditious. The international trade minister is putting heat on me, which means I have to perform. Hence I'm asking for your help, Grace. I know you can handle it. I know you won't disappoint me."

Was he trying to flatter her into agreeing? He was such an unpleasant person even his flattery sounded like a threat. "I'm not sure I — "

He interrupted her. "I don't need to remind you that your political appointment is at the pleasure of this government."

There was no mistaking the threat, this time. She held his gaze, and said, "I feel taking on this case would put me under the microscope of whoever killed Crosby."

"Have you received death threats?"

"No."

"Have you received any annoying phone calls? Callers who won't speak, just hang up when you answer?"

"No."

Jean Cadeux looked thoughtfully at the Liechtenstein on his wall, as if it had a connection to their work. "Grace, you've been on the job now for four years. How many nasty calls have you had in all that time?"

"When I first started, as you know, I was deluged with hate mail from left-wing groups who thought I had sold out because I didn't grant asylum to every applicant who appeared in my hearing room. Since I've been on the Commission I've had to change my telephone number twice. I now have an unlisted number. I've had the odd wacko follow me from the office."

"But, Grace, that comes with the territory. You've faced it before. It's nothing new."

"Excuse me, sir?" The callousness of his remark astonished her.

"Grace, we're decision makers. Judges and parole board staff are always at risk, often threatened and subjected to harassing phone calls. We've had to provide police protection to a few who were followed home by former inmates."

"Are you telling me, sir, that I should accept this kind of behaviour as the norm?"

"You could say that, yes."

Grace wondered why he was railroading her into taking this case. Trying one last tack, she said, "My other concern is that I could be accused of bias from various groups."

"Your record is immaculate, Grace. You've never been accused of bias."

"I was thinking of positive bias, sir. What if my decision went positive? How would that look to the public?"

"If we chose someone else and the case went negative, the multicultural communities would also accuse the Commission of bias. That seems to be the problem Immigration is having right now. In other words, Grace, we can't always factor in public opinion. We just have to do our job the best we can." He leaned forward and smiled at her. He seemed to be trying to make his eyes look appealing and his expression warm, but his smile was false and grating. "I want this hearing to be fair and expeditious. Most of all, I want the public to feel confidence in the system."

"Sir, there is a possibility that I could run into the claimant socially. How would that look?"

"I have faith that you will comport yourself in private so as not to cross that fine line." Jean Cadeux's eyes locked on hers in a determined way.

"Thank you for your confidence in me. But all the same ..."

"You're my choice, my selected candidate for this case." His tone was no longer friendly. "If there's anything I can do, or if you need anything, call me directly. I'll help you out. In the meantime just keep me informed of events since my office will be fielding calls from the press."

"Sir, I decline the case. If that's all right with you."

The look he gave her could have turned water into ice. The veneer of civility was gone from his manner.

"No, Grace, it's not all right with me. You're the presiding judge. The matter is now closed."

"Why wasn't I consulted before this decision was made?"

"There is no need for judges to be involved in the policy or management decisions of the agency. You are assumed to be available for whatever cases are assigned to you. If you decline now, against my express wish, your non-cooperation will be noted, and I'll have no choice but to mention the matter to the judicial discipline committee." There was an unmistakably nasty edge to his voice. "Now, I've an exceedingly busy schedule. Please take this file of press clippings and background information with you. I want you to study it before the actual file comes in. One more thing, if there are any calls from the press, just refer them to my office here. Media lines will have to be developed. I'm sure you can see yourself out."

She gave him the mental fuck-you as she left his office.

Nick got back from New York and headed straight to his office. His cubby hole was bathed in afternoon sunlight and summer humidity. Not yet rush hour, and already the view from his window looked out onto the four lanes of traffic backed up on University Avenue.

"We gotta hit," said Dubois. "Amazingly, the two strands of hair check out. The perp's already in one of our crime databases. Are you sitting down, Nick?"

"Give it to me."

"Mann Lea. Charged and convicted back in 1995 for trying to smuggle a couple of Korean business types across the border into Montana."

"Umm," replied Nick. It was between a grunt and something thoughtful. "What about address?"

"We're checking on that. Back then his address was an apartment building in downtown Edmonton. Needless to say, he's no longer a resident. A young woman who works for the forestry department is the present leaseholder."

"Good work, Dubois. Call me if anything else develops."

BJ and Harry, from the van, watched her as she left her office. They followed half a block behind as she walked to her health club in her short sleeved tunic suit buttoned at the throat.

"Fucking hot and the bitch is wearing a suit," cursed BJ.

"So what? She looks good in that suit."

BJ threw Harry a dirty look. "What the hell do you know about broads? Her legs are okay, but she ain't our type. The bitch's wearing way too much clothes. I like broads to show more skin. And have more tits too."

Before BJ had been incarcerated, he used to work for the Hell's Angels part-time, shaking down small time businessmen, and forcing girls into prostitution. His idyllic life came to an end when he went to prison for killing three of his hookers who were not bringing in enough business. He wondered what happened to the other five girls. After he iced the lady judge, he would track them down. Get free sex and be back in business as a biker pimp.

They watched her turn down a residential street. Harry slowed the van until they dropped back to a safe distance, two blocks behind. "We still don't know if she can ID us in a police line-up," said Harry, sounding depressed.

"Harry. We got to do it. We already decided that. Now all we have to decide is when."

"Yeah. We got to find the right moment. But, BJ, if the broad can't identify us, what's the point of whacking her? She didn't do us any wrong. We don't have a beef with her," protested Harry.

BJ had long ago chosen to live outside the law. He gave his friend an impatient look. "On the other hand, Harry, why take stupid chances?" Yep, he could easily imagine doing her out of spite and cruelty.

chapter fifteen

Dubois's tip led Nick to the zoning office at the City of Montreal. In turn, that call was directed to a property assessment officer for the City, who ran extensive computer searches and called back that very same day with promising results. The house was registered as belonging to a Hispanic family. However, Hydro Quebec records revealed that a Thu Li Mann resided at that address. Other utility records recorded his last name as Vu. Nick wondered, briefly, what his quarry's genuine family name was: Thu or Vu? Maybe neither one. He assigned Rocco to look into it, while he and Kappolis flew to Montreal.

Their flight arrived at 9:45 p.m. Pumped up on caffeine and adrenaline, they drove at high speed from the airport to the address, with RCMP cruisers and two crime scene vans behind them. It was the kind of low-rent neighbourhood where the presence of cops does not raise eyebrows. Even the sight of yellow police tape was common enough that the neighbours just went about their business. However, the sight of the special-weapons-and-tactics team with their paramilitary arsenal had curious teenagers daring each other to worm under the police tape. Nick warned them back, holding up his badge.

The SWAT team led the way, bursting through the front doors. Dressed in Kevlar flak jackets, Nick and Kappolis followed close behind with their own weapons. Once inside, they split into teams. A thorough, cautious circuit of the house verified what the silence had already told them. Nobody was home.

"Seems Li Mann Vu has flown the coop," announced Kappolis.

"Looks that way, doesn't it?" said one of the Montreal SWAT team. The evidence technicians were right behind them, carrying in their metal suitcases full of equipment.

"Toss the place from top to bottom," Nick ordered.

He watched as they slapped on their latex. And left them alone as they reached for their black dusting powder. Hands in his pockets, he surveyed the house, careful not to disturb anything, as the technicians busied themselves taking photographs, dusting for fingerprints, noting the location of objects. One of them carried a video camera, recording the rooms as he walked through.

Nick wasn't quite sure what to make of the place and its absent occupant. The furnishings were genuine Asian antiques mixed in with kitschy fakes. And then there were the four TV screens, the satellite dish, the expensive computer equipment and the police scanner in the dining room, which had been left on. He walked through the rooms trying to get a feel for the man who had taken the life of his friend and colleague. There was nothing to indicate much of a life being lived. There were no photographs of loved ones, no mementos of Li Mann 's homeland. It was as if his entire life was lived only in the moment: on hold for something. One could only guess what. Li Mann Vu's house said he lived a rather pathetic life, that he was a man without an anchor. Crime, Nick thought, must be his only connection with other people.

His other observation as he toured the house was the rigidly ordered neatness and newness of everything. The stove was hardly used, Waterford crystal was still in its boxes, the cupboards were filled with unopened boxes and packages of food.

Bizarre was the adjective that came to his mind. The place was like a movie set.

"Must have been too busy killing people or smuggling illegals into the country to bother with a cooking course," remarked Kappolis, picking up a brand new copper pot.

"No phones, no jacks. The phone company didn't know about this guy," remarked Nick.

Nick always tried to understand the thought processes of his suspects, and he'd developed some very definite ideas about human motivations. The act of committing a crime put things in a different perspective. In his opinion, it was easy to go down the road of being a criminal. The willpower was in staying clean, in not cheating on welfare or unemployment insurance, in not coveting your neighbours' possessions or robbing them blind while they were at work. Nick was used to people who were not exactly what they appeared to be. But in this case, he couldn't get a handle on the exact immorality of the man he was hunting. Somehow the pieces didn't quite fit together.

"Box every slip of paper you find," Nick ordered the evidence technicians.

There were blank entry visas into the United States and Canada, blank birth certificates for just about every province in Canada and a dozen states south of the border. The drivers' licences were kept separately in a drawer along with the health cards. In another room, one of the evidence techs found a box of blank American social security cards.

"Boss, do we notify the Americans?"

Nick did not answer right away. He was thinking about what it all meant. All you needed was a birth certificate. With that one piece of paper, you could apply for a driver's licence, a social security card, and an authentic American or Canadian passport.

"Let's not notify our pals south of the border yet. We'll make the call as soon as we have some answers. No need to upset them right away," Nick replied.

They all knew that they were damned if they called and damned if they didn't call Washington. One way or the other, Canada would be blamed for its lax immigration policy. But if they didn't inform their counterparts, and the news was leaked to the press, they would be lambasted publicly.

"Blank visas, passports, birth certificates. This guy must be the premier agent smuggler of bringing illegal aliens into the country. Are these things real or fake?" asked Rocco.

Nick turned to him. "I want you to run checks and see if there've been any thefts or break-ins lately at any of the Canadian embassies around the world. Leave the American embassies to me."

They checked the house one last time. On the inside door of one of the kitchen cabinets was a pinup calendar of gorgeous Asian girls and Vietnamese recipes. Kappolis passed it to Nick. "What do you make of this?"

Nick flipped through the pages. "A calendar advertising the services of a photocopy shop. Qwik Kopy: Two cents a copy. Could be worth checking out."

Nick took the card from Kappolis. He copied down the address and telephone number before passing the card to the evidence tech.

"So we got ourselves a couple of leads, but still no photograph of what Li Mann actually looks like," said Kappolis.

"Even with a photograph, it would still be like looking for a needle in a haystack." Nick, the last to leave, closed the door behind him.

The Qwik Kopy printing shop was located in a strip mall in downtown Windsor, a stone's throw from the bridge into Detroit. From outward appearances, the photocopy shop primarily catered to university students, and the mom-and-pop businesses in the neighbourhood. Signs declaring "Two Cents a Copy" were plastered on the walls and counters.

"Okay, this is what we got," said Rocco, sitting next to Nick in the Bronco. "According to business records the company is registered to Thu Li."

"Sounds like a play on names. Li Mann Vu. Li Mann Thu. Thu Li. We got enough evidence to search the place."

Nick walked into the printing shop, looking the place over. There was only one employee. The clerk was a small, slight, young man, dressed in worn, outdated clothes that looked as if they came from the Salvation Army or some second-hand outlet. He seemed no older than eighteen or twenty. Probably a university student working part-time.

"This is a criminal investigation. This here," said Nick, shoving an official document in front of the man's face, "is a copy of our search warrant. We suggest you cooperate with us." Nick slapped a couple of blank identity documents and a phony passport down on the counter. "What you're doing is totally illegal."

The young man's face crumpled at the sight of the FBI and RCMP agents entering the shop right behind Nick and Rocco. He looked close to tears. "I have nothing to do with that. I only photocopy what I'm told to copy. Owner handles that stuff. Not me. Please! It's true!"

Nick could see he was telling the truth. He took him into a back office to question him further.

"Your name?"

"Ismet Bakir, sir."

"Where're you from?"

"Turkey, sir. I'm studying at the university. Tuition is expensive and here is the only job I could get. Please believe, sir!"

As an interrogator, Nick was relentless. It was clear the clerk didn't know much, but any information he could get out of him would be useful. This kid was Turkish, the detainee he had interviewed in New Jersey was Sri Lankan, Li Mann Vu was Vietnamese. International borders were either disappearing faster than he thought or the case was morphing in three or four different directions. The implications of it all made his head spin. In frustration, he smacked the palm of his hand across the employee's face.

"What's the name of your employer?" asked Nick.

"Thu Li Mann. Sir, I only work in this print shop," howled the boy, tears running down his face. "I only see owner twice in all fifteen months working here. He comes when shop is closed and I gone home. This is true, I swear!"

Bingo, thought Nick. Thu Li Mann and Vu Li Mann were too close to be two different people.

"Tell me what you know about the man who hired you. This Thu Li Mann. Where does he live? Does he live alone? Does he have family or friends here in Windsor? Have you seen or know of his family or friends?"

"I know nothing about him. Nothing!" Ismet howled.

"Rocco, get the sketch of Li Mann. Show it to him."

The boy held the sketch between trembling fingers. "It could be Mr. Li. I think maybe it is. He hardly ever comes. My job is to run the photocopy shop for customers, students. I print and they pay. My pay-cheque is deposited directly in my savings account. It's the truth, sir."

Several minutes later, Rocco butted in on Nick's interrogation session. "I ran him through the computer, boss. He's clean. No priors and picked up his Canadian citizenship card last year."

One of the FBI agents handed Nick several blank identity documents. "Found these in the back room."

Nick saw that they were blank drivers' licences and health cards.

"Too bad we can't deport the sucker." Nick gave his terrified victim a chilling look. "Okay. Watch him. I'll talk to him again later. Seize every piece of paper. I want bank statements, cancelled cheques, customer files, shipping records and tax information."

The agents had boxed at least two hundred forged blank Canadian citizenship cards, forged American and Canadian passports, three hundred lamination kits to produce European passports, and an assortment of blank identity documents.

Nick closely examined the five photocopiers. All top of the line. He noticed a particular model of Canon photocopier. Dubois had told him that certain organized crime groups favoured that model in printing fifty and hundred dollar bills that were a reasonable facsimile to the real thing. "Get his ass back in here again," he ordered.

Rocco dragged Ismet Bakir in for another round with Nick.

A thought struggled to surface in Nick's mind as he stared at the packed boxes. It glimmered in his subconscious but it refused to emerge into the light. He felt only frustration which he took out on the frightened young man. "You do know something," Nick raised his hand again. "I want to hear it. How did you get the job?"

"Advertise in campus newspaper." His voice rose and cracked. "It's true what I say. Job in paper and I apply. I get two hundred dollars pay a week. Money deposit automatically in my bank account."

"The bank records for the business. Where are they kept?"

"The owner takes them away once a month."

"When was the last time he was here?"

"Last month. But I did not see him."

Nick pulled out a photograph of Sun Sui. "Look carefully, Ismet. Ever see him before?"

"No. Never. I swear it!"

Damn! Couldn't link Sui to the printing of phony documents.

Nick studied Bakir. He was a permanent resident, grateful to have a job, who wasn't going to rock the boat by asking his employer too many questions. His job of running the photocopy shop supported his education at the nearby university. It wasn't a crime to keep one's nose down in order to keep a job.

"This your correct apartment address here?"

"Yes."

"Okay, Mr. Bakir, I'm letting you go on your own recognizance. Your employer was involved in serious crimes and your employment here makes you an accomplice. My suggestion is to find yourself a lawyer. You'll be hearing from us when we need you to answer more questions pertaining to your employment in a criminal organization. Because membership or participation in any kind of organized crime activity is a serious offence in both Canada and the U.S. In the meantime, if the owner contacts you, you call me right away at this number. If I find out that you didn't comply, I'm going to have your ass deported back to Turkey. Hear me?"

"I will. I too grateful."

Before Nick could stop him, Bakir fell to his knees and kissed the tips of Nick's shoes. Nick backed away fast, and barked an order to his officers. "Tell the driver to back the Ryder truck at the back of the store. Then I want you guys to load all the cardboard boxes and shut the place down."

Nick could see from the sheer volume of documents that clearly, what he was fighting wasn't just the crime of illegals entering North America. This was a business. These people made incredible profits smuggling people wherever they wanted to go. Some governments made it too easy to obtain machine-readable travel documents, passports, visas and identification cards. In Canada, you could apply for a passport in the mail. If you were running a criminal organization, you couldn't get a better system than that, Nick thought cynically. Li Mann's passports and work permits were like tickets anyone could buy. There were even FedEx envelopes for out-of-town customers who needed their phony documents in a hurry.

On one hand he felt elated that he had finally connected with his quarry, Li Mann. The evidence — the phony papers they had seized here and in Montreal were sufficient to charge Li Mann Vu with running an international human trafficking network that spanned the globe. On the other hand, he felt weary and beaten by the sheer volume of evidence. And what good was it if he couldn't find Li Mann Vu? And he had nothing, not one shred of evidence, to prove that Li Mann and Sun Sui were in any way connected. Riffling through a stack of papers, Nick swore under his breath. On the one hand he had a suspect — he knew where Sun Sui was, and he could arrest him at any time — but he didn't have enough evidence.

When he stepped out the door a microphone was thrust in his face. News of the raid had brought out the press. Looking straight into the television cameras, Nick threw out one scrap. "All I can say at this juncture is, the raid today was in connection with an ongoing criminal and immigration investigation of a people smuggling operation which claimed the life of a senior immigration officer. Beyond that, I can't get into specifics."

As he loaded a few confiscated items into the jeep, he had the maddening sense that Li Mann Vu was watching him from somewhere. He used so many names: Thu Li Mann. Thu Mann Vu. Lee Mann Vu. It seemed that every time Nick took a step forward, the ground shifted under his feet and he was back where he started.

Before getting on the highway for the trip back to his office, he crossed the bridge and stopped off at the INS border office to file and sign off reports for the use of U.S. Customs Service and INS officers. He also retrieved his messages. Dubois had called and left his RCMP number. Maybe he had tracked down some information on Wa Sing. Nick made speed the whole way back to Toronto.

He wanted to stop and call Grace, but something told him not to.

The night was unusually warm. The radio announcer had said something about a heat wave gripping the eastern seaboard. Right about that. Li Mann moved the telescope, set the crosshairs on the man parking the jeep in the parking lot. The image was so clear he felt he could almost touch him as he walked across the street and into the diner. As he waited for the immigration officer to reappear, he idly examined his hands. The scars, old and new, told a tale of war and experience. He was proud of them. At the base of his left fourth finger was a scar an inch long. There was another scar on the back of his right thumb, and half of the little finger on his right hand was missing. Lost in Vietnam. He felt the calluses on the palms of both hands; they were thick and rough. The softness had gone out of his hands long, long ago. Yes, his hands were like a badge of honour. Those who met him for the first time knew it, felt it in his handshake.

After an hour and a half the immigration officer came out of the diner, climbed into the jeep and drove it across the parking lot to the front entrance of the con-dominium tower. Li Mann swung the telescope around and adjusted the magnification for a better look at what was being unloaded from the trunk. There were no secu-rity guards or police in sight. It would be easy to kill the man who had violated his home and place of business. He would pay. Not now, but soon.

The General smiled. It had been a long time since he had found a worthy opponent. He loved the thrill of the chase, it pumped him full of adrenaline; it was a drug, better than opium. He knew that the Immigration officer was ruthless in pursuit of a goal. He had observed him from the beginning, when he had entered the Mandarin Club. Li Mann had been sitting in the karaoke lounge, nursing a mai tai and trying to take his mind off work and the pain in his body. It was pure luck that he had man-aged to slip out of the club before the raid began.

Li Mann Vu also followed the story of his botched smuggling operation through newspapers and the nightly news. He knew his opponent had no compunction about violating other people's rights and liberties in doing his job. This immigration officer had fingerprinted and detained people with impunity for crossing borders without proper visas and passports, and had ignored criticism from his country's bar association for his actions and decisions. Yes, a worthy opponent. They were two men who took pride in their work. Unfortunately a lasting relationship would not be forged, because the sanctity of his home had been violated.

The temperatures cooled the following day.

Two men in light summer suits walked along the gravel path towards the pedal boat rental booth. By the time they got there, the afternoon sun had already dipped behind the row of crab apple trees that lined the south end of the island. Sailboats dotted the margin of the long meandering shoreline. Behind them was the expressway, which was clogged with cars in the evening rush-hour traffic. The Caucasian and his slightly shorter Asian companion stood in the rental queue. Surrounding them were tourists in Bermuda shorts, armed with cameras and maps.

"I've got something to tell you," said the Caucasian.

"After we're in the boat."

They fought the wind as they pedalled out into the water. The air carried the smell of cow manure. Once out in the open water, it was the perfect place to hold a conversation without eavesdroppers. The nearest sailboat and water craft was a good half-mile away.

"Grace Wang-Weinstein has been assigned to the case," said the Caucasian.

"Will she do what she's told?"

"I believe so, but we can never be a hundred percent sure."

"I need to be sure. What good is she to us if we can't control her?" His enunciation revealed him to be an educated man. His tone was soft but unyielding.

"I don't know if this will do you any good but I've made copies of her bio and file." The Caucasian handed the accordion file to his boating companion. "A word of advice. If you think the case is shaping up to be a negative, then it must not be concluded. Because once a decision is made, it's final. There is never any judicial review of exclusion orders."

The Asian understood. "What strategy would you recommend?"

"If legal issues get sticky, personally, I would recommend a strategy of delay and adjournment. And maybe abandonment. Giving up entirely the claim for asylum."

"What's the reason to abandon? Why would I do that? How can I set up shop in North America if I don't have permanent status? That's why Canadian citizenship is important to me. I need that Canadian passport."

"If it looks like the immigration officer has uncovered damning evidence against you, then you must give up the claim. To keep a decision from being rendered on a case. You can always make an application to have a new asylum claim heard."

They pedalled hard against the wind.

"I can do that?"

"Yes. It says so in the Immigration Act."

"Can she be bought? Bribed?"

"I don't think so."

"Wouldn't it have been easier to assign a judge who could be controlled?"

The Caucasian didn't enjoy the criticism implied by the question. He kept his gaze on the water. He had never been one-hundred-percent comfortable with this man. Now as they sat side by side in the pedal boat, he strained to interpret his companion's every nod, smile, and frown. Even though he was a China watcher and friend of China, he blamed it on cultural differences. The Asian's arrogance drove him crazy. But he kept his frustrations to himself. "I thought you wanted someone of your race," he said, peevishly.

"No, I didn't say that. I said I wanted someone we could either compromise or influence." The Asian crimped his lips into a tight line.

"There may be other ways we can influence her," said his Caucasian companion. He was trying to sound confident but even he could hear the uneasy tone in his voice as he made the suggestion. Under the circumstances, he decided it wasn't the right time to raise the issue of a fee increase.

"No, I think we need a fallback plan."

The Caucasian turned sideways to stare at his boating companion. "What kind of fallback plan are we talking about here?"

"I may have to move south of the border. If I fail to resolve my status here, then it's important for me to seek citizenship in the States. I want you to contact the U.S. Administration. Tell them I have information that they're interested in. The Americans are always interested in ensuring their military might. I've information on China's sale of missile and nuclear technology to Pakistan and Iran."

"And what if they want to meet you before the IRC makes a decision on your case?"

"Have you never played mah-jong? We take it one step at a time. First call them and locate the right person to pass this message on to. Then get back to me. Then we will formulate our second step. It's pointless to second-guess what their move will be."

chapter sixteen

The air smelled like rain. For a long time she stood on the dock of the Hawthorne Yacht Club watching rowers and kayakers as they skimmed across the water. It looked like fun. Now, there was a word that hadn't been in her vocabulary for a while now. What was she doing here? She should never have agreed to meet him. Stupid, stupid. She could have made an excuse. As she argued with herself, she saw him coming towards her. He was late. She didn't expect an apology; nor did she get one.

Wa Sing greeted her warmly, but carefully. "How are you, my dear? I'm glad you could come on short notice."

She submitted to a kiss on the cheek. Up-close and in sunlight she noticed that his skin was pale and blotchy with age spots. Money and power couldn't buy you everything. For some perverse reason that pleased her.

"Why couldn't you talk about this on the telephone?"

"You can't be sure these days. I hear the police are tapping phone lines all the time. Privacy no longer exists."

She waited. She had a pretty good idea what the meeting was all about, but she'd let him broach the subject.

"I'm leaving the country tomorrow. First I'll stop over in Vancouver. Drop in and say hello to Kim. It's been a while since we dined together at our favourite dim sum restaurant."

The heavy, serious air with which he made this statement about her mother was strange — it seemed more like a threat than a passing remark. She made no reply as they climbed the external stairs of the glass-and-redwood structure. Briefly, they traded community gossip until she asked him directly, "Last time we met, you said nothing about leaving the country. Where are you going?"

"I've got to go to Singapore and Malaysia. I'm buying property in the downtown core. A redevelopment project. I've been advised to leave the country for a while."

They stood on the upper deck, looking out on the water. "Advised by who?" Grace interrupted.

With a dismissive wave of his hand, Wa Sing continued, "The political opposition wants to embarrass the government over campaign contributions. I'm told that my name is on the list of those to be subpoenaed. My contributions were all entirely legitimate, of course, but appearances may be against me."

He was obviously getting his information ahead of the public. She pulled her eyes from the water to look at him. He met her gaze calmly and suggested they sit down and order something cold to drink.

Grace followed him to a table with a view of kayakers training for the big race.

"Who's your source? Can you count on the quality of his information?"

"Like you, he has benefited from my support. It's in his best interest that I don't testify at the inquiry. Nor do I wish to."

By process of elimination she tried to figure out who this source could be, but his words pulled her back.

"If I stay in the country, there is a possibility that I'll be charged with influence peddling."

She knew Section 121 of the Criminal Code well enough to know that it was an indictable offence, carrying a maximum five-year sentence.

"And lot of people will get hurt. It could even touch you, Grace. No, I've worked long and hard to make sure that our community has people all the way to the top."

"What do you mean?"

"Not all the money I contributed was mine. Someone asked me to make a campaign donation on their behalf."

"Who?"

"Excuse me, my dear, the less you know the better."

"Why didn't this person make the contribution himself? He could have gotten a hefty tax credit for a political donation. Why?"

He brushed off her question with a dismissive wave of his hand. "Grace, that's not why I asked to see you."

A young, blond waiter appeared and Wa Sing gave the order for two Singapore slings.

"I'll have a Sambucca straight up instead," said Grace to the waiter before returning her attention to the old man.

"It's only a matter of time before the rift between the U.S. and China is healed. Then China will join the World Trade Organization — and that's the outcome we want."

"Who's *we?*"

"Grace, please don't interrupt me when I'm speaking. Listen, please. The Prime Minister's trade mission to China is important. It sends the right signals to the right players." He fixed his pale, old eyes on her. "Grace, your mother's country has 1.2 billion people, a hundred million unemployed. It's an impending disaster. Cities all across China have already eliminated 190,000 state jobs. Job creation is a priority for some very powerful people in those cities."

"Those are staggering numbers. Finding jobs for a million people is already an insurmountable task, let alone a hundred million," said Grace.

"I'm glad you see my point. Massive unemployment in China concerns everyone because China is now one of the biggest players on the world stage. That's why I'm here. To ask for one small favour."

The waiter set down a tall glass adorned with fruit and paper parasols, and a shot glass of clear liquid. Mechanically, Grace put out a hand and wrapped her fingers around the shotglass. Deep down in her stomach, she already knew what he wanted.

"I'm so very glad you're taking Sun's case. He is one of us. He is of our background. And he's now a millionaire who can make a difference in his mother country. I feel that with his money, skills and connections, he's one of the few Chinese who can alter the course of Chinese history to bring us success in the twenty-first century."

She didn't respond. She knocked the Sambucca straight back, savouring the sensation as it went down her throat.

Wa Sing continued, "Sun Sui has not always been a credit to our community. As the black sheep, he brought shame to his parents when they discovered that he had only two interests — dating girls and making movies. But this dabbling in nightclubs and entertainers won't go on forever. He'll settle down and become what he is capable of being: a serious and established businessman. You know, the Suis are very well connected."

It was a horrible feeling to be manipulated. Still, she asked, "Well connected? How? With the Chinese government?"

"Yes."

"But how can the government be his ally *and* the agent of his persecution at the same time? That affects his asylum claim."

"Tell me what he wrote in his asylum claim."

"I can't do that. I took an oath when I assumed public office."

Again he waved her words away, as if they were buzzing flies. "Grace, please listen. I'll give you a little history lesson on our people. Sun's father was purged as a rightist for speaking his mind in 1957. Then his family was purged again during the Cultural Revolution. I know from a mutual friend of ours that his father and first brother spent a good many years in the countryside cleaning latrines and tending pigs instead of working as engineers and scientists. Today, all those who were on the out are sitting pretty inside the Politburo because their technical skills were needed. But after Sun was arrested for his part in the democracy movement his father was pushed into retirement."

"Other than that, his parents didn't really suffer the effects of Sun's participation at Tiananmen Square?"

"Yes, they did. The leadership wanted to strip the family of all privileges and to execute Sun. But then the regime changed hands and Deng Xiaoping took over."

"If he's rehabilitated, why can't he return home?"

"Deng's no longer in power and Sun, unlike his father, has bad-boy ways. The movie business in Hong Kong is the worst of Chinese culture."

"You mean, he's only interested in making kung fu movies and porno films?"

"Yes, his parents feel disgraced by that. Worse, his latest film was banned inside China because it was critical of the new leadership."

"So it didn't pass the Ministry of Culture and Censorship test. That's just one ministry that dislikes him," said Grace.

"That current minister of culture would like to sentence him to the gulag."

"Then, please, explain to me how he can help his people in China if they perceive him as an enemy."

"Because they need him. The new Chinese leadership think he's highly connected to the Canadian government."

"Ahh. I get it. He's used his advisory role on the trade junkets to China to build a higher insider profile than he really has."

"Something like that, Grace."

She nodded as she turned her glass in the wet ring on the paper placemat. That was true, regimes around the world were no longer executing the well-educated and the well-connected from governments they had overthrown. In her own work, she had been turning down Amharic peoples in their refugee claims because the Tigreans who had wrested control of Ethiopia were no longer persecuting them. They needed the expertise of the Amharics to run the country.

"In other words, the regime would still do business with him?"

"Yes."

"Then I suggest he drop his asylum claim!" said Grace, her voice rising.

"Lower your voice." Wa Sing was suddenly icy. "I'm asking you to overlook certain anomalies in his asylum claim."

Arms crossed, she said, "You know I can't do that! That would be serious professional misconduct! I'd like to help you, but this is impossible. In fact, it's inappropriate for me even to discuss the merits of his asylum claim with you."

"Grace, listen to me. Since China took over Hong Kong, Sun has nowhere to flee…"

"What did he do to? Who did he piss off?"

"His wife's family. They're high ranking party members and they're sick and tired of hearing stories of his infidelity. Not to mention, they're not pleased about his movie business."

"What can they do to him except push for divorce?"

"A lot. But that's another story. Right now, Sun needs to get his Canadian citizenship. Remember he's one of us and needs our help."

But I'm not *one of you,* she almost said. But she couldn't. It would sound very ungrateful considering how much he had helped her. She felt no allegiance to the citizens of the People's Republic of China. And certainly none to those with a taint of criminality.

"Why not claim asylum in the U.S.?"

"You know it's much tougher down there. It's great to do business with them but that doesn't mean they want us on their doorstep."

She diverted the conversation. "What is your exact relationship with him?"

"I met him through friends last year when I was in Taipei. He approached me to come in on a joint venture to make serious money. How could I say no? I who have two wives, five daughters and eleven grandchildren. My estate must be sizeable when I die. Not to mention the need for money while I'm still alive."

"What's this partnership of yours?"

Wa Sing pulled out a glossy brochure and a stack of photographs from his jacket pocket.

"Real estate. Business is booming. Shanghai, the Paris of the East, is full of skyscrapers designed by Canadian and American architectural firms. I can honestly say that I would be nothing without his Shanghai government contacts. And they love him because he brings a ton of business to the city."

"But everything you're telling me weakens his asylum claim. If he has such good government connections, then the very same government can't be his agent of persecution."

"In a bloated bureaucracy, it is both. You can have enemies and friends within the government."

"Then surely his friends in high places can protect him," she argued.

"Look at Russia. It's a game of musical chairs," the old man sighed.

"Tell me about your partnership." Grace flipped through the colour photographs and slick brochure.

Wa Sing leaned across the table. "Listen, Grace. I need Sun. Right now, we have a three-way alliance between me as the front man, Sun with his money and connections, and a West German architectural firm to do the actual work. Without him, I would not be as successful as I am today." He handed her another brochure.

She read it: Three hundred condominiums, a hotel complex with roller skating and ice rink, two swimming pools and a complete health spa facility. The ground level was occupied with a shopping arcade. The nineteen-hole golf course project sat on almost four hundred acres of prime land outside Shanghai.

"See here," he said pulling out a photograph from the pile. "This will be a country club condominium project, worth close to six billion dollars. Think of how many thousands of jobs that creates. And the spin-off effects."

Nice work if you can get it, thought Grace. She caught the bartender's attention and pointed at her empty glass.

"Tell me, how did he make his first million? Was it honestly?"

With a brief laugh, the old man said, "Grace, no one gets rich honestly. If you want to know more, ask him yourself."

Grace was starting to understand what it was all about. Sun Sui was playing the two governments, of Canada and China, off against each other, promising the politicians on both sides access to trade and wealth. Everything was going without a hitch until Nick's colleague died, and Nick learned that the Flying Dragons used Sun Sui's club as an operating base. That implicated him as the club's owner in the Dragons' smuggling of illegal aliens. Nick had lost the case to deport Sun, but he wouldn't give up. Grace knew the man all too well. He would find another angle. He would find enough evidence and build a criminal case through the criminal justice system, and sooner or later he would win. There was more than one way to skin a cat.

She could see the hurt and anger in Wa Sing's eyes. It suddenly struck her that neither of them really knew the other. They had known each other for years, but as stereotypes — she as the opinionated and rebellious second-generation woman, and Wa Sing as the hard-working immigrant who had made good in his adoptive country. Beyond that, what did she know? Nothing.

A long silence enveloped them. He tossed back his drink and reached into his jacket for a cigarette, then he spoke without looking at her, as if he was speaking more to himself.

"I know what you're thinking, Grace. What you must understand is, our community is like any other community. We are not all heroes. You've been placed in a position where you can protect this man." He looked at her darkly. "Sun Sui is of our community. And he can save China from becoming a country of sellers. Of old women sitting on streets selling their worldly possessions for a few yuan.

What is the future of a country if everyone is selling and no one is buying? Just look at Russia today."

"Sun Sui has committed crimes," said Grace, thinking about Nick's exclusion order and package of documents on Sun's criminal activities.

"No, Grace, you don't understand," Wa Sing replied condescendingly. "The establishment wants to make a symbol out of him. He is no worse than the successful French or English businessmen of this country. Like any tragic Greek hero, he has built his success on virtues that are inseparable from his flaws. Yes, he has the ambition of half a dozen men. And yes, he behaved badly towards those entertainment girls in his Mandarin Club, took advantage of them sexually. But that's our cultural flaw. We value sons above daughters. And remember, he brought those poor girls out of China, out of their rice-bowl poverty."

For a moment Grace was speechless. Could he not guess her feelings about such behaviour? Finding her voice, she protested, "It's more than that. He's been linked to three murders. An immigration officer, a gang member, and an employee of his nightclub."

Wa Sing made a dismissive gesture with his hands. "Those allegations are not true. How could I do business with such a person if they were true?"

How indeed? She searched his face for an answer, but found none.

His eyes narrowed as he looked at her, but his voice grew softer. "In any case, if one of our group does something wrong, do we immediately cast them out into the cold? No, like good Buddhists, we must stick together and help him find his way into the light."

Tired and angry, she lashed out, "Don't bring Buddhism into this. You used me, didn't you? You deliberately introduced me to him that night at the Yung Kee reception, trying to win my sympathy for him, knowing if push came to shove and he needed to file a refugee claim, there would be a good chance for me to hear the case."

"Grace, how could you think that? At that time I didn't know he was in trouble with the immigration authorities."

She heard the lie in his voice, and realized this wasn't the first time. She wanted to think carefully of all he had told her. She rose to leave.

In the gravel parking lot, he said, "Grace, you're like my daughter. What we spoke of just now, we won't speak of again."

"That's for sure. I'm in a conflict of interest situation already."

"Grant him asylum, Grace. Many people will be grateful to you. And others won't care. There's no need to waste taxpayers' money by conducting a two-week hearing."

How did he know that the case was scheduled to last two weeks? He knew all about the case and expected her to do as she was told. She had no one to blame but herself. Four years ago when she had accepted his help to get her appointment on the bench, she had made a pact with the devil. She was in a hell of a fine fix.

Wordlessly, Grace turned and walked toward her car. He walked beside her, silent too. She was angry, but her feelings were confused, and regret stabbed at her. She was sorry she had spoken so coldly to him. After all, his values were those of another country. And he had been a friend for too long. She stopped abruptly, and turned to him, thinking she would try to make peace with him.

Instead, he grabbed her roughly by the arm. "You're like my daughter. I don't want you to get hurt. I'm telling you now, Sun is a man who always gets what he wants."

With that remark, he was gone. She watched his car moving out of the lot. Just beyond him, she caught sight of a man with a camera. He looked like everybody else, with his baseball cap backwards, and a moment before he had been taking a picture of the sailboats. But now he was taking a picture of the back of Wa Sing's car. Or was he? The man turned and aimed his lens at the river again.

It was crazy to be suspicious of everybody. She got into her car and drove home.

It rained for much of the day. Nick sat in his office, watching the water pour down from the sky. In the middle of his desk was a salami sandwich and the *Law Reporter*. He held down the corner of the page with a bottle of mineral water. Once a week, he tried to keep up with the legal issues and how the courts were voting, particularly in immigration law. Verster's win had not made it into this month's issue. He hated to admit it, but yes, he felt the pinch of his self-imposed need to win. And right now, he was not winning. Philip Wong had sent him an e-mail that morning: no luck in tracking down that travel agent's snakehead contact. Moreover, Verster had won the first and second round of their match. Most of the girls were released from detention, and were back at the Mandarin Club with their entertainment acts. He listened to the street sounds through the open window. The weather matched his mood. The growing pile of files on his desk only made his mood lower. Trying to take his mind off Sun Sui, he sorted through crime scene reports on another case, and leafed through detention certificates of inadmissible aliens.

By two in the afternoon, he was making headway on a third of the files sitting on his desk. The phone on his desk buzzed. "What?" he shouted into the receiver.

"Nick, it's Jon Keiler," said his secretary. "Shall I put the call through?"

"Yeah, do that."

"Hello, Nick. I hear you've been trying to reach me." Jon Keiler was the immigration manager at the Canadian embassy in Hong Kong.

"Where the hell are you, Jon?"

"I'm on holiday."

"Must be nice. When are you back at work?"

"Next week. It hasn't been a great vacation. I dropped three grand to stay at this exclusive resort in Thailand, and it's rained every day."

"Jon, it's been a long two weeks for me, too. Right now I have my own problems to deal with. I really don't want to hear how disappointed you are in your vacation."

"Sorry, Nick."

Changing gears, Nick said, "I've sent you several e-mail messages concerning an application you processed a couple of years ago. The applicant's name is Sun Sui. Look into it for me, will you?"

"I'll look into it when I get into my office next week."

"We'll talk then."

At the end of the day, Detective Kappolis called. "Bad news. Sun's alibied up to the neck. Girls in and out all day and night when Gee Tung got whacked. They've all vouched for him."

"How convenient."

"Yeah. And we got diddly on his wiretap. Like he knows we're listening in on his conversations."

"What about his visitors' list?" asked Nick.

"Mostly girls."

"Maybe it's a front. We should start getting their names and particulars."

"I got them on video camera. My boss says if nothing interesting turns up in another week, he's going to pull the squad teams off surveillance duty."

"Nothing we can do about that. Let's just keep our fingers crossed. Before we sign off," said Nick, "did your team go through Gee Tung's place for prints?"

"Yeah. Nothing usable. Certainly not Sun Sui's. And we got nothing on the guys who killed him. A hired hit done by professional triad members. Looks like it was the perfect crime. The girlfriend can't even remember what they looked like."

"I hate this case," said Nick glumly. "I got a rich nightclub owner with fat political connections, but dirty hands. For all we know, he could've bought the bullet that killed Gee Tung and Andy Loong, but we've got nothing. I can hear him laughing at us now."

"We'll get him."

"Yeah. Let's work on that goal."

After a few more files Nick called it a day and walked over to Hart House. He changed into his swimming trunks, and seventy-three laps later, he was spent and smelling of chlorine. He walked along Wellesley towards Yonge Street, losing himself in the crowd. Evenings on the Strip you were lucky not to get stabbed to death for chump change. He wasn't worried. Hands jammed in the pockets of his chinos, he made eye contact with everyone he passed, daring the scumbags to push their luck. Still feeling restless, he walked the city, pushing past the strip joints where half-naked young girls stood beneath tacky marquees hawking show times. He walked past a newspaper and magazine stand where his gaze wandered to the rows of women's magazines pushing beauty and how to trap a man. To him, it was just another genre of porn. Carried along by the crowd, he observed the massage parlours with their attendants pushing sex toys to passers by. Further up the street, the scent in the air changed — from the fetishistic to the gastronomic. All-night pizza joints and Chinese take-outs.

Fatigued and lonely, he took the short-cut back to his condo. At eleven-twenty, he was sitting alone in the dark on the balcony, the night sky above him stretched out like a black tarp.

Later, just as he was falling asleep, too late, he remembered that Kelly Marcovich had wanted him to call her.

chapter seventeen

"Nick, I think you should walk away from this case."

"Walk away? And let him get away with murder?" Nick switched on the speaker phone and fanned himself with a file folder. The muggy weather of the past few days had turned into a heat wave, and the air conditioning system in the building was too antiquated to work properly. As he talked, he cleared files off his window vents.

"If Sun's got friends at International Trade, my advice to you is, save your breath. Canada is scouring the globe for trade. First it was Mexico. Then Chile. This year it's gonna be China. Bad timing, my friend," said Dubois.

"What the hell are you reading?"

"Go to the International Trade Department's website. It's all there. Check it out yourself. It says right here in the government website, 'when Canadian firms compete for contracts and strategic partnerships abroad, they are not competing against other Canadian firms. They are competing against top U.S., French, and German firms. The race is global.' Nick, we're fucked, my friend."

"Dubois, we know the whole Sun Sui mess is political."

"Listen, I got the full membership list of the Asia Business Council. One thing I found out. Your ex-girl-friend's a member. Maybe you should talk to her."

"Grace? You know she's not so 'ex' anymore. I ran into her again. At the annual tea party."

Dubois groaned. "I thought you looked down on the snobby crowd and their pretentious ways."

"I do." Nick didn't feel like elaborating.

"Hey, it's your life. I don't know what you see in her. She ain't the only woman you can screw, you know."

Nick decided the best response to that was no response.

After the phone call, Nick worked in a desultory way until Kappolis showed up and dropped his six-foot-two frame down on the lumpy chesterfield.

"What's up?" asked Nick, looking up from the report he was writing.

"Good news. That house Li Mann was renting in Montreal. I tracked down the location of the landlord and owner. Here it is." Kappolis handed Nick one of his business cards with the information written on the reverse side.

"Thanks," said Nick.

"I ran a check already. Seems the owners of the building are non-citizens. I think you should be the one who pays them a visit. Throw your weight around a little, know what I mean."

Grace found comfort in rituals. After almost twenty years, the daily routine of putting on running gear, tightening laces, and stretching hamstrings had become a form of indulgence for someone with a sedentary job. Besides, her body was now hopelessly addicted to the endorphins, her drug of choice. She had first started running in university. Back then it had been a means of distracting her mind from dry and musty tomes, and a means of escape from the loneliness of moving east and a crowded dormitory. In the beginning she had run no more than a mile. But as the years passed the mileage increased because she found pounding the pavement to be therapeutic. Not the least of it was that an hour on the road meant an hour of private time to herself. Time to reflect and to make peace with herself and the world. Everything around her became a passing blur, and that was as good as a rest, particularly after a full day on the bench, when she needed to empty her mind of work and worry.

She headed down her street of parked cars in the direction of the park. The moon was just rising in the blue sky as she cut her own trail along the tortuous dirt path, the domain of endurance athletes, masochists and testosterone-heavy jocks. Grace kept her eyes on the ground, on the lookout for outcroppings of rock and roots. Periodically she would look up and be charmed by the floral scenery and the ducks feeding down by the river. After a mile, she noticed that she was the sole runner on the path. Fine with her. By the second mile, she was running at an easy pace and her mind was in another channel.

The sun was sinking across the river. Another beautiful sunset. In another forty, fifty minutes, it would be dark. At the bridge that joins Ontario with Quebec, she turned around. As a city-bred woman, she had a healthy fear of sex predators lurking behind trees and bushes. After she passed the sycamore and the weeping willows, she headed back to urban life by running along city streets.

Crossing Bronson towards Hintonburg, she was on the wrong side of the tracks: cheap real estate, lawns overgrown with weeds, and sidewalks strewn with garbage and broken beer bottles. She ignored the few rude gestures from drivers and pedestrians. Waiting for the lights to change, she noticed a white van and wondered if it was the same white van she'd seen when she started out three miles ago. But what were the chances of that in a city of a million white vans? She wrote it off as coincidence, and the suspicious mind of a person who lived in a city with too many perverts.

Past the tacky billboards promoting underwear and cars, her feet took her down a favourite street of splendid Victorian mansions and through a children's park. She observed lovers holding hands and a child throwing a temper tantrum. She passed a row of park benches and headed for the exit at Lydon park, sidestepping a homeless person panhandling outside the park for change to hit the liquor store. She jogged past a restaurant that she hadn't visited in a while; in the windows were people seated having dinner. When would Nick be coming up to visit her again? She wanted to call him but didn't want to appear too clingy. After years in a marriage, she would have to relearn old dating skills.

Turning right, she detoured down a favourite block of athletic and outdoor stores like Eddie Bauer, Trailhead, and Mountain Equipment Coop — she liked looking in the windows as she jogged by, and why not? She kept them in business with regular purchases of Gore-Tex, polar fleece, and running shoes. It took her less than six months to turn two-hundred-dollar runners into a mush of rubber. As she checked out the latest in shoe technology, she noticed a white van reflected in the window. The same white van again? Only one way to find out. But there was too much traffic for her to wade the street and jot down the license number. Still, she kept her gaze on the van hoping to get a good look at the driver or passenger. But the windows were tinted and rolled up. She watched until it drove out of sight.

Once safely inside her house, she decided she must have been letting her imagination run amok. God help her. Was she so scarred by urban life and lurid news stories of sex maniacs pouncing upon unsuspecting women? She chastised herself for letting her paranoia get the better of her.

chapter eighteen

He drove with one hand on the steering wheel while his other hand held hers. Neither of them wanted to talk about their violation of legal protocol. How they were breaking the cardinal rule of the immigration system: the judicial side just did not fraternize with the enforcement branch. Instead he listened to her banter about the immigrant population in Montreal, and how you could find everything from tandoori houses to Korean grills to tapas bars all within the same block.

After a three-hour drive, he almost lost his cool as they checked in.

"You'd think a five-star hotel like this, in a cosmopolitan city like Montreal, would have at least one English-speaking clerk at the front desk," he complained.

She squeezed his hand. "My French will get us through the weekend. Let's not ruin a perfectly good romantic getaway by talking Quebec politics."

Once inside the hotel room, he took her in his arms. "Let's go to bed."

"What about dinner?" she asked, exploring his mouth with her tongue.

"Later."

He didn't bother closing the drapes. Outside the window, the sky to the east was a steel blue tinged with pink and black. He looked down at the woman in his arms; her eyes were closed. A good part of their relationship was carnal; he liked that. He had had sex with other women and remembered enjoying it. This was different. He moved his hands up her skirt, exploring the feel of her thighs.

Slowly they undressed each other. The sight of her naked brought a rush of desire so powerful that for a disconcerting second, he felt like a teenager again, overwhelmed with lust and longing.

Her hands worked the length of his body.

"Mmmm. I've had detailed fantasies about this all week."

"Which part?" she grinned naughtily. "This part?" Her hands had stopped between his legs.

"You might want to apply for the job as my personal masseuse," he moaned.

"I didn't think there was a position open."

"For you babe, anything," he said as he flipped her over on her back, pinning her down with his body and hands. Her body felt like silk underneath his tongue. He started from her breasts and worked his way down.

He was just the kind of lover she wanted, just as he'd always been. Attentive and unhurried. Unhurried, even in their desperation to have each other.

Later, in the darkened hotel room, she broke the silence. "So tell me why you invited me to Montreal."

"I want us to try again. I want you to be in my life. But I don't want us to have secrets from each other. There's another reason. I have to interview someone. I think you could be of help to me."

"Work. It figures," she sighed, running her hands on his body. "Where're we going tomorrow?"

"I'm checking out the landlady who rented a house to a snakehead called Li Mann. Maybe she has a good photo of her tenant, because we sure as hell don't."

"Stop. I don't want to talk about work anymore."

They made love again. Afterward, they ordered dinner from the room service menu because neither of them wanted to get dressed. Nick wanted to talk.

"I want you to know everything about me," he said, with his arms around her, he began telling her about his parents' flight from Czechoslovakia in 1968. He had never told her the whole story before. "My parents used to talk about the Russian tanks advancing into the city. They were very apprehensive because they'd lived through that kind of thing before, with the Nazis. My father's parents were both arrested by the Gestapo. My father was just a boy — he never saw his parents again."

Grace lay quietly listening.

"My father went to live with his uncle. He met my mother in university. In '55, they married and lived on campus. The following year my dad became faculty head of the economics department. I was in grade school when the situation in the country changed from bad to worse. My parents knew they would be among the first to be arrested. They planned their escape along with others from the university. In the final days, we hid in the homes of friends. Dad had befriended someone at the American embassy, who in turn helped them emigrate to the United States. They came for freedom, but somehow I think they left their hearts behind in Prague."

Grace put her arms around him, snuggling into his shoulders.

"Dad found work at the University of Rochester teaching economics. It took him another eight years to make faculty head. He retired last year. You should've seen the big retirement party they threw him."

He adjusted his position, facing her, cupping one breast in the hollow of his hand. "No complaints. I had a good life. Dad made me join Scouts. I spent just about every summer hiking in the Adirondacks and skiing in Vermont."

"So how did you wind up in Canada?"

"My parents thought it would be a good idea if I saw something of the world. Their idea of this was to have me do my undergrad studies at the University of Toronto."

"We missed each other like two ships in the night. I came to do graduate studies," said Grace, clasping one hand over his. "Besides, we probably needed to marry other people to appreciate each other."

"There's something to that," replied Nick. "Anyway, I slunk back home to study law at Columbia. How about you?"

"Osgoode Law School in Toronto. What happened after Columbia?"

"I practiced for two years in the prosecutor's office in New York, and then in Boston. When I got married, we moved to Toronto again because her family lived there."

"How long were you married?"

He sighed and stared out the window at the moonless night. "Seven years. I'm surprised it lasted as long as it did. The relationship was built on sand."

"How?"

"It was superficial. She thought I had a good pedigree and would be a great breadwinner. And that I would wine and dine her practically every night."

"That's pretty unrealistic."

"Hmmmm. Tell me," said Nick, touching her cheek with his lips. "What about you and this David guy I spoke to on the phone once?"

She twirled a lock of hair around her fingers as she spoke. "David Rikeman. We were both stationed in El Salvador. He was with the American embassy. We met at one of the diplomatic parties and matched up for a whole string of reasons. Sex and friendship and playing the part of the white knight in shining armour."

His eyebrows rose inquiringly.

She elaborated. "At the time I was in the country on a United Nations human rights project. I was part of a team of anthropologists digging up the bodies of those killed by the military. Mass graves. The army did their best to threaten and intimidate us. David used embassy resources to protect us. He gave us use of his bullet-proof Mercedes. Dating him provided some sort of diplomatic immunity. That made a big difference." She had a far-away look in her eyes as she talked. "At times it was very scary being there. But I cared about the work. I come from a family whose mantra is, service to others. I believe in it too. So I renewed for another term."

She sat up in bed and reached for a water glass. "Dave and I, our relationship really clicked in El Salvador. Our relationship thrived on the fear and adrenaline. It was the coming home that was a relationship killer." She shook her head sadly. "Strangely, marriage counselling only made things worse. And then I met you."

"Well, I'm glad you did," said Nick, sliding his hand under the sheet.

After breakfast the next morning, she consulted a map as Nick pulled the rental car out of the underground garage. "You know Montreal?" he asked.

"A bit. This is one of my least favourite parts of city. You can be sure that the neighbourhoods along this strip don't make it into glossy tourist brochures. See," she pointed. "By day, the strip looks normal enough with fruit stores, bakeries and hanging salamis and smoked meat briskets hanging in the windows of delicatessens. But at night, God help us. The cokeheads, prostitutes, and the paedophiles are out in full force."

She stopped and grimaced, pinching her nose shut.

"Whoa!" Nick exclaimed.

The smell of baked urine was overpowering. Down the next street, the sound of sewing machines buzzed feverishly as immigrant women turned out piecework to anonymous contractors in the shmatte business.

Nick parked in front of the address they were looking for. After ringing the doorbell, they listened to the sound of heavy footsteps pounding down the stairs, then the sound of chains being released. The door opened a crack. Nick flashed his badge and launched into his immigration spiel.

The woman was unimpressed. "Me already speaka to polica. Big francophone men come to door. I say to the stupid one whose English is worse than mine; I not know tenant. Asian man good tenant. He rents house and give post-dated money. Very good. That's all I care about."

Ramona Santiaga was her name. She rolled her chubby shoulders while her big-boned frame blocked the doorway entrance to her house. She reminded Grace of the stereotype Latino hired help portrayed in Hollywood movies with her heavy accent, thick black hair and flashing eyes, and the small white apron that circled her stocky waist. A pair of pink mules incongruously adorned her feet.

It was obvious that she distrusted and feared authority at the same time. Nick seemed to know what she was thinking. "I'm not the Montreal police," he assured her. "I'm with Canadian immigration. This isn't a police matter."

He tried to disarm her with a friendly smile but Grace could see it wasn't working.

"Do you mind if we come in for a few minutes?"

The face hesitated. The door began to close. Quickly, Grace introduced herself, woman to woman, and Ramona looked at her, weakening. "I've much work to do. I give you maybe five, ten minutes only."

"My friend only wants five minutes of your time."

Ramona stepped back from the doorway and allowed them inside.

Nick looked at Grace with an expression that said, "How the hell did you manage that?"

Grace smiled and followed Ramona into her house. The hallway was covered in clear vinyl plastic, but Ramona asked them to remove their shoes. The living room furniture was also covered in vinyl. The end table and a fringed floor lamp were still adorned with the store price stickers.

Ramona pointed to a sofa covered in a moss-green polyester fringed throw. At that moment, a man wearing an undershirt and stained denims came down the stairs.

"Who are these people?" he yelled and pointed.

Nick stood up and they introduced themselves again.

"This is Orlando," explained Ramona, "he's my brother."

Orlando turned to his sister, a torrent of Portuguese burst from his lips. Grace had picked up enough of the language in Brazil to know that he was chastising Ramona for allowing government officials to enter their home. The gist of what he said was, you couldn't trust government officials. They started off investigating other people and ended up investigating you. They would have the damnedest time getting her and Nick out of their house.

Ramona smiled nervously as her brother heaped verbal abuse upon her.

"We won't stay long," Grace suddenly pleaded, in Portuguese.

Orlando directed his attention at Grace. Once he understood that he couldn't exclude them by speaking his mother tongue to his sister, he switched to English, but he was still furious.

"Ramona is too friendly. She talks to everybody. I keep telling her that we're not back home in the Azores where we could walk down the street barefoot and say hello to everybody," said Orlando, chopping the air with his workman hands. "But what does she know? All she knows in life is bathroom and kitchen cleaners." He spat out the word kitchen cleaners as if it was synonymous with anthrax and Ebola.

Grace and Nick exchanged glances, but Ramona didn't seem offended. She excused herself from the conversation, disappearing into the kitchen.

Orlando huffed and puffed a few more times, then said grudgingly, "What can I do for you?"

While Nick was explaining, Ramona reappeared with cold drinks and a plate of cookies for four.

Orlando turned on her in another torrent of abuse, this time in English. "In the name of the Virgin Mary, Ramona, these people are not our guests! We want them out of our house as soon as possible. Holy Mother of Mary! When will you learn!"

Ramona glanced at the Virgin Mary on the wall and quickly crossed herself.

Nick deftly produced the police sketch of Li Mann Vu.

"Is this your tenant, Mr. Li?"

"Yes, but face much older," said Ramona holding the picture in her hands.

"How did you come to rent your house to Mr. Li?"

Orlando spoke up. "We had an ad in the *Montreal Gazette* two years ago. He said he would take it for two thousand a month. Give us cash for one year in advance. You'd be stupid to turn down such an offer."

"You didn't check references?" asked Nick.

Orlando shot Nick a look implying that government officials were indeed stupid creatures.

"What is there to check? Post-dated checks can bounce. Cash is king, and he paid in advance." His tone was contemptuous.

"Did you drop in regularly?"

"Why?" asked Orlando. "He did his own repairs and paid for it himself. He never called us. Only once to say that he was renewing the lease for a second year. Then he came by the house and gave us another year's rent in cash."

"Yes, we only see him twice. He was perfect tenant. Neighbours no complain about loud parties or women. He said to me when he signed the lease for the second year that he travelled much in his job," said Ramona.

"He was our best tenant," confirmed Orlando. "Why you asking? To deport him?"

"The Immigration Department has a few questions to put to him. Did you know he was housing illegal immigrants in your house?"

"No, we didn't know and if we did, we wouldn't care," snapped Orlando, making a show of looking at his watch.

"What is he guilty of? He was a good tenant," said Ramona.

"We suspect that he's a ringleader in smuggling illegal immigrants into this country."

Orlando interrupted Nick's explanation. "That is government talk. Yesterday, more government people took up my time by wanting to see the house. The house is empty. The government has driven out my best tenant. Will you reimburse me? No, I didn't think so. You people in government have lost touch with society all around. You should be lucky the illegals are here to pick up garbage, wash dishes in restaurants, pick fruit on the farms. These people work for peanuts and you people benefit. I'm sorry we can't answer anymore questions. You go now."

Grace broke into the conversation. "You've got a big house here. The two of you must've worked like dogs and penny-pinched yourself silly to afford two houses."

"Two houses? We own seven houses," spat Orlando, beating the air with his muscular arms. "Since separatist politics began, we've been buying up good houses cheap. Anglophones have been leaving the province. If Quebec separates, then we lose our shirts. We gamble and pray that Quebec can't afford separation."

Ramona further explained that she and her brother owned and lived in this house while their other siblings lived and owned other homes. She also owned her own cleaning company, and her father and brothers worked in construction.

"You've done well since emigrating. Your family is an immigrant success story," said Grace.

"There'd be more success story like us if Immigration didn't keep deporting hard working people." Orlando shot Nick a dirty look.

You couldn't win. Grace got up and moved toward the door.

Nick graciously ignored the last remark. "I appreciate your time."

Sitting behind the steering wheel, Nick commented, "What a pair of characters. We were lucky not to meet the entire family."

"Come on, Nick. It wasn't that bad. Sure, they could've used an interior decorator. But I kinda liked Ramona."

The day was a scorcher. The air fanned out around them like heat from a pizza oven. Nick had the air conditioner going at full blast as they drove around downtown Montreal, looking for a parking spot and a place to eat.

"I know I shouldn't ask," said Grace, "but who is this tenant Li Mann?"

He gave her a quick look. Then, careful in what he revealed, he said, "I'll tell you what I can. I believe he pulled the trigger on Walter. Naturally, I want his head. Given the blank visas, birth certificates, and other documents we found at his house, I have reason to believe he's the mastermind behind some of the smuggling of illegals into this country."

"So you have two reasons why you're out to get him."

He didn't want to reveal any more. Instead, he turned the tables. "I've got a question for you, Grace. I was told that you're a member of the Asia Business Council. In fact, you use to sit on the board. Tell me about it."

"You could say it's a community association for Asian business leaders. Many of these businessmen have a hefty net worth. They tend to use the council as a lobby group, to go after government contracts. Just like any other lobby group. Some of them would like North America to take human rights off the table when discussing trade. Personally, I disagree with that. Why do you ask?"

"A name came up on our system. I have to run a check on him."

"Who's that?"

"Wa Sing. You know him?"

There was the tiniest of pauses before Grace said, "I know of him. Through my mother. They belong to the same benevolent association."

Nick wondered if her momentary hesitation meant anything. But why should it? She hadn't refused to answer, which she could have done if she wanted to. They both knew they couldn't tell each other everything about their work.

Days later, the full extent and meaning of what she said and didn't say would become clear to him. But for now, as he listened to the lovely sound of her voice describing her childhood in Vancouver, he was distracted from all suspicious thoughts.

Back at the hotel, they were a man and a woman secluded in the privacy of a room on the twenty-ninth floor. On the radio, some kind of marvellous Brazilian-African music played. The beat of the drums was like a drug. The singer's voice was like a spiritual cantata. He was lost to her as his hands touched the exquisite smoothness of her neck, the curve at the base of her throat, the perfection of her breasts. He loved her. Nothing else in the world mattered.

He entered her like a sweet dream. Lips, hands and bodies intertwined. He had never known sex like that. And if she left, he probably never would again.

chapter nineteen

After Nick dropped her home, she walked through the door to a fat cat who cursed her absence as he rubbed his flurry flanks against her legs. Eating dry food for two days straight was not to his liking. The first thing she did was to open a can of turkey dinner for her fat boy before releasing him onto the deck. At the sight of his feathered friends, his atavistic instincts were raring to go. Then she picked up her voicemail. Five calls. One from her mother wanting to complain about her children, no doubt. Grace sighed, no matter how hard you tried to accommodate your parents, it was never enough. Ellen called twice, wanting to do lunch on Tuesday. And two other callers who hadn't left messages.

Just as she was about to unpack, the phone rang. The call display on her bedroom phone said it was her mother. She didn't have the energy to return all the calls but she knew better than to ignore calls from her parents.

"Grace, your father and I have been trying to reach you."

"I know, Mom. I've been very busy with work."

She knew what was coming. Why be the first to bring it up?

"Yes, your father and I read about you in one of the Chinese dailies."

"You mean, you read about me and the Sun case, and you told Dad. We both know Dad can't read Cantonese."

Her mother ignored the correction.

"I had drinks with Wa Sing yesterday while he was waiting for a connecting flight to Taipei."

"I thought he said he was going to Singapore? Not Taiwan."

"Grace, don't change the subject."

Silence.

"I don't know this Sun person, but it seems he's a philanthropist in the community. Whatever his sins are, I agree with Wa Sing that you can't judge him as harshly as the rest of the country."

"Mom, please! You know I can't go into the merits of the case with people outside the Commission. Not even with my own family."

Long pause.

"Grace, I think it's best if you don't hear this case. As an elder in the Chinese community, I don't want to have to keep defending your actions. It isn't right to deport someone back to a place that could kill him. Particularly China. It may be just a job for you, but for other people, it's their life. If you order him deported, it could cause a lot of trouble for you. As your mother, I'm suggesting that it's not wise to judge your own. You understand, darling?"

Silence. No matter how old you are and how much distance you've put between yourself and your parents, they can still reduce you to a state of adolescent rebellion.

"Yes, mom, I understand. Unfortunately, it's not as simple as that. I can't turn the case down without incurring disciplinary action from the judicial committee. I have tried and have been warned."

"Then, Grace, you must choose who you want as your enemy. Better to choose the anger of your boss, who's only one man, than the wrath of a community."

"Mom, I hear you. I'll take that under consideration."

"Grace, don't give me that judge talk. Remember, I'm still your mother."

She held her annoyance in check and diverted the conversation. "How's everybody doing? Can I talk to Dad?"

"He's out. He's helping the Buddhists raise money for another temple. And volunteering at the hospital twice a week."

"I thought he was volunteering already in the Buddhist community?"

"He's doing that as well. Your father likes to keep busy. We're retired, so why not give back to the community?"

You sure drummed that into me as a kid, Grace thought. I must have been the only teenager who volunteered for four summers in a row as a candy-striper at the Vancouver General when all my other friends got paid summer jobs.

Instead she said, "Dad must be the only Jew who's also a Buddhist."

"No, apparently there are others like him."

"Really?"

"Yes, your father says there's a small Jewish Buddhist community somewhere in Nova Scotia. He wants to take the train out to the east coast next summer."

Long pause.

"If I'm not doing anything next summer, maybe I'll tag along."

"That would be nice. But, Grace, you should start thinking about finding a companion of your own. You're not getting any younger. Call Auntie Ming. In fact, she came for dinner last night and asked about you. I'll tell her to call you."

"Auntie Ming" was no blood relation. The two women had met volunteering at the Resettlement Program for Newcomers. They had discovered that they shared the same ancestral village in China. Since Auntie Ming was childless and twice widowed in China, Kim had brought her into the family fold. When Grace was a teenager, Auntie Ming had joined them for supper every Sunday evening. A few years later, her dad had read them a newspaper story about a Jewish marriage broker who was making a killing running a matchmaking business. The story inspired Auntie Ming to do the same thing.

"Mom, I don't need Auntie Ming's marriage broker services. We're not living in the old country. And I'm old enough to find someone for myself."

"I know you are. But Auntie Ming has a dentist she's trying to match up."

"Too bad and no thanks."

"He's second generation like yourself. Handsome and with money."

Mom, I like the man I'm sleeping with just fine, she wanted to say. She would tell her mother about Nick later, when they were further into their relationship. Right now, she couldn't handle the pressure of daily phone calls from her mother wanting a status report of every date and encounter.

"He's also a half-and-half."

"A half of what?"

"He's half Chinese and half Irish. Come to think of it, I see his mother regularly in Chinatown. Next time, I'll show her a picture of you."

"Mom, please! I'd appreciate if you didn't pass my photo around to every desperate mother and grand-mother in Chinatown."

"Okay, we'll do this in person. Come down for Thanksgiving."

"Fine, but I don't want to be matched up. Hear that, mom? I gotta go now. I've got another call hold-ing," she lied.

"You buy your ticket and we'll pick you up at the airport so you won't have to spend money on a cab."

Right after the Sun Sui case. Home for the holidays. Terrific!

Before the sun went down, she clipped a bouquet of blue rhododendrons from her front garden and stuck them in a vase of water for her dining room. Then she did two loads of laundry and cleaned her kitchen.

The rented sedan stopped a few hundred feet short of the house with the wraparound porch. Li Mann climbed out and stretched his legs. He had trailed the immigration officer from Toronto to Montreal, and then to Ottawa. Finding the girlfriend judge so easily was a bonus. His orders were to kill them both. The problem was the opportunity. He had had the opportunity in Montreal, inside the Notre Dame cathedral. Just as he was about to release the safety catch, a busload of tourists from Yonkers, New York had entered the church.

Now that he was standing across the street from her house, he noticed that she was already under surveil-lance. Interesting. He strolled down the street, past the white van, glancing at the two men inside. He had thought it would be easier to kill the judge first. Now there was a complication. But an interesting complication. Li Mann cracked his knuckles as he strolled around the block. By the time he got back to his car, he knew what he was going to do.

Back in Toronto, Nick reverted to hunter mode. He rented a car at the airport and drove straight to the office. The building was empty except for a lone security guard watching the Sunday football game on a portable television.

He was doing everything he could to oppose Sun's claim for refugee status. Sun's asylum hearing was a mere week away. Worse case scenario, if Sun won his claim, Nick would have one last kick at the can to have him prosecuted in criminal court, but given the backlog in the courts, it could be a hell of a long wait. Personally, he hoped it would not come to that. Deportation was much easier on the taxpayers' wallets. And he'd given way too much time on one case already when the stack of files kept growing on his filing cabinet.

He pulled out the Sun file and began to peck away. You would think after spending a weekend with the presiding judge he'd have an inkling of where the case was headed. But no. She could compartmentalize her life to the point of utter discretion. The perfect judge. That certainly didn't help his case any. What he needed was a coherent strategy that he or one of his officers could sell to her to help her deny Sun refugee status. But then again, with a well-paid lackey like Verster, Sun already had a foot in the door.

Nick spread the entire file folder across his desk. Good thing Judge Egan had consented to the confiscation of Sun's passport. He picked it up and studied it.

Couldn't get him on a forged document. It was an authentic Hong Kong passport. The seal and stamp over the photo were real. The date of issue was 1992. He then flipped through the middle and back pages, where the entry and exit stamps and visas were found. There were many. Reaching for a pad, he made a list of countries, broken down by time period.

In 1994, Sun's investor immigrant application had been approved by the embassy in Hong Kong. That would have been Keiler. Nick consulted the computer records: Keiler's visa officers had approved the applications and visas of 2,609 people that year.

Sun had travelled in a circuit from Hong Kong to Taipei, Jakarta, and Moscow and back to Hong Kong. Taipei and Jakarta Nick could understand. But what the hell was he doing in Moscow? Was there a Communist link in this? His itinerary was a good question to put to him in the hearing room. From the Russian border stamps, he noted that Sun had been in the country for a total of twenty-eight days in 1995. A long stay for a man travelling on business. Most businessmen are in such a time crunch, they're in and out without having seen anything of the country they're in. But what kind of business would have taken him to Moscow? People smuggling? Drug smuggling? Looking for sex workers?

He went back and forth on several of the pages, studying the dates and entry stamps. The border stamps told him that Sun left Hong Kong on February 12, 1994, but didn't arrive in Canada until April 4. He stopped in London for several days, and flew to Peru. Why? He stayed in Lima for almost two weeks, then it was Argentina and Chile, no more than three days in each locale. Afterwards, he flew to Panama.

He turned the pages. In 1995 and 1996, after he had received landed immigrant status, he flew back to Latin

America. Mexico, Argentina, Columbia and Panama
again. Once to Costa Rica and Venezuela. Why? The
only reason Nick could think of was that Sun was buying visas and passports from those countries. It was a
common enough practice among people smugglers.

Nick counted all the trips. Sun had even taken a trip
to the Congo. And had been back in China several times.
That information certainly affected his asylum claim. He
claimed he had trouble with the Chinese authorities, but
if that was the case, why go back to China? And five
times at that.

He set the passport down and took a breather, grabbing a pop from the machine in the basement cafeteria.
On his way back up to his office, he guzzled down half
the can and thought about Sun's passport. How much
time had Sun actually spent in Canada? Then, as the elevator rose slowly, with its usual ominous wheezes, it hit
him. Of course it would be in the fucking dates and
places! He ran back to his office, grabbed his notes and
did some quick mental arithmetic, then banged his fist
on the desktop in triumph. This might be a strategy to
defeat Sun's asylum claim. The evidence had been staring at him in the face all the time. According to the residency requirements of the Citizenship Act, an applicant
must have spent at least three years in Canada before
applying for citizenship in the fourth year. According to
Sun's passport, he had spent a mere total of 136 days in
the country during the three-year period. In his department, an appellant could be turned down for citizenship
on the ground that he had failed to meet the country's
residency requirement. But Sun had to apply in order to
be turned down. However, the evidence of his non-resi-
dence could affect his asylum claim, as a man seeking
Canada's protection. Nick's momentary elation was fad-
ing. But at this juncture, anything was worth a try.

He looked at his watch. It was Monday in Hong Kong. He dialled the embassy in Hong Kong and left a message for Jon Keiler.

"Jon, call me ASAP when you get in tomorrow. Need you to run a couple of checks. Also, got your package of docs, but where is the security certificate on Sun? Need to know what level of security checks you conducted on applicants fleeing the colony right up to the Communist handover. Reason I'm asking is, the applicant has more than a whiff of triad activity attached to his name. Does the Flying Dragons triad set off any alarm bells? What about people smuggling activities?"

He didn't want to accuse Keiler of not doing his job. But in the past twelve months, his officers had come across a large number of applicants who had been approved at overseas missions but had failed to pass security checks. And that raised one big fat question mark.

On his way out, he left instructions for Rocco to pull up entry and exit dates for the dead snakeheads, Gee Tung and Shaupan Chau. He was looking for a match or link to Sun's travel itinerary. It might help to prove membership in a criminal organization such as the Flying Dragons.

He called Kappolis before shutting off the lights. After bailing out of his office, he grabbed the eastbound subway for the Danforth, where the detective lived.

The Danforth was once home to a large enclave of Greek immigrants. Over the years it had changed to something resembling Yuppieville though the Crete Café was still a male hangout of retired Greek freedom fighters escaping their stay-at-home wives. The place was usually smoky and packed. But they always managed to find a table for Nick, thanks largely to his acquaintanceship with Kappolis's father, who now lived on memories and his veteran's pension.

Nick walked through the dining room to the pool hall at the back. Kappolis was already having a game with several regulars, who were knocking back ouzo and retsina. Nick joined in.

"Called you on the weekend. Where were ya?"

"In Montreal. Checking up on Li Mann's landlord."

The detective threw him a quizzical look. "Since when does the boss leave town for two days to do legwork?"

"I killed two birds with one stone. Had a date."

"Ahh. Now the truth comes out," the detective smiled knowingly. "With who?"

"Old girlfriend. Grace. Remember her?"

"Ahh, shit, man!"

Kappolis was not a fan of lawyers and judges, but now was the time to come clean.

"I'm seeing her again."

"Shit, Nick!" Kappolis said again, and pointed at the balls and the old geezers grinning at him across the pool table. "See what you made me do? You made me lose!" he tossed Nick a stick. "Play."

As he cued up the balls, Nick said, "You think I'm consorting with the enemy."

"What do you see in her? Apart from good sex."

The last thing Nick wanted was to choose between a woman and an old chum. Changing the subject, he said, "I went through Sun's file. We know he was born in China and he was never given British citizenship in Hong Kong. At least there's no record of it that I can find."

"I thought that Patten, when he was governor of Hong Kong, made British citizens of the crème de la crème of Hong Kong society. Maybe you can't find it because the government records are a mess. They're disorganized, chaotic, they lose information, misplace it, misfile it — you name it! It's the same all over. Down at Metro Division, we even lose things in the evidence room. Bulky computer equipment. Can ya believe it?"

Nick eyed his friend. "I'm not sure if he was made a British citizen or not. What I'm saying is, if Sun lost his asylum case and he had British citizenship, then we could either deport him back to Britain or Hong Kong. Right now, I have two files of Chinese criminals in Vancouver detention that China is refusing to accept. China says their jails are bursting with their own criminals. They don't need any more."

"You're in a fine fix, my friend."

"You know what?" said Nick, cueing up his balls. "I'll cross that bridge when I get to it. All I'm doing right now is building a case to make sure Sun loses his asylum claim."

"Attaboy, Nick! Now play."

chapter twenty

Grace had a late breakfast. The view from her kitchen windows was a dark, overcast sky. Remembering what Wa Sing had told her about Sun Sui, she dragged her feet in picking up the file. He was abusing the system, pulling out all the stops to keep from getting deported. That made her angry. She procrastinated as long as she could, cleaning her kitchen and doing laundry. Finally, she sat at the dining room table and began to read Sun Sui's narrative:

> I was born into a family of land-owners. In the 1950s all of my grandparents' land was confiscated by the Communists. In the 1960s, during the Cultural Revolution, my parents were accused of being Rightists, and were subsequently persecuted by the Communists. They were sentenced to life in a labour camp.
>
> In 1986, I enrolled in the engineering pro-

gram at Beijing University. There, I came to know another world. The world of democracy. To satisfy my curiosity, I joined the Beijing Universities' Student Movement. On June 4, 1989, I participated in the democracy demonstrations. I was arrested and held for several months and accused of sedition against the government. After my release, the Public Security Bureau regularly dropped by my house to harass and remind me that they were monitoring my democracy activities.

I wanted a son badly. In 1990, my wife became pregnant again. My son was born in December of that year. In January 1991, the PSB discovered that I had two children, and arrested me for violating China's one-child policy. I was found guilty and fined 100,000 yuan. On the day of sentencing, the court official said the state had just found out who my parents were. Given their political backgrounds, the state wanted to make an example out of me for my democracy activities and breaking the one-child law. Instead of being fined or doing time, I was to be executed for my crimes. I was then handcuffed and jailed.

A week later, in my incarceration, I was taken down to the jail administration office. Outside the office I was very surprised to see Captain Lei, the administration deputy. I knew him: our fathers were friends. He told me that the order for my execution had been signed. Captain Lei suggested to me that I should ask to have my execution take place in Ningxia instead of Beijing. I didn't ask why because I knew he was trying to help me. Besides, there were soldiers in the room. Captain Lei said that the transfer would have to be done by proper procedures and that this would cost me money.

Later that day I was escorted by a guard to an interview room with a telephone. Captain Lei told the guard to wait outside. The transfer to Ningxia had been arranged, but someone else would have to be involved and bought off. Lei arranged on the phone with my father to pay two million yuan for my prison transfer. That night, he came to my cell and told me that I would travel by bus, under armed guard, at the end of the week. He reminded me that I was facing execution. I took this to be his indirect way of telling me that if I tried anything en route I had nothing to lose, as I was going to die anyway.

The next day, Jiang and my children came to visit me. I told her about my execution and prison transfer. I explained to her that I would be travelling by bus to Ningxia. Since Jiang didn't know how to drive, I asked her to find a driver, preferably a total stranger who could accompany her on this trip. Together, they were to follow the bus.

Grace wondered, who exactly were his parents? What had they done? Or hadn't done? She poured herself another cup of coffee and wondered about the extent of the truthfulness of his narrative. This coincidence or stroke of luck in running into Captain Lei, was it plausible? And what exactly was the nature of the relationship between Captain Lei and his father? Two men who appear to be on the opposite ends of the politically correct spectrum. Under what circumstances had they met? And why would Captain Lei risk jail or execution to help a man facing execution?

The story didn't have the ring of truth. But that didn't surprise her. From her years on the bench, she knew that every claimant embellished his story. The truth and lies were woven together. Over the years, she had dealt with too many champion liars in the witness box.

She continued reading:

On the day of my transfer, I was accompanied by two armed Revolutionary Guards. I was handcuffed to one of them. As we left the prison, I saw Jiang standing next to a car with the driver she had hired.

On the way to Ningxia, I made a point of being well-behaved during the six and a half hour trip, I kept thinking, how was I going to overpower two armed guards and make a run for it? When we stopped at a roadside restaurant for dinner, I asked the guard I was handcuffed to if I could use the washroom. He accompanied me into the washroom and removed my handcuffs so I could use the stall. When I closed the door behind me, I immediately saw my escape route. Above the toilet tank was a broken window covered over with a piece of plastic. I tore the plastic, opened the window and climbed through it. Then I ran around the side of the restaurant. Jiang and the driver were parked at the far end of the parking lot. I raced towards them, climbed into the car, and we drove off.

I don't know whether the Revolutionary Guard purposely allowed me to escape or not. Possibly, Captain Lei had instructed these men to be lax in guarding me. Again, I don't know. Nor did I ask Jiang where she found the driver. However, he was astute enough to put the car in the opposite direction from Ningxia, using a different route than the one taken by the bus. We drove to a town called Xiam, approximately two and half hours away from the restaurant.

At Xiam, I asked Jiang to return to Beijing. She left me a bag containing money and clothes. I then asked the driver to go to Henan, where I hid in the house of my third cousin.

I learned through Jiang on the phone, shortly after her return to Beijing, that the Revolutionary Guards and the District Public Security were making numerous visits to my parents' house to interrogate them about my escape. Later they arrested my father at his workplace. However, they couldn't break him because he had no idea where I was hiding. Only Jiang knew, but for some reason, she was never questioned about my escape. Maybe the PSB took pity on her as a single mother with two children. I knew she kept a very low profile, rarely going out, spending most of her time in the home of her parents, and looking after our children. A year later she moved to Fujian and stayed in her brother's house.

I lived in Henan without incident for several months. The driver who had assisted my escape stayed with me in Henan. It was he who found a fisherman who took us to Hong Kong in his boat.

Grace snorted as she put the file down. Was his claim of persecution pure fabrication? Or was he a master of weaving the truth with the lies? Too many thorny questions were raised. Like how had Sun's family gotten their hands on two million yuan so quickly? Then there was the relationship with the driver who assisted in his escape. What happened to him? Why had he jeopardized his safety to help a complete stranger? And how had Jiang found him? Want ads? Word of mouth? Sun said his wife was never questioned or targeted by the PSB, though his aging parents were. In the hearing room, she would have to tear it apart, lie by lie. As for the dozen or so affidavits attesting to Sun's moral character and sharp business acumen, that was pure bullshit, in her opinion.

She didn't want to burn up any more energy thinking about his case. After all, the burden of proof rested squarely on his doorstep. Sun would have to support his narrative with documentary or other proof. Grace stared at the bankers' boxes sitting on her dining room floor. Sun's hearing was one huge paper chase: affidavits, letters, financial statements, government documents from Nick's office, police reports and court records of his deportation hearing. The total ran over 15,000 pages.

If his entire claim was fraudulent, then this was his strategy. He was burying them in paper.

Enough of that nonsense.

She slipped into her running shoes and went for a three-kilometre run. On her return, she showered and made a jug of sangria to quench her thirst. Through her kitchen windows, the sky was clearing, and the sun was filtering through the leaves in brilliant shafts of light. Glass in hand, she sat down on the deck and began to read from where she left off.

An hour later, she couldn't take it anymore. She stood up and stretched her legs. "Where does the truth end and the lies begin?" she screamed.

Assuming that the story of political persecution was true, then he fled China like a common criminal, arrived in Hong Kong with nothing but the shirt on his back, but somehow he managed to start a nightclub. Where the hell did he get the money to do that? Did he borrow it? Did he obtain it through criminal activities? Or was he merely in the right place at the right time? And if he made his money honestly as all those affidavits seem to attest, then the puzzle was, why would he throw it all away by becoming involved in the Flying Dragons triad and people smuggling activities? Good questions to put to him in his hearing.

Pouring another glass of sangria, she composed her thoughts. Even if she were to give him the benefit of the doubt, the claimant's background wasn't all that dissimilar from her mother's. Surely he would share some of her mother's cultural neuroses. One's good name should never be tarnished. Reputation was all-important. When you had millions, why take the risk of chasing after a few more million through crime? Simple greed? She shook her head. His narrative was pure fiction. Like one of his movie scripts. Maybe it was a movie script he had adapted for his refugee claim.

Still, she had no choice but to go through the charade of hearing his claim. Sitting in her dining room, she switched on her laptop and created a file, then spent the next hour banging out notes to herself and all the questions from his claim that jumped out at her. When the battery died, she called it quits and grabbed a late lunch of Digby smoke herring and crackers.

Wanting to finish the job, she drove into work. It was ten to three. She noted that her secretary had already left for the day. In fact, half the office was empty. So much for manning the borders. Sitting at her desk, she logged on and tapped into several databases where she cross-referenced historic dates and places with Sun's narrative. As she reviewed some of the documentary evidence, she had to admit that some of it paralleled the history of her own family. In the early 1940s, her mother's relatives had known that their country was going to fall into the hands of the Communists. Her great-uncles and aunts had even bought air tickets out of the country. At the last minute, her grandfather had cashed in his plane ticket and decided to stay. According to her mother, her grandfather's reasoning had been, they had survived Nanking and the evils of the Japanese occupation. How could his own people, even if they were Communists, be worse than the Japs? But when the Communists marched in, he was immediately arrested, along with his wife, his daughter, Kim, and scores of relatives. They were all sentenced to life in labour camps.

And if my mother hadn't escaped, Grace thought, where would I be today?

In search of a snack, she headed down to the lunchroom, where she brewed a cup of coffee and helped herself to some stale chocolate chip cookies. Back at her desk with a cookie in her mouth, she tried to pull up the file on Sun Sui she had just created.

"Whaat? I don't get it?"

The file was gone. Her coffee got cold as she tried to locate it. Frustration and hope washed over her in waves. Welcome to the wonderful world of computing! No wonder people hated computers.

She dialled up the systems operator who — lucky for her — was located in another building. A great face-saving device. She was angry with herself for being computer stupid. Things like this — revealed to her that she wasn't as smart as she thought she was.

"I've got a problem. With this new legal software. Again," she paused. "I just created a file, saved it, got out of the menu for half an hour. Now I'm back in but I can't find the file. It's disappeared."

"Didn't you call me last week with computer problems? The software is new, maybe you need to sign up for a course to learn it. Because files don't disappear. Gimme the information and I'll locate it."

"Well, the old software was much easier to use. Frankly, I hate the new software."

"A lot of users are saying the same thing, lady," said the tech support operator. He worked with her for several minutes until he found it.

"Thanks." She saw that the file had been saved twice. She checked the time. The second save had been when she was making coffee. That was strange. Was it her own techno-stupidity? Or had someone sneaked into her office while she was in the lunchroom?

On the way out she mentioned it to one of the few clerical staff sitting in the bullpen area outside her door.

"No, Grace. No one went into your office."

"Hmmm. Okay. See you tomorrow."

Weird. She hated technology. What she really hated was how absolutely stupid she felt over her inability to keep up with the wired world.

A large brown envelope with the RCMP logo in the left-hand corner was sitting on top of the heap of papers on Nick's desk. Ignoring it, he picked up a file that one of his officers had flagged for his attention. He didn't have to look at the date to know that it was an old outstanding file. The reports inside looked like they'd been archived to death. Dog-eared, torn, and coffee-stained. Tilting back his chair, he was just about to start making case notes when the phone rang.

"Got the envelope I couriered to you?" It was Dubois.

"If you're referring to this big brown manilla thing, it's sitting right here. I'll get to it later in the day."

"Open it now, Nick. Take a good look at it." It was an order.

Holding the phone between his ear and his shoulder, Nick sliced open the envelope and quickly flipped through the photographs. He suffered a quiet shock when he realized who the female subject was. Grace. Sitting at some kind of outdoor café table talking intensely to the other person, an old Chinese man. Then standing in a parking lot with the same man. There were twenty-four pictures, some in sharp focus, some blurred and off-centre. Two had been blown up. All were in colour and some been taken with a tele-scopic lens. He had seen the old man's face before, but where? Dubois's voice in his ear answered the ques-tion for him. "His name is Wa Sing. You asked me to ring a check so I assigned one of my rookies. You said you're seeing her again. She ever mention that she knows him?"

Nick didn't answer. Grace's words came back to him: *I know of him.*

"Nick, this is what you get for consorting with the enemy."

Dubois's words hammered into his consciousness. He willed himself to listen.

"This case has political written all over it. It's not your usual agent smuggling case of illegals. This one's about money and power. Not poverty and desperation." Dubois's voice was hard and unforgiving. "We may live in a democracy but it's the power of a buck that makes society go around. Let's not kid ourselves. We know those with money also have influence and power. And right now I smell bullshit and coverup!"

"Coverup?"

"Yeah. This Wa Sing character has been subpoenaed to testify at the inquiry into illegal political payoffs and under-the-table campaign contributions. That scandal's spreading like an oil slick. The guy's a hair's-breadth from being arrested and indicted on influence-peddling charges, and guess what? He flies the coop three hours before our cops show up at his door. The question is, pal, who warned him?"

He was following Dubois's drift a little too well. And he was going to be sick to his stomach.

"One of the things we're gonna check out is, whose campaigns was he bankrolling? You can bet your ass the opposition wants to know that too! Ask yourself, Nick, how do people get political appointments to the bench? I don't know of any average Joe or Josephine getting any kind of appointment to any kind of bench. Hell, the average Joe can't even get his city councillor to return his phone calls."

Dubois's voice cut right through him.

"Look hard at the photos, Nick. What the fuck do you know really about this broad?"

Good question. Well, for starters she was great in bed. And she was the only woman he had ever come across who was good with a chainsaw. She was a bit of a butch-femme and he found that sexy. One time she had been mugged in broad daylight by two skinhead punks. Not only had she refused to give up her handbag after they had torn her clothes and knocked her to the ground, but she had gone after them in an unrelenting chase, even pinning down one of them until the cops arrived. Then she appeared in court as a witness and buried them with her testimony. He had watched her on television, standing on the steps of the courthouse, playing the part of the helpless little woman. Talk about going for the jugular.

"Face the facts. She's fucking you both ways, pal! Have you ever asked her just who the hell her political backers were? Ask her for her entire goddamn list of supporters!"

No, he had never asked her that question. He had never even thought of it. Why? Because his dick got in the way, that's why. What an asshole he was. He didn't think he was one of those guys who couldn't keep it in his pants, but he would have one hell of a time explaining that he wasn't if his entire case went down.

His eyes were watering. He could feel his knees buckle as he fell back into a chair. Thank God he was in the privacy of his office.

Dubois's voice whined on like a buzzsaw cutting through him. "I want you and me to ask ourselves this question: of the two hundred adjudicators on the bench who could hear this case, how come it gets assigned to her? I think the decision is already cooked, Nick. I think it's already going positive, before one piece of evidence is heard. The fix is already in."

chapter twenty-one

A difficult day on the bench. Several times she almost lost her professional composure, it was a relief to adjourn the case. To add to her troubles, she couldn't reach Nick. Just wanting to hear his voice, she had left three messages on his home answering machine and called him at work four times. For some reason, she couldn't get past his secretary. What was going on? Was this his way of dumping her?

Maybe she was going crazy, but on three occasions she'd noticed an Asian man with a pockmarked face. He was standing right behind her in the coffee-shop this morning, as she grabbed a café latte to go. Was he following her or was it just her imagination working overtime? Maybe she was losing it. Too much stress. The Sun Sui case on top of a full docket of cases. Seventeen decisions to write, and dreadfully late on five of them. A new legal software package she had yet to master. A boss she didn't like or trust. A man she adored but who

was no longer speaking to her. Too many white vans
everywhere. And a dead colleague whose killer was still
at large. The last thing she wanted, at the end of the day,
was her own company.

She navigated the Volvo through downtown traffic.
God, she hated this stretch of Bank Street, bumper to
bumper from the Hill all the way south to Sunnyside.
But she had only herself to blame for the fact that Ellen
lived in the Glebe. She had helped her friend find the
duplex one Saturday afternoon, driving around the
Glebe's ten-mile radius of book stores, boutiques, outdoor cafés and renovated brick mansions. Taking a
wrong turn, they had cruised down Fifth Avenue and
had found themselves lost on a quiet cul-de-sac. The
previous tenant was in the midst of hammering an
Apartment for Rent sign on the lawn as they drove by.
Ellen had just been complaining that she needed a bigger place, so they circled the block and stopped. Ellen
had immediately fallen in love with the place. Grace suspected its charms had little to do with the size and layout of the rooms and more to do with the fact that the
previous tenant was a disciple of Martha Stewart.

The only thing the two of them differed on was
their politics. Ellen was one of those feminists who in
Grace's opinion had fallen victim to a rigid feminist
ideology. Grace did not see herself as a feminist. She
liked to think that she did not suffer the sins of ideology. Rather, she preferred to look at the issues on a
case-by-case basis. Ellen, however, had paid the price
for her ideology as a feminist who believed that marriage and childbearing were the enemy of women's liberation. She had lost out on the man she loved over the
issue of children. Now, at forty-seven, she was haunt-
ed by her lost chance at motherhood. In the end, she
became a victim of biology. Then last year, her body

had further turned against her when she discovered that she had breast cancer. It was this disease that had cemented the bond between two women from different worlds. She had been there at the hospital when Ellen had gone in for surgery to remove the lump in her breast. When Grace's marriage had collapsed, Ellen had been there for her.

She parked in front of the building, a renovated three-storey Victorian house. Celtic music wafted through open windows, Ellen's or maybe the tenant above. The planters she helped Ellen haul up two flights of stairs were now full of black-eyed susans, petunias and begonias from the farmers' market. She rang the bell and was buzzed in. Grace double-locked the front door behind her. Picasso prints lined the stairs going up to Ellen's flat.

"Thanks for the dinner invitation. I was getting tired of my own cooking. And ordering in Chinese. And hanging out with myself."

"Sounds like my life," said Ellen. She had taken two chilled wineglasses out of the fridge and was opening the bottle of South African white that Grace had brought.

After thirstily knocking back half a glass, Grace turned her attention to the food. "Mmmm. Yum, yum." She salivated at the pesto pasta chicken salad, and an earthenware dish of appetizers filled with potatoes, garbanzo beans, chorizo, and eggplant. She helped herself to a piece of chorizo and a leaf of radiccio from the wooden salad bowl.

"Guess what I heard from one of the justices? You know the illegal campaign contribution scandal that's been brewing?"

Grace stopped eating and gave her undivided attention to her friend. "What've you heard?"

"A man named Wa Sing was at the top of the witness list. You know him, don't you? Not too well, I hope. He apparently contributed heavily to the government winning in the last election. There are even rumours that he was just a front man for some of that money, that it came from an unknown source."

Her heart skipped a beat. In a small voice, she asked, "Where did you hear that?"

"I'm dating this guy who works as a researcher for the opposition. Adam says that several of those big contributors are under surveillance." Ellen popped a morsel in her mouth.

"Surveillance?" If Wa Sing had been under surveillance prior to leaving the country, did that mean that she was caught in the net as well? Could the white van be an unmarked police van? Nick had asked her about Wa Sing. Was that a test question? Did he know that she had lied to him about not knowing him? If it was a test, she had failed. Grace lost her appetite.

Ellen sampled her own appetizers. Picking up a square of bruschetta, she said, "I heard Jean Cadeux on a radio interview this week. He announced that you're presiding on the refugee case of that nightclub owner."

Grateful to change the subject, Grace said, "Yeah, I was forced to take that case. He leaned on me. Almost threatened me."

"Threatened? Can he do that?"

"Well, he did."

"Too bad. I wouldn't take the case. Too controversial. The public has swung way to the right. Some of them have a lynch-mob mentality."

"Don't I know it," said Grace, pouring herself another glass of wine. "If I grant, they'll say I'm biased, too left wing. And if I say no, the Asian community will be royally ticked with me. I'll be made into a modern-day version of Uncle Tom," said Grace, eyeing the dish of chicken salad.

"Damned if you do, and damned if you don't. Great for your career, Grace, but don't expect to win a lot of friends."

"I love this Middle Eastern stuff," said Grace, pointing at the eggplant dish. "What's it called?"

"Babaghanoush. I made too much of it, so you're going to have to eat lots of it," ordered Ellen, setting out plates and utensils. "I've been reading cookbooks lately."

"Beats reading case files."

"Speaking of case files, yesterday we heard the appeal of a sex crime case. Tomorrow is the appeal case of that neo-Nazi group charged with defacing Jewish tombstones. Both highly controversial. Already the press are hounding us, wanting to know our verdict. I saw a clip of myself on the news. Grace, I looked really fat!"

"I know what you mean," Grace nodded sympathetically. "The camera can be very unkind. There's nothing worse than coming home after a long day, wanting to veg on the couch with the remote, and seeing nothing but yourself on television, with a mug shot of the claimant in the upper right hand corner. God, I'm looking forward to the end of this case and it hasn't even begun."

"Are you ready for the big day?"

"No, I'm not. I'm very nervous. Ellen ..." said Grace, looking at her friend. "I had contact with the claimant. I was introduced to him at a dinner party. It was just the one occasion, and we talked about nothing, just made chitchat. Last thing I need is to be accused of positive bias. That is, if by some weird stroke of fate I go positive on the case."

"One meeting?"

Grace nodded.

"You're making a big deal out of nothing. I wouldn't worry about it," said Ellen as she poured the rest of the marinade on the pork-chops and brushed the kebabs of zucchini and eggplant with olive oil.

Grace reached for a piece of chorizio.

Ellen continued, "If I were you I'd spend more time worrying about my appearance. You know. Hair, mascara. And use some eyeshadow, too."

"Ellen, that sounds so — not serious. So frivolous."

"After seeing myself on television, I'm giving you the best advice. Do you want to look like a dog on national television? Coast to coast?"

"I hear you. I was thinking more about the Judge Ito factor."

"What does O.J. Simpson have to do with your case?"

"I watched the O.J. trial and I couldn't help thinking about poor Judge Ito. Sitting through nine hours of testimony in appropriate judicial repose, day in, day out. Can't even run your fingers through your hair or slouch in your chair while hearing evidence. I don't need that kind of scrutiny. The jury's already out on the kind of decision I'm going to render. I don't need to be judged on my looks and my judicial demeanour as well."

"I've never thought of it from that perspective," said Ellen, handing her an I Luv New York booklet. "Want to go to New York next weekend? Take your mind off work, and all your worries."

"Speaking of worries," said Grace. "Did you find anything out about that licence number I gave you?" She had managed to jot down the plate number of the white van she kept seeing, and had passed it to Ellen.

"Right," her friend said. "The creepo in the white van. My cop friend says it's not in the system. It could be a phony plate or it could belong to an undercover cop. But, Grace, I really wouldn't worry about it. There're too many cars on the road with phony plates, and too many drivers with no car insurance, not to mention a gazillion white vans in this country."

"You're probably right, but I can't shake the feeling that I'm being followed," said Grace.

"Grace, that's not a good feeling to have. You've been working flat out for the past year. When did you take holidays last?"

Grace threw up her hands. "I don't remember. Whose got time for holidays?"

"We're taking holidays. We're going to drive down to New York. Hit Bloomingdale's. Take in a few plays and art galleries. I hear there's a great play on Broadway."

"Ellen, have you read the business pages? Our Canadian peso is worth sixty-seven American cents. We can't go anywhere south at those prices. Remember the last time we went down to New York for the weekend? We spent three thousand apiece. And don't forget that's in U.S. dollars!"

"But didn't we have fun? Didn't we get some fantastic clothes? Live for today. Stop penny-pinching for your tomorrows."

Grace sighed. "Maybe. After the case is over. End of September."

"Don't let me down. I'll call the travel agent tomorrow and book tickets."

So much for vacationing with Nick. Despite being a liberated woman, Grace wanted him to do the asking. What had happened to them? She hadn't heard from him since their weekend in Montreal. "I'll light the barbecue," she said, carrying a tray of wine and glasses out onto the porch.

Ellen followed, carrying plates of marinated chops and vegetable kebabs.

After refilling their wine glasses, they swung back and forth on the loveseat glider, watching the street life below. Pigeons cooed from the rooftops of houses. Kids played hopscotch on the sidewalk. A gang of teenage boys wearing oversized jeans whipped down the street on skateboards. Lovers embraced on park benches a block away.

Halfway through dinner, Grace asked, "Have you heard anything from your cop contacts about the investigation into Crosby's death?"

"I meant to tell you, Grace. It's cold. It was a working day, and there were no witnesses. The cops have got nothing. Just one more unsolved murder this year in the nation's capital. But one detective thinks it's the work of a right-wing group."

"A right-wing killer? Killing over ideology?"

"Don't underestimate ideology, Grace. I see it every day at work. Why do you think lawyers judge-shop? They know which judges tend to take a hard line, and which ones have more liberal sympathies, like yourself. Naturally they try to manipulate the system to get the decisions they want."

"I see it too. And I abhor selective justice. But there's not much I can do about it," said Grace. She ruminated on Ellen's words and she shifted her weight in her chair, to better accommodate the plate on her lap. "Maybe you're right. It's just hard for me to grasp the taking of a life over an issue of ideology."

"It happens. You and I have always tried to interpret the law in a spirit of humanity, even generosity, but a lot of people out there no longer agree with us. They don't trust us. This country isn't the nice, kind, sleepy place it was when we were growing up. Your ex-boyfriend, on the other hand, I bet right-wing coalitions just love him. They see him as some big white defender. Keeping the barbarians at the gate. I've met him. He appeared at the federal court on a case to deport an accused Nazi. He's very open-minded. Not a racist at all. But there're groups out there that think he is, because they themselves are. People see what they want to see."

BJ and Harry watched as the Volvo took the last parking space on the street.

They rolled by slowly. BJ could see the two broads out on the porch, chatting and drinking wine. Something was cooking. The smell made him hungry. He knew she'd be there for several hours. He knew broads. When they started talking, it'd be an all-nighter.

They had almost decided to let her live, until they read in the newspapers about the refugee case she was hearing. It was about some nightclub owner who was implicated in three murders. One of the victims was an immigration officer killed in the line of duty. A white guy. To make matters worse, Harry had cruised the internet, and found that there was a list of left-wing lawyers and judges. Just like the list of abortion doctors. Yep, on the Net, there was a two-pager on the Hamas terrorist case she had tried. A member of Hamas had been involved in a terrorist bombing in Israel. Hamas did plenty of killings like that. Harry told BJ about what he read: how she had granted the terrorist asylum. He didn't quite understand all the legal gobblegook or her arguments about there being a fine line between a terrorist and a freedom fighter. All he needed to understand was, some foreign terrorist was now a citizen of his country, enjoying the perks of that status when his wife and daughter were dead. Harry hated her and that was enough for BJ.

He was pleased with Harry's decision. He hated left-wingers and the middle class. He wanted to kill the broad right now and move on. He had seen enough of her house and that fat furball. He leaned back in the front passenger seat, getting comfortable as he cleaned his .44 Smith & Wesson.

A little after eleven, she and Ellen said goodbye. Traffic on Bank Street was busy. It took forever to get onto the 417 and get out of the city core. As she finally got on the off-ramp for the Island Parkway that would take her home, she nearly ploughed into a slow-moving, 10-tonne tractor-trailer hauling its produce. On a two-lane, dark highway, there was really no safe way to make a pass. She had no choice but to put up with driving at a snail's pace. As she dropped her speed to fall two car lengths behind the rig, the blast of a horn behind her drew her attention to the irate driver on her bumper.

Damn it! Tailgating wasn't going to get him to his destination any quicker. Through her outside mirror, she saw his flashing lights. Okay, the idiot was signalling to her that he was going to pass. Good luck, Bozo, driving into the path of oncoming traffic.

As she watched him pull out and begin to pass, the car swerved right into her lane, until it blocked her path forward. Lucky for her, her foot immediately hit the brakes.

The driver stepped out of his car and walked towards her. Window down, she yelled at him. "What the hell's going on?"

She didn't have a chance.

"Get out of the car!" The man raised a gun at her.

I'm dead, she thought. Dead.

"Get out now!"

Reluctantly she climbed out of the security of her car. Pitch blackness whirled around her as her brain tried to process what was happening. A car jacking by an Asian thug?

"Here're the keys to my car. Take it!"

"I don't want your car."

"If this is a robbery, I'm cooperating. Take my purse." Grace held out her bag to her assailant. She got a good look at his face in the moonlight. There was something familiar about it. But what? For a brief second, she shifted her gaze and looked around her in the darkness. There was nowhere to go. Nowhere to run.

"What do you want?"

"I have to kill you."

"What do you mean, you have to kill me? What the hell have I done to you?"

"Move off the road ... over there."

Her vision was sharp and her heart kicked in strong. The last thing she wanted to do was to walk willingly into the woods to lie down and die.

As he came toward her, he reached into his pocket and came up with what looked like a large barrel of a suppressor.

Okay, what next?

Just as he finished tightening the suppressor to his gun, they both heard and saw the sound of a vehicle approaching.

Help was on the way.

She turned her head sideways and saw that it was a van — a white van! Maybe, as Ellen said, it was an undercover vehicle on surveillance duty. She waved an arm as the van approached. Two men climbed out. Undercover cops?

Almost casually, her assailant turned his hand and raised his gun at the man approaching closest to him. She heard a popping noise, and saw the man blew backward against the van. The sight of a man being killed in cold blood sent a shiver of fear and nausea through her. What followed next was an exchange of gunfire, several shots in rapid succession.

She ran.

Her legs pumped in rhythm with her lungs. She heard more shots, but she didn't feel them hitting her body. She wished she had worn her running shoes, wished she could trade her Birkenstocks for a pair of wings.

Running forward into the darkness, she fell. She fell through the air for what seemed like an eternity. And then without warning, her body dropped down the embankment and slammed against shrubbery. Instinctively she spread her arms backward to catch her fall.

Ten feet above her, on the Parkway, she heard more shots fired. Footsteps running. She sucked in her breath.

Be still. Don't let him find you.

Seconds later, she heard the sound of an engine backfiring before tearing into the night. Then the sound of the second vehicle speeding away.

With a gasp and a moan she rolled herself onto the ground. Pain shot through her body. She felt herself for the telltale wound and the wetness of blood. No bleeding but she couldn't stand. She must have twisted her left ankle as she fell. Crouched on the ground, she fumbled into her bag for her cellphone, and dialled 911.

The important thing was not to get hysterical. Calmly, she explained to the 911 operator what had happened and her location. About fifteen minutes later, a police cruiser spotted her car on the side of the road.

"I'm down here!" she yelled.

It was only when the officer helped her into her car that she realized there was a dead body lying on the gravel by her back passenger door. The officers asked her about the dead man. She could barely understand what had happened to her, let alone explain it to the authorities. The cops found no weapon at the scene of the crime. And certainly found no weapon in her car. Her story of a carjacking by an Asian thug was met with a healthy amount of scepticism. After all she still had her car. She couldn't understand it herself. But then, she was just happy to be alive.

By the time she was released from the police station and the hospital, she hobbled into her house and crashed into her bed. Despite her physical exhaustion, she had insomnia and lay wide awake staring at the ceiling. Her mind churned with the thoughts and images of the past few hours. Just as her eyes got heavy, she remembered why her Asian assailant had seemed familiar. It was the face in the police sketch of the man who was wanted in the death of that immigration officer. Why was he targeting her? What about the white van? Were they targeting her too? Nothing made sense. The world had gone mad.

After tossing and turning, she finally fell into a restless sleep.

chapter twenty-two

She dreamed. The exhilaration of speed and freedom filled her soul. She flew past undulating forests, over mountains a billion years old. As she flew north in a land of shifting tectonic plates, she could see the trees diminish in size and height until, finally, she saw open tundra stretched beneath her. Once upon a time prehistoric bison hunters had travelled here. Herds of caribou came thundering down endlessly each winter.

Look! Over there! Bogs and black-water ponds. Now she was flying over pre-Cambrian rock. She marvelled at the way the granite peaks ran from lake to sky. Here in the big, clean rivers, the pike, pickerel and trout swam in abundance. And the water was so clean you could drink it straight from the stream.

Now it was a warm summer night, and she was lying on her back on a carpet of reindeer moss, watching the northern lights, and the night sky filled with galaxies of stars. In the quiet of this northern landscape she could hear the earth breathe. Yes, in this beautiful, raw, exquisite place, she was home. Lord, let me stay like this forever.

Then the phone rang. Damn! She opened one eye and squinted at the clock. Past nine in the morning.

It was the RCMP calling, bringing back last night's terror to her. "Ma'am, we identified the body. His fingerprints belong to a Harry Kitchin. Heard of him, ma'am?"

"No, never. Do you know why he was stalking me?"

"Ma'am, I'm getting to that. We have reason to believe that he killed your colleague Mark Crosby."

"Oh, my God."

"It seems that Crosby overturned a deportation order on a man who later killed Harry Kitchin's wife and child in a highway accident. The drunk driver got off on a technicality. After that, Kitchin went to his house and killed the man. Kitchin was tried and sentenced to nine years at the Kingston Penitentiary. But he got out early on good behaviour."

"I see." Her mind churned with images of the previous night. "What about the other man who was with this Harry Kitchin? Both of them were stalking me. Do you think they were trying to kill me? Why?"

"Ma'am, at this point in the investigation we don't have all the answers. We still don't have a clear description of Kitchin's assistant. However, we'll comb prison records and talk to the warden. Don't panic in the meantime. My hunch is, Harry Kitchin's companion has taken off across the border. Put distance between himself and Ottawa. If we come up with anything, we'll call you immediately."

Long after the call had ended, she cradled the phone to her ear. So many emotions raced through her. The wretched incompetence of the criminal justice system had convinced this Harry Kitchin that it was his duty to mete out justice to the killer of his wife and children. In prison, he grew harder, angrier, and more dangerous. Crosby's death had been a revenge killing by a man whose life had been ruined — and by what? By the court's inability to prosecute.

She sat at the edge of the bed and reached for the knife under one of her pillows. She had double-locked her doors and windows last night, and gone to bed with the phone and a knife beside her. Now it was daylight and these precautions seemed a little silly, but.... Maybe she was overreacting. The man who had been stalking her was dead. Sure he had brought someone else with him, but that man had no motive to continue tormenting her. Or did he?

She hit the shower and then slowly got dressed, rubbing ointment on her bruises and scratches. Then she wrapped her ankle in a tensor. Hobbling downstairs, she looked out across the street for her Asian assailant and Harry Kitchin's companion, even though she thought it unlikely they would show up in broad daylight.

As she made herself a breakfast of toast and eggs, she thought about Kitchin's companion and wondered how much of a threat he was? She could see how Mark Crosby and Harry Kitchin had had a relationship of sorts, but there was no relationship of any kind between her and Kitchin's companion. On the other hand, Li Mann had wanted to kill her. Why? What had she ever done to him?

Was last night's incident connected to the Sun case? Hold that thought. If so, was it because Sun didn't want her to hear his case? Why? Because he was afraid that she would see through his fraudulent claim and decline his asylum application. If so, then she should figure out a way to weasel out of hearing his case.

Wait a minute. Why should she let him and his goons terrorize her like that? To do so, would mean that he would've won. Fuck him! After all, she had survived last night's terror. And she wasn't the only survivor.

The world was full of survivors. People who had lived through hellish experiences, tragic losses, and dislocations. One only had to look at the taxi drivers in the city; they were all from somewhere else. The Pakistani who had journeyed through villages and evaded corrupt policemen, only to board a cargo ship for a month-long voyage across oceans and continents, who now worked fifteen or eighteen hours a day driving a cab in order to put food on the table for his family back home in some dusty village. Or the immigrant women she saw in Montreal, who worked in sweatshops, turning out clothes as fast as they could, because the more they sewed the better their miserable pay would be. The only difference she could see among such survivors was that some were changed for the better, and some for the worse.

She poured the last of the coffee into her mug and reflected on Wa Sing. Even he had survived terrible experiences, though you would never know it by his serene, expensively dressed exterior. Her mind turned to Sun Sui again. He was a survivor in a different way. Her mother had often said everyone in China had suffered some kind of persecution under the Communists. If you missed out on being persecuted by the government, just wait a few years she'd said; governments change hands. But those with money always find ways to accommodate the new political reality, Grace thought; particularly today, when money can buy almost anything. She saw it every day at work: the moneyed class everywhere simply left and bought citizenship in other countries. These people weren't the only ones who had one foot at home and one abroad. Even her parents were a good example of that. Making the pilgrimage back to China and Israel every few years. Others wanted nothing to do with their past. To them it was the source of all of their troubles. Some went to great lengths to change their national and ethnic identities. Or converted to a different religion. But no one could shake their past. Worse, sometimes their past caught up with them.

Nick hated the thought of being bested by some Chinese gnome. Dubois's words were still fresh in his mind as he yelled to Rocco, sitting outside his office.

"Drop whatever you're doing. He's left the country. I want to know when, where, and how. When you've located him, call me. We need to have plans in place to arrest him."

"We have an immigration warrant out for his arrest," said Rocco, taking a seat next to another enforcement officer on the lumpy sofa.

"We also have one on Li Mann. And look where it's gotten us. Nowhere. I want you to put together a team and check every airport and every passenger manifest on every airline for a Wa Sing," ordered Nick.

A couple of hours later, a call was patched to Nick that Wa Sing had already boarded a Cathay Pacific flight from Vancouver to Taipei.

"How the hell did he slip through our fingers?" Nick straddled a chair and crossed his arms over the back.

Two enforcement officers stared back at him. One of them said, "God only knows. Maybe he's travelling on a false passport."

"Rocco, call our embassy in Taiwan. Fax a photo of the old man. Let's hope we can catch up with him when he lands in Taipei."

Somewhere down the hall, someone was smoking. Nick could see a thin cloud of blue fog hanging over the lighting fixture. He was fine with that as long as it wasn't in his office. His irritability about the cigarette smoke threw off his concentration, and allowed the other torment that was gnawing at him to flood into his mind again. Grace. The smell of her hair and the feel of her skin. No, he would not think about that now. She had lied to him about Wa Sing. Now the old man had slipped through their fingers. Walter was dead. Loong and Gee Tung's name were added to the homicide list, and still the killer or killers of these men were at large. Sun's refugee hearing opened in two days. If Sun won, Nick didn't know what he would do.

His frustration mounted. He paced the office. Finally, he decided to make productive use of his waiting time. He concentrated on the stack of reports and files sitting on the side credenza. Now was as good a time as any to comb through them. Every month he made an effort to go through enough of a sample to give him a general picture of the arrests, detentions and removals of non-citizens across the country. As he read, he made notes on his desktop computer.

Several hours into his files, the phone rang.

"Our guy never got off the plane in Taipei," said Dubois.

"How many stopovers before Taipei?"

"Two. Vancouver to Singapore. And another stopover in Manilla."

"He could've gotten off either in Singapore or the Philippines. Son of a gun. I'll leave it to you to alert the RCMP officers there."

"All righty," replied Dubois. "I'll see you in two hours."

"Where're you now?"

"Airport. I'm handing the attendant my boarding pass as we speak. Meet you at that Irish pub down the street from your office in two hours. I'm counting on huge rush-hour traffic on the 401."

Nick continued chipping away at the files in his office.

Dubois was sitting at the bar, nursing a double on the rocks, when Nick walked in.

"Sorry I'm late," he said, and ordered a Molson Dry.

Dubois was inspecting him, critically. "You look bloody tired."

Nick didn't deny it. He shrugged.

"You're working too hard, Nick. You're starting to put on a little weight there, buddy boy. If you don't take care of yourself, you'll start looking like me." Dubois grabbed his love handles. "Me, I've been trying to lose forty pounds for the past ten years. Do I look like I'm succeeding? Not one bit."

"Your problem is grease. My problem is too many files." Nick gulped down his beer. "Do we have a table?"

Dubois was scowling into his Scotch. "We had one, but you weren't here and it's gone. I flew in and got here on time. You're just around the corner, and still you're late."

"Sooorry."

"Sitting at the bar's fine with me." Dubois raised his empty glass at the bartender. Turning to Nick, he said, "About your girlfriend. I thought you should hear this from me."

So that was it. What the hell had she done now? "Grace? What about her?"

"She said someone who looked like Li Mann tried to kill her last night. Instead, he killed someone else. Dead man was Harry Kitchin. Turned out he was Crosby's killer. Kitchin's gun was a perfect ballistic match from the slug taken from Crosby's body."

Dubois filled Nick in on what he knew of Harry's history, adding, "My guess is, she walked in on Harry just after he whacked Crosby. She says she didn't see anybody but he coulda been hiding in the house. Him wanting to get rid of her was his way of tying up loose ends.

"Problem two. No weapon at the crime scene. No idea who Kitchin's partner is. That means he's still on the loose." Dubois reached into the second bowl of peanuts. He stuffed his mouth and chewed furiously. He eyed a group of students as they noisily filled the table across from them.

The bartender slid two more drinks down towards them. Nick knocked back the last of his beer before passing the empty mug to the bartender. Then said, "I follow you so far. Why do I get the feeling that there's a lot more to all this?"

"Back to Li Mann. Tire tracks show that there were three vehicles. Why does he want to kill her? He doesn't know her? And you're the one tracking him. So why's he targeting her? Are he and Sun using her to get to you? We know your girlfriend went through some confrontation because she fell down the parkway embankment, and twisted an ankle. Got a few scratches on herself from the brambles and bushes."

Nick nodded as he pointed at the empty peanut dish to the female bartender.

"We're missing a piece of the puzzle here. Maybe Grace knows something that she's not aware of herself. That's why her life's in danger," said Nick, instinctively coming to Grace's defence.

Dubois shrugged as he started on the bowl of olives. "If she's got people trying to kill her, she's knee deep in shit of some kind. Maybe you should talk to her. Find out what she knows and why people want her dead?"

While Nick was thinking about that possibility, a waiter reappeared.

"How about some food?" Nick said, changing the subject.

They ordered a large pizza with every known variety of protein. It took less than twenty minutes for it to arrive. When it did, they stopped talking. They only resumed speech after they had eaten at least four slices each.

Dubois wiped his fingers on a napkin, then pulled out a pad from his jacket pocket. "I got RCMP officers at all our embassies in Asia on the lookout for this Wa Sing character. They're all putting in double time. But you know that already. This is what I want you to see." Inside the pad was an unsealed envelope with a folded document inside. "This was sent to me by the RCMP officer at the Hong Kong embassy. I thought you would find it interesting."

Nick took the document out and laid it flat on the table.

"It's your copy to keep," said Dubois, "but don't read it here. Level V clearance. Don't lose it, 'cause my ass could be in a sling."

As they parted company, Dubois said, "I got an e-mail from Kappolis that Sun Sui was flying up to Ottawa this weekend to prepare for his hearing. He asked if the RCMP would take over the surveillance. I already assigned two squad cars to the guy."

"Thanks."

A half moon dominated the late-summer, dead-of-night sky. It hung low and forbidding under the dark-inked canvas of midnight. For a long time Nick watched the night sky from his balcony. Stretched out on the couch, he finally picked up Dubois' document and read it.

Law enforcement and intelligence officials on both sides of the border had launched a secret operation to gather evidence of Chinese interference in American and Canadian politics through political donations. So far, the FBI had already investigated over 500 American companies to determine whether they were being used by the Chinese government to funnel illegal campaign contributions to politicians they favoured. The Communists liked to use this strategy to increase the power of their own lobby groups and to buy influence in North America. What else was new? He did not find the report shocking. Maybe he had been in the job too long. Or had lived too many lives.

On the second read-through, he allowed the implications to sink in. The information was explosive, no doubt about it. The theft of technological and political information by Chinese spies was accelerating. Not only that, but the Communist Party leadership clearly had links with triads and Asian tycoons who were thought to be infiltrating and gaining influence in important sectors of the North American economy by buying up companies.

The only thing that struck Nick as significant was why Jon Keiler hadn't brought this investigation or report to his attention?

Guilt, maybe. That he and every visa officer in every embassy had accepted one gift too many from grateful and successful visa applicants.

He knew that his people were short-staffed. But backlog or no backlog, his immigration officers were doing sloppy work, cutting corners way too often. He wondered if he should recall every officer home for retraining, with Jon's name at the top of the list.

chapter twenty-three

Monday was the first day of Sun's hearing, and the Immigration and Refugee Commission building had become a security nightmare. Anti-immigration demonstrators had staked out their turf on the north side of the street in front. Ethnic representatives, refugee advocates, and hangers-on milled around on the other side, waiting for their five minutes of televised fame.

Every parking spot was taken. News crews from CNN, CBC, ABC, and all the others were parked and double-parked wherever they could find room. In the first floor lobby, studios with pull had set up television cameras. A pack of newshounds, baying for blood, greeted Grace the moment she appeared. She had to run the gauntlet of flashing lights all the way from the taxi to the lobby, into the elevator and to the door of the hearing room.

She kept an expression of bland calm on her face but inwardly she was swearing at Jean Cadeux. This was what the commissioner had dumped on her. The press would be sticking like burrs to any aspect of the case that they could use to generate controversy. At least until a new crime scandal emerged. She prayed that would happen soon.

Counsel for the claimant had asked for a last-minute prehearing conference. Seated on the bench, she took the opportunity to study Donald Verster, Sun Sui's high-priced hired gun. In the cab, she had done a quick-and-dirty scan of Nick's notes on Verster. He was not what she had expected. From everything she had read, she had envisioned a big man, with the height to match his ego, but standing before her was a bantam rooster in a good suit wearing the male version of platform shoes.

"Counsel, how are we today? I trust you had a pleasant flight up to Ottawa."

"No, I drove up on the weekend. Thought I'd kill two birds with one stone. Do a little sightseeing before the case started."

They smiled tensely at each other. Grace had always believed in the value of exchanging social pleasantries; it was important to set the tone of the judge-lawyer relationship, to keep things cordial over the next two weeks. But she disliked Verster on sight.

Her ally, in-house counsel, known as the refugee claims officer, or RCO, sat across from the claimant's table. This morning, it was Piraro, an eager but inexperienced, young lawyer. His role was to present evidence pertaining to the claimant's background and conditions in the country from which he fled. Like the prosecutor in a criminal trial, he prepared the Crown's case, but his role was not adversarial.

The hearing room was wired for sound. Electronic technology had taken place of the traditional court reporter. Grace turned on the system and

began. "Counsel, we're now on the record. You mentioned in your fax that you had a few concerns going
into this hearing?"

"I do, Your Honour. But the minister's representative, Nick Slovak, isn't present. Should I proceed?"

"Mr. Slovak has informed my office that he intends
to forgo the first, and possibly the second, hearing. He'll
be here to present exclusion evidence. In my opinion,
this will make for a more expeditious hearing."

"I agree," said Verster. He and his client exchanged
smiles.

"I think we can proceed to swear in the claimant
and the witnesses. Counsel, we don't need to hear oral
evidence from each and every one of those witnesses
who have submitted affidavits. I find the affidavits are
sufficient. I would suggest that you select two or three
witnesses for cross-examination. And I'll leave the
choice to you."

"Your Honour, in regard to Mr. Slovak's package of
documents, I wish to point out that the Provincial Court
and Immigration Appeals Division have rendered a decision favourable to my client — "

"Counsel, save your arguments," she interrupted,
rudely cutting him off. Then, mindful that every word
was being recorded, she paused to choose her words
carefully. The last thing she wanted was to lose the
case because counsel for the claimant had miscon-
strued some innocuous remark as biased. Mildly, she
continued, "Immigration has raised exclusion and the
evidence is sufficiently serious in nature. Given that
the minister's representative isn't present at the first
hearing due to his workload on other pressing cases,
I'm asking you to save your arguments pertaining to
exclusion until the end, when we're canvassing the
exclusion issues."

"In that case, I would like to instruct my client and witnesses to a date when they could present evidence to counter the allegations and charges made by Mr. Slovak in his deportation order."

"Fair enough. Let's proceed with the inclusion issues and the evidence. The time factor depends on you, counsel. Let's be thorough but efficient in our examination."

Verster and Grace exchanged meaningful looks.

After the prehearing and a fifteen-minute break, Grace formally opened the proceedings. "Counsel, you may now begin your examination in chief."

Grace listened to the evidence with a straight face and inscrutable expression. She would have to try like the dickens to keep an open mind and bleach Wa Sing's conversation about Sun's business activity in China from her memory banks.

"In 1988," Sun was saying, "Zang, one of my classmates at the University of Beijing, asked me if I wanted to become an active member of the Student Democracy Movement. Zang made me membership secretary."

"What did you do as membership secretary?" asked Verster.

"My first task was to do an informal survey on campus, to find and recruit those who were favourable towards democracy." The claimant paused to measure the effect of his words.

"What else did you do?"

"I arranged meetings, always at different locations, which would be made known to members only at the last minute, because we were afraid of being raided by the PSB, the Public Security Bureau. These precautions were necessary. At these meetings I would take minutes by hand. My other job was to videotape the student democracy rallies. I was at the demonstration at Tiananmen on June 4th 1989. I filmed the events."

"Would you please describe what you witnessed that day?"

"I saw many of my friends killed, some rolled over by army tanks. Others shot. After the demonstrations, I ran to hide at my parents' house. I was worried very much for myself. The next day, the Public Security conducted a mass arrest of demonstrators by coming into the university and seizing the membership list of the Student Movement supporters. I knew I was in danger, because I had already been the subject of frequent inquiries by the local District Public Security Office."

"Was anyone else in your family under investigation?" Verster intoned.

"Counsel, that's a leading question," interrupted the refugee claims officer.

The claimant looked at his lawyer and the RCO before glancing at Grace. Grace indicated that he should go on with his testimony.

Sun explained, "Yes, around August 1989 my father, who worked as a lecturer at the university, was suddenly detained for inquiry. Public prosecution officers came to our house one evening and arrested him."

"Do you know why this happened to him?"

"I think it was because at his workplace he expressed support for me. After all, I'm his son. For that, he spent two weeks in jail and was only released due to poor health. After his release he was demoted at the university to part-time lecturer. This affected his benefits w…"

Grace intervened, "Counsel, this asylum claim concerns Mr. Sui and not his father. Let us limit the evidence regarding the father's occupation. Particularly when the father isn't present to give corroborating evidence."

"Very well."

Verster turned his attention back to his client.

"When did you come to the attention of the authorities?"

"In November 1989 the PSB came to my parents' home. They ransacked the house looking for the video-tape that I made that June."

The RCO sprang up from his seat like a jack-in-the-box. "I wish to put the claimant on notice that he made no mention of any videotapes in his asylum application or earlier testimony. I'd like to raise the issue of legal credibility regarding new evidence that is being brought forward only now."

"You have a point there," Grace agreed. "But since this is counsel's examination in chief, I'd prefer to have him lead the questioning as to why this videotape evidence wasn't mentioned in his asylum application."

"Thank you, Your Honour," said Verster. "I'm afraid that I'm to blame for this. I was remiss in not including that bit of evidence. It was an oversight on my part as counsel. In this, I have failed in my duty to the courts and my client."

Grace wasn't quite sure what to make of Verster's confession or of his abject but insincere-sounding apologies. Was he planning to shoulder the blame for other gaps in the claimant's evidence, to keep credibility from rearing its ugly head? He knew the court had little choice but to accept his explanation. Not a bad strategy.

"Are there any further omissions of evidence, Mr. Verster? If so, I want them brought before the hearing room now. Are there, counsel?"

"No, there are no further omissions or errors in the written evidence, Your Honour."

Turning towards his client, Verster continued, "Sun, please tell the hearing room how many men from the PSB came to search your house."

"I think four or five men."

"Could you give us the general scenario of the event?"

"Yes. It was just after lunch on a Saturday or Sunday. My parents were visiting. My wife was about to serve dessert when the knock on the door came. My mother went to the door, and when they asked for me, she lied, saying I wasn't home. They didn't believe her. That's when they burst into the house and started searching. By that time I was hiding in a storage basket in the kitchen. When they found me, they beat me, asking me where was the videotape. I had no choice but to give it to them. After the tape was in their possession, they threw me into the back of their van."

"Thank you, Sun. Your Honour, I'm finished with the area of evidence concerning my client's political participation and the aftermath of Tiananmen. I'd prefer to examine area by area in order not to confuse my client over the chronology of events."

"That's my style as well, counsel. Mr. Piraro, you may begin your examination on this area of evidence."

Piraro preferred to stand. He looked straight at the claimant and asked, "Excuse me, Mr. Sui, you were in your own house when the PSB came. Where was your wife?"

"She was there in the house with me but was too terrified to speak."

Grace arched her eyebrows in Sui's direction. His oral evidence was incompatible with the written evidence in his narrative describing his wife's chutzpah in finding a driver and following the prison bus. She noted the inconsistency on paper.

"I'm going to take you back to the events at the Tiananmen Square massacre. What was your role in going to the square?"

"I was there as an organizer."

"And you made a videotape of the demonstration?"

"Yes. I ran out of tape after four hours. Afterwards, I gave the tape to a friend who showed it to an American journalist."

"Did you ever get the videotape back?"

"Yes, the journalist made a copy and my original was returned to me. I kept it at home. When I was arrested, they found the videotape in my possession. During my interrogation by the Security Bureau, I was labelled one of the greatest enemies of the Communist government."

The RCO paused. Then, turning to Grace with a boyish smile, he said, "Your Honour, if you permit, I'd prefer to conduct the remainder of my examination after the lunch break."

Verster sprang up from his chair. "I'd like to request a break, too. It's almost one o'clock. I'm famished and so is my client."

What the hell was going on? Grace glanced from Piraro to Verster. She would have preferred that the RCO complete his examination without stopping halfway, which would give Verster and the claimant the opportunity to formulate their responses. But she could hardly insist that they go on. So much for the element of surprise. Was Piraro that incompetent? What kind of trick was he trying to pull? In her book, his conduct was grounds for a reprimand. She made a note to have a little chat with him.

After lunch, the RCO picked up where he had left off.

"Do you remember where the May 1989 memorial parade was held?"

"We went to Martha's Park in Beijing."

"What happened?"

"First there was a silent prayer. Then someone made a speech, then there was a group discussion and exchange of opinions. It went on all day. Afterwards we went home or back to the university."

"Could you explain how you became involved in the student movement?"

"The universities of Beijing and Canton came together for joint demonstrations. I was asked to coordinate a group demonstration."

"Could you explain where and when these demonstrations took place?"

"After the May parade there were other parades in the same month. One was at City Hall, then another at the Provincial Government Building. In Canton, it was at Haizhu Square near the bridge. Those were practice demonstrations before the June massacre."

"Do you remember what precipitated the June 4th 1989 incident?"

"I'm not sure. It was many years ago."

"I'll give you a minute. Think back to that day."

"My memories are confused ... I really don't remember what started it."

"Describe what you do remember."

"At eight in the morning we met at the university. Then about nine-thirty we went to Tiananmen."

Piraro turned to Grace, and said cheerfully, "Those are my questions for the claimant."

That was it? Less than two hours and he was done? Grace couldn't believe it. She'd like nothing better than to pop him one from the bench. Only the need to maintain an appearance of judicial neutrality kept her in check. She had a score of questions she needed answers to. Questioning the claimant herself might be imprudent; judges were advised not to act as researchers, prosecutors or court reporters while on the bench. But she couldn't just let the questions go unanswered because the RCO had failed in his duty to the court and the state.

"Counsel, with your permission, in order to clear up my own confusion, I'd like to ask a few questions of clarification."

"By all means, Your Honour."

Testing his credibility, she asked, "Mr. Sui, why exactly did you make a videotape of the event?"

"I was asked to."

"But it was dangerous. Why did you agree? You don't do everything that you're asked to, do you?"

"No, but I did in this case, because I thought it was important to record history in the making. I was excited and proud to be a part of that history. I believed that the march at Tiananmen would be similar to the fall of the Berlin Wall. It was important that we have a record of it to show the world and our grandchildren."

Good answer, she thought. Testing him again, she asked, "But wasn't the square crawling with foreign journalists? Weren't they filming the event as well?"

"They were. But a Chinese perspective was very important."

"The events were the same in everybody's videotape. That means the perspective was the same. So I don't understand your remark about a Chinese perspective. Do you care to explain?"

"We wanted to take the footage and use it for a documentary. We wanted to explain to the people that when Deng talked of reform, he meant economic changes and not political ones. We wanted to wake up the people."

"What happened after you ran away from the square?"

"I went home and I destroyed all the documents in my possession that the government might have used against us."

"What documents would those be?"

"Anything with the signatures of people who participated in demonstrations."

"Was your signature among them?"

"I wrote some of the slogans, but I don't remember if I signed all the documents." Sun stared straight at her. For a moment their eyes locked. She couldn't read his expression.

Grace wanted to ask more follow-up questions but she stopped herself. To do so was to slide down the slippery slope of prosecutor-judge. Changing tack, she said, "Counsel, I suggest you redirect. Could you ask the claimant what he did after he destroyed the documents?"

"Very well, Your Honour."

Verster turned to Sun. "Given the passage of time, Sun, I want you to try and recollect the sequence of events."

"I went back to the university to find out what was going on. There were many rumours that some of the democracy leaders had disappeared, and some of the demonstrators had already gone into hiding."

"Now, Sun, I'm jumping around here. After the massacre at Tiananmen, did the government or students engage in any kind of protest?"

Grace immediately slapped him down. "Counsel, that's a leading question. I suggest you confine yourself to asking open-ended questions in my hearing room."

"Sorry, Your Honour."

"No, nothing further happened," replied the claimant.

Verster turned to her. "This ends my examination on the issue of political opinion. I'd like to make a small request on behalf of Mr. Sui. We'd like to reconvene for Wednesday instead of tomorrow. Mr. Sui has a doctor's appointment. He has a respiratory condition and the high smog levels in the summer are affecting him adversely."

Grace stared incredulously at Verster and Sun. This was a transparent ploy to buy time. Time for what? To produce favourable evidence? More witnesses?

Sun Sui explained, "I have a chronic cough, which needs medical attention."

Cough, my ass! He hadn't coughed once in the course of a hearing that had run from nine to five. If she wanted to apply the credibility test, she could've gotten him then and there. But she agreed to the request, because it would also buy Nick time. As the minister's representative, he should have faxed her notice of his absence and the date of his appearance to intervene.

Where was he? What the hell had she done to tick him off? She had called him again last night. She got nothing. To be precise, she got fourteen rings, unanswered.

"Wednesday morning. Nine sharp."

"Thank you, Your Honour," answered Verster.

Sun smiled at her as if he and she were on friendly terms. She wished he'd stop doing that. She had already secretly breached the rules of judicial conduct by sleeping with the minister's rep. The last thing she wanted was for the press to start sniffing around her private life because she appeared to be chumming with the claimant! She looked at the reporters for a long moment. Those hungry hounds would snap at any scrap of scandal to stay on top of each other. The case was already a powder keg. She didn't want to supply the press with a lighted match.

"As of Wednesday, this hearing will be an in-camera proceeding," she announced. "I know members of the media have filed an application to have these proceedings conducted in public. While I hadn't made a decision on that application, I'm doing so now. I understand that the claimant and his counsel have waived their right to privacy; nonetheless, I'm disposed to invoke Section 69

(3) of the Immigration Act, which states that, if there is a serious possibility that the life, liberty, or security of the person would be endangered by reason of any of the case proceedings being held in public, the court may take measures to ensure the confidentiality of these proceedings. At the end of each hearing, the press may request copies of the hearing room tapes."

Protests immediately erupted from the reporters and from Verster because it was he who had invited the press. Leaping to his feet, he said accusingly, "Your Honour, it was our understanding that such an application was usually made by the claimant and his counsel."

"Generally it is. But this isn't your average asylum claim. You just have to step outside this hearing room to see that. This claim has already generated a fair amount of public attention, thanks to you, counsel." She glared down at them from the bench. "Too much attention could adversely affect Mr. Sui's claim."

There! Put the spin that it was in the best interest of the claimant.

"Lastly," Grace intoned, "I want to make it clear to counsel and claimant that I don't want any release of information concerning this case to interest groups or the media. Anyone doing so will be charged with serious misconduct. Is that clear?" Grace levelled her gaze at Verster, daring him to object. After a moment she won the staring contest. He reluctantly nodded assent.

Back in her office, she waded through papers in her in-basket, hoping to outlast the waiting media types, but at six o'clock, she realized they weren't going to leave until she delivered a few soundbites. Since there was no way to avoid them, she ran a comb through her hair and reapplied her lipstick. At the security doors, she paused for a moment to collect her thoughts, then pushed the doors open. Lights flashed in her eyes and microphones were pushed in her face. They pursued her all the way out the building.

"Ms. Wang-Weinstein, we don't understand why you have overturned Mr. Verster's application to have the hearing heard in public?"

"Are all your cases always in-camera proceedings?"

"Can you give us your opinion of the first day of the hearing? Can the Immigration and Refugee Commission discuss the legal issues presented today?"

"What about proof? Does the Refugee Commission intend to use the RCMP and the police to obtain evidence of illegal activities?"

The distance from the security doors to the outside world had never been longer. The questions came at her like bullets in a firing range. On the steps of the building she decided to turn and face the cameras.

Trying to keep her remarks brief and as unexciting as possible, she droned, "The IRC recognizes the right of the public to be kept informed about the quasi-judicial proceedings of Mr. Sui's claim. However, that right must be balanced against other rights. In this case, particular sub-sections of the Immigration Act require that the Immigration and Refugee Commission decide whether there is a serious possibility that the life, liberty, or security of any person in this case would be endangered by reason of any of its proceedings being held in public. In this case, I believe that such a serious possibility exists. And I have granted such an application to ensure confidentiality. For that reason, the remainder of the hearing will be conducted in-camera. That's all I have to say. Good day, everyone."

"Could you comment on the uniqueness of the situation? Isn't it highly unusual for a judge to close a hearing that the lawyers and witnesses want open to the public?"

"Some members of the media are considering taking this case to the Federal Court on the grounds that insufficient notice was given for an in-camera hearing. Would you reconsider if the media presented arguments to you on this issue?"

The questions were being fired from all sides. Damn! The cordon of reporters and their bulky equipment had closed around her. Using her briefcase as a weapon to hack her way through the crowd, she kept her eyes straight ahead of her, and once out on the street jumped into the first available cab going in any direction.

Time had passed and Nick could not remember the list of questions he had given Rocco for his examination of Sun's witnesses or what his thoughts had been, except that those thoughts circled around Sun Sui and Li Mann Vu. He wanted to get out of his clothes, which were sticking to his body, but he had to stick around for the phone call from Jon Keiler. As he waited for the phone to ring, he scribbled notes into case files, from sheer habit. He sorted through detention certificates and applications. As he reached for the next file folder, the phone rang.

"Nick, how ya doing, fella?"

"Jon, I don't understand how it could take you almost a week to return a call. Particularly to your boss." Nick thought he knew why Jon Keiler in Hong Kong was deliberately avoiding him. His immigration manager at the Canadian embassy didn't want to discuss Sun Sui's investor immigrant application because he had made an error in judgement.

"Well, I'm sorry, but it's not like we got nothin' to do around here, you know. Anyway, I had to pull up that investor immigrant application you wanted. What do you want to know?"

"The RCMP thinks Sun Sui has connections to the Flying Dragons triad. How could you approve his application? I don't need to remind you that the Immigration Act prohibits the admission of any person who engages in criminal activity. In other words, Jon, we're trying to keep criminals out of the country."

"I hear ya. But this guy's a movie mogul. Everyone here in Hong Kong knows that there's heavy-duty triad involvement inside the entertainment industry."

"Just because everybody's doing it doesn't make it right," snapped Nick.

"Nick, you don't know the Hong Kong mentality. I'm telling ya, just because someone knows triad members doesn't mean he's a member. Because just about everybody here is a member of some triad or other."

Nick cut him off. "Just send me his entire file."

"His entire file? It was handled by four or five of us. A lot of those papers have been archived in another building across town. It's gonna take several days and two bodies to do record searches. Nick, you know how short-staffed we are here."

"Then do it!" He was losing patience with Jon. In his book, it was one thing to screw up, another thing to try to bury it. That was the problem with being in the same job too long. Complacency settled in. One's judgement became dull. When you add a government employer to that, you had that extra layer of secrecy to shield the poor and stupid decisions.

"I'm giving you three business days to toss it into the diplomatic pouch."

Jon tried to argue but Nick interrupted him again. "How come you didn't tell me about the joint Canada-U.S. operation into China-sponsored espionage and their illegal campaign contributions?"

"Because it's bullshit. It's nothing more than a

make-work project for law enforcement guys in the two embassies here."

"Still, I'm ticked that you didn't even brief me on it. Now get on that Sun Sui file."

It was past six when Nick rode the office elevator down. His mood was sombre. His immigration manager in Hong Kong was beginning to look more and more incompetent with each passing week. And the idea that Sun and Li Mann were getting away with Walter's murder was intolerable. Walter had been torn from life so brutally, in a second, with no time to prepare himself. Because of that Nick saw, more than ever, the sacredness of life. He saw, too, the elusiveness of justice. Outside, people rushed by him, a blur of movement. He headed home, his loneliness made worse by the empty beauty of soaring architectural patterns of glass, granite, and steel.

chapter twenty-four

Ottawa, like Washington, was a political town. It was just smaller, that's all. She stared out the window, taking in the surrounding glass buildings and headquarters of blue chip companies. She knew that when she had first arrived here, her ex-husband's name had smoothed her way. It was a city of insiders, and only insiders could get things done. If you had contacts, doors magically opened and calls were returned promptly. Insiders knew their contacts' gatekeepers by their first names; they schmoozed with the spouses of their contacts. The ones who were really in the loop even knew all about their contacts' extramarital affairs. But being an insider took a lot of work. It was almost a full-time job in itself, to maintain one's network of contacts. For an insider, hell was finding oneself outside the gate, looking in.

Outsiders cooled their heels sitting in public reception rooms as they waited their turn for interviews, permits, approvals and appointments. They waited and waited, because the wheels of the Byzantine bureaucracy that is the federal public service turn with excruciating slowness.

Cadeux's secretary intruded upon her thoughts.

"Monsieur Cadeux will see you now."

She tried to do "upbeat and perky" as she walked into his office. "Commissioner. How are you?"

"Grace, how are you?" He looked grim.

"Fine. I'm just preparing for tomorrow's continuation. I hope this won't take long."

"Oh no. I just wanted to ask you how things are going."

"We've only had one day of hearing. I should get a better sense by day two or three on how the case is shaping up. We'll talk at the end of the week perhaps."

"Wonderful. Now, I want you to bear in mind, Grace, that the situation is ... difficult. As your political superior, I'm ultimately responsible and, well, the ministers are breathing down my neck. Reminding me to be careful with taxpayer dollars."

"Which ministers, sir?"

Exasperated, he said, "What does it matter which ministers? Foreign Affairs and the International Trade, as it happens."

Keeping an even tone, she said, "I'll keep that in mind." Inwardly, she was raging. Cadeux was such a flunkey, so obsequious to the "ministers," so rude to the judges and adjudicators who reported to him.

"I've read the framework you've laid out. The exclusion evidence so far is entirely circumstantial. Keep in mind that we're not the police! If the police don't make their case on criminality, then it's not for us to make it for them. I don't need to remind you of that, do I?"

"No, sir."

"Moreover, the claimant is only a year or so away from getting citizenship. If we can save the taxpayers' money by cutting out the circumstantial evidence, then you should do it."

"I'll see what I can do. Is that all, sir?"

"There is one more consideration. Right now, my office is being deluged with calls from the business community criticizing us for harassing a businessman who has created hundreds of jobs for Canadian citizens. Not to mention the various Asian communities that have called us with accusations of racism. Therefore, I've issued a press release with a little background on yourself."

"In other words, you're using me to fight the racism charge."

"Grace, please, I don't need this kind of hostility. I'm walking a fine line here as it is."

"But is that one of the reasons why you assigned the case to me? You're using me to deflect the racism charges?"

Cadeux gave her a pained look. "Just bear in mind that the claimant is a very highly regarded man. And that the allegations of criminality are just that. Allegations."

"Until proven."

"But there is no proof, Grace."

"Yes. One more thing, sir."

"What else?"

"It's Piraro, the RCO. He's not as thorough in his cross-examination as I would like. Is it possible at this late stage to replace him with someone who's more knowledgeable about China?"

"Piraro may not be a China expert. But his competence as a lawyer will do much to advance the case."

"I disagree."

"Damn it! Grace, I'm not going to replace Piraro now. I don't need the bar and the public service union on my back. Now, call me at the end of tomorrow's hearing and give me a synopsis of how things went, so I can advise you on how to proceed. And that's an order."

As she closed the door behind her, she released a inaudible groan. That was all she needed. A micromanager.

First Wa Sing, then her mother, now Cadeux. Who was next? The prime minister? Obviously there were a lot of players who were willing to rubber-stamp Sun into the country. The only exception to that rule, apparently, was Nick.

The undercover officer assigned by Dubois to babysit her was standing in the lobby. "I'm parked in the underground. Never mind taking a cab and me tailing you. I'll give you a lift home."

Grace waited for him to back the Chrysler out of the parking spot before jumping in. "Any developments on finding Harry Kitchin's partner?"

"Nothing. But we did track down Kitchin's sister and brother. Both said that he had few friends. With criminals, friendship isn't a deep thing. This partner of his is probably on the other side of the country by now."

Grace was silent for a moment thinking about this. Then she nodded, her throat relaxed. After all, the RCMP was always thorough in what they did. The officer's reassurance eased back the knot of fear that had taken up residence in the back of her head.

Later, at home that night, she called Nick again. Nothing. His answering machine had been disconnected. Since their weekend tryst, she had left umpteen messages with his secretary. No return phone calls.

Okay, she got dumped. She was a big girl, she could take it … but shouldn't she know why? Dark thoughts niggled at the edge of consciousness. What had he found out about her? Did he know about Wa Sing? Did he know about her social exchange with Sun Sui? Did he assume the worst — that she was going to go yes on the case? Damn him for his lack of faith in her.

Harry was dead. That wasn't supposed to happen. His best friend had been taken away from him. So what was the difference between the lady judge and him now? And where had that gook killer come from? Was Harry's killer her bodyguard? What did it matter now? Murder was murder. They were even. Except that he was going to better the score. Now he had reason to hate the bitch. Yeah, he would hit the lady judge real good. He opened the glove box of the Chrysler he had just stolen, and pulled out a map. He had dumped the white van at a national park, near a garbage dump. It would be a while before anyone noticed that it was abandoned. When Harry was alive, he had the whole thing all thought out. Steal cars, use them for two weeks or so, dump them, and steal another one. It was a good plan. After this job he would abandon the Chrysler as well.

He drove down her street and noticed that the house was pitch black. He kept the engine running as he got out of the car. The obese tabby was stretched out on the front steps. It would be nice to kill the cat too. He walked up to the front steps. Just then, the porch and living-room lights came on. He checked his watch. The timer was set for eight.

Boldly, he paced the streets in her neighbourhood, daring the police to find him. He looked into the faces of the people passing by. So arrogant, their eyes, so judgmental. The kind of people he despised. He imagined what it would feel like to pump a round into their faces.

As he drove away, he plotted his revenge. This time he would have to plan. No more nasty surprises. Back on the highway, BJ checked his speed. The last thing he wanted was to be caught on a traffic violation. He tapped on his steering wheel along with the radio and smiled to himself as he thought of half a dozen ways of icing the bitch.

Day two of the hearing. Grace was impatient to get to exclusion and the evidence of Sun's criminality, but she couldn't until they had wrapped up on inclusion issues.

Verster announced at the beginning, "I'd like to close off on religious identity."

"It's a peripheral issue," Grace warned, "so don't take all morning, counsel."

"I'd like to enter the Amnesty International documents as exhibit C-24, if you'd indulge me, your honour. This document also covers the legal issue, return to his country of former habitual residence, Hong Kong. Paragraph 4 states that Hong's Kong's reversion back to China, freedom of worship is no longer taken for granted. The Mainland authorities have intensified efforts to suppress unsanctioned religious activity. As my client stated yesterday, he's an Anglican by faith. Therefore the next page also pertains to him. 'Scores of Christians have been arrested in a brutal crackdown on worshippers within its borders and beyond ...'"

"Counsel, this isn't kindergarten class. We can all read, thank you."

"I wanted to bring those points to your attention."

"Mr. Piraro, do you have any questions to put to the claimant regarding this document or the religious issue?"

"Only one." Turning his attention to the claimant, the RCO asked, "Since coming to Canada, what church have you attended?"

"The United Church on Beverly Street."

"Do you attend service?" asked Piraro.

"Unfortunately not. I'm either too busy or out of the country."

Piraro announced, "I've no more questions but I'm willing to make observations at this point on the religious identity."

With a sigh, she said, "Go ahead." Grace found Piraro so incompetent in his cross-examination, she wondered when exactly he was called to the Bar.

"The claimant may very well be a practising Christian, but he has not met the burden of proof on religious grounds. Therefore, his claim that he has would suffer persecution as a practising Christian if he were to return to either China or Hong Kong is not proved."

Verster banged a fist on the table, and jumped to his feet.

"I'd like to point out the documentary evidence in Tab 11 which states that the harsh treatment of Christians dates back to the 1950s when Mao Tse Tung's Communists expelled the last papal representative, driving Christians underground. Turning the page at the top, it continues, stating that religion and religious activity are perceived by the Communist Party authorities as a vehicle for political organization, dissent or outright opposition to the party's rule. Your Honour, the operative word here is perception. One doesn't have to be a practising Christian, only a nominal Christian, to be targeted by the Communist authorities. Therefore on religious grounds alone, the IRC should find my client to be a genuine asylum seeker."

"Noted," said Grace. It was a good point. But that didn't mean that the claimant squeaked in under the religious issue. His religious identity was a peripheral issue. The central issue was his political opinion.

After lunch, Sun answered his lawyer's questions in a straightforward manner. "I have a daughter but I wanted a son. In the culture I come from the bureaucrats are corrupt. Everything can be achieved through bribes. Even two or more children. I know this because my friends have paid bribes to the officials at the Family Planning Agency to look the other way. I was prepared to pay the bribe money. What I wasn't counting on was the events of Tiananmen Square and my own role there. I didn't expect the authorities to make an example out of me because of the background of my own parents and grandparents. I had assumed that with Deng the Cultural Revolution and the past were behind us. I thought we were moving ahead as a country. I was wrong in my assumptions."

This evidence had been covered in his narrative. Her mind wandered. From Inner Mongolia to the Yellow Sea, from Shanghai to Tibet. Beijing's one-child policy meant a country where hundreds of thousands of baby girls were either killed or sent abroad for adoption. The one-child policy was domestic law. The Chinese government was harsh. But it was also two-faced, apparently. One face of the government wanted to kill Sun Sui, while the other wanted to lure him back with promises of wealth and privilege. But was it so different here? She suddenly saw an image of Jean Cadeux's face, irritably telling her that government ministers wanted her to go easy on the claimant ... and then Nick's face, as he told her about the death of his friend Walter, and Sun's possible role in that murder ...

His oral evidence was consistent with his written narrative. Nothing new here.

"Counsel, I've a few questions of clarification," Grace interrupted.

"You may put them to my client."

"Mr. Sui, in your narrative, Captain Lei helped you escape from prison. He was a friend of your father. Could you tell us about the relationship between Captain Lei and your father?"

"Captain Lei was a former student of my father at the university. Their relationship dated back at least twelve or thirteen years. After he graduated, he often returned to the university to play in the ping-pong championships."

"Where did your father get the two million yuan on his lecturer's salary?"

"My wife borrowed the money from her eldest brother. She then passed the money to my father, who then delivered it personally to Captain Lei."

The claimant delivered his testimony straightforwardly and without hesitation. So much for trying to trip him up and rule against him on credibility. She glanced over at the Piraro and noticed that he was doodling on the legal-size pad. In a curt voice she asked, "Mr. Piraro, do you have any questions to put to the claimant?"

"None."

"Before you make arguments on this issue, counsel, I'll reveal to you the thinking from the bench. I'm well aware of the documentary evidence on the one-child policy. The purpose of this one-child law is to contain the country's population growth. Basically the claimant will have to further show why he should be entitled to international protection after breaking the laws in his own country."

Claimant and counsel exchanged stricken looks.

"I'll prepare those on closing."

"Fine by me. At tomorrow's hearing, counsel, you'll conduct examination on the claimant's life in Hong

Kong. Particularly in the area of asset accumulation."

"Your Honour, my client can't attend tomorrow. I was wondering if we could reconvene on Monday."

"What's wrong with tomorrow?"

"He has a doctor's appointment."

Again? Grace critically stared at the claimant. He didn't look sick to her. She was ticked with counsel and claimant. "Very well." She swallowed to regain a normal pitch, then, thinking, fuck with me and this is what you get. Voice tightly under control, she went on, "When we resume, I'd like you to canvas the claimant's residency in Hong Kong. From there, the minister's representative will open the exclusion issue of the claimant being a high-level crime figure at the helm of a multi-million dollar smuggling empire."

"But Your Honour ..."

Before he could finish his sentence, Grace had risen. "This ends our hearing for today." She flicked off the recording devices and stepped down from the bench.

Nick listened to the phone ring twelve times. He made no move to answer it, because it might be Grace, and he couldn't talk to her. He hoped she was all right, that she was taking care for her safety. The story of the carjacking made his blood run cold whenever he thought of it. But he knew she'd be careful, she was no fool.

He read the card again. He had in fact read the card a dozen times. Each reading brought her closer to him, while taking them further away from each other. To see her loopy handwriting, to read her message announcing her love for him was exquisite torture. All of the distance he had put between Grace and himself closed again, when he read her words of how much he meant to her ... until Dubois's words came back to him. And he remembered the roll of twenty-four prints sitting in his desk drawer.

"General, it's me."

Li Mann Vu recognized the voice of the Red Prince on his cellphone. "Yes. How are you?" he asked neutrally.

"Have you done it?"

"No. I'm afraid to say that I botched it. There was a surprise. Seems that she was stalked by two men. They pounced on me and I had to kill one of them."

"Stupid! Fucking stupid of you!" The Red Prince swore into the phone. "Kill them both in case they can identify you. We can't afford to fail. Do you want their government to send in tanks in against us?"

"We aren't in China. Not even Vietnam is like that," Li Mann Vu snorted.

"I don't care where we are. All I know is, for an old soldier, you're losing your edge," the Red Prince said derisively.

Changing topics, Li Mann Vu said, "I heard on the radio that the dancer who escaped from that immigration raid has turned herself in. And she's dancing in your club again."

"Yes. After the club paid a stiff penalty for her actions. We'll have to dock her pay to recover the money."

"How much did you pay in penalty? Five hundred dollars? A thousand? For someone who's already made over $300 million smuggling three thousand people into North America this year alone, you're acting very petty towards someone who's got nothing."

Not deigning to reply to that, the Red Prince asked, "Where are you right now?"

"I'm in a motel in Ottawa. On the outskirts of town."

"Stay and finish the job. Kill her!"

"What about Toronto and taking out that immigration officer?"

"All in good time. I want her killed first."

"After I kill him, I want a vacation. Harvest season is coming up. I need to get back to my village. Besides, the village is counting on my return."

"So am I. I want you in China. Preparations must be made before the first cargo ship sails from Fujian next year."

"Not before I go home."

"And I'm telling you that there's a lot of work we've got to have in place before that flotilla of migrant smuggling ships makes its way to North America. There's a lot of money riding on that. Just think of your share of the profits. But before we see any of that, we need to work out the details. Like where's the best place to bring the illegals ashore."

Li Mann Vu sighed into the phone. "I need three weeks in Vietnam. Then I'll go to China. Don't ask me to do anything else right now."

"Don't call me at my hotel. The immigration officer and his police friends have me under watch, and my line is tapped. And the cops have confiscated both my cell-phones. Right now, I'm trying to get another one."

"Where're you making this call?"

"I'm at a pay phone at the IRC right now." The Red Prince chuckled. "Right under their noses, but they don't dare wiretap their own phones."

"In other words, I can't reach you?"

"No. Just wait for my calls."

After Li Mann Vu hung up the phone, he lit a cigarette and thought about his life. First he had been a soldier. That was honourable. Now he was an enforcer. Not so honourable. A lot of people feared him. Some even hated him. Like he hated the Americans.

He lit another cigarette and inhaled deeply. Let me count the ways on how I hate the U.S. government. They had helped rebuild the economies of their former enemies in Germany and Japan. But not Vietnam. His people had won the war, and lost the peace. The U.S. continued to punish them with an economic embargo. Half the country did not have enough to eat, and the other half was dying from the corrosive effects of Agent Orange.

Like Agent Orange, over the years, the hate had corroded his insides. He felt nothing. Worse, he could no longer distinguish right from wrong.

chapter twenty-five

Jean Cadeux barged into her office without knocking. He stretched his lips into something that only he would pretend was a smile.

"What the hell are you trying to do, Grace? Do you want the General Accounting people to can the entire Commission? Or maybe a Senate inquiry into professional misconduct?"

"What're you referring to?"

He spat the words out. "I've been informed that you're having an affair with the minister's representative who is assigned to the Sun case. Is this true?"

Oh shit! thought Grace. She'd been found out. What could she say in her own defence? She momentarily took refuge by staring out the window and tried to let the blue skies and cirrus clouds inhabit her. They didn't.

She turned her attention back to Cadeux. What a slimebag!

Was he spying on her? Had he seen her in Montreal holding hands with Nick? So what? Just because she was in public office didn't mean she wasn't entitled to a personal life. She wanted to tell him to fuck off, and despite all she'd been through recently, she managed to restrain herself. "Where did you hear that, sir?"

"Never mind where I heard it! It's a clear violation of conflict of interest guidelines. I'm not inclined to be tolerant of this, Grace. I could very well lose my own job!"

Of course, that's what this was all about. His job. "I assure you that I'm not having an affair with him." That was not quite a lie. He hadn't called her back, after all. It seemed that he was no longer speaking to her. Which meant that everything was off.

"You should have disclosed everything to me when I handed you the case."

Like a queen bitch, she argued, "I thought my personal life was my personal life. I didn't think the state had a right to intrude on who I was seeing. Or who I was fucking! And for your information, when I was handed the file, I didn't know that Mr. Slovak would be representing the minister's office personally. I thought the assignment would go to one of his officers. I assure you I have never discussed that case or any other case with any unauthorized person."

The commissioner mulled over her words and as he looked at her. He could see the anger hovering around her clear brown eyes. He hated to fight with her when she was a bitch because it diminished his reputation as a supreme adjudicator. At the same time he had to consider his political reputation. Nothing else mattered to him.

"All right. It's probably best to keep quiet about this. But you will not see him again, privately or publicly, until this hearing is over. If we stay out of the papers and just do our job, the ministries will have to leave us alone. If not, they can close down the entire commission. If General Accounting doesn't do it first. The public isn't happy that they're footing the bill to allow more newcomers in. Never mind the ones who are committing crimes. Watch your step." He wagged his finger at her. "Don't fuck up, Grace!"

Fuck you too! She coolly studied him. He looked old and tired, but that's exactly what he was. An aging asshole who spent his energies spinning his lines to justify his own actions to the press, public and powers that be up on the Hill.

She cut the tension by raising the issue of Piraro's performance again.

"I know, I know." He tried to brush aside her criticisms of Piraro's weakness in the hearing room. "He's a good lawyer but he's a rookie RCO, Grace. He needs practice."

"Christ almighty!" That was too much. She blew up. "I'm taking it on the chin every day from the media on a public case like this, and you assign me someone who's wet behind the ears! So he can get some *practice*?"

"If you overlook exclusion, you'll be fine with him on inclusion."

"That's no fucking way to conduct a hearing! And I can't overlook exclusion." They tried to stare each other down again. "Why the hell wasn't Raymond Fong assigned as my RCO?" she demanded.

"We asked him, but he declined. He said he didn't want to be blacklisted from his own community if he cross-examined too hard and the claimant got turned down."

"That's real swell! And you had no fucking qualms about dumping it on me and forcing me to accept it!"

"That's different! You're a judge. Paid to take heat and flak. An RCO is only an in-house lawyer, paid to do our bidding. At a much lower salary, I might add."

She glared at him, but he ignored her. He put on his bifocals and flipped through a handful of transcript pages of the Sun Sui case.

"I've been following the hearing closely."

Now what?! She knew her body language was bristling with impatience and anger, but he was oblivious.

"It seems to me that you're wasting time on a weak exclusion case. It looks as if he has a very strong case for asylum. Am I correct?"

Who was presiding in the hearing, her or Cadeux? Calm down, Grace, she told herself. Don't lose your temper. You could have your ass hauled before the judicial discipline committee. And all because of a brown-nosing slimeball like Jean Cadeux? Not worth it. She took a deep breath.

"The case does have some merit on some of the inclusion issues."

"Then what the hell are you waiting for? Rubber-stamp him in! If there's merit on the inclusion issues, why are you making the claimant go through rings of fire?"

"Because there's a hefty package of documents on exclusion. Evidence of alleged criminality runs almost five hundred pages. While the evidence is yet to be tested in ..."

"Those damn documents were tested and tossed out by the court of appeals. We are not the goddamn police! How many times do I have to tell you that?"

"In all fairness, sir, I'd like the minister's rep to briefly canvas his issues before we make a determination that his evidence carries no weight."

"Almighty Christ, Grace, if you really want to believe in fairness, you might as well quit and go join the peace corps." His eyes locked on her. They sat in awkward silence. Grace looked away first. Why challenge him? Just don't give in.

"Sir, I'd like to think that I know how to do my job." Her words were dry and precise.

"Job? Don't give me that, Grace! You know and I know that this political appointment of ours is a way station."

Was he trying to bribe her now, after his threats hadn't brought her into line? "I'm not sure I understand, sir ..."

He cut her off before she could finish.

"I think you do understand! We didn't get into public office without being political animals." He slapped both hands on his desk and stood up. "Our politics may not be the same but I've no intention of letting you make me look like a fool!"

"It's not my intention to make either of us look like fools."

"Then let's get one thing clear. This man has fucking influence. We're only doing this because of a fucking technicality. If this had happened a year or so from now, he'd already be in. He'd be a citizen and this hearing wouldn't be happening. The fact that he's been granted investor immigrant status says a lot. The fact that he sits on three corporate boards in this country also says a lot." His eyes flashed as he leaned forward, hissing at her like an angry snake. "Money talks, Grace. This claimant is here to stay, whether you like it or not. All you and I can do is ensure our own survival. Do I make myself exceedingly clear?"

"Yes, sir. Are we finished?" She returned her attention to the computer screen. It was the clearest signal she could give that she no longer wanted to talk about it. Their meeting was over.

He turned his back and stormed out of her office.

She left the building and joined the thronging flow of people on the sidewalk. She walked fast, not caring where she was going; she just wanted to get away, to work off her anger, to lose herself in the anonymity of the crowd. But even here she thought she felt eyes drilling into her back. She looked around, fully alert. A whirl of faces passed. She studied the Asian faces, looking for Li Mann.

What about Harry Kitchin's partner? The police didn't have a name or a composite sketch, so how could they ever locate him? And the undercover officer Dubois had assigned to her for the past four days had reported that everything was quiet. So much for trying to bolster the argument that she was being stalked.

Still, she had been somewhat successful in containing her hysteria. For the past several days she had managed to shoehorn her anxiety into a side compartment of her brain so she could think about the larger problems of work. But in the open like this, her nerves were screaming. Today, of all days, the feeling of being watched was overwhelming. She was sure that one of them was on her trail again. Which one? Kitchin's partner? Or Li Mann?

Get with it, Grace! When your life is being threatened, who cares about the identity of the assailant?

Would he try to kill her here in broad daylight? On a crowded street? It had been done before. Desperate for a diversion from her thoughts, she walked towards the outdoor blues concert in Majors Hill Park. Finding an empty bench underneath a row of elms, she sat and turned the facts and events of the past three days over and over in her mind. Finally, picking herself up, she walked south toward Sparks Street. The summer music festival was still on, and the streets were crowded with tourists and the sounds of rhythm and blues, and jazz. She took careful note of the faces until she was satisfied that the picnickers, office workers, street musicians and other pedestrians had no devious intentions against her.

She crossed four lanes of traffic, which was bumper to bumper. She passed a man with a ferret on a leash, and a young woman with a Mohawk cut walking her Rottweiler, all muzzled up. The crowds of people suited her fine. They made it easier to blend in, lose anybody who might be watching her. Periodically she glanced back over her shoulder, searching the sea of faces for a pockmarked Asian man, scanning the street constantly for a white van. If only she had gotten a good look at the other assailant.

She entered the World Exchange Plaza and crossed the atrium. The lines in front of the tellers were six deep. It was lunch hour. A bad time to go to the bank, particularly if you wanted to deal with a human being. She marched up to the service and reception counter and pushed her way to the front.

"Excuse me, but I need to get into my safety deposit box. I'm in hurry. I've got to get back to work."

"Everybody's in a hurry these days. Join the club, lady," snapped the clerk.

So much for the customer being right.

The vault of safety deposit boxes was set behind the counter to the far left. A set of massive metal doors gleamed like polished silver. She caught the eye of the manager, who recognized her, and sent someone to help her.

"Follow me," said another, friendlier clerk.

They entered a small windowless room filled with files and metal cabinets. Sitting behind a desk was an elderly man, who looked to be only a couple of years from retirement.

The clerk pointed her towards the desk. "Talk to Thomas."

Thomas, the clerk, entered her safety deposit box number into a terminal.

"You Grace Wang-Weinstein?"

"Yes, that's me. Here's my ID." She handed him her driver's licence.

He gave it a cursory glance. "I believe ya."

No, please, don't believe me. Trust no one. I'd sure hate the thought of someone stealing my key and getting access to my box.

"Would you like my social insurance number so you can match it to whatever's on the screen?"

"Okay."

She recited her SIN number to Thomas.

"Good enough. Follow me."

He guided her through a set of doors into another room which was really a vault. Outside the vault stood a security guard wearing a sidearm. Thomas walked past him and found the K boxes. He stuck the bank key into the slot, then pulled out the box and dumped it on a wooden table.

"How much time you need?"

"A minute or two. I'm just getting some jewellery from my box."

She waited for Thomas to leave, closing the door behind him. Then she inserted her key and lifted back the lid. Inside were only three items: a handgun, a box of ammunition, and her wedding ring. She wrapped her hands around the cold blue steel of the Sig Sauer .38. Once upon a time in El Salvador she used to wear the .38 as part of her uniform. Between her thighs, tucked neatly under a garter belt, and no one was the wiser. No need for that now. She loaded a clip of ammunition then dropped the gun into her bag.

"I'm done," she called out as she gave the key a good turn.

She watched Thomas insert the bank key and slide the box back into its slot. Then she left. On the way out, she counted the number of security cameras. There were twice as many security guards. You'd want to think twice before robbing this bank.

She walked back to the office. It was amazing how safe an illegal, unregistered gun could make you feel.

BJ glanced at his watch as he stood in the throng of picketers across the street from the IRC. He had a front-row seat for the show; the press ambushing his target on the steps of the IRC. He followed her, on the opposite side of the street. He watched as she grabbed a cab. He put the stolen car into gear.

He remembered how, when he was a teenager, he and his uncle had stalked a moose for over a week in the forest. A week of crawling on his stomach, sleeping out in the open, being eaten alive by deer flies, black flies, and mosquitoes. Compared to that, this was nothing.

The uniformed man behind the glass at passport control pulled him out of the line. He was asked to wait in another line, while the man picked up the telephone. Wa Sing saw himself reflected in the glass divider. He knew that he would soon feel the sting of humiliation. Staring at his reflection, he was glad that he was dressed in the elegant navy blue silk suit, white shirt, and a tie that he had picked up in Milan last year. It would not do to be splashed across the international dailies looking like a poor man, a failure. Looking like a rich businessman caught in a government sting operation was better. He would still be able to hold his head high.

The customs officer hung up the phone and waved to someone off to the side. Wa Sing did not bother turning his head. He knew. A moment later, two policemen with submachine guns slung over their shoulders approached him. One of them motioned to him to rise from where he was sitting.

"Please, sir, come with us."

Wa Sing obeyed. At least they were polite. They didn't grab him and rough him up the way policemen usually do. Passengers moved aside quickly, staring hard at him as he walked past.

As Wa Sing followed them meekly through the passport control booths, he saw his two guards visibly relax. One of them entered a security code into a black keypad and waited. A buzzer sounded and all three men wordlessly walked through a pair of automatic sliding doors. They passed a series of doors before one of them knocked on a steel door. A moment later, Wa Sing entered another room where another group of uniformed policemen were already waiting. His passport was taken away from him, and handed to an officer who, though a very young man, looked like the commanding officer.

"You're Wa Sing?"

"Yes."

Wa Sing noticed that the inspector spoke English with a perfect American accent. He must have attended an American school, or had gone abroad for his education. His eyes remained on the inspector as he examined the passport carefully, page by page.

"I'm Inspector Ben Lim. I see that you've been here for several days. Do you mind telling me where you've been staying? We searched for you but you weren't registered at any hotels."

"I was staying with some friends at their home. You know Chinese hospitality ..." Wa Sing smiled and shrugged.

Inspector Lim smiled back. "Yes. There's no need to explain further." He glanced at the door and said, "I'm sorry, sir. The RCMP officer at the Canadian embassy here has asked me to detain you for questioning. I'm to turn you over to them now."

"Could you please tell me what this is all about?" asked Wa Sing.

"They told me that it's a political matter."

"Why can't I answer these questions over the phone?"

"I don't know. An RCMP officer should arrive shortly. You can ask him that question. As far as Singapore is concerned, your passport is in order, and you haven't committed any crimes in our country."

Inspector Lim handed Wa Sing's passport back to him. Wa Sing slipped it into his pocket. The two men waited together. Then the door slid open, and the Caucasian face of an RCMP officer appeared.

"Mr. Wa Sing, we need to ask you some questions. You'll have to accompany us to the Canadian embassy."

"Please, I've a plane to catch, why not ask your questions here?"

"We can't do that. We're acting under orders. Gather your things and follow me."

chapter twenty-six

He stood in front of the peephole, so she could see
who he was. After a moment the lock was turned
and she came out of her house wrapped in a bathrobe,
her hair wet and slick down her back.

"Nick." She looked at him uncertainly, but a
smile was pulling at her lips. Was she laughing at him?
"What a pleasant surprise," she said, and leaning forward she kissed him lightly on the lips. "Close the
door behind you, I was about to have dessert. How
about an ice cream cone?" Her voice was soft, pleasant to the ears.

Nick closed the door behind him. He remained
silent and followed her into the kitchen. As she turned
to speak to him, he dropped the black-and-white photographs of her and Wa Sing on her kitchen table.

"Look at these."

She stared at them, a stunned look creeping into
her face.

"You had answers to most of my questions all along. I could have saved days in my investigation if you hadn't withheld vital information. Or lied to me outright." His voice was bitter and coiled tight as a piano string.

She clutched at the opening of her bathrobe. "I can explain."

"Good God, Grace. I trusted you. I believed in you. Instead I found out you're a liar. A fucking liar!" She crumpled into a chair. "Worse, I fell in love with you. Fell for you. I was blinded by that."

"Please, Nick. I can explain everything."

"You mean if I hadn't found out, then I wouldn't be worth an explanation?"

"No, that's not how it is."

"God, you must've been laughing at what a jerk I am."

He walked towards her and lifted his hand as if he meant to strike her but instead he pulled her out of the chair and against his chest. "I confided in you. Told you everything about my work. Tipped my hand way, way more than I should. All that time, what were you doing? Using that information against me? Was that it? Did you give this Wa Sing a blow-by-blow account of my movements?"

"Nick, stop it! I may have withheld some information from you. But I had good reasons. And I never lied to you. Not once did I ever jeopardize your safety. Or the safety of your officers."

"Fucking me was convenient for you and your friends."

"Shut up!" she screamed. "Sit down and shut up. You want the truth? I'll tell you the truth." She knew a lot was riding on her answer. He was asking about faith and trust, and their future together. She knew it was important that her answer be honest yet correct.

"Where do I begin? How do I know Wa Sing? Through my mother. She's known him since she was a young woman, more than half a lifetime. He helped me get my political appointment on the bench. Yes, he did." She pushed a wet strand of hair out of her eyes. "I was practising law then. Just another lawyer in a big downtown law firm. I hated it. I hated adding up the hours and the minutes, right down to the seconds. I hated the concept of billable hours. I felt sleazy as I wrote out huge invoices and pushed them into my clients' hands. I didn't know what else to do with my law degree. I had to do what the firm required." She dropped her head into her hands. After a long moment of silence, she looked up. "Then I met Wa Sing. He told me I was wasting my time. He offered to help. To resurrect my career."

Nick understood perfectly. He saw it at least once a week, all the ambulance-chasers outside detention centres, looking for business among the jailed and the deportees. The ones who thought that they were hot shit spent their time in plush surroundings, kissing asses as they begged for appointments to the political trough or on corporate boards. The roster of just about every corporate board and government agency was over-represented with lawyers. A glut of them on the market had made it impossible for any but the seasoned veterans to earn a comfy living. He knew too many lawyers too well. He knew the ones with connections had fled the profession, moved on, like rats fleeing a sinking ship.

Her head was turned away from him, looking out the window into some middle distance. After a long silence, she continued, "Just before the present government took power, he came to me, like a fairy godfather, and said he could get me a political appointment to the bench. I asked him how. He told me that he had made generous campaign contributions to half a dozen politicians running for office. Fortunately for him and for me, he had backed the right political party. After they won, Wa Sing called in his favours. The politicians he funded now owed him. Within a matter of months, Wa Sing started dispensing favours. Out of friendship for my mother, he did this for me. I'm not the only one he blessed. But I don't know who the others are. He's never told me and I've never asked."

Her voice was even and filled with resignation. "It's not a subject that I bring up because it isn't always understood. I don't think I was unqualified, or that I didn't deserve the appointment, but I didn't work for it. I'm not exactly proud of that. I felt that I had lost integrity. It made me ashamed. In my family, we work for our achievements. My family and friends treated me as if I had done something special. Something extraordinary. I hadn't."

She exhaled, and slumped lower in her chair. Her hands twisted the sash of her robe.

"In our family, if someone does you a favour, you owe them one. It's that simple. Wa Sing never brought it up. Not until now. Until now I never had to choose between bringing integrity to my work and showing my gratitude for a favour done years ago." Finally she looked up and met his eyes. "No, I never told you any of this. You've always kept your integrity intact, always lived by your own strict code, each and every day. How could I tell you? I thought you would think less of me. You see, I wanted you to think I was worth having."

"What deal have you struck now? To go positive on Sun Sui?"

"I was asked to. But I haven't struck any deals. I can't, and I won't. If I do go positive, it will be because of the merits of the case. But if I found in Sun Sui's favour, and you knew about my history with Wa Sing, how could I ever be sure you believed in me? But I've longed to tell you about it. It's been very hard. It's not just Wa Sing who's pushing me."

"There's someone else?"

"My boss. He says his boss is pushing for a positive decision."

"Your boss's boss? That would be the minister of immigration? My boss?"

"I suppose so, Nick," she said in a soft voice. "Can you get past this? Can our relationship get past this?"

He walked to her side and reached for her hand. She gave it, looking up at him tentatively. Had he forgiven her?

"It's not over yet," he said. "I've put out an arrest warrant for Wa Sing. The RCMP at the Singapore embassy have finally caught up with him. He's on a plane home as we speak. I thought you should hear about it from me."

"Why, Nick?"

"I'm going to subpoena him to testify against Sun."

"What makes you think he will?"

"If he doesn't, I'll treat him as a hostile witness. But I'm hoping he'll cooperate. I'll dangle immunity in front of him."

"Then we're on opposite sides on this one Nick. I can't stand idly if he's been arrested and is locked up in detention somewhere. I have to help him. Then my debt to him will be repaid. It'll be easier than going positive on Sun Sui."

Nick fell silent as he stood by her side.

"I guess we shouldn't see each other until this case is over."

"I guess you're right."

She sighed deeply.

"The first time our relationship ended it was because of David. But my marriage was over, really. I let it be about my husband, as an excuse. In a way I was relieved when you ended it, because it meant I wouldn't have to come clean on this. The truth was, I simply didn't know how to. David understood how these things are done. Those plum diplomatic jobs are all by appointments. In that regard we deserved each other."

He reached out his hand to her again, but she ignored it.

"God, if I had known I would have to pay this high a price for a job I accepted years ago, would I have said yes?" She ran her fingers through her hair, and wrapped the sash more tightly around her waist.

He watched her, feeling sorry for her. Accepting one favour, years before had taken a huge personal toll on her emotional well-being.

"I believe you, Grace."

"Thanks, Nick. Now I've no more secrets in my closet. And I'm not in cahoots with anyone."

He reached out to her and pulled her into his arms. As he embraced her, as he spoke the words of forgiveness, another part of his mind was working, thinking.

"I've got an idea, Grace. I think it would be very useful if we found out who else benefited from Wa Sing's benevolence."

"You mean who also received political appointments and favours?"

"Yes."

"How am I going to do that?"

"I don't know, Grace. You know him, I don't. I'll leave that to you."

"I'll think about it. If I get the chance, I'll ask him. If he refuses to divulge names, then that's the end of that. I won't push him."

Nick nodded. "His flight touches down in three hours."

After he left her house, he went for a long walk in a nearby park and ruminated on what she had told him. He had always suspected something along those lines, except he had thought it was her ex-husband who had sponsored her political appointment. But in light of her membership in the Asia Business Council and her mother's friendship with Wa Sing, it made perfect sense for the old man to sponsor her. But what he was left with was exactly what she feared. He doubted her. How could he be sure she would not be influenced by her obligation to repay a favour owed? Could he really trust her to be an impartial decision maker, to judge Sun's case on its exclusion merits? He was pretty sure that Sun was the ringleader, the Don, of the Flying Dragons. If she rejected his asylum claim, Nick would know she was honest. Or would he? Wasn't he putting pressure on her now, just as the others were, from the other side? One thing he knew for sure: Grace was in a difficult position. He hoped she would be able to make a fair and impartial decision. And when the decision was made, he hoped the trust between them would be restored. He wanted to believe in her.

The afternoon sun hovered between the buildings. Heat and humidity filled the air. Li Mann Vu checked for signs of a tail as he left the travel agency. The street scene around him appeared normal. A low rent district with its share of transients on the street. Weather-beaten apartment buildings owned by slumlords. A soiled ribbon of storefronts that catered to immigrants and the down-and-out. Li Mann smiled to himself as he tucked the one-way ticket in his back pocket. He fitted right into the neighbourhood in the east end of Ottawa.

After the woman, one more job and he was going home. Soon he would be back on Vietnamese soil. Soon he would hail a truck that doubled as a taxi and take the road leading into Ho Chi Minh City. He would see farmers in conical hats who were already hoisting baskets of produce to market, and animal vendors were peddling cages of parrots, monkeys, and wildcats.

If his luck held out, he could be in Da Nang at the end of the week or early next week. He just had one more job to do. The trick was, how to kill three birds with one stone. He mulled on that thought as he walked toward his car. He reached for the parking ticket stuck to his windshield wiper, ripped it in half before tossing it in the gutter.

At the end of the day, Nick and Dubois were at the airport to greet Wa Sing as he disembarked from his flight from Singapore. Wa Sing's lawyer, a flamboyant-looking man in his late thirties, was waiting, too.

"Mr. Sing," said Nick, pausing. "I trust your flight wasn't too taxing."

Dubois remained silent. Diplomacy wasn't his strong suit. But at least he held his rudeness in check.

Nick wondered briefly when Wa Sing had had the opportunity to alert his lawyer, Mulcahy, to his predicament. Dealing with lawyers would make his work all the more difficult. The goal in bringing Wa Sing back into the country was to find out what he knew about Sun Sui. Now every scrap of information would be given out warily, after long consideration. It would be like a chess match.

Wa Sing looked down glumly at the handcuffs on his wrists.

"You can make life easier for yourself if you cooperate," said Nick. "We're not interested in you, but in what you know."

Mulcahy jumped in. "Before my client provides any information, we want to know what's on the table. Because as we all know, my client has not been charged with any offences. You allege that he made illegal campaign contributions. If he's charged, then it should only be fair that those on the receiving end of campaign contributions be charged as well."

"Our investigation isn't about him. After he provides us with the information we need, he's free to go."

"Showing good faith by removing the handcuffs would be a nice start," said Mulcahy.

"We can accommodate that," replied Dubois, reaching into his back pocket for the key.

Wa Sing whispered something in the ear of his lawyer.

"Excuse me for a minute," said Mulcahy, as they walked toward a bank of telephones. After a brief conversation, he returned and spoke a few words to his client. Then they all climbed into the back of an RCMP paddy wagon.

"My client wishes to ask a friend to meet him at the police station."

"I see nothing wrong with that," said Nick. Would the friend turn out to be Grace?

The lawyer made a quick call, and they were on their way. When they got to the RCMP headquarters, she was already there, waiting for them. She did not greet him, or look at him. Nick watched her engaged in conversation with the old man. For the first time, he saw the deference in her manner. And wondered if it was the same for all the others who had benefited from the old man's largesse?

Dubois found a room large enough for all five participants. Nick, in his shirtsleeves, sat at the head of the table. He and Dubois laid out the terms of the deal they were prepared to offer.

"We'll give him immunity from prosecution if he cooperates and provides us with the information we need."

Wa Sing shook his head vigorously. "No, I can't cooperate."

Grace grabbed his armed and whispered furiously in his ear. But the old man kept shaking his head.

She stared straight at Nick, "He doesn't have the information you want. That's why he can't help you."

"Bullshit!" announced Dubois.

Nick directed his gaze at Mulcahy. "If that's the game he wants to play, then more than one can play it. I'm going to subpoena him as a hostile witness to give evidence on what he knows about a man claiming asylum whose case is currently being heard. When I'm finished with him, the RCMP will take him into custody and grill him on the details of his campaign contributions. There's a paper trail of close to a million dollars moving from offshore banks to his account, and then out again as cheques he wrote to political parties. Particularly the present government."

Nick saw a look of shock cross Grace's face. Was she only now realizing that Wa Sing wasn't just an unimportant minor player in this, but one of its kingpins?

Mulcahy ordered Wa Sing not to answer any questions.

Dubois had been leaning back in his chair, listening and watching the proceedings. Now he took over. Nick knew how much he loved doing this — pushing people up against the wall and watching them crumble. Only the strongest survived. "We want to know who he's fronting for? Is it the Chinese government? The Taiwanese government? The triads? And which politicians he was told to back? And what the politicians have to do in exchange for winning? I want a lot of info. Else he ain't gonna see the light of day anytime soon."

The negotiation of the prisoner's rights versus information given continued throughout the evening. At points in the discussion, it turned nasty, with name calling on all sides. Wa Sing didn't seem overly concerned with his plight. He sat stoically, with lips pursed, chin jutting out, while his lawyer spun argument after argument. Grace spoke little, just sat and watched the players in the interrogation room. Nick observed her watching the point-counterpoint match between the participants. It gave him an idea. Maybe the way to reach the old man was through her. He called for a recess and asked to speak to her privately.

"Grace, he's in a difficult situation. I don't want an old man sitting in some jail cell all night. I can tell Dubois that if you put up bail, we can put him up in a hotel. A warm bed is better than a jail cell. But I want you to talk to him, get him to cooperate. It's a *quid pro quo* kind of thing."

"Believe me, I don't want him sitting in a jail cell either. With a bunch of hardened criminals."

"We both know he's in serious trouble. First, his name shows up on a list before a senate inquiry and he's asked to testify on illegal slush fund contributions. Next thing you know he's left the country. Not good. He's got quite a few strikes against him, I'd say. Cooperation is the only thing that's going to save his bacon. Grace, you know where I'm coming from. I'm gunning for Sun Sui. I want to know what he knows about Sun. That's all. I don't care about whose campaign he contributed to. My advice to you on this is remember it's Dubois' show. Satisfy him with names and he'll deal."

Grace looked at him directly for the first time that day. "Nick, I'll talk to him."

She talked to Wa Sing alone while Nick, Dubois, and Mulcahy waited outside the interrogation room.

After twenty-five minutes she emerged and asked them to come back in.

Wa Sing spoke up, looking at Grace. "I made several contributions to politicians in the last federal election. You're right. The contributions totalled just over one million dollars."

"The names of those who received contributions?" Dubois had his pen poised over paper.

"Your boss," he said, glancing from Nick to Grace.

Dubois dropped his pen on the floor. He didn't bother picking it up, as he pushed his chair back. He and Nick left the room to confer, discussing Wa Sing's information and where it pointed.

"Where the money went to is bad enough, never mind where the money came from. I wouldn't be surprised if the government told him to take a long vacation outside the country. I've been in this business too long. It's obvious that the politicians want one thing and the bureaucrats want to call an inquiry. No way the politicians are going to allow a senate inquiry to go ahead and bring down one of their own. A cabinet minister like the minister of immigration carries a lot of weight in the government. No way we'll be allowed to press charges. It's way too political. Career suicide for all of us. Nick, we walk away. Put it all behind us."

Nick said nothing for a moment. He looked at Dubois with an expression the RCMP officer couldn't read. "Let's go back in there," he said.

Back in the room, Nick ignored Mulcahy as he spun Wa Sing's chair around until the old man came face to face with him.

"Tell me about Sun Sui."

"What's there to tell?"

"Don't toy with me, old man."

Finally Wa Sing sighed and said, "Sun is a Red Prince. He comes from one of China's hundred or so elite families. I can't speak ill of him. He has the ear of the Mandarins in power over there. He's good to do business with, but there's much to fear if one is on the receiving end of his displeasure."

"What about his triad links to the Flying Dragons? Where is he on the ladder of people smuggling?"

The old man shook his head. "I can't say more."

"I'm sorry, but you'll have to testify. I've already prepared documents to subpoena you," said Nick.

"I can't speak against Sun. You don't know what he's like. The last person who spoke against him was his business partner in Hong Kong. And he was shot dead."

Dubois interrupted. "Nick, let's go slow here. His testimony in refugee court could cause political damage."

"Do I give a shit about political damage? All I want to know is the link between Sun Sui and Li Mann Vu, the man who pulled the trigger that night Walter was killed. Since I can't get my hands on Li Mann, I'll settle for Sun."

"I don't know anyone called Li Mann."

"Don't lie to me!" yelled Nick.

"Stop badgering my client," Mulcahy warned Nick.

Dubois turned to Nick and said, "It smells bad to me. That's all I'm saying. But if you're prepared to get him on the witness stand, I'll back you. But for me, I ain't gonna waste energy on pursuing charges of illegal campaign contributions 'cause I know better. I've been in the business too long."

Grace stared directly at Nick. "Mr. Sing is tired. Not to mention he's suffering from bad jet lag. He's going to need a doctor if he doesn't get some rest. If you look at his feet, they're already swollen with edema from sitting on a plane too long."

"She's right. You have to release my client now," ordered Mr. Mulcahy.

"I'll post bond," said Grace, looking at Nick. "We'll take him to any hotel that you have in mind. We'll continue this again tomorrow."

Nick and Dubois reluctantly assented. They could see the prisoner was very fatigued.

Grace sat in the back of a police cruiser with Nick and Wa Sing. The lawyer had gone home. A second cruiser followed behind the prisoner's.

They rode in silence. Grace's mind was racing. The information Wa Sing had provided about Sun Sui had stunned her. If Sun was a Red Prince, how could he think he would get away with claiming the Chinese government as his agent of persecution.

Their first stop was at a nearby hotel. When Nick got out of the car to check with hotel management, Wa Sing quickly said, "Listen to me, Grace. There isn't much time. Do you have a pen and paper? I'm going to give you a phone number. Call him and tell him about my situation."

Grace looked at him questioningly.

"Never mind who the number belongs to. Write it down, quickly, before he returns."

After jotting down the number he told her and slipping the piece of paper into her shirt pocket, Grace looked out the window, keeping her eyes on Nick, who appeared to be having a heated exchange with the front desk clerk. She took the opportunity to ask a few questions of her own.

"When we talked that day at the yacht club, were you doing it for yourself or for Sun?"

"For you, Grace. This man is the lord of the Flying Dragons. He asked me to pass the message on.

And Sun is a dangerous man. He wouldn't hesitate to kill you."

Grace felt a sudden chill. She was silent for a long moment. So many thoughts were firing inside her head at once.

"I wanted to protect you, Grace."

"Why did you get involved with criminals like Sun in the first place? Why did you do it?"

The question seemed to take Wa Sing by surprise. He leaned back against the seat and closed his eyes. She thought she had lost him, but a moment later, he began to speak.

"I knew what I was getting into, in a way. And in a way, I didn't. You must understand, Grace, things are done differently in China. You can't do business there or in Hong Kong until you find the right person. Or make the right contact. In Hong Kong, I knew I had met the right contact in Sun. He'd only been there for about a year, but you could tell that he was a real operator. I was very impressed with him. And he had the right contacts inside China."

"Did you know then that he was a triad member?"

"Yes. When I met him, I had heard through various sources, that he was being groomed to take over the organization. Since he was anointed the Don, the tentacles of the Dragons now circle right around the globe. And they have legitimized themselves by partnering with clean companies."

Grace looked at him and nodded a little encouragement. "Back then when you met him, didn't you realize that he was reeling you in?"

"I wanted to be reeled in. The joint venture deals were huge. No way I could get them on my own. I was seduced by all that money that kept pouring in. For the first time in my life it started to sink in how much power is derived from the amount of money you have. After I signed the $145 million deal on that office tower in Hong Kong, and the British governor threw a party in my honour, I was hooked. The British prime minister was there. So was the French prime minister. Hollywood celebrities came out to shake my hands. The more I got, the more I wanted. It became a drug. And guess what?"

Grace shook her head, keeping her eye on Nick.

"The more deals I got, and the more money I made, the more he wanted. He started to expect big things from it."

"Like funnelling campaign contributions to political parties?"

"Yes, I cooperated. And I did some other things for Sun that I'm not going to talk about right now. Not with you, Grace."

"Shhhh," said Grace. "Nick's coming back."

As Nick approached the car, Wa Sing suddenly squeezed her hand hard. "Grace," he said in an urgent whisper. "If anything happens to me, look inside the red dragon in my house." She darted a questioning look at him, but he had turned his head away.

Leaning down to the car window, Nick said, "No deal here. Apparently they don't want our business if it comes with round-the-clock security guards. The hotel's under new management, trying to go upscale. We're not the kind of business they're trying to attract."

He gave the driver another address and got into the passenger seat beside him. The driver put the car in gear and they moved out into the evening traffic.

Grace tried to think, but all she heard in her head was the roar of motorcycles in the distance.

She loved the old man. He had worked with Sun Sui. He hadn't known that the price to be paid for the gifts received would be so high. Neither had she. She gave Wa Sing's hand a comforting squeeze.

At the intersection, Grace turned toward the old man, and spoke in Mandarin.

"The number you want me to call. Is that Sun's number?"

He turned and looked at her severely, silencing her with a sharp look of his eyes. Grace knew that he was telling her with his eyes that he was afraid for them both, and that some things were better left unsaid in the company of others. Even in a language their escort didn't know. She could tell from the slight turn of Nick's head in the seat in front that he had seen the exchange in the rear-view mirror. Not much was lost on him.

At the next hotel on the list, Nick abruptly told Grace to get out of the car and accompany him. Wa Sing was left in the car, handcuffed to the door. The police officer got out from behind the wheel and walked away a few paces, lighting a cigarette.

After the night manager of the hotel agreed to accept a guest who would be under armed guard, Grace and Nick walked out of the lobby together. Grace turned to him and said in a low, angry tone, "You know, there's no need for you and your RCMP friend to belittle him like this. Treating him like a common criminal."

"We're treating him the way we treat everyone," said Nick, in a neutral tone.

"Oh? He hasn't been charged with anything. He's got no criminal record, but you guys demeaned him. You took him down for fingerprinting. And if one set wasn't bad enough you had to get two copies of his fingerprints. Talk about extreme humiliation, Nick."

"He should have thought of that before he ran like a common criminal."

The explosion knocked them flat on their backs on the sidewalk. For a minute they lay on concrete and bricks, stunned. Slowly they became aware of a ferocious fire in the prisoner's car. The force of the explosion had shattered the glass panels at the front of the hotel and nearby buildings. As well, it shattered the car windows and windshield of the second police cruiser, and several cars parked nearby. An empty tour bus was also caught in the fiery explosion. It was like a scene out of Dante's *Inferno*.

Grace gaped in horror at the flames licking the first cruiser, Wa Sing was trapped inside. She screamed for him, ran towards the car, trying to save him. Nick pulled her back from the flames and the heat.

"Call 911!" someone yelled.

Nick dragged her back to the sidewalk, away from the acrid smoke. Dazed-looking survivors lay on the ground, covered in blood. A crowd was beginning to appear. The fire trucks were the first to arrive, but there was little they could do. In a matter of minutes, several police cruisers were on the scene followed by the wail of an ambulance. A cop shoved his way through the crowd of onlookers. Nick approached him with information. Grace remained sitting on the ground, too shocked to stand. A policewoman sat beside her, and attempted to comfort her.

There was debris spread over a fifty-metre radius. The entire crime scene took on a different personality when Nick became part of it. Within an hour, two RCMP officers had assembled several facts from witnesses in the area. The parking lot attendant next to the hotel described seeing a car and motorcycle parked across the street just before the explosion. When the lot attendant saw the flames shooting towards the sky, he simultaneously heard the roar of a motorcycle engine. The car and motorcycle turned eastward. Two passers-by also noticed the car and motorcycle. That was all the witnesses remembered. No distinguishing characteristics, no plate numbers.

Nick approached the blanketed form of the chauffeur's body, and knelt beside it. Then he slowly rose and walked toward the smoking wreckage of what was left of the car. He stood studying the wreckage for a long time before walking away.

Finally he came over to Grace and put his arms around her. Her shock gave way to grief and she wept uncontrollably. Nick tried to comfort her. He felt her body tremble against his. Reporters were milling around them. He pushed them away, and led her into a car. She insisted that there was no need for her to go to the hospital but Nick could see that she was in no shape to take herself home. Instead, he took her back to his hotel room.

Nick sat next to Grace on the bed and held her. "Do you know what this is all about, Grace?"

"I thought I did. But now ..." Her voice trailed off.

"It's about power. It's about winning elections by fair means or foul," said Nick. He stood and began pacing across the room, from the door to the window and back. "It's about money," he said in a tight, angry monotone. His voice rising, he went on, "Those with the big bucks to run a campaign win the elections. This is the great tradition of politics in the free world. It's cloaked in fancy dinners, campaign contributions, owing favours to supporters and money men. It's no longer about the best man winning. It's those with the best connections who can reach those with the deepest pockets. We're no better than Iran or Russia. Do you know what happens when we let rich men buy politicians, Grace?"

She didn't speak.

He continued with his tirade. "Then they own them. The real bosses are the ones who funded their political campaigns. In this case, Wa Sing was killed because they wanted to keep him quiet. But it's not about whose campaign he funded. That information is in the public record somewhere." He turned to look at her. "I think, he was killed to keep quiet on what political favours were received in exchange for the money."

"Do you think he fronted for people like Sun?"

"Yes. And for foreign governments like China and Russia. Probably did it through shell companies."

"Now we'll never know what information died with him."

Grace thought of Wa Sing's last words to her, not really sure what he had meant, but resolved to try and find out. She owed him that. She shuddered as she remembered his words that Sun Sui wouldn't hesitate to kill her too, and she didn't want to die. Wa Sing didn't deserve to die like that.

Nick watched a tear run down her cheek. He squeezed her hand and brushed it away with his lips, then kissed her. She returned the kiss, and they fell back together on the bed. The connection between them was immediate. His hands were in her hair, on her breasts, pushing up her dress. After they made love, Grace wept again for her old friend, as Nick held her in a tight embrace. Gradually she relaxed, and they fell asleep, entwined and exhausted.

chapter twenty-seven

The day after the bombing was day three of the hearing. Sun was dressed for victory in an expensive blue-grey tailored suit, gaudy diamond cufflinks, and a Rolex. He exuded confidence as he took his seat in the witness chair.

Grace was angry and vengeful. She felt like an actor playing the part of a judge. No way she could forget what Wa Sing had told her about Sun before he died. Much of what he had told her was confirmed in Nick's package of evidence. Her mind was made up as she took her seat on the bench, but she had to be careful about revealing her hand. Her strategy was to allow Verster to open with his examination-in-chief before she hijacked the examination from him. As Sun took the oath to tell the truth, Grace wondered how much coaching he'd had. He picked up his story where he had left off, describing his escape from his prison guards. But after last night, sitting in a hearing room and listening to Sun portraying his younger self as an idealistic young student seemed unreal. Her mind floated as if she was travelling through a dark tunnel. It was dangerous to do this, she could lose the thread of questioning.

"Counsel, I've several questions of clarification to put to Mr. Sui before we move on to his time in Hong Kong."

Verster gave his consent reluctantly.

Grace changed the tempo of the questions so that Sun wouldn't have time to remember everything he'd said in the previous two hearings.

"Mr. Sui, I want to take you back to the day of your escape while you were being transferred from one prison to another. In your narrative, your wife found the driver to drive the getaway car."

Sun Sui relaxed his posture, he nodded his head.

"The driver of the getaway car stayed with you for a long time. Why did he risk his own safety to do that?"

"I paid him well. Actually my family and my wife's family paid him well."

"Still, money is one thing. And freedom from jail or capital punishment for abetting a felon is another. What's his name?"

"Li Mann Vu."

The man who had tried to kill her that night on the Parkway! Grace wondered if he had played a role in Wa Sing's murder. She was sure that Sun Sui had ordered his death. The trick was to keep bias out of her language, tone of voice, and demeanour. She quickly jotted a few notes on the legal pad.

"How did your wife find this Li Mann?"

"I don't know. I never asked her. I was just grateful that she found someone to help," said Sun, studying his nails.

Liar. Keeping an even tone she asked, "Li Mann Vu stayed with you in China and fled with you to Hong

Kong. Am I right?"

"Yes." He shot her an angry look. He did not want to go through this door.

Too bad. On the record she established his criminality through his association with Li Mann Vu.

"I can understand why your wife would want to hide from the PSB. But why did she go to Fujian to be with her brother? Why not Shanghai?"

"She's only my wife in name. We've been estranged too long and divorce is frowned upon in my family. Jiang stayed with her brother in Fujian. As head of the port authority there, she thought he could protect her against other high level government officials."

Bingo! The Fujian connection was another nail in the coffin to his illegal smuggling activities.

Verster quickly bent toward Sun to silence him. Turning to Grace, he asked, "Your Honour, may I ask where you are going with these questions?"

"Bear with me, counsel." Turning her attention back to Sun, Grace said, "On question 15 of your asylum application, you state your father-in-law's occupation as army. You mean, the People's Liberation Army?"

"Yes."

Grace furiously leafed through pages of evidence. "In exhibit package 9, fourth paragraph down, it states that the corruption inside the People's Liberation Army is terrible. In many regions, the army leaders and troops live in nice houses, drive new cars, and are flush with cash. Care to comment on that, Mr. Sui?"

"It's not that China is corrupt."

"No?" asked Grace, raising one eyebrow at him.

"China has merely reverted to the old system of doing business. Everything is done on personal relationship and commission."

That jibed with what Wa Sing had told her. She

reached for exhibit package 21 of Nick's documentary evidence. "Given your family history, the documentary evidence states that you're a Red Prince. You belong to that special class of children of well-connected former revolutionaries. In the new China, there is an emerging axis of power between Communist party officials, the army, the Red Princes, the taipans in Hong Kong, and triads. Would you agree with that?"

"Yes, that's quite true," said Sun in a flash of arrogance.

Obviously he enjoyed being a Red Prince. It was starting to jell. "That being the case, did you belong to the Flying Dragons at any time when you lived in Hong Kong or here in Canada?"

"No."

"What the hell?" shouted Verster, jumping up from his seat. "Sun, don't answer any more questions."

Grace had no intention of asking any more questions about triads. It was enough that she had opened the door for Nick. At the same time, Sun had perjured himself under oath. Gottcha on credibility. If Nick failed to make his case for whatever reason, she could always turn his asylum claim down, citing his failure to pass the credibility test. Wa Sing deserved that.

Preparing a trap for Verster, she said, "Regarding the issue of exclusion, I'd hate to waste Mr. Slovak's time by having him fly to Ottawa to canvas the claimant on his alleged criminal links to the Flying Dragons." She paused.

"I totally agree with you," replied Verster.

Good. Now she had him. "That being the case, I'd like Mr. Sui to submit his phone records going back to his arrival in Canada."

"What? Why should we submit phone records?" demanded Verster, nervously tapping a pencil on the table.

Meeting Verster's gaze, she answered, "The court needs to be satisfied that Mr. Sui doesn't have criminal links with the Flying Dragons or with any other criminal organization. What better way than to produce phone records and examine who he communicates with. After all, we all want to save Mr. Slovak a trip up here."

When Verster realized that he had made an oversight, he said in a bullying tone, "I want it noted on the record that I strenuously object to this."

"So noted," replied Grace, watching the busy movements while trying to eavesdrop on the constant whispered interchanges between Sun and his lawyer.

After some time, Verster barked from his table, "Your Honour, phone records have nothing to do with this asylum case. Therefore we won't be submitting any phone records."

Pumped up for battle on this point, Grace said in a calm, clear voice, "Then I'll have to subpoena them."

"You can't be serious!" shouted Verster.

"I am. And I just did." She smiled smugly to herself. The subpoena had caught them flatfooted. Fuck with me and kill my friend and this is what you get. Yes, she had gotten them by the balls.

Back in her office, Grace heard the radio newscaster announce in sombre tones the death of one of the country's philanthropists. She said a prayer as she picked up the phone and called her mother.

"Mom, I've something to tell you."

"Grace, it's all over the news. Your father and I have been trying to reach you all morning."

"Mom, I'm at work."

"Take leave, Grace, and come home."

"I can't, mom. Not right now."

"Grace, answer me. The newscast said that there was a woman with him in the car. Was that you?"

"Yes, it was." Grace gave her mother a sanitized version of Wa Sing assisting the police in the illegal campaign contribution inquiry, and how they were booking him into a hotel when the car blew up. And how she had happened to be in the hotel while Wa Sing waited in the car for her to return.

The sound of her mother sobbing into the phone unleashed a fresh wave of tears. Grace reached for the box of Kleenex on her desk.

"The newscaster said it could be the work of triads. Is that true, Grace?"

"There's a strong possibility of that, mom," said Grace reluctantly, not wanting to discuss the specifics of the case with her mother.

"We don't need Asian trash in this country."

Grace said nothing. It was not the time to remind her mother of an earlier conversation where she wanted her to go positive on Sun Sui.

Her mother's voice was stronger now. "If Wa Sing was murdered, and you know something, Grace, you'll have tell the authorities. You can't do nothing."

"Mom, I'm doing everything I can. Trust me on that."

In the beginning, BJ had worried about getting caught. But over the years he'd learned to enjoy the cat-and-mouse game. It was like a challenge — he dared the cops to find him.

He stood with the throng of noisy picketers outside the Immigration and Refugee Commission. This time, he had brought a sign. It read, "Criminals Go Home." He pulled his Dodgers baseball cap down low over his sunglasses.

The bald man picketing alongside him asked, "You coming back tomorrow for the rally?"

"Maybe. What's it about?"

"Against immigration policy."

"Yeah, I guess so."

"Me too. I drove all the way in from Kingston. We gotta defend the country for our white brothers and sisters."

"I'm with you, brother."

They gave each other a high five.

"She has to come out soon," said the bald man. "Unless she's going to sleep on her office floor."

Someone yelled, "Everybody get into position for the cameras. Hold the placards high so the cameras can read them."

The crowd roared, capturing the attention of the TV crew. Someone in the crowd yelled, "We ain't got enough food to feed our children. But foreigners can come here and steal food from us by sitting on the dole or stealing our jobs and putting us in the soup lines."

"Yeah! And if that ain't bad enough, they do the crime but not the time. I say we save public money and deport the sucker!"

The placard-carrying crowd cheered. Then they joined hands as if they were in a national unity rally, and started to sing "O Canada!"

Building security warned Grace to delay her departure from the building by five or ten minutes. Enough time for the police to break up the crowd. When they got there a few minutes later, officers with bullhorns called on the crowd to disperse. "Move on, before we charge all of you with trespassing on public property."

After another police unit showed up, the crowd began to thin as people left for the day, but not before grumbling to the reporters.

BJ hung back and waited for the judge to exit the building. As soon as she did, the press pounced on her. He watched from across the street. Then he decided to trail the media who were trailing her. Piece of cake. The icing came when he spotted the goon who had whacked Harry that night.

Across town that afternoon, Nick was meeting with Dubois and his colleagues at RCMP headquarters.

"This whole damn thing sucks," said Dubois.

Nick nodded.

They waited as the other officers filed into the room. When everyone was seated, Nick opened the meeting. "According to Rocco, Li Mann Vu posed as Li Thu and left Pearson International on a direct flight to Seattle the same day that Wa Sing was flying in. From the ticket he purchased in Chinatown, his final destination was Vietnam." He threw up his hands. "That means we've lost him. We can go through the motions and seek extradition, but I'm not holding my breath on that. Vietnam is a whole different ball game. The leadership does whatever they want to do. That means our entire focus is on Sun Sui. He's all we've got."

Nick sat down, turning over the meeting to Dubois. It was his show. He stood and paused for effect before beginning, "Not only is this a murder investigation, but it's also an investigation into a cop killer," said Dubois. "And an investigation into organized criminal activity." He picked up a manual, which he waved in the air as he spoke. "The bomb was detonated by remote control. We know Sun Sui ordered the hit even though he didn't push the remote. Right now, Sun's got our own officers as an alibi."

"I don't get it. How did he plan it if he was under round-the-clock surveillance and his hotel phone was tapped?" asked one of the junior officers.

"Nick, feed the videotape into the machine, will ya?"

As Nick adjusted the channel on the television, Dubois went on, "The guy's no idiot. It's us who fucked up. Here he is. First day of his hearing at 10:30 a.m., according to the timer, he's downstairs in the lobby of the IRC and he's making a phone call in the pay phone just down from the elevators. Call lasted ten minutes. Unfortunately the phone company ain't too helpful on getting us a list of numbers dialled on that phone."

Dubois ejected the tape and fed another one into the machine. "Same thing here. Our guy making a phone call from another pay phone on day two of his hearing. From the security camera, this call lasts about fifteen minutes. Who the hell is he talking to? Whoever it is, it's the one that takes the orders and passes it down the line. From the way he's standing we can't get a good look at the numbers he's dialling. That means, we don't know if it was a local call or long distance. Either way, our guy's barking the contract kill order into the phone, and our people are alibiing for him."

Nick said, "A motorcyclist was seen in the vicinity just before the bomb went off. But he was wearing a helmet and goggles. My hunch is it was Li Mann tying up loose ends. However, we can't prove it. Nor have the Flying Dragons admitted responsibility for the bombing. But we're sure they were behind it."

One of the officers pessimistically remarked, "So what if it was a Flying Dragons hit? What are the chances of us catching this cop killer? We've been up against organized crime long enough to know of cases where these killers fly in on phony passports, do a hit, and get on the next plane out. Maybe he's already left the country."

"Maybe he hasn't and we'll get lucky," snapped Dubois. "We lost one of our own, remember? That means we're going to work the case to death. Now I suggest we contact police detachments across the country and pull every member of every triad in for questioning. Extensive questioning."

"We can do that," said one of the homicide detectives. "Not only questioning, guys. I also want the lieutenants of the Dragons under watch."

"Good idea," said Dubois. "I want it set up ASAP, before midnight."

The meeting ended and the officers went to work immediately. Nick was pessimistic, but at least, he reflected, with bitter satisfaction, the bodies were piling up around Sun Sui. There was no way Grace could grant him asylum now. Sun's knowledge of police movements, even when he was under house arrest, was infuriating. He was goading them, mocking them.

He made it back to Grace's place at six that evening. He found her leaning against the kitchen counter, talking to the funeral home. She was dressed in a black T-shirt and jeans. Her hair hung loose around her face. There was exhaustion and gentleness in her face, and a certain vulnerability.

"Let's go out for dinner," said Nick.

"You buying?"

"I'm open to persuasion." He pulled her into his arms.

Hand in hand they walked down her neighbourhood street. Fuck Cadeux! She was going to see whomever she pleased. Her personal life was her own business.

They walked in silence down to her favourite Indian curry house. The evening was relatively cool, with a fresh breeze coming off the river. Rollerbladers rushed by them and joggers cut across their path, all on their way somewhere.

Over dinner he told her about the meeting at RCMP headquarters. Grace could not reciprocate with news of her day. Nick understood this. Still, he found her mood vague and distant throughout the meal. When coffee was on the table, he took her hand and said, "We're going to get the man who killed Wa Sing. I promise, Grace."

"I know, Nick. I'm just thinking about this number Wa Sing gave me in the police car before he was killed. He told me to call the number. I did. Twice from a pay phone. Both times, no answer. Not even a recorded message." Grace shook her head. "There wasn't enough time for him to tell me who the number belonged to. You were getting back into the cruiser."

Nick took the number from her. "It's a government number."

"I know."

He jotted the number down on a paper napkin and gave her back the original. I'll have Rocco look into it."

She squeezed his hand affectionately. "Thanks, Nick."

"We'll survive this thing. And we'll get him. Don't worry, Grace."

Outside the restaurant, she reached up and kissed him. "What about us? Do you think it's too late for us, Nick?"

"You know I still love you. I know we've hurt each other and there's some scar tissue. Grace, I'd like us to start all over again and be more careful about us."

She nodded. "I love you."

Nick kissed her on the lips, softly at first, and then passionately. "Come on, let's go home."

chapter twenty-eight

Jean Cadeux banged down the phone and ordered her to shut the door. He scowled at her under heavy brows. "You've disobeyed my instructions."

"What instructions were those?"

"I told you to get this hearing over with quickly. Instead, I hear that you've now subpoenaed the claimant's phone records. Phone records from the claimant's household are meaningless."

"Sir, I'm surprised that you would monitor the progress of the case on a daily basis." She groaned to herself. The man was a true micro-manager and control freak. For the first time she wondered if he might be something worse. She'd always assumed he was concerned only with protecting his own skin. Could he be protecting someone else as well?

"I've no choice but to file a grievance to the judicial committee regarding your conduct in the hearing room," he was saying in a threatening tone.

"What conduct is that? Doing my job? Looking into his membership in a criminal organization such as the Flying Dragons?"

He glared at her with steely eyes. "None of this speculation is relevant. We don't have enough hearing rooms as it is, and some of the lawyers are starting to complain that adjournments are taking too long."

"I find that hard to believe," she countered, trying to figure out what was behind this latest hissy fit. She held her silence as he grabbed a copy of the subpoena off his desk, his hands shaking with anger.

She began to relax. If he wanted to reprimand her over subpoenaing his pet asylum claimant, fine. The publicity would reflect badly on him. What was her crime? "Too thorough an examination of the evidence and legal issues." Whose side would the court of public opinion take? She didn't see any point in defending her actions. His mind was already made up.

"Will that be all, sir?" She didn't wait for an answer. She rose and walked toward the door.

"You can expect a letter next week from the committee regarding your judicial conduct."

She didn't bother responding as she closed the door behind her.

On the way out, she made a mental note to watch her back more carefully with him. In this town, no one got power without seeking it out, or hung onto it without compromising in some way, big or small, and Cadeux was the personification of the slow and steady accretion of power and privilege at the expense of others. Always seeking the next connection that would pull him into the light. The kind of man who would serve his master with slavish devotion until the day he could stab him in the back and take his place.

Back in her office, she switched on her computer. Sun's claim was heading south. She found it more efficient to update the findings of fact electronically, and while the evidence was still fresh in her head. She took care in composing her legal arguments because she wanted them to hold up at the Federal Court of Appeal. It took her over two hours to write the first draft. Since it was a controversial case, she knew the media would file for a copy through an access to information request. Last thing she wanted to do was to embarrass herself with sloppy thinking and writing. Three quarters of the way through the analysis, she took a break and made a cup of Darjeeling tea. Half an hour later, back at her desk, she clicked on the keyboard.

Shit!

Her file was gone. Not again. She hated to call Systems. The last time she called them, the young man on the help desk had told her disrespectfully that she had saved it in the wrong subdirectory or something like that. Something he considered childishly dimwitted. After several frustrating minutes she gave up and impatiently punched the number for assistance.

"Look, I can't find a file. Help me." She was angry with her techno-stupidity.

He took her through the paces.

"I should clean out my directory. Look, I know I saved it on the hard drive and I've checked every subdirectory. Now I can't seem to get back into my menu to pull up the file. I think my machine is frozen. Damn! Just look for the Sun Sui file for me, will you? What?" Graced tugged at her hair. "Shit! It's going to take time? Time I don't have. I'll call you back in an hour." After hanging up the phone she stood in front of the window and screamed at her reflection. "You're losing it!"

She thought she knew the procedure to get into the new legal software. Grace sighed, if only that was all she had to contend with. But no, Wa Sing was dead. The claimant was a criminal, lying through his teeth under oath. Her lover had found her out to be a cowardly liar. Cadeux wanted her to be a sycophant, not a judge, the pompous little turd. If he fired her, what next? She didn't know, but she knew that she couldn't put up with him as her boss for another two years.

She stared out the window, clutching an elbow, cheek propped up in her hand. According to the newspapers, Li Mann had fled the country. She prayed that the RCMP was right about that. What about Harry Kitchin's accomplice? She hadn't had another incident since the night of the fatal shooting from either of them. Those thoughts led to the next two questions: Could she be sure that that was the end of being stalked? And what beef did Kitchin's accomplice have with her anyway?

She tied her unruly hair in a ponytail, and sat in her chair, eyes closed. She carefully considered the situation and decided that Kitchin's accomplice was not a threat. Li Mann, on the other hand, could be a problem if he was still in the country. Obviously, an international arrest warrant wasn't much of a deterrent in his case. After several minutes of deep breathing exercises, she opened her eyes again. Reaching into her jacket pocket, she stared at the telephone number again. She was tempted to dial the number but did not want to reveal her identity. With caller ID, that was impossible from her work phone. She would try again from another pay phone on the way home .

While she waited for the systems people to run diagnostics on her machine, she reread her handwritten notes. She wondered if it really was plausible that the authorities could be both Sun's agent of persecution and his business partners. Who knew? Maybe it was possible. Maybe he fucked his partners over, and that's why he feared returning home to Hong Kong or China. But with Wa Sing dead, she didn't want to give Sun the benefit of the doubt. All she wanted now was to turn him down and deport him out of the country. Hopefully, those phone records would be the noose she was looking for. Yes, she had made the right decision to subpoena them.

An hour and a half later, she was still waiting for her computer to be up and running. It sure would be nice to go for a walk in the park. But she couldn't even do that because the press was waiting to ambush her downstairs.

In short, she was a prisoner in her own office. And in her home. Grabbing a legal size notepad, she decided to work at her desk the old fashioned way; she wasn't up to facing the newshounds downstairs.

The Red Prince tore off the chauffeur's jacket. He was already late for his meeting, and he grumbled as he got caught at the lights. Everything was unravelling too fast. His charmed life was disintegrating before his eyes. He sighed heavily as he sat in traffic. Finally, the green light winked. He stamped on the gas and took off. A few minutes later he pulled into the far end of the parking lot at the golf course. His contact was already there, waiting for him.

Cadeux climbed into the Mercedes. He looked disgruntled. He loved money, but apparently murder unnerved him.

Sun turned an ironic smile on Cadeux. "A perfectly planned operation, wouldn't you say? Of course, I should have killed her too. Sometimes life can be measured in minutes. If she and the immigration officer had remained in the car for a few more minutes, all three would've died."

"You don't think we went too far?" muttered Cadeux, not looking at him.

Sun said, "The old man was my business partner, but in the end he started to behave like a foolish old woman. Trying to balance profit statements with moral good and philanthropy. An amateur, really. Not like you and me, my friend. Besides, I couldn't trust him once he was apprehended by the police."

A line of sweat formed on Cadeux's brow and upper lip. He looked uncertainly at his companion. "Yes, I — I think you did the right thing."

"Thank you. The only smart one in all this is the woman. You should've heard her in the hearing room. She's the only one who understood the connections between the Communists and the triads. You know, the Flying Dragons and the Young Yon both competed for me to join their organizations. At first I was flattered, but then I realized it was my military connections. My in-laws are high up in the PLA, and the triads wanted to use army trucks to move heroin and drugs across China. One phone call to my brother-in-law was all it took." Sun snapped his fingers.

Cadeux stared at him. Sunlight slanted through the tall trees in the distance. Clearing his throat unhappily, he said, "And now you're the Don."

"Of course, I'm the Don! I played my cards right when I found out the old Don had stomach cancer. And now my in-laws put up with me. Particularly my brother-in-law in Fujian, who's not pleased that I've reduced his percentage in the smuggling operations," Sun concluded, laughing.

Cadeux said nothing as he gazed up at the sky for a moment.

Sun got straight to the point. "I need asylum in North America. After I screwed my wife's family and my friends, no way I can return home. Besides, I want to transfer my base of operations here. What did you get for me?"

"Well, the State Department wants to meet with you and listen to what you have to say. I told them that you had a list of American companies that were controlled or affiliated with Asian gangs and the Chinese intelligence service."

The Red Prince rubbed his hands together. "Aren't I clever? Have the law enforcement agencies take out the competition for me. That'll give the Flying Dragons a monopoly on human smuggling. Good, good."

"I also mentioned that you had information about the sale of Chinese missiles."

"Unfortunately, I've to fuck over my brother-in-law for this information. It's his own fault. For a high ranking military man, he has loose lips. But for me, it's good, because the Americans are worried that China will go to war over Taiwan. The most powerful country in the world will need an insider's perspective on this. Colin Powell, here I come."

"I've rented a car for you. It's waiting at the duty free shop just before the border." Cadeux handed him a set of keys.

"What else?" demanded Sun, holding out his right hand.

"Oh, yes. Your Panamanian passport came last week to my house."

Sun examined his passport mugshot. "Thank you."

"How did you get it, you mind my asking?"

"How else? By investing in the banana republic." Sun shrugged his shoulders.

"Why?"

"I never put all my eggs in one basket." Sun slipped the passport into the jacket pocket.

Cadeux extended his hand. "Let's keep in touch."

After they parted, Cadeux vowed to himself that he would do whatever it took not to outlive his usefulness to this crime boss. He drove to the office to perform one more task. He didn't bother signing into the security log. In his darkened office, he flicked on his computer.

He had to find a way to squash her subpoena because Sun's phone records would reveal the extent and length of their communication. That was the last thing Cadeux wanted.

Li Mann Vu stumbled out of the karaoke diner. He had drank too much and smoked too much opium. He could barely stand as he tried to insert the key into the car door. The minute he climbed into the driver's seat, he knew something was wrong. He felt the cold metal pressed against the back of his neck.

"How's it feel now, asshole?"

Li Mann didn't reply.

"Let's take a drive out of town. Turn west on this street and keep going until I tell ya."

There was too much drink and drugs in Li Mann's body. He could not clear his mind to think. Like an automaton he drove into the night, following orders from the killer sitting behind him. He knew in his gut that time was meaningless to him now. He would not be flying home on his one way ticket. He would no longer be a part of the Flying Dragons. In time, Sun Sui would find someone to replace him.

"At the end of this road, take the dirt road on the left of ya."

Beyond the wildflowers and the weeds was the woodlands, a thicket of trees and shrubs inhabited by deer, rabbits, and other wildlife.

Li Mann cut the engine. "What're you going to do to me?" he asked, staring in the rear view mirror. He could see the eyes that blinked back at him. Li Mann realized that the man who held him captive was mad.

"Get out!"

Li Mann climbed out of the car. Emotions welled up inside of him as he climbed out of the car. He looked up at the night sky, it was dark enough to see the stars. That meant he was no longer in the city. That meant there was no one to see or help him. For the first time in a long time, he felt a shudder of fear move through him.

"You killed my best friend, you dumb fuck! Now I'm gonna take your life. An eye for an eye."

"I can explain," said Li Mann. He could still feel the effects of all that booze and smoke in his body. He forced his mind to think. He had to find a way to reach the knife that was strapped to his right calf.

His opponent was crazy, shouting obscenities at him. Li Mann racked his brain as he was marched a hundred yards into the woods, gun pressed into his back. Then about eighty yards further into the dense forest, the path disappeared. The trees became thick around him. The terrain became surprisingly familiar and he had a flash of clarity about what he needed to do. After all, he could have written the book on jungle warfare.

Like a good soldier, he would refuse to stand still for the bullet. The important thing was to keep moving, to look for the chance to make a run for it into the woods and darkness. Eyes alert, he saw his opportunity to the right of him. He parted a strong branch as he moved forward, and waited for it to snap in the face of his opponent.

He ran, breathing fast and shallow. He heard the stream of curses behind him. He knew his opponent was gaining. He heard the sound of bullets as he scampered over rocks and fallen tree trunks. Then his legs faltered. He held out his arms to brace his balance. Too late, he stumbled, felt the trunk of his body swaying for balance, and then a long fall. As he turned his head to protect his face, he thought about his wife and his parents. He saw the ground rushing up at him and sensed himself slipping into the soft earth, into a void of darkness. Huddled in the dark underbrush, he concentrated his mind on mastering the pain. One ear pressed into the earth, he could hear the nasal croak of the bullfrogs and the sweet music of the crickets. He was breathing frantically as his mind went back in time to his comrades buried deep in the forests, and those in the Da Nang cemetery.

He closed his eyes. Despite the pain, he felt relief. There was no more separation. He was going home. He felt himself being pulled down a long dark tunnel.

chapter twenty-nine

Nick was roused from his sleep by the ringing on the bedside phone in Grace's bedroom. Without thinking, he reached for it. Dubois was on the line, yelling.

"Nick, Sun Sui has escaped."

"When? How? He was under surveillance!"

"Seems he switched places with his chauffeur. Got dressed in his uniform and cap. That's how he got past the guards posted outside his hotel room and in front of his hotel."

"Shit! Shit!"

"Nick, we're looking for him as we speak. Got a countrywide and international warrant out already. Photos of him plastered from coast to coast. Something should turn up."

Grace stirred, lying next to him. She turned to give him a sleepy, concerned look.

"What about the chauffeur? Does he know anything?"

"We interrogated him till we were all blue in the face from bullying and badgering. I don't think he knows anything. He was just following orders when he was asked to strip out of his uniform. That was about three hours ago. That's a good lead. Sun could be anywhere."

"I'd better call Rocco." Nick watched Grace roll out of bed and pad into the bathroom. "Do me a favour. Keep it out of the press for twenty-four hours. No news could have the effect of lowering his guard. He might be less careful. Less watchful."

He wasn't hopeful of catching Sun. He knew he had all the stolen authentic documents he wanted. Failing that, near-perfect forgeries.

Wrapped in a bathrobe, Grace asked. "What happened?"

He downplayed Sun's escape. "I wouldn't be overly concerned. Sun can't go far. It's just a matter of time before he's caught."

"Don't bullshit me, Nick."

"Babe ..." He threw up his hands. "It never ends. It just comes at you from all sides." He had just woken up, but God, he was so tired. His career seemed like a never-ending landscape of chess moves with an invisible opponent.

She ran her fingers through his hair. "We need a holiday together. When it's all over. Let's go back to Malta. Or rough it in Patagonia."

"I'm too old to rough it, Grace." He fell back onto the bed, pulling her down on top of him. He needed solace. He needed her one more time.

"You go where you need to go," Grace insisted. "Do what you need to do. And don't worry about me, I'm a big girl. I can look after myself." She was pushing the speed limit, weaving in and out of lanes trying to get him to the airport to catch his 10:40 a.m. flight to Toronto. He had to agree that she was a woman of impressive confidence.

Little conversation passed between them on the way. He sat with a cellphone pressed to his ear, giving instructions to his staff to check all domestic and international flights, and to issue an immigration warrant for Sun Sui's arrest on both sides of the border. When they parted at the airport, he made her promise to keep him in the loop while he was gone.

"This is Dubois' personal number. Don't hesitate to call him." He pressed it into her hand.

"I'll be fine, Nick."

"No, Grace. Promise me you'll call him if anything goes wrong."

"Okay, okay. Promise."

The commuter flight to Toronto was jam-packed with business travellers. Wa Sing's words stayed with him throughout the flight. Running for office was a risky venture, but besides that it was enormously expensive. For those who failed to win an election, the cost was huge, sometimes measured in the years it took to overcome a mountain of debt. But if you had the backing, and you won, you were laughing all the way up to the Hill. And that was the trouble with this case — it wasn't a simple case of illegal alien smuggling any more. No, it was rotten to the core. Even if the asylum hearing had been completed and Grace had turned down Sun's refugee claim, the minister would have overruled her.

He got no respite when the flight attendant offered him a newspaper. The lead story was the government quashing their own inquiry into the campaign contribution fiasco. The words swam in front of him as his mind kept coming back to one question. Exactly how much and what kind of influence had a million dollars in campaign contributions bought the old man and Sun?

The flight attendant offered him a choice of beverage. It was too early to be drinking, but what the hell. He had a Sleeman's.

Where did all this leave him and his office? He had given up on Keiler being cooperative in sending anything to him through the diplomatic pouch or regular mail. Keiler was stalling, covering up his stupid decisions to grant visas and approvals to those he shouldn't have. He had taken short cuts by not running extensive security checks. At the same time, Nick knew he would have the damnedest time firing his employee. Simply put, the government did not want their stupidity aired for public consumption. Particularly this present government, which had done much to foster an even deeper culture of secrecy.

Still, as Keiler's boss, Nick needed to know exactly how Jon Keiler could have approved Sun's application and God knows how many more applications from triad members. Criminal underworld figures were incredibly wealthy. Their net worth sometimes reached the billions, and political payoffs were as easy as buying groceries. Was this a case worth fighting for? Yes, he decided, it was. His goal since the beginning had been justice for Walter Martin, and that still mattered. They had had good times together, until a bullet had made Walter's wife a widow and rendered his children fatherless.

He took another sip of beer. He knew what he had to do next. But at the same time, he had the feeling that something ominous was gaining on him.

After dropping Nick off at the airport, Grace headed to the office. From Nick's conversation with Dubois, she already knew what awaited her. Still, the microphones and cameras jammed in her face were hard to take. Reporters assaulted her with questions about Sun Sui.

"No comment. No comment," she said, all the way up into the elevator and along the corridor to the security coded doors that led into her office.

Just as she took off her raincoat, the phone rang. It was Verster. "Ms. Wang-Weinstein, this is a courtesy call to tell you personally that my client, Mr. Sui, is abandoning his asylum claim."

"Why, counsel?"

"You know, I'm not exactly sure why. He communicated that to me early this morning, and I'm merely passing on the message."

"I see you've already informed the press before you called me."

"No, that's not true. For the record, they called me first, wanting to know our strategy for the continuation of the hearing. Naturally, I had no choice but to tell them that there was no longer a hearing."

"Well, for the record, counsel, if you appear before me in future cases, keep it firmly in mind that I'd like to know before the press." To say anymore would be judicially inappropriate, Grace dropped the receiver back into the cradle.

She sat at her desk. Then got up and wandered to the window. She looked down into the rain-drenched streets below. Sun would be on every network, on every local news, and newspaper. Why had he decided to walk away from his hearing? Why hadn't he waited for the decision to come down and appeal the negative?

Turning away from the window, she considered her next move. Last night, she had called Wa Sing's daughters. Lorraine Lu, Wa Sing's oldest daughter, answered the phone. She told Grace that neither she nor her sister was interested in keeping the house. They had already taken what keepsakes they wanted. The proceeds of the house and its contents were to go to cancer research. As a favour, Grace had agreed to handle the real estate transaction and the content disposal.

"One more thing, Lorraine. Wa always told me that he wanted me to have the 'red dragon'. Do you know what he was referring to? I just thought I'd ask so I wouldn't spend hours searching for something I can't recall seeing."

"No, Grace. Nothing comes to mind. But if it does, I'll call you back."

Now, with time on her hands and feeling at loose ends for the first time in months, she decided to head over to New Edinburgh, to Wa Sing's house. Years ago, when Wa Sing had decided to live several months of the year in Ottawa, Grace had gone house-hunting with him. They had found the large bungalow set back majestically from the street. It was the most promising house they had seen after touring at least a dozen houses all over the city.

In her jalopy Volvo, she drove down a leafy street, where the houses were set on large lots. An occasional FedEx truck passed, otherwise the street was empty. She knew the house well, and it was easy to find by the hedge of azalea bushes that flanked the driveway. She pulled into his driveway.

For a while, she didn't know how long, she sat in her car calling up old memories. Then, fighting the wind and rain, she walked around to a side door and let herself in with the spare key hidden underneath the deck. The house had been closed up for only a week. Already it had the feel of a mausoleum. Removing her shoes, she walked through the house, flicking on lights, and opening a window for fresh air. She made a mental note to call the cleaning lady as she scooped up the heap of mail lying behind the front door. She went through it. Bills and junk. Still procrastinating, she made herself a cup of tea. As she waited for the water to boil, an idea came to her. Picking up the phone, she dialled the number Wa Sing had given her just before he was killed.

Sure enough, someone picked up the receiver on the other end. "Yes?" said a man's voice. A very familiar voice. The voice of a very famous, powerful person.

Without identifying herself, Grace quickly hung up the phone. It was enough to know that the rot went all the way up to the top.

Now she had to find the red dragon. Cup in hand, she marched up the stairs to his study.

At the top of the stairs, Grace stopped. In front of her was an open window; underneath the white carpet was still damp, with traces of mud and dirt. As if the intruder had removed his shoes, to keep from tracking water and soil into the house.

Dread. Was someone still in the house? Wa Sing's murderer? Most likely.

Grace stopped breathing and stood still to listen. Nothing. Not wanting to take chances with her life, she took the .38 out of her bag, and released the safety catch.

She wondered what his killer had been looking for? A red dragon?

To her left was a narrow hallway. There was a door at the far end. It was closed. Taking a deep breath, she put her hand on the knob and turned it. Her senses immediately told her something felt wrong. She could feel the sweat forming on her back and the dryness in her mouth. Stepping into the room, she saw papers scattered on the floor. Just a few sheets. As if someone had been in a hurry. Or her presence had alerted them. She kept the gun in her hand as her eyes swept the room looking for a red dragon. What was it anyway? A book? A picture? A statue?

First, the filing cabinet. No doubt about it, the old man was a pack rat. Jammed in the first drawer were old letters, going back decades, from friends and "those from the old country." The second and third drawers were filled with assorted loose papers. Some of them were receipts from various charities he had supported regularly, and others he supported sporadically; all seeking charitable donations, or sending him charitable contribution slips or thank you letters for his donations. But no red dragon.

What exactly was it? And where could it be?

She didn't want to linger in the house longer than necessary. Pushing the bedroom door opened, she walked in.

One step forward. My God.

On the bookshelf in his bedroom sat a pair of bookends. Two red dragons. She grabbed them both. One was heavier than the other. She would examine them later. Stuffing them both in her bag, she raced down the stairs and out of the house.

Sitting at her breakfast table, she looked over the bookends carefully. The irony of the old man's secret hiding place was not lost on her as she pried open the false bottom of the red dragon bookend. Finding a plate that moved slightly on the bottom of the heavier "red dragon" she pried it open. Inside she found two diskettes. She loaded the first diskette into her Toshiba laptop. It contained files of financial statements broken down by quarter, going back several years. As she stared at the fields and the numbers, the revelation was too fantastic to believe. She was looking at the financial records of illegal immigration operations by the Flying Dragons. The old man was either the bookkeeper or secretary. Either way, his involvement in the triad came as a shock to her.

The zeros on the balance sheet far exceeded mere millions. The money the triad was raking in was a testament to the profitability of the triad, and the exodus of people leaving their homelands. In the case of illegal migration from China, Beijing's market reforms had cost millions of farmers and industrial workers their jobs. That was what the old man had been trying to tell her. Ironic really. China's bid to enter the World Trade Organization would further hurt millions of people, driving them to leave the country by whatever means they could. And on this side of the world, the sweatshops were clamouring for cheap labour; one of the ugly side effects of globalization that no one talked about.

The second diskette was a breakdown of expenses. It was more damning than the first. The entries spoke of payoffs and campaign contributions to individuals. It was all here. The campaign contributions crossed political party lines. The old man and Sun had been hedging their bets. Nothing wrong with that. Legitimate companies and honest businesspeople did that all the time. No, the damning evidence was the payoffs made to corruptible border guards and customs officers for entry visas and to look the other way at immigration checkpoints.

If it hadn't been for the subpoena, Wa Sing would still be alive today. The subpoena had been his death warrant. Sun didn't want to take chances. The last thing he wanted was to have the old man name the names of those who had been bought off in the human smuggling racket. That would have destroyed the Flying Dragons crime empire. Too many parties would kill to suppress this information. The evidence laid out before her was what the intruder had been looking for in Wa Sing's house.

Sweat from her palms was dampening the keyboard. There were multiple entries to a numbered account. Huge sums of money paid on a regular basis. Paid to whom? She had an idea. But first she had to prove it.

The old man had died to prevent this information from getting out. What should she do? At first, Grace wanted to shut down the machine, destroy the diskettes, and forget she had ever seen them. She turned her head and eyed the phone. Whose advice should she seek? Who could she trust? If only Nick was here.

She closed her eyes. What if she had been followed from Wa Sing's house? She stood, and with elaborate casualness, checked the street outside. No one. She went out the front door and observed the comings and goings of her neighbours. Nothing out of the ordinary. She went back inside.

She already knew that illegal immigration was a multinational, billion-dollar business. The old man had allowed himself to act as a front for Sun and his crime gang. Damn! That's what all of this was about. Money. Making money illegally with murder on the side.

She nodded to herself, her eyes staring into the middle distance as she thought more about it. Organized crime groups like the Flying Dragons offered a one-stop-shopping approach to smuggling. From Nick's adversarial evidence, she knew that the Dragons not only handled travel and other documents for their migrant clientele, but also rented and bought old cargo ships, and refitted them. She also knew that criminal organizations like the Flying Dragons had corrupted government officials around the world. The whole damn mess was a Pandora's box. Breach of trust. If any of it ever hit the press ... God, she didn't want to go there right now.

None of this would have surfaced if Walter Martin hadn't died that night, and if the Mandarin Club's telephone number hadn't been found in that snakehead's shirt pocket. Funny how chickens have a way of coming home to roost.

Knowing what she knew, what should she do? She dialled the telephone number again. In the space of a few hours, the line had been disconnected. What did it mean? Was someone onto her?

Nick was bone tired when his flight crossed the international dateline. He had taken a risk in leaving the country without seeking permission from the director general or the minister of immigration himself. Only his secretary, Rocco, Dubois, and Grace knew of his departure from the country. For all he knew, his career would be over when he returned. That was not something he would lose sleep over in light of the fact that his political masters had committed greater crimes.

Twelve and a half hours after leaving San Francisco, the plane began its descent into Vietnam.

Darkness. How he loved the darkness.

BJ rested his head on the back of the driver's seat of the gook's car. It was a much nicer car than the stolen piece of shit he'd been driving around. For starters, it had air conditioning.

He stared at her house. He had been watching the house for days. He knew about the burglar alarm system. All the windows were wired too. Middleclass people could be so stupid. Installing an outside door in glass. Smash the glass and get into the house. Or go through a basement window. But that would trigger the alarm. After casing the house thoroughly, he knew exactly how he would get in without triggering the alarm. The stupidity of never-ending middleclass people.

BJ oiled his gun. He was tired of the game. He had originally planned to kill her tonight but had changed his mind after he saw the boyfriend. He didn't have an axe to grind with the boyfriend. If it was the Chinaman, it would have been a different story.

Tomorrow night it would be time to finish the job. In his head, he choreographed her death. He would let her watch as he killed her fat furball. The death of a pet drove them crazy. He'd learned that when he'd killed his neighbour's cat back in the sixth grade.

Should he use a gun on her? No, maybe a knife. With a gun it was over in one shot. But a knife, the possibilities were endless. Pleasure surged through him as he started the car.

"Lady judge, you and me, we got a date tomorrow night. Are you good and scared?"

You should be.

chapter thirty

The plane accelerated down the runway and lifted off. Nick's twenty-four hour layover in Vietnam had been surreal, as if it had happened to someone else. It was a mixture of the *National Geographic* and Conrad's *Heart of Darkness*. Looking out of the plane window, he could still make out the pretty water lilies floating in the round ponds. As a student of history, he knew they weren't just landscaping. They were craters, left by the U.S. bombers.

He leaned back in his seat and accepted a drink from the flight attendant. He nursed it, thinking of the citizens of Vietnam, who lived in a hand-to-mouth cycle of poverty. How to choose between begging, borrowing, and stealing? Or working in brothels? In Ho Chi Minh City, beautiful young girls could be had for less than the price of a beer back home. The story of American foreign policy could still be read on the zombie-like faces of people who had survived one horrific tragedy after another.

He had tracked down Li Mann Vu's village but no one there knew where he was. In Da Nang, he met a couple of smugglers who bragged about their routes. Phnom Penh and Bangkok were major snakehead staging grounds where officials were easily bribed into providing illegals with fake documents. One of the smugglers who had worked with Li Mann said, often times, illegals were flown to cities like Mexico or Moscow before being rerouted into the United States and Canada. What Nick really wanted was more information about the safe houses and the clearing houses for the illegals. In that regard, he got zippo.

Now, flying above the country, Nick meditated on what he had seen. What a paradox, he thought. In the West, snakeheads were vilified for smuggling hundreds of boatloads of illegal immigrants into countries. Here they were looked upon by the desperate as saviours. Goes to show, nothing is ever black and white. Even though he had never fought in the war, he could understand why the country still loomed large in the consciousness of America. He was leaving a place that had blown through him like a hot desert wind.

He closed his eyes.

Grace spent an almost sleepless night and passed the long hours of the next day at home, her mind only partly occupied by the backlog of files she was working on. By nine o'clock that evening she knew what her next move had to be. Accelerating down the Parkway, she turned music on her car radio up loud to cancel out her thoughts. By the time she parked in front of the IRC, her neck and shoulders were stiff with tension.

The security guard at the console nodded to her before returning to his fourteen-inch black and white.

Grace tried to breeze past him. "I'm in a hurry — is it okay if I don't bother to sign in? I'll only be here two minutes. I forgot something in my office yesterday morning."

"Miss Wang-Weinstein, we got to do it by the book. You gotta sign it, else I could lose my job," said the security guard.

Sighing impatiently, she entered her name and falsified her destination into the log book. At least she'd tried. At the bank of elevators, instead of hitting the up button, her finger pressed the down indicator. She was nervous. As a non-administrative person, she needed permission to go down to the bowels of the building. The knowledge that she might be challenged by a guard sent a shiver of anxiety through her body, exacerbating the tightness that had settled around her neck and shoulders. But she needed to know. She needed to check the Archives for clues about Cadeux's duplicity. She needed exact proof of his breach of trust.

Inside the elevator, she slowly exhaled as she hit the button for Level II of the basement, where old cases were archived, going back ten years. She closed her eyes momentarily. Dear God, don't let me get into trouble over this. Nervously, she swiped her electronic keycard through the slot. The steel door to the archives clicked open. The room was L-shaped, with a low ceiling. Its walls were lined with rows of filing cabinets that went on for about a hundred feet or so. At the other end of the room were computer workstations. In her opinion, the room was laid out wrong. The computer workstations should be reversed. After a search for records was completed, one would then cross the room to retrieve them from the filing cabinets.

She only flicked on half the lights as she moved across the room because she did not want to attract attention of security. The room was still in gloomy darkness as she sat down at one of the workstations. Turning on the computer, she typed in Cadeux's name and the year he was appointed as head of the IRC. She needed to get a full flavour of the cases that had passed through his hands. He had assigned particular cases to specific adjudicators, and signed off on completed cases and their outcomes. She needed to see if there was a pattern, somewhere. Anywhere.

The databases showed that he had had a hand in more than eight thousand cases over a five-year period. Her task was huge. She'd have to compress years of cases into a couple of hours of search time. For the next two hours, she mined the system, doggedly pulling up statistics, cross-referencing fields, and databases.

Gradually, inevitably, it came together. It was all there. Buried under half a dozen programs and a couple of databases. Cadeux had used his deputy ministerial powers and that loopy signature of his to facilitate visas at various embassies around the world. He had allowed people with possible criminal connections to enter the country under the guise of business investors and foreign students. The microfiche confirmed his signature on the signed applications. God knows how many of those then went on to file refugee applications, or used Canada as a back door entry into the United States.

She could not help murmuring as she re-read the list several times. So much power in the hands of one unprincipled, ambitious little sneak. In the Convention Refugee Database, his fingerprints were easier to identify. He had assigned rookie lawyers on tough cases, and without supervision. In short, he had stacked the deck against the government that employed him. He didn't always win. That would have looked suspicious. But there was no doubt he delivered what his bosses wanted.

Talk about breach of trust. Thanks to officials like Cadeux, the lucrative flow of human traffic would never slow down.

On a hunch, with several strokes at the keyboard, she went into her own case system. After typing in the names of several claimants she had turned down, she waited for the system to do a search. After a long minute, the screen changed. There it was. Several of the claimants she had turned down had somehow had their decisions reversed. So the little shit did always win, in the end. He had taken advantage of the weakness of the IRC. With a backlog of a thousand or so asylum cases, she had never given much thought to those claimants she had rejected. She and all the other adjudicators had trusted the system. Cadeux had constantly reminded them that they were not administrators. But now she saw that Cadeux sometimes directed the last few administrative links to his own doorstep. With a click of the mouse, he had power to overturn failed asylum claims. Like the fox guarding the hen house.

He had made the country's generous immigration and refugee system even more generous. God knows how many people he had granted Convention refugee status too. Or the numbers who had obtained citizenship by fraud. Nick and his colleagues were working frantically to stem the tide of illegals pouring into the country. Walter Martin had died in that battle. But had they ever suspected that it was operatives inside their own government that had opened the floodgates?

Still unable to believe what she had just read, she hit the print button for a hard copy. She needed proof.

BJ was outfitted in dark clothing. He had followed her to the office. Nine-thirty in the evening and she was going to work? Then she'd be home late, probably alone. An ideal opportunity.

With her goon out of the way, tonight would be the night. He drove back to her house in a station wagon he had stolen from an underground parking garage. He knew exactly how to get into her house without triggering the burglar alarm system. He owed it to that fat lump of fur. From watching the cat, BJ knew that there were no motion sensors in the kitchen, and no electrical contacts at the trap door. He knew it because the last time he was here, he had tried to kill the furball, but it had gotten away from him, scooting into the house through the animal trap door.

Deliberately stomping through her flowerbed, he made his way around to the back of the house. Sure enough, the cat was sitting on top of the kitchen counter, next to the stove. At the sight of him, it stood up, arched its back and hissed. BJ smiled to himself, there would be plenty of time to kill it when he got inside the house.

Unwrapping the handsaw, he began to enlarge the cat entrance, which was nothing more than a swinging trap door built for a large cat or small dog. Forty-three minutes later, he had cut through vinyl siding, wood, insulation, and drywall. He squeezed his hundred-and-eighty-pound frame through the enlarged mess of a hole. Methodically, he checked out the house. He needed to find a good hiding place and surprise her. Nothing too cramped. He might have to wait a long time for her to come home. His gaze swept the living room and dining room, then he headed upstairs towards her bedroom.

Boy, was she going to be surprised. The thought brought a cruel smile to his lips.

"Such dedication. Eleven at night. In the sub-basement of a downtown office building reading dusty files and staring at a computer screen. It would be admirable, if you had security clearance to be here at all." Grace shot up in her seat at the sound of Cadeux's voice behind her. "Curiosity killed the cat, Grace. What exactly are you doing?"

She struggled to speak. "I'm looking at old files."

"I know that much. Why?"

The hard copies lay on the desk. She shifted her position to stand in front of them, blocking Cadeux's line of vision. The ruse didn't work. He walked towards her, pushed her aside, and picked up the documents.

His expression hardened as he flipped through the printouts. "What were you planning on doing with these? Brown bag them to the press?" His voice shook with anger. "Not a very smart idea, Grace. You disappoint me."

"You're the bigger disappointment," she said defiantly. "How could you rubber-stamp thousands of phony asylum seekers into our country? How could you destroy the integrity of our immigration and refugee system? How could you?"

"Oh, don't pretend to be so pure. In my shoes you would've done the same. If I hadn't let them in somebody else would have. Why shouldn't I be the one to get the rewards? Besides, I had no choice. I needed the money. Do you know how much I pay my ex-wife in alimony? I was royally fucked. Wa Sing was my lifeline. What was there to think about when someone offers to pick up the tab?" He met her gaze head on.

"You think I wanted this appointment to the IRC? You think I care about the luckless and the losers? You think I care about refugees and their precious persecution? I wanted the Transportation Commission but the old man wouldn't hear of it. I never forgave him for that."

"No one was holding a gun to your head. You had free choice."

He gave a bitter laugh as he pulled a gun out of his suit jacket pocket, and pointed it straight at her. "What do you know about it?"

"What are you doing?" she asked, squeezing her hands together in an effort to fight the waves of panic washing over her.

"You, Grace, are a loose cannon. And unfortunately, with the old man dead, you've got no one on your side."

"Did you kill him?"

"No, I didn't, though there are benefits to him being dead. One master is always better than two."

"You're now working for Sun? That's why you were trying to railroad me into going positive on his case."

"You could put it that way."

Grace stared at the gun. "So what's next? Are you going to kill me now?"

"Don't tempt me," said Cadeux with an angry twist of his lips.

"The guard knows I'm in the building and you'd be caught immediately." She thought fast. Maybe she could get him to believe she'd work with him. "Why don't we talk it over? Do a trade."

"Trade what?"

"I've got evidence that's very incriminating. Notes that Wa Sing left behind regarding payoffs that you received."

"Ahh, the voice from the grave. The computer diskette the old man kept talking about. You'll hand that over."

"If I die, they'll be found."

"I think you're bluffing. You'll give me what you got from the old man's house."

"Jean, whatever crimes you've committed, you don't want to add murder to the list," said Grace, racking her brain for a way out of this mess.

"Who said anything about murder? You hand over the notes and whatever else you took from the old man's house, and we'll talk about it. If we can't reach an understanding — well, maybe you'll kill yourself."

"Why would I do that?"

"You were distraught over the old man's death, and full of shame after I fired you. You can put it all in a suicide note." He waved the handgun in front of her. "Come on. Let's go get it."

Don't panic, Grace told herself. Thinking fast, she said, "Before we go back to my place, I'm afraid I need to use the ladies' room. I've got my period."

He eyed her suspiciously. "It's true. If you don't believe me, I'll pass you my dirty tampon," she bluffed.

As he weighed the situation, she bravely walked away from him, turning right towards the ladies' room. He followed her inside.

"Don't try anything funny because I won't hesitate to shoot you," he said, waving the gun at her.

"If you shoot me, I warned you, the evidence goes to the press."

"Grace, you don't scare me. Let's get this over with."

Closing the stall door, she sat on the lid and collected her thoughts as she unwrapped a clean tampon and pushed the wrapper underneath the stall. That would enhance her credibility and buy her a precious minute or two. Holding the cellphone close to her, she dialled Dubois's direct number that Nick had given her, and whispered a help message while she flushed the toilet simultaneously.

"Hurry up in there." Cadeux banged on the stall.

"Almost done," she said as she hit the redial button

before dropping the cellphone back into her bag. She contemplated the gun for a second, but unfortunately, she was dressed in T-shirt and jeans, and there was no place to hide it on her body. After she had washed her hands, they left the ladies' room and silently rode the elevator up to the lobby level. "Don't speak as I sign us both out. Let me do the talking," ordered Cadeux. "Remember, I'm going to have the gun pointed at your back."

He signed them out in the log book and said goodnight to the security guard.

Sitting behind the wheel with a gun pointed at her head, Grace let out a deep breath, trying again to fight the panic rising in her chest. If she was going to come out alive after tonight, she had to keep her wits about her. Slowly, she pulled onto Wellington Street. No police cruiser in sight. Where the hell were they when you needed them?

"You don't have to keep pointing that thing at me. I can only do one thing at a time."

Out of the corner of her eye, she watched him place the gun in his lap. "Don't try anything stupid, Grace."

"Would I be that stupid?" Her heart was racing. What to do next? Not one cop car on the Parkway. "It's not too late to negotiate this thing. We're two reasonable people," pleaded Grace.

"Too late."

For once in her life she wished that she lived further away from the office. Nope, it didn't look good as she pulled up on her driveway. The police had not yet arrived.

"Get out of the car!"

Her head was pounding with every step she took into her house. As she disarmed the alarm, she noticed one of the numbers on the panel was flashing. Did that mean the police were coming? But she had too much on her mind to sort it out. She had to keep Cadeux talking, to buy herself time for Dubois to get here.

"Did you know or ask about these people you were fast-tracking? Were they criminals on the run from their own country? Or were they merely opportunists?"

"I never asked because I don't care. When you're getting five grand for every application you sign, does it matter who they are? Besides, it wasn't like I was the only one. How do you think this government came to power? Who do you think contributed to their election campaign?" He gestured with the gun, indicating that she should keep moving. "There's big money to be made in smuggling. It takes money to get power, and to stay in power."

"And how does it feel when you look at yourself in the mirror?"

Cadeux was standing in her living room, looking at her vindictively. He seemed almost happy, now that he was pointing a gun at her.

"You've no idea how I hated you, Grace."

"Pardon me? What did I ever do to you?" She put her shoulder bag down on a side table, acutely aware of the weight of the gun inside it. How to get at it?

"It's what you didn't do. The old man wanted to keep you clean. He didn't mind soiling my hands in the least."

"Have respect for the dead. Wasn't it enough that you were on the receiving end of his largesse when he handed you this plum appointment?"

"You call it a plum appointment? I call it crap — I deserved better. I was right in the line of fire. The old man didn't give a damn about asking me to do his dirty work."

That explained the animosity he had always shown towards her.

In an effort to deflect his anger, she said, "So they used you. What I don't understand is, when exactly did you meet Sun Sui?"

He followed into the dining room. "A couple of months before the *California Jupiter* dumped 634 migrants off the B.C. coast."

In a pretence of showing empathy, she said, "You mean, they deliberately set you up for that? So that you could sign off on all those migrants on that ship?"

"Yeah."

"When Wa Sing was arrested, the RCMP asked him to name names. He looked at me and said my boss. All that time I thought it was the minister of immigration. He was really referring to you. My direct boss. Not the minister himself."

He shot her a nasty look. "Shut up! You know too damn much. I could kill you right here. Give me whatever you took from Wa Sing's house now!"

Was Dubois even on the way? Had her message been received?

"I left some of the papers at his house."

"Well give me what you took." She felt the gun pressed into the small of her back. She couldn't help wondering if she was going to be alive after tonight. The truth was, she was scared of him. Psychologically and practically, his back was already against the wall. It would take very little to push him over the edge, and make him pull the trigger.

She handed him a diskette. "Aren't you going to look at it?"

"What for? I believe you."

Just then, the phone rang.

"I think I should answer that." She quickly moved towards the phone in the hallway. "I'm expecting my mother and boyfriend to call. It could be either one of them," she lied. Luckily, the phone in the hallway was the only one in the house without caller ID. "If I don't pick it up, they'll suspect something's not right."

"See who it is," Cadeux said impatiently. "And make it quick."

"Grace, it's Dubois. Is everything all right?"

Cadeux leaned next to her to eavesdrop on the conversation. How to tell him that she was in trouble? In a trembling voice she said, "No, honey, it's not all right. I'm so sorry about last night."

"Ehh?"

She could hear the RCMP officer's confusion on the other end. Quickly, she added, "Listen, André, I can't talk to you right now. There's someone here. And yes, I think we should resume our relationship. I'll stop seeing Nick. Promise, promise. And I'm so sorry that I dumped you through e-mail. That was real shitty of me."

"Huh?"

"We need time to sort out our affair. I've got someone here with me. This is not a good time. Can you understand that?" She quickly hung up the phone. Oh please, God, make him realize that something's wrong. Her shoulders slumped forward, and her body sagged against the wall. Hurry, Dubois.

"Let's write that suicide note now."

She ran her sweaty palms down the sides of her legs. She needed to give Dubois time to get here. Taking a deep breath she said, "Can I ask you something? There are one or two more questions I'd like answers to before I leave this world."

"That's always been one of your problems, Grace. You want to know too much."

"Whose idea was it that I preside on Sun's claim?"

"Sun's idea. He had this stupid notion that just because you're cute, you'd be a pushover. I went along with it because I wanted to dirty your hands. I had to keep tabs on you."

"What do you mean?"

"I had your phone line tapped and periodically I would go into your computer and check your files."

"All those times I couldn't access my files, you were reading them?"

"And reporting to Sun everything I learned."

"But he was under police watch the entire time."

Cadeux smiled. "That may be so. But on two occasions he gave the cops the slip when he switched places with his driver by putting on the man's uniform." He turned up the dimmer. "Pick up the pen."

"Isn't there any other way we can do this? As long as I'm on the bench, I can do you a lot of favours. If I'd known what was going on I could have helped you more. I still could." If he believed that she was as corruptible as he was, he might be tempted.

"No, Grace. You know and I know that isn't going to happen."

She sat down and slowly picked up the pen. What if she just refused to write it? Then there would be no suicide note, and he would have to shoot her right there and then. That way, at least nobody could mistake her death for anything but a homicide.

The doorbell rang. They both jumped out of their skins. She almost wept in sheer relief.

"Who the hell is that?"

"My boyfriend. I told him not to come. You heard me tell him." Grace could hear the panic in her own voice. Would he lose control and start shooting?

Dubois's face peered in through the living-room window. "He's seen us. I've got to open the door."

"Get rid of him." He walked behind her, with the gun pressed into her back.

She opened the door.

"Grace, what the shit is going on?"

She tried to signal him with her eyes to be careful of Cadeux. "Nothing's going on, André. I wish I could invite you in for a cup of tea, but it's late and as you can see, I'm not alone."

Dubois looked blank for a moment, but he picked up on her body language. In a voice full of bonhomie, hand extended toward the other man, he said, "Hi, I'm André. Don't tell me she's seeing you now." He shook his head. "First me, then Nick. Now you."

Cadeux did not offer his name and his right hand stayed behind her back. Dubois's hand was still outstretched but Cadeux made no move.

Her breath coming fast, the bubble of fear inside her on the verge of bursting, she said, "André, this is not a good time for me. Really."

Dubois dropped his hand to his side and shifted his weight from one foot to the other, hand on the door knob. "If that's the way you want it, Grace, I'm going." He observed the other man visibly relax his posture. In an effort to separate them, Dubois took a step toward Cadeux. "Watch out for this girl, friend. Don't get burned like I did."

Cadeux moved to Grace's other side. "Thanks for the advice," he said. The gun was now in his left hand but in the second before he could press it into her back, Dubois moved, quick as a rattlesnake. Cadeux tried to maintain his balance as he lashed out at the RCMP officer, but he was awkward. Dubois deftly delivered a punch to Cadeux's solar plexus. The blow sent Cadeux reeling backwards. As his knees buckled from under him, he fell against the radiator. As he went down, the gun fell clattering on the floor.

Grace dived for the weapon while Dubois handcuffed Cadeux. As they waited for police backup, she quickly explained the situation to the RCMP officer.

As two uniformed officers led him away, Cadeux snarled at her. "You're fired, Grace."

"Coming from you, thanks."

Dubois said reluctantly, "Grace, I have to ask you to come down to the station to make a statement. I realize you've been through a lot, but there're rules."

Grace slumped forward with her head in her hands. "Do you mind? Could we do it tomorrow? I'm completely wrung out."

Dubois hesitated, but nodded. "Okay. But I'm leaving a car here to keep the place under surveillance. Who knows what else is out there?"

"Thank you for that," said Grace, accompanying him to the door. "As a backgrounder, you'll want to look at this." She handed Dubois the diskettes from Wa Sing's house. "It's all there."

She closed the door behind her and sat down in a raggedy heap at the bottom of the stairs. She was emotionally and physically exhausted. What a bloody long night. It was after two in the morning. All she wanted to do was to crawl into bed, if only she had the energy. For a long moment she sat still. She was falling asleep where she sat. Drowsily, she tried to open her eyes but they were too heavy. As her head nodded forward, she was grabbed from behind by her hair. Out of nowhere a hand whipped across the back of her skull, leaving a stinging, hot band of pain.

She felt a pair of arms lift her and slam her forward against the wall.

"Bitch."

She couldn't imagine what was happening. She tried to scream but could barely draw breath. Was this a dream?

"I've waited so long for our date, lady judge. Too bad your friends didn't stick around."

He spun her around until they were face to face. She was awake now. It was the stalker. His eyes were white with flat black irises. Dead eyes.

His large, hairy hands gripped her tight around the neck.

"You got my friend killed that night on the Parkway. We offed your friend Mark Crosby. Guess we're even, bitch."

His beard loomed above her. It stank, and his breath was hot and sour on her face. Her field of vision was growing black around the edges.

"I saw how you let that boyfriend of yours run his hands up and down your body. I want the same from you, bitch." He partially loosened his grip on her. "Take off ya damn clothes."

Her body went rigid. He was going to rape her before he killed her. There was a police guard outside! How could this be happening? She tried to look compliant as her brain worked overtime, trying to figure out how to save herself. If she could only get to the window.

"Let me take my shoes off first."

He released her other arm, backed away to take a seat on the hallway bench. In that instant, she sprang up the stairs two at a time. The bedroom had a deadbolt. She had to get into her bedroom. Just as she reached the top, she felt the back of a hand come down on her head.

"Bitch, don't ya do that again." Knife in one hand, he pressed the blade into the space just between the bottom of her T shirt and waistband of her jeans. The coldness of the steel made her body go rigid. The cotton parted easily under the blade of the knife.

As she struggled in his grip, she saw the glint of serrated metal in his hand.

"Oh God, please don't do that," she begged. How to reason with a madman?

She started to whimper when he flicked the blade upward against her brassiere. Slowly he circled one breast with the tip of the blade.

"God, no, please," she begged.

Then she felt the cold sharpness of steel against her ribcage. She could feel the warmth trickle down her belly. Oh God, to die like this.

She felt abandoned. What were they doing outside?

"Strip those jeans off your body, bitch."

"Please, can't we talk about this?"

"Shut the fuck up! We ain't got nothing to talk about. After I fuck ya, I'm gonna slice and dice ya."

He tore the jeans from her body with the knife. She started to cry. If only she could signal to the officers sitting in the cruiser outside her front door. Flash the lights on and off — anything. Through her tears she could see him release his belt and unbutton his fly. Oh God, help me. He displayed himself proudly to her. Nick, Dubois — why weren't they here to save her? Her body started to shake.

He bore down on her, pinning her arms down with his. His glassy eyes leered at her.

Begging for her life, she cried, "Please, don't do that. Oh, God, help me," she begged. Just as she started to scream, she heard a hissing sound. A feral snarl came from behind her.

Suddenly her attacker gave a yelp of pain, letting go of her as he tried to shake Buzby's claws off his back. Buzby hissed again, and sank his claws deeper into BJ's back. Quickly, Grace brought her legs up to her stomach and kicked him hard in the groin. He rolled off her, howling in pain and obscenities.

"Fucking cunt! You and that cat of yours are dead!"

Adrenaline coursing through her body, she pushed herself onto her feet and pitched herself down the stairs.

Buzby was fighting him but her cat was no match for a madman with a knife. If she was going to die, she would die fighting. She dived for her bag, and the gun.

Take a deep breath. Relax. Damn it! Try again. Remove the safety catch. Her nerves were screaming. She didn't want to die. She didn't want Buzby to die. Where was her cat? Had Buzby died trying to save her?

Cock the hammer.

Her assailant moved towards her, his face disfigured with rage and hatred. Holding the gun with both hands to steady herself, she fired just as his enormous hands reached out to her with the serrated edge of steel. She fired again.

Those few minutes would be her nightmare forever. She would always remember how his dead eyes opened in shock as he dropped his weight on top of her. And the gurgling sounds that escaped from his throat. There was blood everywhere. She was bleeding. He was bleeding.

After that, her mind went blank. She had no recollection of the policemen bursting through the front door and hauling the dead man off her, of the cruisers, the ambulance, of falling into Dubois's arms, or of the chaos of sirens racing through the city that night.

chapter thirty-one

The plane landed at 10:17 a.m., Hong Kong time. Waving his Immigration identification, he zipped through customs and Hong Kong immigration in a matter of minutes. As he went through the revolving doors he left the artificially cool atmosphere of the airport terminal building, and was greeted by a warm blast of monsoon humidity and smog. By the time he climbed into a limo, his clothes were already clinging to his body. Obviously not the best time of year to come.

The last time Nick had audited the Hong Kong mission was the year Jon Keiler had taken up the post. That was before the handover to China. A lot had happened since the Beijing bosses had taken over Hong Kong, and it was at least three years since he'd been here. The uniforms of the soldiers from the People's Liberation Army and Chinese flags were everywhere. Even his limo driver flew the flag on his dashboard.

The taxi was a Mercedes. Nick leaned back against

the seat and enjoyed the smooth ride. Hong Kong might be a cosmopolitan city, but you wouldn't know it from the neighbourhood they were passing through. One in every four persons was dressed in pyjamas. Maybe he was missing something from the fashion magazines. Maybe this was the year of the floppy drawstring pants.

At the hotel, he took a shower. He was jetlagged up the ying-yang. Lying naked on the bed, he tried to get some shut eye. Lately his nights had been filled with frustration and longing. He willed himself not to think about her. Focus on the country he was in. And what he needed to do. An hour later, borrowing an umbrella from the hotel front desk, he braved the torrents of rain washing down from the sky and headed for the Canadian embassy.

At the embassy gate, he stood directly in front of the security cameras, and the doors were beeped open. He flashed his ID and allowed himself to be frisked and searched. After that, the staffers inside kow-towed to him. Membership had its privileges.

The ambassador remembered him from another posting and greeted him warmly. For the next fifty minutes he was corralled in a spacious office with a fantastic view of the harbour, being grilled for news on the home front. He was only released when the phone on the side desk rang with a call from the British high commission. The ambassador waved goodbye to Nick then gave his utmost attention to the caller on the other end.

Jon Keiler was on the phone when he walked into his office. He was stunned at the sight of Nick standing in front of his door.

"I'll call you back," he said, quickly cradling the receiver.

"You get a failing grade for follow through with orders. That stuff you were to put in the diplomatic bag, what happened to it?"

"Nick, I'm sorry, never even got to it. I've been swamped with work. We've all been up to our necks. Can I just get through this before we talk? Or even leave it till tomorrow instead?"

Keiler's opening gave him bad vibes.

"I'm here to talk about the other half of the Sun Sui file. This won't take long. Half an hour at most. In fact, show me where it is and I'll sit quietly somewhere and go through it myself."

"Yes, I looked for that, but it's archived in another location and I haven't been able to get over there. I've got too many deadlines coming up this week. Let me try to rearrange some priorities, clear some of this shit off my desk."

Nick dropped into a chair and watched him shuffle files around his desk. "Fair enough. In the meantime, let's see what's left in the system."

"Okay, but I'll lose half an hour, maybe more, if you need to use this screen. The whole system is slow."

"Jon, do I have to remind you who you work for?"

"You want to put it that way, fine," said Keiler, throwing a harassed look at Nick. "Gimme the spelling."

Nick watched Keiler enter Sun's name into the database. There was a lengthy silence as they waited.

"There's nothing to pull up. It's not there," said Keiler.

"Let me try something," said Nick. He typed in a few letters and waited for the screen to change. It came back blank. He frowned. "Explain that to me," he demanded, looking at Keiler.

Keiler's face was so nervous it twitched. "What can I say, Nick? We must have overlooked him in running security checks."

"Are you telling me that security checks were never done?"

"Nick, since the budget cutbacks, I don't have the

staff. We run the regular background checks, but others get postponed. What can I say?"

"In other words, you're not doing due diligence. You're not complying with my specific instructions."

"Shit, Nick, it's not like that at all." Keiler's voice rose defensively. "With our limited resources, we only do it if we're not sure about something. Like their language skills, or something that catches our attention in their application."

"Funny, when I read his file bright red flags came up all over the place. You mean to tell me nothing caught your attention?"

"This is a different class of people. These people have all got wealth without signs of traditional work."

"And what does that tell you, Keiler? Because it sure tells me that maybe a tiny percentage of them have an uncanny knack of making lots of money. The rest have got links to organized crime."

"Come on, Nick. Not all of them. That's a racist attitude. We once thought the same thing of Italians. We thought they were all cousins of the Mob, remember?"

Silence. Nick had thought of Jon Keiler as a friend, someone he could rely on. He made no effort to conceal his disappointment. He reached into his briefcase. "Okay, Jon. Look what I brought with me. This is what we have on Sun Sui at our end." He flipped through the file. "We don't have much, but listen to this: 'Hong Kong police failed to uncover any legitimate sources of income prior to the establishment of the nightclub.' And he's never filed a tax return. And here, right here, it says he's bringing three mil into Canada. You didn't think that was odd for a refugee fleeing Communist China to make that kind of dough in only four or so years of living in Hong Kong?"

Keiler refused to make eye contact with Nick. "I guessed I fucked up a few of the files."

Nick kept his voice soft, but he didn't mince words. "Jon, you fucked up big time. You barely followed the goddamn processing guidelines I had implemented for all of you SIOs in the field to follow. You of all people should have known better."

"You don't understand!" Keiler was almost shouting now. "I do know better. But I can't do better, because theory is different from real life. And Hong Kong's a whole different planet. What works everywhere doesn't work here. Here we got the richest people in the world and the lowest income tax system. We got the best free market economy and the worst government corruption. Most of these rich bastards in the Territory are either in bed with the Communist Party boys or, as you say, they're international crooks. And I don't mean the ones with criminal records. There's no way to tell an honest man from a crook by the records. That's why I didn't bother running him through security. His file would most likely come back clean."

"That's no reason not to run security checks." Nick glared at Keiler.

"Just about everybody in Hong Kong belongs to some kind of secret society. The whole goddamn place is disreputable, from company presidents to the top guns that run this colony. I agree that I made a few wrong judgement calls. I'm sorry."

Nick pulled another stack of documents from his briefcase. "Jon, these are some of your approved applications that I pulled out of the system. Look at this one. Here's someone who claimed to be a taxi driver but he's recorded net assets of $2.1 million. Alarm bells aren't going off inside your head?"

"Come on, Nick! He met the criteria to enter Canada as an entrepreneur!"

"A taxi driver is an entrepreneur? Maybe in Hong Kong. Not in Canada. When I get back home, I'm going to reassign you."

"Nick, please ..." Keiler turned white.

He looked frightened, Nick thought, and began to feel a little sorry for him. "You've been in the job too long. You've lost your judgement. It happens to everybody. Look, let's meet later and talk about reassignment. We'll work something out."

Keiler seemed abjectly grateful. "Nick, thank you. Thank you for that. Can we meet at my place? There's a restaurant around the corner where we can talk privately. I don't want my staff eavesdropping on my problems."

"Fine."

Keiler jotted down his address and handed it to him. "You know how to find it?"

"Don't worry. I'll see you later."

Walking back to the hotel, Nick tried to make sense of what Keiler had told him. But it didn't add up.

What did he know about Jon Keiler when he had hired him? Keiler was already on the civil service track, and had been trying to get into the foreign service for years but couldn't pass the interviews. Because there was a manpower shortage at the time, Nick had personally brought him on board and posted him to Egypt. After that he had been shuttled to Kenya. Two hardship postings later, he'd been rewarded with the cushy posting of Hong Kong. In his last performance evaluation, he had been written up as a conscientious worker.

But he wasn't popular with other diplomatic staff. According to the chargé d'affaires, Keiler was the kind of guy who attended a high level function and asked the kitchen help for a doggie bag. The chargé had also heard that the expatriate women's network had written Keiler's wife off as a member of the polyester and acrylic crowd. She'd showed up at cocktail parties and other diplomatic functions in track suits. That kind of mean-spirited gossip didn't really make Nick like the guy less, but it sure meant he didn't fit in.

Unfashionable and unhip, Keiler didn't come from money. He was the son of a Hydro linesman from a small town out west. Cattle and farming country. His wife probably had a similar background. So what? Nick had judged him to be honest and intelligent.

But now his suspicions refused to die a quiet death. Could Keiler be on the take? Was he accepting bribes from members of organized crime so he could look the other way, and not run security checks? Was it possible?

Nick didn't know. But he would confront him tonight.

In his hotel room, he phoned Grace and left a message, then tried again to catch some shut-eye. When he finally fell asleep with the remote in his hand, the Hong Kong stock markets were closing for the day, spitting out the last of the numbers.

He roused himself from his nap a little past seven in the evening. Rain still drummed against the window. Monsoon weather.

After lacing up his running shoes, he grabbed the umbrella the hotel had courteously left him. At the front desk, he asked for directions to Keiler's house. A front desk clerk passed him a map with a line of arrows showing him the route to take. He strolled through a neighbourhood of East meets West. Golden arches, waiters on roller blades, DKNY stores alongside Chinese temples and gardens.

He took an almost empty ferry across the harbour. On the other side, he decided to walk instead of hailing a taxi. After the park, he found Keiler's address. Even in the dark, he could see it was a large house. The expensive area, the size of the house, and its attractiveness only deepened his suspicions of Keiler.

He walked through a well of darkness between the elms and the dividing wall. Was Keiler cheap? Why couldn't he turn on the patio and outside lights?

He rang the doorbell and waited. Nothing. He rang it again. He was growing angry. Keiler was avoiding him. He badly wanted to give one of his officers the benefit of the doubt. As he was about to walk away, he heard a sound like furniture falling. Keiler was there, all right. Maybe he'd just changed his mind about meeting Nick.

Since the front door was locked, Nick went around the side and tried the patio door. It was open. He was in luck. He entered, calling Keiler's name. "Keiler. It's me. Nick. I hope you don't mind that I came around the back."

No answer.

The house was in darkness. Something was not right.

A shadow staggered out from behind one of the closed doors. It stumbled toward him. Nick groped for a light switch and flicked the light on. The forty-watt bulb cast a pale light on Keiler's face as he lurched forward. Was he drunk? And why was he so filthy looking?

Keiler fell into his arms, then slid down on the floor at his feet, Nick bent down to grab his hand. God! It wasn't dirt. It was blood.

He felt the stickiness on his hand, between his fingers. Keiler was covered in blood. He made soft gurgling sounds as blood poured out of his mouth, from his slit throat. It pooled in a deep red puddle at his feet, staining the rug underneath. Nick tried to staunch the flow of blood but he knew it was useless. Another gurgle. Nick tried to make out the words, but couldn't. With one last Herculean effort, Keiler directed Nick's hand to his pant pocket where Nick could make out the outline of a computer diskette. He strained to understand the choked syllables Keiler was trying to utter, but then they stopped. Reaching, Nick pulled the disk out of Keiler's pocket and tucked it into his own.

He never looked back. He ran like the devil from there. But he wasn't fast enough. He heard the gunshots behind him, felt a bullet whiz past his head. With no place to hide, he tried to zigzag along the sea wall. Suddenly he felt a sharp pain in his shoulder. And another in his back. Something tore through his body. Then his legs went out from under him. The last thing he remembered before he blacked out was jackknifing into the cold, inky darkness of the sea.

His breathing slowed. Then it stopped. The twenty-four-hour duty nurse monitoring his vital signs sounded the alarm. She called for the crash cart.

The sky opened. He was being lifted upwards. Then the light burst into a rainbow of colours. He opened his eyes and saw his body from a distance. He listened to the emotional voices around him.

"His pulse is weak. Very erratic. Prep him for surgery now!"

As a spectator, he watched the medical team rushing him into the operating theatre. He watched himself being prepped for surgery.

He saw a vision of Grace.

He saw the haggard faces of the doctors and nurses as they worked on him. He was hooked up to all sorts of machines. He watched from afar, as the medical team tried to revive him. Then the thread of consciousness snapped.

epilogue

At nine-thirty the following evening, Grace finally opened her eyes. She was greeted by the sight of Ellen sleeping upright by her bedside, in a hospital room filled with flowers and secured by a police guard. The first question she asked was, where's Buzby? Ellen told her that her cat had been stabbed trying to save her, and was recovering nicely at the animal hospital.

Then she was given the message from Hong Kong. Nick had been shot, but he would be all right, and he sent her his love.

In the days that followed she learned that Cadeux was facing multiple charges of corruption, fraud, and breach of trust. Ellen told her that the RCMP operation on the illegal campaign contributions had captured Cadeux on camera on several occasions in the company of Wa Sing.

Working with Ellen, Kappolis and the local police force, Dubois gave up jurisdictional turf to assist in uncovering the identity of Grace's assailant. They learned that his name was BJ Carmody, and that he had already served time in the penitentiary for murder and manslaughter. In his dingy basement apartment, they found ample evidence that he had intended to kill her. Ballistics was able to match his gun with the bullet taken from Mark Crosby's body.

As a favour to Nick, Dubois downplayed the weapon Grace used to kill her attacker. Her handgun was quietly tagged and bagged in the evidence room. After the case was consigned to dust, the handgun was quietly returned to her where it made its way back into the safety deposit box.

Nick languished in the critical care ward of a Hong Kong hospital, hovering between life and death. He had almost died from a massive loss of blood. Afterward his body had gone into anaphylactic shock, causing his heart to stop from one of the transfusion drugs. An emergency team was assembled for around-the-clock care. As well, a certain Dr. Quang and his prayer warriors had been called by the pastor when it was feared that the patient would not make it through the night. They had chanted by his bed until the early hours of the morning when the emergency team pronounced that the patient had pulled through the worst. His recovery made the front page of the *South China Morning Post*, and within the span of forty-eight hours, he inadvertently became the poster boy for the prayer warriors.

The Hong Kong police had arrested two of Keiler's colleagues. From his hospital bed, Nick ordered them sent back to Canada, and made Rocco the immigration manager at the embassy.

Two months later, Nick found himself reporting to a new immigration minister. He handed Keiler's diskette over to his minister, along with a hard copy of the evidence. The disk contained the names of Canadian and local staff at the Canadian embassies, in Hong Kong and China, who had accepted bribes from many underworld characters to delete their criminal backgrounds from government computers. That way, applicants with links to triads did not show up on the system.

Despite their best efforts, the following summer, the largest human smuggling operation from China arrived in Canada. Three cargo ships carrying close to a thousand illegal aliens landed off the British Columbia coastline.

Then one day, out of the blue, on a perfectly good fall day with the leaves turning colours, a phone call from Kelly Marcovich ruined Nick's entire week. His immigration counterpart in Washington called to inform him that Sun Sui had received asylum in the United States in exchange for ratting on the competition. He had handed over names and the inside dope of other triad gangs. And he was working with the U.S. Attorney-General by giving evidence against his Panamanian associates and their roles in issuing visas to a hundred or so Chinese intelligence agents to enter the U.S. To add insult to injury, Sun got immunity from prosecution for his role in Walter Martin's death in exchange for his testimony before the Foreign Affairs Subcommittee on Organized Crime in Washington. Once more he grassed on former friends and associates by naming names of Communist officials and Chinese gangsters who had made donations to American political parties.

One late fall day, a couple of hikers came across the remains of a body in the woods. It carried a driver's licence in the name of Lee Man. The cause of death was unknown due to the advanced decomposition and disturbance of the remains by wild animals.

Nick asked Dubois to fill him in on all the details. Li Mann Vu's false identification on a badly decomposed body seemed too convenient to him. However, the DNA taken from the remnants of a body found in the woods was a perfect match from samples taken in Li Mann's house. Officially, the search for Walter Martin's killer was over. Unofficially, both men viewed the human remains as nothing more than a skin Walter Martin's killer had left behind.

Jon Keiler's murder was never solved. The Hong Kong police wrote it off as another gangland killing in the Colony. Like Wa Sing's murder, there was not enough evidence to pin it on Sun Sui or the Flying Dragons.

There is only the now.

This was a lesson in life that Grace had learned the hard way. Nick, too, realized that he had been unconsciously living for the future. What good would that have done him if he hadn't pulled through in Hong Kong? Since his brush with death, his dreams became more colourful. At times he would awake in the morning and retain fragments of memory of being in another place, travelling through a tunnel of bright light and rainbow colours.

Grace and Nick booked a flight to Malta, and returned to the place of their first tryst. In a seaside village, they found a quiet church, and tied the knot. Later, neither could remember what the church's denomination was. It could have been Martian Orthodox for all they cared.

It was the best month-long, honeymoon-vacation they'd ever had.

acknowlegements

There are a number of people to whom I owe a great deal. Those who believed in the book from the onset were my friend Jim Dahl and his sister, Stevie Cameron. I want to say thank you to Stevie for introducing me to her lawyer Marion Hebb and her associate Sally Cohen. Sally has been a terrific cheerleader, boosting my confidence through the slow and daunting process of getting a manuscript published.

Among those who contributed enormously to the editing process was Doris Cowan. She worked on the book, page by page, scene by scene. There is no finer editor than Doris, a gifted critic of language, characterization, and dialogue. I cannot thank her enough. Taking over from her at the next stage was Julian Walker. This book would not have happened the way it did without his discerning editorial suggestions.